THE HOPE OF VITALITY
THE STONE CYCLE BOOK 6

THE STONE CYCLE SERIES

The Stone of Knowing (Book 1)
The Cost of Knowing (Book 2)
The Stone of Authority (Book 3)
The Struggle for Authority (Book 4)
The Stone of Vitality (Book 5)
The Hope of Vitality (Book 6)

Companion Novelettes
The Seer: A Prequel to The Stone of Knowing
The Rending: A Prequel to The Cost of Knowing

Other epic fantasy by Allan N. Packer

THE RUPTURED KINGDOM SERIES

The Hard Edge of Magic (Book 1)
The Riven Land (Book 2)
...other titles to come

Companion Novelette
The Renegade: A Prequel to The Hard Edge of Magic

THE HOPE OF VITALITY

THE STONE CYCLE
BOOK 6

ALLAN N. PACKER

LUMINANT PUBLICATIONS

To Nick and Mary,
fellow travelers and valued friends on the journey into eternity.

Baron Island
Savage Strait
Castel
Castel Citadel
Deadman's Pass
Steffan's Citadel
Arven
Maranelle
Duchy
of
Erestor
N
W
E
S
Arvenon
& surrounding Kingdoms

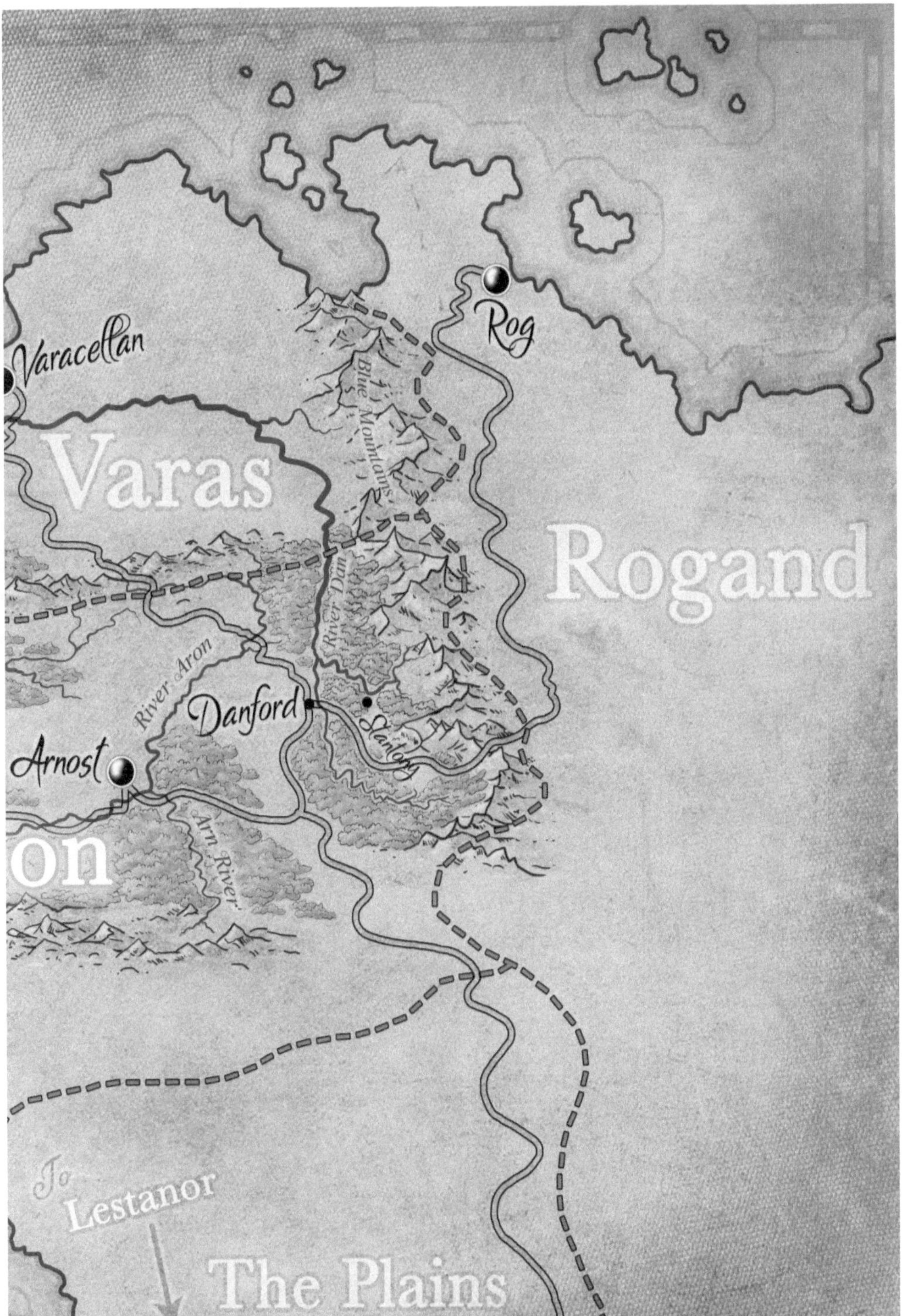

Varacellan
Rog
Varas
Rogand
Blue Mountains
River Dan
River Aron
Danford
Santon
Arnost
Arn River
on
To Lestanor
The Plains

VOLUME 1—A HARVEST OF CONFUSION

1

The sun had disappeared below the horizon, and its afterglow was slowly fading from the sky. Kamash sat spellbound beside the tiller, gazing upward as the lesser lights emerged, unveiling their grandeur in a dazzling display that stretched from horizon to horizon. The moon was yet to rise, and not even a wisp of cloud intruded upon the brilliance of the tiny stars that winked down at him.

The boat rolled ceaselessly beneath him, plowing swiftly through a low swell kicked up by a steady breeze. A dorsal fin abruptly broke the surface, and dolphins sported exuberantly about the little craft. They were no sooner gone than a new delight presented itself. Glancing back over the stern, he found a glow of phosphorescence trailing in the wake of the boat.

Had the ocean and the heavens collaborated in a salute to the old man's return?

Facing forward once more, he noticed a dark mass on the horizon —a telltale sign that his destination was almost within reach. Kamash's heartbeat quickened in anticipation. He had never been so ready to say goodbye to the complexities of civilization and the incessant demands of other people.

A part of him wondered if he would miss contact with his kind, but he thrust such thoughts aside. Long years of isolation had shown him he could manage very nicely on his own.

A full moon obligingly appeared as he drew near at last to the familiar little beach. As the hull scraped across the sand, he was confronted again with a question that had plagued him for weeks. Should he release the boat, allowing it to drift away the moment he landed?

The little craft was a thing of beauty. It had served him faithfully in the brief time since he took possession of it, returning him speedily and without incident to his island. Even the idea of abandoning it felt somehow disloyal.

It was a crucial decision—one with the potential to define his future. While he could not imagine another foreign princess appearing suddenly to confound him, the day might come when he himself needed help of some kind. And in spite of his eagerness to escape Rog and its relentless bustle, an entirely different thought had been nagging away at him. Would a time ever come when he craved human contact once more?

A reckless streak in him wanted to simply set the boat free and ignore the consequences. The cautious side to his nature firmly resisted any such notion.

In the end he settled on a compromise—he would defer the decision until the morning.

Leaping onto the sand, he pulled the boat clear of the waves. After sitting for so long, activity felt invigorating, and he found himself eager for more. His restless feet took him to the location where he had previously stored his boat. He'd moved his former craft using thin tree trunks as rollers, and they were still where he'd left them. Carrying the makeshift rollers to the beach, he laid them out and upended the little vessel onto them. He had brought a range of supplies from Rog, and after placing them on top of the hull he carefully pushed the load across the beach and into the trees. Having maneuvered the boat into its resting place, he relocated his supplies beneath it with the intention of retrieving them in the morning.

After first arriving on the island so many years earlier, he had woven a large mat, throwing it over the boat to protect it from the elements. He had replaced the mat more than once over the years, but the most recent version still appeared usable. Tossing it across the hull, he piled some fallen branches on top for good measure.

He had told himself he would defer any decision about keeping the boat, and securing it in this way was hardly consistent with that plan. But he didn't care.

After a long voyage followed by tiring exertion, he was more than ready to lie down. The prospect of exploring his old dwelling in the dark held little appeal, and the weather was mild. Exploration could wait until the morning. Heading back to the beach, the old man made himself comfortable in the sand. He was soon asleep.

DAYLIGHT WAS SHINING BRIGHTLY when Kamash awoke. He opened his eyes to the sight of a stranger staring down at him. Startled and alarmed, he leaped to his feet and took a hasty step backward.

The observer, bearded and unkempt, didn't move. Ragged clothes hung from him, and long hair dangled untidily about his face. He appeared quite wild.

"Who are you?" asked Kamash nervously.

For a moment the man said nothing, then an animated flow of words burst from him. Kamash could not understand a word of it. It didn't sound like Arvenian.

"Ahr?" he asked.

The man nodded vigorously, responding with a simple question of his own. "Rogand?"

Kamash nodded in his turn.

The Ahran began speaking again, slowly and loudly, as if to a child. He pointed first toward the sea, then back to the island. His efforts were fruitless—Kamash could only shrug in response.

Deciding they needed to start somewhere simpler, the old man pointed to his chest. "Kamash," he said.

"Kumm-ash," the stranger repeated. A finger jabbed at his own chest. "Ghar-pin."

"Gharpin," Kamash repeated, before adding pointedly, "Welcome to *my* island."

A frown of puzzlement came to the Ahran's face as he scanned the little beach. He swept a hand toward the sea before pointing at Kamash. When the old man offered no response, Gharpin's hand bobbed up and down rhythmically, as if riding waves, before plunging precipitately. Then he turned expectantly to Kamash, his eyebrows raised.

Gharpin was plainly wanting to understand how the new arrival had reached the island. Almost certainly a castaway himself, he appeared to be asking if Kamash's ship had sunk. Such an outcome must seem incomprehensible in view of the mild weather, but what else could the Ahran conclude with no ship visible anywhere?

Language barriers had their frustrations, but at that moment Kamash was glad he had no way of explaining his situation to the stranger. Witnessing the intensity of the Ahran, it didn't take much to guess what Gharpin might do if he knew a seaworthy vessel was present on the island. And his brief exposure to Ahrans had given the old man more than enough reason to exercise caution.

In concealing his boat the previous night, Kamash had acted on little more than a whim. That action suddenly took on a new significance.

For the moment it might be safer if Gharpin remained ignorant about the boat. That revelation could wait until Kamash better understood who the Ahran was and what his intentions might be.

GHARPIN WASTED no time in taking Kamash on a tour of the island and its facilities. The Ahran's efforts in rejuvenating the cultivated strips were impressive, and his careful labor had already seen reward. The bones around the cooking fire also suggested he had used available materials to good effect in catching fish.

The remodeling of Kamash's dwelling was another matter

entirely. The old man was shocked to discover that large sections of two walls had simply vanished. Apparently oblivious to Kamash's reaction, the Ahran chattered away proudly as he pointed to his supposed improvements.

Kamash could only shake his head in dismay. He tried to remind himself that Gharpin could not guess he had caused offense—he had no way of knowing he was talking to the original architect.

Over time the rationale for the Ahran's changes became apparent. The dwelling was now considerably more light and airy than before, and much better ventilated. That might be well and good, but Gharpin had never needed to weather the storms that buffeted the island during the rainy season.

The building would need to be repaired before bad weather set in. Assuming they remained on the island.

Learning to respect his new companion didn't take Kamash long.

It wasn't difficult to warm to Gharpin. Hardworking and capable, the Ahran was also generous and considerate. He freely shared everything he had, and he graciously yielded to Kamash the single bedroom in the dwelling. Perhaps he had concluded that the older man needed its limited comfort more than he did.

Thus far Kamash had reached no understanding of why Gharpin was so driven. For driven he certainly was. Although the castaway was making the best of his situation, he seemed impatient—at times desperate—to escape from the island.

The life of a hermit did not appeal to everyone, of course, but that didn't seem to be the issue. Although Kamash's interactions with Gharpin were almost entirely limited to hand gestures, he nevertheless sensed a passion burning just below the surface of the man. There was something he wanted to do, and he wanted to do it badly.

Not long after Kamash had arrived on the island, Gharpin had beckoned him over. Using a stick to draw in the dirt, he scratched out a rough depiction of a raft. Staring intently at the new arrival, he had waited for a reaction.

Kamash responded by using one hand to represent the waves, rising and falling rhythmically. He then used his other hand to represent the raft, riding the waves. The wave hand began to rise and fall more vigorously, causing the raft hand to buck and sway wildly. Then the wave hand smashed repeatedly into the raft hand, eventually causing it to sink below the waves.

Gharpin understood the meaning well enough, and he walked away with a long face.

The following day Kamash noticed Gharpin carefully examining the trees on the island. It came as no surprise when the Ahran showed him a sketch of a boat in the dirt.

The design might have been simple, but it was nevertheless a commendable effort. Unfortunately it was also worthless. Without suitable tools they had no way even to begin such an undertaking.

Escaping the island was clearly an obsession for the Ahran. With a perfectly seaworthy vessel readily to hand, the old man began to feel increasingly guilty about concealing it from his companion.

However, with no way of knowing what Gharpin was planning, Kamash concluded the only safe course was to remain silent.

"SAND," said Kamash, lifting a fistful of tiny white grains and allowing them to flow between his fingers back onto the beach.

"Cahn," responded Gharpin.

The old man pointed to the water. "Sea," he said.

"Ahr," the other replied.

"Ahr?" asked Kamash in surprise.

"Ahr," Gharpin repeated firmly.

So the Empire of Ahr was named for the sea. Interesting, but perhaps not surprising since it encompassed a cluster of islands.

Then it occurred to the old man that he might not have been sufficiently specific. Was it possible that Gharpin understood him to mean "water" when he pointed to the sea? Might "The Empire of Water" also be a possibility?

Shaking his head at his own slow-wittedness, he headed along the beach toward the stream, beckoning to the Ahran to join him. When they reached it, Kamash pointed to the flow and said "stream." Then he splashed into it and bent low. Filling his cupped hands, he stood up and said "water," as the liquid spilled through his fingers. Finally he strode across the sand and repeated the exercise in the shallows of the sea.

Gharpin appeared to understand. Scooping water into his own hand, he said, "phlu." Then he added, "nath-ahr," indicating the stream.

Kamash nodded with satisfaction. So "ahr" did mean "sea." And the Ahran word for stream appeared to be a derivative of it.

In spite of this small success, language acquisition was not coming easily to Kamash. His advanced age was undoubtedly hampering his endeavors, but he was willing to acknowledge that his limited improvement had more to do with a lack of ability. After a couple of weeks of growing frustration, Kamash decided to give up the struggle and abandon his attempts entirely.

Learning Ahran hardly seemed necessary anyway, considering Gharpin's steady progress in learning Rogandan. Redirecting his energies toward helping the other man offered Kamash a more useful focus.

The two men spent several hours each day cultivating, catching, and preparing food. The bulk of the remaining time was occupied working on Gharpin's Rogandan. Highly motivated to learn and surprisingly proficient, the Ahran worked hard on vocabulary and pronunciation while wrestling with the rudiments of grammar. Fortunately for both of them, Kamash proved to be a better teacher than a student, and he derived almost as much satisfaction as Gharpin from the Ahran's achievements.

From the beginning the two men had made extensive and effective use of sign language. Engaging in simple interactions in Rogandan expanded their communication enormously.

As the days turned into weeks, the outline of Gharpin's story slowly took shape. By the time a month had passed, Kamash knew that Gharpin had commanded a ship, that he and his crew had been the victims of sabotage, and that someone of high rank had been responsible. Details were far from clear, but Gharpin may even have been suggesting that the perpetrator was the most senior official of the Empire of Ahr, the Grand Vizier.

As they interacted, a number of tantalizing hints also suggested that Gharpin might have been involved directly with Princess Neira. On occasion Kamash thought he recognized her name, but when he repeated it Gharpin looked at him blankly. Perhaps the problem lay with his pronunciation, or perhaps the Ahran had simply been using a word that sounded similar. Either way, language was proving an insurmountable barrier, to the frustration of both men.

Even without knowing the full details of his story, Kamash had now seen enough of Gharpin to feel confident the Ahran did not represent a threat to Rogand. Accordingly, he decided the time had finally come to show him the boat.

Fearing that his companion would want to sail away the moment he saw it, Kamash waited until the sun had almost set before leading him to its hiding place. Throwing aside the branches and pulling off the protective mat, he revealed the little craft.

Gharpin's eyes went wide. "You have boat!" he said. Then he turned to Kamash. "*We* have boat?" he asked.

Kamash nodded.

The Ahran gazed thoughtfully at the little vessel for several minutes. "Now, I think," he finally said, before adding, "Tomorrow, we talk?"

Kamash nodded again, and they turned their backs on the boat, setting off for their shelter.

That night the old man's thoughts churned restlessly as he waited in vain for sleep to take him. He had been more than a little relieved at his companion's restraint—Gharpin had not even attempted to closely examine the boat. For all his drivenness, the Ahran was apparently less impulsive than Kamash might have expected. Nevertheless, Kamash didn't doubt that the shipwrecked captain would want to leave, and soon.

A difficult choice lay ahead.

Gharpin was an accomplished sailor who needed no help from an old man. The simplest option would be to give him the boat and remain on the island when he left. The loss of the craft was of no real concern to Kamash—he had never made a final decision about keeping it anyway.

While it might be the simplest solution, somehow it didn't sit right. If he understood correctly, Gharpin had lost his ship along with his entire crew as a result of deliberate sabotage ordered by an Ahran official. The most likely reason was that the official wanted to silence him. What secrets was Gharpin hiding? And what would happen when he suddenly reappeared after mysteriously escaping a watery grave?

And where would he go? Sturdy as the little boat might be, Gharpin would never be able to sail as far as the empire. If he tried, then sooner or later he would encounter an Ahran ship. Any such encounter could prove fatal if a powerful official wanted him dead.

His future would be equally uncertain if he sailed to Rogand. He couldn't pass himself off as Rogandan, and Ahrans were not exactly held in high honor in Rog at that time.

Kamash sighed. He would never be able to live with himself if he abandoned Gharpin to his fate. That left only one practical alternative—he would need to accompany his new companion to Rog and advocate on his behalf to King Krasmir.

In his innocence the old man had imagined he'd escaped human turmoil and intrigue forever. With a heavy heart he faced the reality that he was about to be thrust back into human society once more. And right into the center of the maelstrom.

2

———

King Rupert of Castel stirred, waking from a nightmare that lingered at the edge of his awareness. Where was he?

His world lurched suddenly, accompanied by the loud creaking of timbers and the swaying of a hammock beneath him. Everything abruptly came flooding back.

Was Tasha still at his side?

Propping himself up on one elbow, he peered into the darkness, trying to make out the other hammock in the storage room where they had been imprisoned. He could see nothing. The single candle left by their captors had gone out, and no light penetrated this deep into the bowels of the ship.

Rupert lay back quietly again, confident he could not have slept through Tasha being removed from the room. She was most likely asleep. If so, he saw no reason to disturb her.

With nothing else to distract him, a torrent of thoughts raced through his mind. He knew King Krasmir would be searching for them; the Rogandan monarch would never rest until he had freed his daughter. The Ahrans had made that task much more difficult by removing the captives from Rogand though. He wondered if they were being taken to the capital of the empire, Kat Ahket.

The disruption would by no means be limited to Rogand. Castel would be forced to continue without its king. In his absence, Count Gordan had been acting as regent, and Rupert had every confidence in him. But what would Gordan do if the Ahrans decided to bargain with Rupert's life? And how would King Krasmir react if he was forced to choose between his daughter and the interests of his kingdom?

What would become of them all? As for Tasha and him, they had fallen into a deep, deep hole, and Rupert wondered if they would ever make it out again.

Unwilling to dwell on the worst possible outcome, he reminded himself that Princess Neira was under heavy guard in Rog. Perhaps an exchange could be arranged.

"Are you awake?" a soft voice asked.

"Yes, I am," he replied eagerly. "Did you manage to get any sleep?"

"Not much. Not as much as you."

He frowned in the dark. "How do you know how much sleep I got?"

Her reply was blunt. "You snore."

A deep flush warmed his face. For reasons he couldn't understand, this simple pronouncement did almost as much to deflate him as everything that had happened so far.

"Not loudly," she added belatedly. "Just enough that I knew you were asleep."

With his perspective restored, he confronted his own sensitivity. How did princesses manage to be so effective at discomposing him? Did it come naturally to them, or did they learn it as part of their training? He ran a hand across his face, grateful that the darkness concealed his embarrassment.

For a time there were no sounds apart from the noises of the ship.

A quavering voice eventually broke the silence. "Do you hate me, Rupert?"

Taken by surprise, he responded as cheerfully as he could manage. "How could I hate a person who's joining me on the adventure of a lifetime?"

Her choked off response might have been an ironic snort. More likely it was a sob.

When she said nothing further, he added, "We're not going to let them beat us, Tasha!"

A full minute must have passed before she responded. "No. We're not." Her words were accompanied by a loud sniff, but her voice was steadier.

WITHOUT DAYLIGHT it was difficult for Rupert to judge the passage of time. Their isolation was interrupted only when their captors brought food and water, occasionally leaving behind a flickering candle to chase away the darkness for a while.

It might have been two or three days before they were eventually led from their prison and rowed to what appeared to be a small island bustling with activity. Uncomfortable after so long in the dark, they climbed out of the longboat onto the beach, covering their eyes against the dazzling light. Having delivered the prisoners, their captors returned immediately to their ship, leaving them to the dubious mercies of the men already on the island.

Glancing around uncertainly, Rupert saw a large group of men hard at work erecting several structures, directed with unruffled efficiency by a wiry man with a thick beard. Building materials lay scattered about an open space beyond the beach. After a brief glance toward the newly arrived prisoners, the workers and their overseer ignored them entirely.

Glancing out to sea, Rupert saw a second ship lying at anchor off the beach, presumably the vessel that had transported the men and materials already on the island.

Released into an open space at last, he began pacing back and forth restlessly.

It took a supreme effort to calm himself for long enough to check on Tasha. "Are you well?"

She responded with a halfhearted nod. Emotionally exhausted by the ordeal, she seemed wooden and detached.

· · ·

BY THE TIME the sun set, workmen had erected several simple huts.

The bearded overseer strode purposefully toward them. "My name is Dessue," he said in passable Rogandan. "I am in authority on this island. Please follow me."

Two huts had been built apart from the others, and he led them to the nearest. "This will be your hut," he told Rupert. Turning to Tasha, he pointed. "Your hut is behind it."

"Thank you," said Rupert tightly.

Speaking courteously to any of their captors cost him an effort, but he remembered his father saying that a king should behave like one, whatever the circumstances.

Dessue assessed him. "You have spent a long time in the dark." His tone was gruff, but not unkind. "Hot food will be brought to you as soon as my men have prepared it." He nodded once, then he left them.

Rupert and Tasha sat together outside Rupert's hut. More comfortable in the dim light of dusk, they gazed out at the waves breaking endlessly onto the rocks.

Some life had returned to Tasha. "Our situation seems to have improved," she observed.

Rupert nodded once. "Let's hope it stays that way."

Food was brought to them as Dessue had promised. Simple as it was, the meal seemed sumptuous after the provisions tossed indifferently into their prison room on the ship.

The events of the previous few days had taken their toll. Rupert felt weary beyond words. Tasha was clearly in no better state. "I need to sleep," he told her. "I won't be far away. Call if you need me."

She returned a sleepy nod, and they retired to their huts.

Rupert's sleeping quarters might have been basic, but at least the low bed was not swaying. The guards did not disturb him, and he slept soundly for the first time since his captivity. In the morning he discovered that Tasha's experience had been similar.

After another meal was delivered, Dessue paid them a second

visit. "I trust that your huts are adequate." After a nod from Rupert, he told them, "I have been given responsibility for keeping you safe and in good health. You may wander the island freely. Two guards will accompany you at all times, but that is purely for your own safety." He addressed Tasha in particular. "My superiors have made it clear that you are not to be interfered with in any way, and I have made sure the men are aware of that."

Rupert managed another muted thank you. But whether he showed it or not, he was greatly relieved by Dessue's assurance to Tasha.

"You will not be treated badly if you behave well," Dessue promised curtly.

The moment he had gone, Tasha stood up and stretched. "Shall we see if he was serious about letting us explore the island?" She sounded remarkably buoyant.

Rupert did not hesitate. "Certainly! I need exercise!"

Leaving the beach and the huts, they headed into the trees.

"We're being followed," he whispered, jerking his head behind him.

She peered back over her shoulder at two guards who had set off after them. "Should we try to lose them?"

He shook his head. "Let's not push the boundaries. We don't want Dessue deciding he's been too lenient."

The guards followed at a distance, but it soon became apparent they had no intention of intruding. After a while Rupert was almost able to ignore them.

They hadn't walked far when a steep hill rose before them, its tree lined slopes obscuring the summit.

Tasha gazed up at it. "I wonder if that might give us a view across the whole island."

After a glance back at their guards, he shrugged. "Let's find out." He had no idea if the hill was off limits. If it was, it would soon become obvious.

The guards made no attempt to stop them, and they reached the top puffing from their exertions. Peering back down the slope, Rupert saw the two men leaning against trees some distance below them. They had avoided the steepest part of the climb while choosing a location that would allow them to see whenever he and Tasha left the hill. Eavesdropping did not appear to be on their agenda.

Putting the Ahrans from his mind, he allowed himself to appreciate the view. Blue ocean could be seen in every direction. Three smaller islands lay not far away. Apart from visible greenery—presumably trees—none of the three appeared to be any more than featureless lumps of rock. Tiny smudges on the horizon hinted at other islands further away. As far as Rupert could tell, no landmass of any size lay within reach.

Their own island was modestly sized and covered with vegetation. Birdlife was plentiful, and the barking of sea lions carried faintly to their current position. He guessed that a range of marine birds and animals used the island as a breeding ground.

Apart from the beach where they had landed, only one other strip of sand was visible. It was small and inaccessible from the surrounding cliffs. The rest of the coastline appeared rocky and forbidding, at least to humans.

"Where are we?" asked Tasha.

Rupert shook his head. "I have no idea. We might be halfway to Ahr-chitani for all I know."

The princess peered off into the distance. "If we hadn't been sailing for so long before we arrived, we might be near the Rogandan coastline. There are plenty of islands to the north of Rogand."

"There are islands off the coast of Castel and Varas as well," he replied. "It would take longer to sail there, so I suppose one of them might be a possibility."

She peered around at the island, screwing up her face. "It certainly isn't appealing, wherever it's located. Unless you happen to be a sea lion, I suppose."

He snorted. "No. I imagine the Ahrans wanted somewhere that wouldn't attract attention. If so, they chose well."

. . .

FOR BETTER OR for worse this place was now home. As the days slowly passed, they did their best to adjust. Dessue occasionally visited them. The visits were brief, and Rupert saw no point to them, but the Ahran was at least making an effort to be accessible. Although neither he nor his guards showed them any particular deference, they served an adequate meal twice each day while apparently expecting nothing in return.

The first sign of change was the arrival of an Ahran ship. Having spotted it in the distance from their hilltop lookout, they made their way to the beach, curious to see what was happening. Keeping out of sight among the trees, they watched as supplies were unloaded and the boat returned to the ship carrying several passengers.

"Is that Dessue in the longboat?" asked Rupert in surprise.

"It appears to be. Perhaps he's meeting with the ship's captain."

As they watched, half a dozen men they didn't recognize were rowed to the island. The men had all the appearance of new arrivals intent on settling in. The impression was confirmed a couple of hours later when the ship raised anchor and departed. It left with Dessue still on board.

Rupert couldn't shake off a sense of foreboding, but he decided to put a positive face on it. "It looks like we're going to have a change of administration," he said, speaking as cheerfully as he could manage.

"So it appears." Tasha sounded less than enthusiastic.

Dessue's replacement wasted no time in making his presence felt. Within the hour he approached their huts, surrounded by guards. Assessing the captives through narrowed eyes, he spoke to them in Rogandan. "I am told that my predecessor treated you as guests. You are not guests—you are prisoners."

He eyed them coldly. "Your food will be provided, in keeping with the emperor's benevolence to prisoners throughout his empire. However, I will not tolerate laziness. You can no longer expect my men to do menial tasks on your behalf. Do them yourselves. The work of preparing your meals will, of course, fall to you."

With that he turned on his heel, leaving them gaping open-mouthed.

Tasha made no attempt to hide her contempt. "He didn't even bother to tell us his name!"

Rupert gazed uneasily at the retreating form of the Ahran. "I wonder if he's planning to restrict our freedom of movement."

It didn't take long to find out. To Rupert's surprise, nothing was done to hinder them when they next set off on a walk. Two men followed them as before. The guards had now become blatant in their efforts to listen in on Rupert and Tasha's conversations, but apart from that no obvious differences emerged.

For the next few days, life continued much as it had under Dessue. Everything changed when they went for a long walk.

Having climbed the tallest hill on the island, they stood gazing at the horizon.

"I'll race you to the bottom!" said Tasha with a grin, bouncing off toward the trees below without waiting for an answer.

Rupert hesitated for a moment. Then, throwing caution to the winds, he set off after her.

Careering down a steep slope dodging trees was more than enough to occupy his full attention. But he was drawing close.

Hearing him coming, Tasha put on an extra burst of speed. As she drew away from him, her laugh turned into a cry of alarm as she lost her footing and tumbled down the slope.

Rupert watched in horror as she rolled helplessly downward, her head barely missing more than one tree. Tumbling into a ditch, she came at last to a jarring halt.

Frantic and agitated, Rupert hurried to her side.

She stared up at him, pale and wincing with pain. "My ankle! I think I might have broken it."

Rupert called to the guards. "Come and help me!"

To his astonishment, they ignored him completely. They must surely have witnessed the whole episode. Yet they appeared unmoved by Tasha's plight.

"Your master will hear of this!" Rupert growled.

Their response was a harsh laugh.

Helping Tasha upright, he placed her arm around his shoulder.

She took a tentative step forward, Rupert bearing her weight as best he could.

"Can you manage?" he asked.

She nodded tightly, and they set off for her hut.

Every hop jarred her injured ankle, and more than once she cried out in pain. The indifference of the guards and their refusal to help incensed Rupert. He gritted his teeth and tried to limit his focus on where to place his next step. Nevertheless, his fury grew as the minutes dragged painfully by.

By the time they reached her hut, Tasha was barely able to cope with the pain and the shock. After making her as comfortable as he could, Rupert hurried off to find the Ahran leader.

The man was not alone when Rupert found him. Wisdom dictated that any interaction should take place in private, especially since most of the guards understood at least some Rogandan.

Rupert was too angry to care. "The princess has seriously injured her foot! She needs urgent medical attention! Your guards have done nothing whatever to help!"

The two guards had arrived at the same time, and the leader immediately addressed them in their own language. After a rapid interaction, he turned to Rupert indifferently. "The prisoner has injured herself as a result of her own foolishness. I do not regard that as an emergency—for me or for my men."

Rupert's tone became icy. "Your predecessor told us he had been given responsibility for keeping us safe and in good health," he snarled. "If the princess is crippled or worse because of your neglect, you'd better kill me! Because if you don't, when I eventually meet your master I'll make sure he fully understands your attitude toward your responsibilities." He fixed the leader with a furious glare. "And if you do kill me, you'd better have a good explanation for killing one hostage and crippling the other."

Rupert spun on his heel and left without waiting for a response.

No Ahrans appeared, and Rupert spent an anxious night trying to care for Tasha.

Not long after the sun rose, a small group of Ahrans arrived. The leader was among them, and he glowered at them both. Rupert ignored him.

One of the Ahrans approached Tasha. "May I examine your ankle?" he asked calmly in Rogandan.

When she responded with a tight nod, he worked the ankle carefully from side to side. Then he probed it thoroughly. Rupert could see he wasn't trying to be rough, nevertheless the princess winced with pain as he worked.

The healer finally completed his work. "Your ankle is badly sprained, but not broken," he told Tasha. "You need to avoid putting weight on it until the swelling goes down."

The leader spoke sharply to the healer in their own language. The exchange was brief and terse. When it was over, the leader turned to Rupert with a sneer.

"Since you have demonstrated that you cannot take proper care of yourselves, I must treat you like children. My men will be instructed to prevent you from climbing hills or trees. They will also make sure you never go out of your depth into the sea. If you do not comply, your movements will be severely restricted."

He left without offering them an opportunity to reply, striding swiftly away. His guards followed close behind him.

"How did you convince them to examine my ankle?" asked Tasha.

Intent on avoiding details, Rupert responded with a noncommittal grunt. He managed to present a calm face, but inwardly he was on edge.

He felt sure he had made an enemy of the leader. And sooner or later the Ahran would find a way to hit back at him.

3

———

A week after Tasha's accident, Rupert sat beside her as they prepared their evening meal over a crackling fire.

Tasha aimed a wry smile at him. "The Ahrans seem to have lost interest in us entirely."

"I'm very happy to be ignored by our enemies," he said grimly. "Especially since we're essentially helpless."

She tossed the hair from her face. A couple of stray locks remained, and he had to restrain himself from reaching out tenderly and tucking them behind her ear. The impulse was a welcome distraction from the simmering anger that constantly threatened to overwhelm him of late.

"I don't really mind being ignored," she continued. "It is an adjustment though. When I became a princess I was instantly surrounded by fuss. It was so irritating! I used to long to be free of it. Now that the fuss has gone, it feels strange."

Rupert grunted. Having been surrounded by fuss from the moment of his birth, he understood perfectly.

"I'm happy to do routine tasks though," she said with a smile.

He shrugged. "It isn't as if we have anything more meaningful to do."

She ignored his bleak mood. "I've never needed to cook for myself before. Some of our early attempts were forgettable, but I think we're becoming quite good at it." A dimpled smile lit up her face as she sniffed the food before them.

He fixed his full attention on her, gazing at her in frank admiration. "I don't know how you do it, Tasha. Cheerfulness seems to bubble out of you." He shook his head. "I'm struggling to find anything positive to focus on. I don't think I could do this without you."

ONCE TASHA HAD FULLY RECOVERED from her injury, the two of them resumed their daily walks. Although they were no longer able to scan the horizon from the highest point on the island, they were otherwise still permitted to wander freely. They soon established a routine that incorporated at least one extensive walk around the island each day.

The benefit to Rupert went beyond exercise. He discovered he needed a change of scenery to help lift the grim mood that typically settled on him when he woke each morning. He hadn't been accustomed to thinking of himself as moody, at least not in the years that followed the dark period of Lord Eisgold's betrayal. The captivity, especially under Dessue's replacement, had changed that along with so much else besides.

RUPERT AND TASHA set off on their daily walk with two guards trailing them as always. To all appearances the guards followed without enthusiasm.

The small party took a route that led them past a pool fed by a reliable spring. The crystal clear water of the pool had called out to them from the moment they first discovered it. On that initial occasion, finding that their guards had no objection, they had jumped in and enjoyed a brief swim. The water was bracingly cold at first, but they soon adjusted. A swim became an important part of their routine whenever the weather permitted it.

Shallow at the edges, in its deepest section the water reached to Tasha's chin. The pool was wide enough to allow plenty of room to swim or splash about as their fancy took them.

Having arrived at the pool on their latest walk, Rupert stood beside it mustering the courage to brave the cold and plunge into the water. Stepping up behind him, Tasha pushed him squarely in the back, pitching him bodily into the water. He emerged shivering, a howl of protest on his lips. Tasha looked on unrepentantly, giggling with glee.

Slapping the surface of the pond with the palm of his hand, Rupert directed a stream of water at Tasha. His aim was perfect, and she squealed as cold liquid doused her. Taking advantage of her distraction, he surged from the pool and dragged her in. Both of them were now completely soaked, and after a brief wrestle they fell apart, laughing helplessly.

Dripping from head to toe, Rupert stood in the pool with hands on his hips, shaking his head in mock outrage at Tasha's surprise attack.

At the same time, he couldn't help but be grateful to her. Once more her buoyancy and cheerfulness had lifted his mood, granting him a moment's respite from the harsh realities of their situation. How could he have endured these weeks without her?

"While I'm here, I might as well take the opportunity to bathe," Tasha said in Rogandan, glancing pointedly at the guards as she said it.

The guards had been ignoring them, apparently finding their behavior foolish and beneath their attention. Now they shrugged and turned away, retracing their steps back through the trees.

The guards had previously respected Tasha's need for privacy when she bathed, and that occasion proved to be no exception. Rupert was grateful for their consideration, much as it surprised him.

Curiously, while the guards accommodated the princess's need for privacy, they still showed concern for her safety. The first time she had set out for the pool to bathe, the guards made no move to follow her. They had, however, insisted that Rupert accompany her. When he refused, they had made it clear they were not offering him a choice.

The situation raised challenges of its own for Rupert. Tasha was a beautiful young woman he cared deeply about, and it wasn't easy to remain detached as she undressed to wash herself and her clothing. He kept his back to her and tried to fix his mind on other things.

When she finished, he took his turn to bathe. She had always shown him the same courtesy, and without any apparent struggle. If he was honest, he found the discrepancy unsettling.

Pushing such thoughts from his mind, he focused on washing himself.

A deep sigh of contentment from Tasha interrupted his thoughts.

"I needed that!" she said. "In the palace there was always someone to prepare my bath and whisk away my dirty clothes. I took it far too much for granted! Now that it's gone, I can't pretend I don't miss it. I'm not myself in filthy clothes. Cleaning them properly is impossible here, but some attempt is better than nothing. And I can't tell you how good it is just to rinse my hair—I try to pretend it's been properly washed. Now I feel ready to face the world again."

He chuckled. "I'm ready to face the world too," he told her.

Stepping from the pool he made his way to her side. Seeing her smiling up at him, he reached for her hand. She placed it in his without hesitation.

He glanced around. "This wasn't exactly what I had in mind when I set out to court you."

"Our island exile hasn't exactly been romantic," she acknowledged. "But we're in an impossible situation. Thank you for helping me through it."

He returned a wan smile. "You've helped me much more than I've ever helped you. I couldn't have survived without your cheerfulness."

They stood in silence for a time, staring off into the distance.

"What are we going to do, Rupert?" she eventually asked.

He shook his head grimly. "I don't know. But as soon as an opportunity comes I'm going to seize it, however slim the chances."

RUPERT PAUSED to stretch his back, wincing at the protest from muscles he hadn't known he possessed. A steady breeze nagged at the untidy locks draped across his brow, and he wiped irritably at the sweat that dripped incessantly down his face.

A group of Ahran guards lounged idly no more than a stone's throw or two away, watching the captives with bored expressions. Rupert aimed an angry glance in their direction.

"Ignore them, Rupe," urged Tasha quietly. "They're not worth it."

For her sake he wiped the scowl from his face, shifting his attention to their shelter. Before bending to the task once more, he briefly glanced up at the sky. If he knew anything about cloud formations, wild weather would be upon them before long. They needed to work faster if they had any hope of completing the repairs to Tasha's shelter by nightfall. Perhaps sensing his unease, his companion quickly resumed her own labors.

From the moment their captors had ceased helping with practical tasks, the Rogandan princess had insisted on working alongside him whenever they needed to exert themselves. She asserted that she had become physically stronger as a result and more capable than ever before, and it was undeniably true. But the calluses on her hands confronted him with a persistent reminder of the disrespect shown her by their enemies.

To be fair, their small huts had been erected by the Ahrans. But that felt like an age ago. As time passed, more and more dwellings had been damaged by storms. The worst storm so far had descended on them the previous day, and by morning few buildings remained habitable. The guards quickly repaired their own huts, but they made it clear they had no intention of working on the huts of their captives.

Thankfully Rupert's hut had remained largely unscathed. The same could not be said for Tasha's dwelling. Perhaps her structure had been unlucky; perhaps less care had gone into its construction. Either way, they were left with no choice but to attempt a repair job themselves.

When Rupert asked for tools, the guards handed them over willingly enough. Their only requirement had been that the tools must be returned before nightfall.

He had the impression the guards didn't believe them capable of making effective use of the implements. They weren't far from the mark—with or without tools the task was almost beyond them. Rupert and Tasha had watched their huts being built, but neither of them had any personal experience of building, and they found repair work much more challenging than they had anticipated. Nevertheless, they persevered with dogged determination.

Rupert perspired profusely as he worked. He had long since stripped off his shirt in an attempt to cool off, although it made little difference. There was a time when he would have felt embarrassed to be so exposed before Tasha, but the trappings of refined society had rapidly been peeled away in the weeks of isolation. The changed reality demanded a different set of practical priorities.

"What if we don't finish in time?" Tasha asked, a trace of anxiety in her tone.

"Then you can have my hut," he replied evenly.

"But what will you do?" she asked.

"I'll sleep in the open."

She shook her head. "That won't work. If there's no other option we'll share a hut. We can find a way to make it work."

"I'm not going to even consider the possibility of failure," he said grimly.

Glancing once more at the sky, he bent his back and began again with renewed energy.

THE STORM HAD PASSED. Tasha's hut had taken a battering, but their makeshift repairs had done the job, and it had survived intact. With the sun shining once more, Rupert and Tasha took the opportunity to bathe at the pool. They welcomed the chance to forget about buildings and manual labor, and especially to leave behind their guards.

After visiting the pool they returned to the beach and gazed out to sea. Open ocean stretched off into the distance, not even the tiniest speck of land intruding upon the blue expanse. The emptiness only served to emphasize their isolation.

Then a ship sailed slowly into view around the island, anchoring off the beach. A boat was lowered into the water, and sailors rowed it toward the beach.

Were their guards being relieved again? It was an uncomfortable thought after what happened last time.

The Ahran leader met the new arrivals and conferred with them for many minutes. Then a group of guards headed purposefully toward the huts.

"What are they going to do?" asked Tasha uneasily.

Rupert stood up resolutely. "I have no idea. But I intend to find out."

Even before they reached the Ahrans it became clear that they were demolishing Tasha's hut.

Hurrying to the site, Rupert confronted them indignantly. "What is the meaning of this? We worked ourselves to the bone repairing that!"

An unfamiliar guard stepped in front of him. "Two huts are unnecessary," he growled, speaking in Rogandan. "One is more than sufficient for you both."

"Surely you're not suggesting we move in together!" Rupert retorted, shaking with anger.

Tasha placed a hand on his arm, but he refused to be placated. "This is unacceptable!" he shouted.

The new guard glowered at him. "You think yourself so high and mighty," he sneered. Switching effortlessly to Arvenian, he taunted, "Where is your kingdom now, pitiful little monarch? You deserve no more honor than a flea!"

A cold fury rose up in Rupert. The guard didn't wait for him to do something foolish. A fist smashed into his gut, causing him to double over in pain. A heavy blow to the head sent him crashing to the ground. The guard began kicking him viciously, and he curled into a ball, trying to protect his head with his arms.

The last thing he remembered before losing consciousness was an enraged Tasha leaping at the guard, screaming at the top of her lungs.

Rupert groaned. His head throbbed unmercifully, and waves of pain flooded his body.

When he opened his eyes, Tasha's face swam into view. Her look of concern was marred by an angry welt over one eye.

"What did they do to you?" he managed weakly.

"Not much. That brute of a guard slapped me hard enough, but I wasn't badly injured." She snorted. "He went away with some injuries of his own. He pretended not to feel it, but those scratches won't heal for a while." Her lip curled in grim satisfaction.

A damp cloth appeared in her hand, and she dabbed gently at his forehead. It stung, and he winced involuntarily.

"I'm sorry," she said.

He waved aside her apology, closing his eyes again in an attempt to settle himself.

"Where are we?"

"In your hut," she told him.

Speaking was difficult. He closed his eyes to rest some more.

After a while he rallied enough to ask, "Why?" His head was too fuzzy for him to better express his confusion about the new dramatic downturn in their circumstances.

"I've been asking myself the same question," she said with a sigh. "The new guards apparently came with new orders. We'll find out before long what that means in practice. I suspect we'll end up with a lot less freedom. The guard who beat you speaks Arvenian, too, so we won't be able to talk so freely anymore."

Everything had changed so abruptly. Their previous situation seemed almost pleasant by comparison.

His mind was spinning. "They destroyed your hut," he managed.

Tasha didn't respond immediately.

"Perhaps they're trying to force us together," she finally offered.

"I don't understand," he said with a frown, wincing when it set his head throbbing even more.

"We'll need to share a hut from now on."

He stared up into her face, uncomprehending.

She shrugged. "I don't know anything for certain, Rupe. I can't pretend to understand them."

Still unable to think straight, he waited patiently for her to say more.

After a pause she asked him, "Have you ever wondered about their behavior when I bathe?"

"They stay away," he replied, remembering not to frown again. "That's worth something." They were doing it out of respect for her privacy. Weren't they?

"They insist that you accompany me," she said. "Why?"

It seemed obvious. Even though they'd been ordered not to interfere with her, it made no sense to let her wander the island alone. "They wanted me to keep you safe. Why else?"

She went silent again.

He worked hard at marshaling his thoughts. "Are you suggesting the guards wanted us to sleep together?"

She gazed down at him. "Why else did they leave us alone at the pool?"

The idea made a weird kind of sense. He'd respected the boundaries, difficult as it had been. They probably hadn't expected that.

Thoughts began to come in a rush. From the beginning the guards had stayed well clear of them at night. Then it occurred to him that more than once he'd noticed the guards sniggering as the two of them headed toward the stream.

Even after Rupert had provoked Dessue's replacement, the Ahran had never forced them apart. It would have been an effective way of hitting back at Rupert, and the leader must surely have realized that.

Their captors' next step had been refusing to repair the damaged hut. With a storm closing in, Tasha herself had voiced the possibility of sharing the other one. Somehow they had managed to repair the hut themselves.

Perhaps the new guards arrived with orders to speed up the process. Since the two captives weren't taking the hint, the Ahrans had abandoned subtlety. The first step was to demolish Tasha's hut. Assaulting Rupert completed the picture.

It all added up. Separate sleeping quarters were no longer an option. Even if both huts had still been intact, Tasha needed to care for Rupert. They had literally forced him into her loving arms.

A number of things had previously seemed bewildering, but everything was slowly becoming as clear as a mountain stream.

How could he have been so blind?

From the beginning he'd believed the Ahrans were holding them for political leverage. The captivity offered an ideal opportunity to manipulate the kingdoms of Castel and Rogand. Now Rupert wondered if he understood them at all.

What could they possibly achieve by driving Tasha into his bed? Were they trying to weaken his standing in the eyes of the Rogandans? Or was there a different agenda?

Thoughts and possibilities rattled around in his head until he felt dizzy.

Try as he might, he could make no sense of it.

4

———

Bisri Ahuzza stepped forward into the throne room of His Imperial Majesty the Emperor Hourahn II of Ahr. He had positioned himself to one side of the Grand Vizier and a couple of paces behind him. As soon as they approached the throne, both men came to a halt and stooped low.

Ahuzza had always found the throne room intimidating. He couldn't help but be struck once more by the casual arrogance of its splendor, and the menace of the endless ranks of armed guards clad in imperial attire. He wondered if Rheibas ever experienced a similar reaction.

The emperor did not look pleased to see his most senior official. If the chief minister was aware of the emperor's mood, he gave no indication. As ever, The Grand Vizier presented a calm and unruffled demeanor.

The emperor fixed Rheibas in a glare. "I have been informed that my daughter is currently in Rog. What have you done to ensure her safe return to Kat Ahket?" he demanded.

"I regret to say that the Rogandan king has imprisoned her, Your Imperial Majesty. After the duplicity shown by the Rogandans in her original disappearance, it is difficult to predict what they will do next.

It is safe to say that restoring her to Your Majesty is not currently high on their agenda."

"And what of the disappearance of the king of Castel and the Rogandan princess?"

"I hardly know, Your Majesty," the Grand Vizier replied with a puzzled frown. "But it seems to be a vulgar business."

The emperor frowned. "The Rogandans claim that they were abducted by Ahrans!"

Ahuzza tried to mask his surprise. He was not aware of their disappearance, much less any claim that Ahrans were involved.

He could only admire the effectiveness of the emperor's intelligence gathering. The chief minister was head of the empire's spy network, but the emperor clearly had independent sources of his own.

Rheibas did not falter. "Any such claim is a monstrous falsehood, Your Majesty," he said firmly. "The Castelan king was apparently courting the princess. It has been suggested that he absconded with her, perhaps out of fear that his suit was about to be refused by her father. I imagine the two of them will be discovered sooner or later in some remote bolt hole. It would not shock me if the Rogandan princess is found to be expecting a child."

The chief minister dipped his head sadly. "The shame of such behavior must be difficult for the Rogandans to bear. But blaming the empire is dangerous folly. Perhaps it is an attempt to divert attention away from their own actions in making a hostage of Her Imperial Highness Princess Neira."

The emperor did not seem happy, but the chief minister was unfazed.

"If you would assign to me four or five thousand soldiers and the necessary ships to transport them, Your Majesty, I believe I could quickly resolve the current impasse."

The emperor's eyes narrowed. "I will approve no such thing!" he protested. "Do not expect me to support a military adventure in Rogand, Chief Minister. Not without much stronger cause. Get back there promptly, and find a way to resolve the matter without squandering the lives of my soldiers or plundering my treasury."

Rheibas bowed. "My diplomatic efforts will be redoubled, Your Majesty."

"You are dismissed," growled the emperor.

As the chief minister backed away, the emperor added, "Remain here, Ahuzza!"

Bisri Ahuzza stayed where he was, bowing respectfully.

As soon as the Grand Vizier had gone, the emperor turned to his envoy. "What do you make of this business involving the Castelan king and the princess, Ahuzza?" he asked.

The bisri shook his head. "It is the first I've heard of it, Your Imperial Majesty. My ships were not able to dock at Rog, so we remained at sea the whole time. We had contact with Ahran trading vessels, but the news I received through them might have been little more than hearsay. Do you believe your sources are reliable?"

The emperor waved a hand indifferently. "In this particular case the information is third or fourth hand—I wouldn't have let Rheibas off so lightly if I had real reason for concern. Nevertheless, this situation has provided me with an opportunity to remind him that I have sources of my own. I lean heavily on him, but I will never allow myself to become entirely dependent on one official, however effective."

Ahuzza nodded. "I understand, Your Majesty. You instructed me to operate independently when you gave me three ships and sent me to the region, but in practice the chief minister was my only source of reliable intelligence."

The emperor grunted. "That situation has to change!"

He directed a troubled glance at Ahuzza. "What have you learned of my daughter?"

"I am aware that she was taken by pirates—or perhaps by the Rogandans—and is now being held in Rog by the king. Beyond that I know very little, Your Majesty. According to the reports I received she is quite well. I doubt that the Rogandans would risk mistreating her.

As to what it would take to retrieve her, I cannot speak with any authority."

The emperor scowled. "There is far too much I don't understand about what is going on in Rogand," he said. "And I find some of the priorities of my chief minister perplexing." He shook his head. "Rheibas is a master at resolving political crises with little fuss and minimal loss of life. Why hasn't he been able to secure the release of my daughter? Why his fixation with a military solution? And on the other side of the world! There are subtleties here I don't understand."

The bisri decided it was wisest to say nothing.

The emperor continued, "When Rheibas sails for Rogand, you will return as well with the ships you commanded last time. As before you will operate independently from the chief minister. But this time you are to establish your own contacts with the Rogandans."

His face set hard. "I want my daughter back! And I want her back without a war! I cannot be expected to make sound decisions without reliable information, and I am no longer willing to limit myself to one person's perspective on such a delicate situation. Too much is at stake! Make no representations on my behalf, but ferret out everything that is happening. Do it discreetly. When you learn anything of relevance, I want to know about it immediately."

Bisri Ahuzza bowed.

"You are dismissed," the emperor ordered.

THE GRAND VIZIER'S summons to the royal palace had not extended to Bolnyk. Accordingly, Rheibas's senior agent made his way to the Grand Vizier's palace to await his master's return. As soon as the audience with the emperor came to an end, Bolnyk expected the chief minister would want to meet with him.

He was not disappointed. Rheibas appeared sooner than the agent expected.

The chief minister pointed the way to his private conference room, and Bolnyk followed him in.

Calling for a servant, Rheibas ordered refreshments before adding, "Make sure I am not disturbed! Under any circumstances."

The servant left, closing the door behind him.

"We have work to do, Bolnyk," the chief minister said grimly. "As I expected, the emperor is not inclined to give me a free hand in Rogand. We will need to use other means to achieve our goals."

Dipping his head in silent acknowledgment, Bolnyk aimed an inquiring look at the chief minister.

"Applying military pressure is not an option in the short term," Rheibas told him, a sour look on his face. "Nevertheless, we have the resources we need. It is a simple matter of applying appropriate leverage in the right place at the right time."

"I await your command, Your Eminence," Bolnyk assured him.

Pulling out a map labeled "Arvenon and Surrounding Kingdoms," Rheibas bent low over it. "This is what I need you to do."

WITH THE CONFERENCE AT AN END, Rheibas met his senior agent's eyes. "Do you understand?"

"I do, Your Eminence," Bolnyk replied, pushing himself to his feet and offering a tight bow.

Attentive as always, he waited patiently for the chief minister to dismiss him. He intended to allow himself a few minutes to relax in his own modest quarters in the palace. Any respite would have to be brief. There were things he needed to do.

The chief minister had other ideas. "Come with me," he barked.

Following Rheibas through a seemingly endless succession of echoing corridors, Bolnyk eventually found himself before a metal door in an unused wing of the palace.

Two guards stood outside. At the approach of the Grand Vizier, they snapped to attention.

"Open it," growled Rheibas. "Then leave us."

One of the guards unlocked the door. Tugging hard, he pulled it open. Given its thickness and weight, it must have been soundproof.

A dimly lit room lay within. Bolnyk caught a glimpse of a miserable and bedraggled man, his face vaguely familiar, sitting on a low bed. Bolnyk decided he had spotted him on at least one other occasion, although he knew nothing of the man's history.

Rheibas flicked a hand, and the guards withdrew, positioning themselves out of earshot. Rheibas ordered Bolnyk, "Wait here." Entering the room, he leaned heavily on the door to push it closed. In spite of his efforts, it remained slightly ajar.

A brief conversation ensued between the two men. Bolnyk caught no more than snatches of it.

Rheibas's growl reached him faintly. "You...accompany me...Rogand...convince me or...sharks."

"But...but I...I showed you...the..." the man sputtered loudly.

"Silence!" shouted Rheibas, cutting him short.

Bolnyk heard no more than muffled voices until Rheibas emerged.

Waving over the guards, the chief minister waited until they had secured the door, then he headed off, Bolnyk beside him.

As they walked, Rheibas issued a rapid series of instructions. "I am making you responsible for this imbecile. Bring him to my ship just before we leave for Rogand. Place him aboard in a secure location where no one can talk to him. The man is deranged, but in Rogand I might be able to find a use for his ravings, given the right audience. I expect him to arrive safely and in good health, but beyond ensuring that, do not speak to him or waste a minute of your time with him. Do you understand?"

When Bolnyk responded with a nod, the chief minister turned on his heel and walked briskly away.

The senior agent watched his master turn a corner and disappear. Then he gazed thoughtfully back the way they had come.

What possible interest could Rheibas have in the bedraggled creature hidden away in the room? What had the two men been talking about? And what audience could possibly benefit from the ravings of a madman? Was Rheibas looking for ways to confuse his enemies?

Bolnyk set off for his rooms absorbed in his thoughts. He knew better than anyone how dangerous it was to pry into his master's business, and he had no intention of crossing that particular line.

Nevertheless, the situation was intriguing. A lunatic held no interest for him, but he couldn't pretend his curiosity wasn't roused, if only because the chief minister usually confided in Bolnyk, yet the senior agent knew nothing of this prisoner.

RAGING seas made the voyage unusually hazardous for Bolnyk and the other passengers on the ship that bore the Grand Vizier toward Rog. Tossed about unmercifully, the senior agent had ample opportunity to ponder darkly the strange fascination that drew his master so far from home once more. Rheibas had invested considerable resource into establishing a presence in the region, to say nothing of the elaborate scheme involving the princess. Yet his senior agent had no idea what he was striving to achieve.

After a series of unusually mountainous waves had slammed into the ship, Bolnyk remembered the prisoner. He had seen him safely aboard, but Rheibas had also given him responsibility for delivering the prisoner to Rogand safely and in good health. Accordingly after collecting a loaf of bread, a lump of cheese, and a skin of wine, he lurched his way below decks to the section of the hold where the man was located.

Unbarring the door of the prisoner's room, he pulled it open and stepped inside, holding high a candle. The flickering light revealed the prisoner standing in a dark corner, swaying unsteadily with the rolling of the ship. The chains clanking around the man's ankles confirmed there was no risk of him escaping.

He threw the food onto the floor near the prisoner.

The man was eyeing him curiously. "You're the Grand Vizier's lapdog," he observed, speaking in Rogandan.

"You have no idea who you're talking to," Bolnyk growled, firmly gripping a nearby beam of wood in an attempt to stay in one place.

"Probably not," the man acknowledged. "But I do know that the Grand Vizier trusts you implicitly."

"How do you conclude that?"

The man might have been shrugging, but it was impossible to be certain with the pitching of the ship. "He allowed you to see me, and he hasn't executed you yet."

The senior agent scowled. It was infuriating to think that a miserable lunatic might be privy to information the chief minister had kept from him.

He wondered again who the man was and what the chief minister wanted him for. He hadn't forgotten either that Rheibas ordered him not to speak to the man at all.

Strangest of all, if the man was insane, he certainly hid it well.

Curiosity kept him lingering.

The man seemed to sense it. "He hasn't told you, has he?"

With no response from the senior agent, a mocking grin came to the man's face. "Of course not," he smirked. "He would never share the knowledge with *you*."

Anger welled up inside Bolnyk. Who was this cur to flaunt his secrets? He stepped closer, raising a hand to wipe the smirk off the ugly face.

The man shrank away, wincing fearfully. "I'll tell him!" he shrieked.

Bolnyk stopped short before landing a blow. Turning his back on the prisoner, he staggered away, reeling with the motion of the ship.

Galling as it might be, the man was right. Bolnyk had been ordered not to communicate with the prisoner. He would have some explaining to do if he left the man with an injury.

The interaction had left him with more questions than ever. Still simmering, he headed away, acknowledging to himself that his anger was directed as much toward Rheibas as it was toward the prisoner.

5

______

Will Prentis sat with King Steffan and Queen Essanda of Arvenon in the king's private audience chamber in the castle at Arnost.

"Can you describe the mood in Rog?" the king asked Will.

Will's face grew grim. "Even before we left, King Krasmir was upending the city in his search for the princess and King Rupert," he replied. "He found no sign of them."

"Has he tracked down more of the Ahran agents?"

"He has. He somehow came into possession of a document listing the safe houses of Ahran agents throughout Rog and the surrounding countryside. He asked Lord Kulferan to surreptitiously observe a few of the sites to verify the document's accuracy. When it checked out, Lord Kulferan carefully planned a series of raids before dawn one morning. The locations were raided simultaneously to prevent agents from warning their comrades. They netted a couple of hundred Ahran agents."

The king looked shocked. "So many!"

Will nodded. "Lord Kulferan's investigations revealed that some of the agents had been there for almost two years."

"This has been long planned," King Steffan observed grimly.

"Why would the Ahrans take the risk of writing down the locations of their safe houses? Much less leave such a document lying around? It makes no sense."

Will shrugged. "It probably wasn't the Ahrans. The document was written in Rogandan, and it seems more likely that it was put together by someone else. The priests of the dark gods have their own sources of information, and the Varasans have a very effective network too."

Will didn't say so, but he himself was the author of the document. He had prepared it not long before he left Rog with his family. The information had come entirely from Thomas through the agency of the Stone of Knowing. Bolnyk, the man in charge of the Ahran agents, had unwittingly revealed the locations when Thomas finally got a good look at him. Not being literate in any language, Thomas had called upon Will to write it all down. Will had left the document where he knew King Krasmir's people would find it.

"Did they learn anything at all about the likely whereabouts of King Rupert and Princess Teylee?" asked Queen Essanda.

"Unfortunately not," Will replied, shaking his head. "They were able to identify what appeared to be the headquarters of the Ahrans, but the leader of the agents wasn't there when they raided it. There were signs that the king and the princess had been held there, at least briefly. At the time we left Rog, Lord Kulferan's men were still interrogating the Ahrans. I suspect they will discover that King Rupert and Princess Teylee were taken away by ship."

This last piece of information was much more than a suspicion. Having seen the Ahran prisoners himself not long before leaving Rog, Thomas knew that several of them had witnessed the two captives boarding an Ahran vessel.

Will had decided it was wisest to let Lord Kulferan extract this information for himself. If the Rogandan commander failed to arrive at the truth, Will could always arrange for the information to be passed on indirectly, as he had done with the locations of the Ahran safe houses.

"Are you still planning to return to Rog?" asked King Steffan.

"Yes," Will told him. "I made a promise to King Krasmir, and I intend to keep it."

"How does Amyra feel about that?" asked Queen Essanda.

"She isn't excited about me leaving, of course, but she understands. She will remain here in Arnost with the children this time." He shook his head with a sigh. "Both of us have great sympathy for King Krasmir and Queen Deka. We have some idea of what they must be feeling."

For a moment the queen's own grief showed plainly on her face. "I am every bit as eager as the Rogandans to see the captives returned safely," she said quietly. Her eyes had become moist. "I am anxious for my brother! And for his kingdom!"

The king quickly moved the conversation in a different direction. "Will anyone else be returning with you, Will?" he asked.

"Just Thomas," Will replied.

The king raised an eyebrow, but he offered no comment on Will's choice of companion.

"You're not taking Rufe?" asked the queen.

Will shook his head. "It wouldn't be fair to him. He would be the only one who can't speak any Rogandan. And if it ever should come to fighting the Ahrans, you'll need him here."

The queen seemed satisfied.

"Reluctant as we are to let you go, Will," said the king gravely, "all of us want to do whatever we can to support King Krasmir and Queen Deka in their efforts to retrieve King Rupert and Princess Teylee."

WILL STOOD HOLDING Amyra at arm's length, drinking in the sight of her. He wanted to remember her just as she was while he was gone.

After a few moments he turned away with a sigh, gazing out of one of the tall windows that illuminated their rooms in the royal castle.

"Are you sure you want us to stay here in Arnost?" Amyra asked. "I expect we would be safe back home in Erestor."

He shook his head. "I'd prefer to wait until our whole party can return together, with an armed escort," he said. "These are uncertain times, and it would be risky to make assumptions about how safe it might be to travel."

She shrugged. "Since Thomas is going with you, I am sure Elena will stay in Arnost with their children as well."

"You'll be able to enjoy a bit of relaxed time with her," Will suggested.

Amyra winced. "I have some distance to travel before we can truly relax together. I'm not proud of the way I behaved at times when we were in Rog. I'll be grateful for an opportunity to make it up to her."

"I don't think you need to be too concerned," Will told her. "Elena is a remarkably gracious person."

"She is," Amyra agreed. "Although that doesn't absolve me."

After a few moments' silence, Amyra casually added, "I will, of course, be sending the Stone of Authority with you."

Will didn't try to hide his shock. "But it's yours!" he exclaimed. He shook his head stubbornly. "I've never wanted responsibility for any of the stones. You know the reasons."

"I understand perfectly, Will," she replied. Stepping closer and slipping an arm around his waist, she rested her head on his shoulder. "The fact that you *don't* want the stone is a good reason why it will be safe in your hands."

He received her embrace, but he remained unconvinced.

"The stone is the reason I needed to go to Rog with you last time," she reminded him. "Having access to it will be just as important when you return."

When he still didn't respond, she became animated. "We don't know what will happen! The stone might play a crucial role."

"I have no experience whatsoever in using it!" he protested.

"Then practice!" she exclaimed. "We'll make time before you go."

Clearly recognizing he wasn't convinced, she added insistently, "It's perfectly sensible, Will. Thomas and Elena have been sharing their stone for years now, and nothing but good has come from it."

He grunted.

Having long since concluded that possession of a stone would be especially perilous for someone in his position, he couldn't simply ignore his misgivings. The more so with that particular stone. Who could guess where it might lead?

———

THOMAS STOOD with Will at the rail of the Nomad Lady, gazing out over gently rolling seas. A steady breeze had been driving the ship forward at a rapid clip, and the favorable weather showed no sign of changing.

It felt like an age had passed since Thomas had parted with Elena at Arnost.

"Try to be careful, Thomas," she had said, a nervous frown creasing her lovely face.

He had contented himself with a reassuring smile in response. He knew better than to make promises about the future.

Neither his children nor Will's children seemed too troubled by the departure of their fathers. They had the run of the castle. Crown Prince Aiden, Prince Leonid, and even little Princess Charlotte had quickly been drawn into their games. Not surprisingly, it didn't take long before squabbles broke out. Amyra and Elena would have their hands full.

In spite of his ambivalence about sea voyages, Will had decided the most straightforward journey to Rog was by sea. After riding west to Maranelle, they had once again found Captain Yordin available and willing to transport them. The Nomad Lady had begun to feel like an old and trusted friend.

As if alerted by Thomas's thoughts, the captain joined them at the rail.

"We're making excellent time, M'Lord," he told Will. "Baron Island is behind us, and we should clear Savage Strait before long."

"That's encouraging news, Captain," replied Will. "As you know, I'm eager to arrive in Rogand as soon as possible."

Captain Yordin glanced briefly at the seas and up at the sky before nodding in satisfaction. "I see no reason to put in at Varacellan, M'Lord. If these winds continue, we can sail directly to Rog."

Will dipped his head in acknowledgment.

A puzzled look came to the grizzled face of the old sailor as he gazed up at the sky. "The wind seems to have settled down nicely. It was beyond understanding earlier." Peering over the rail, he added, "And I've never seen so many dolphins."

After shaking his head in bafflement, the captain offered a respectful nod and headed away in the direction of the wheel.

Thomas grinned at Will. "Was that you playing with the wind earlier?" he asked.

A pained look came to Will's face. "Yes, it was," he admitted. He frowned in frustration. "I can't get the hang of it at all! Controlling the elements is Amyra's thing."

"And the dolphins?" asked Thomas.

Will's mouth twisted in an impish grin. "That's me."

He flicked a finger, and two dolphins burst from the water, chittering loudly.

Thomas gaped open-mouthed.

Will returned a wink. "I seem to be having a bit more success with living creatures."

"And people?" asked Thomas after a pause.

"Never!" growled Will fiercely. "I will *never* forget what it's like to be compelled against your will."

His face became calm again. "After insisting for years that I had no desire for a stone, you must be wondering what I'm about, Thomas."

Thomas raised an eyebrow.

The commander sighed. "I told Amyra I didn't want it. *And* that it wasn't safe for me. She refused to listen." A wry smile creased his face. "Some of the blame falls on you, Thomas! You and Elena gave Amyra the idea. You're so effective at sharing the Stone of Knowing." He gazed at the dolphins sporting around the bow wave. "This arrangement isn't permanent though. After this is over, she'll be getting it back. For good."

.   .   .

THE WINDS HAD CONTINUED to be favorable. Varacellan lay behind them; they had entered Rogandan waters.

Thomas's conversation with Will was interrupted by a cry from the lookout. "Ships on the horizon! Three-masters!"

"How many?" shouted the captain.

"Three o' them, Cap'n!" the lookout replied.

Will made his way to Captain Yordin, Thomas trailing behind him.

"We need to be wary," the captain told them soberly. "Sightings of Ahran vessels in these waters are on the rise. Some of them are warships."

"What do you propose to do?" asked Will.

"Outrun 'em if we can," the captain replied determinedly.

Sailors began dashing about as the captain shouted orders. Sails were unfurled until every available piece of canvas was catching the wind.

"They've spotted us, Cap'n," shouted the lookout.

The masts were now visible to everyone on board. It soon became apparent that the ships were heading directly toward the Lady.

"Can you do anything to help?" Thomas quietly asked Will.

He shook his head. "I'd likely slow us down," he said grimly. "If Amyra was here it would be a different matter."

Tension grew as the three-masters drew ever closer.

"They're Ahran ships—no doubt about that," grumbled the captain.

Eventually, the tall ships began to overhaul them. Captain Yordin had long since passed out weapons to his crew, but it was going to be a one-sided battle if it did come to fighting. The decks of their pursuers were lined with soldiers.

As one of the foreign vessels drew alongside the Lady, shouts of command rang out, and the Ahran soldiers withdrew, lining up to take their turn descending into the hatch. After a few minutes the deck was almost empty.

"Let's find out what they want, Captain," said Will. "I'll talk to them. It appears that they're not looking for a fight."

The captain frowned in response, but he didn't argue. Ordering a couple of men to prepare to launch a longboat, he shouted orders for the other sailors to reef the sails.

As the Ahran sailors slowed their own ships, a man appeared on the deck of the nearest vessel. If his dress and bearing offered any indication, he was a nobleman. Twisting the clasp beneath his tunic, Thomas brought the Stone of Knowing into contact with his skin.

Will appeared at his side. "What can you tell me about our friend over there?" he asked quietly.

"He has access to the emperor," Thomas replied, "and he shows no sign of aggressive intentions."

The captain joined them before Thomas could say more. "The longboat is ready to launch."

Will nodded. "I'll take Thomas with me. We'll go unarmed. No need for guards—we don't want to send the wrong message."

Captain Yordin looked doubtful, but he nodded curtly.

A rope ladder was lowered when they reached the other vessel, and they climbed aboard. The Ahran nobleman stood ready to receive them.

Another man stood at the nobleman's side. It quickly became clear that he was there as an interpreter. He nodded a greeting. "Do you speak Rogandan?" he asked politely.

"We do," Will replied.

"Are you the captain?" he asked Will, pointing to the Nomad Lady.

"I am not. My name is Lord Torbury. I am an Arvenian nobleman. This is my friend, Thomas Stablehand."

The interpreter bowed before speaking rapidly to the Ahran nobleman. After they had conversed briefly, he bowed again.

"My name is Ronizah," he said. He indicated the nobleman. "This is Bisri Ahuzza."

At the mention of his name, Bisri Ahuzza performed a tight bow of his own.

"Could you please accompany us to the bisri's cabin? He would welcome the opportunity to speak with you."

Will shot a brief glance in his direction, and Thomas returned an untroubled expression. Will knew him well enough to take his meaning.

"Certainly," agreed Will, returning his attention to Ronizah. Sending a cheerful wave to the men lining the decks of the Nomad Lady, he set off after the two Ahrans, Thomas at his side.

6

———

Of the Arvenians, only Brother Ander remained in the Rogandan capital. Kamash had sailed away to his island, leaving the Stone of Vitality in the monk's care. Will and Amyra and Thomas and Elena and their families had gone as well, no doubt impatient to consign their Rogandan misadventures to the past. Count Ranauld had long since departed with the rest of the delegation.

As the days passed, Brother Ander could have found ample opportunity to regret his decision to stay, had he been willing to entertain such thoughts. But he felt sure there was a reason why he needed to be there. It just remained to discover what it was.

The palace grounds held mixed memories for him, but he frequented them anyway, appreciating the opportunity to stretch his legs in the fresh air. Two armed guards trailed behind him every-where he went—a visible legacy of the Rogandan king's unwilling-ness to allow further mishaps to befall guests staying at his palace.

His friendly attempts to engage the guards proved futile. One of them, known as Kyleth, rarely said a word to him, although he had plenty to say to his companion. The other, Ghonik, scarcely spoke at all. In time the monk learned to ignore them.

A couple of weeks after the other Arvenians had left, Brother Ander received a message through Kyleth. Given the soldier's obvious reluctance to speak to him, the monk wondered why Kyleth passed it on at all. Perhaps whoever sent the message had called in a favor.

The message requested a meeting at his earliest opportunity. He saw no reason to refuse. He had time aplenty on his hands, and King Krasmir had placed no restrictions on his movements. Accordingly he invited Kyleth to arrange a meeting.

Whoever sent the message must have felt a pressing need for urgency, because the monk found himself being led to a secluded setting in the palace grounds that same afternoon.

The location surprised him, given that access to the palace and its grounds was heavily restricted. Quite apart from the location, Brother Ander couldn't account for anyone wanting to meet with him at all. As far as he knew, very few Rogandans were even aware of his existence. He therefore approached the interaction with considerable curiosity.

Kyleth and Ghonik seemed more reserved than usual as they led him to the meeting place. While not exactly furtive, they didn't appear relaxed. He felt no undue concern about his safety, but the clandestine nature of the interaction had thoroughly roused his interest.

It soon became apparent that their destination was a heavily wooded section of the palace grounds. As they approached, he caught sight of a cloaked figure standing restlessly among the trees. The petitioner proved to be a soldier in late middle-age. Once Brother Ander came into view, the man made a visible effort to calm himself.

Kyleth was inquisitive to the point of being nosy, and even Ghonik hovered close at hand. The gray-headed inquirer glared at them until they moved out of earshot, Kyleth mumbling audibly under his voice.

The moment they were gone, the man turned to the monk. "My wife is very ill," he said, not even pausing to introduce himself. "I would be grateful if you would come and heal her."

Brother Ander's eyebrows went up in surprise. "Why call on me?" he asked.

"My nephew is a soldier. He was with you at the ford," the man replied. "When you healed the boy."

When the monk didn't respond immediately, the man became restless again. "The boy was dead—my nephew had no doubt about it!"

"I will visit your wife," Brother Ander said reassuringly. "I don't know if I can help, but I am willing to pray for her. If she is healed it will be God you need to thank, not me."

"Will you come now? She doesn't have much time."

"If you wish."

The man nodded in relief. "My name is Tarvek. My wife is called Vehmina. Please come with me."

He set off rapidly, checking frequently to assure himself that the monk was following. Kyleth and Ghonik trailed along behind.

Tarvek led them rapidly out of the palace grounds and onto a thoroughfare that led toward the heart of Rog. He moved so quickly that Brother Ander was almost forced to run to keep up with him.

They turned off the main road and wound through a number of side streets, eventually reaching a modestly sized house. Pushing through the front door, Tarvek held it wide for the monk. He ignored the guards entirely. They made their own way in.

Brother Ander followed Tarvek upstairs into a dimly lit room, the guards close behind them. A woman lay on a low bed, unmoving and deathly pale. He examined her closely, touching her forehead, examining her eyes, and listening to her breathing. His extensive experience as a healer told him she was close to death.

He knew there was little he could do, but while weighing up the limited options before him, he decided to offer a prayer of blessing. The Stone of Vitality lay in a pocket of his robe, and he fingered it absently with one hand as he prepared to pray. Placing the other hand on Vehmina's head, he mouthed a blessing followed by an entreaty.

The change in the patient's condition was as swift as it was astonishing. Opening her eyes, she looked up at him and smiled.

"I'm thirsty," she announced.

Tarvek bustled about the room in agitation, alternately hugging his wife and plying her with water and wine. He tried repeatedly to press payment into Brother Ander's hands, and it was only with great effort that the monk prevented him.

The situation quickly began to feel uncomfortable to Brother Ander. Anxious to leave, he murmured a farewell and made his way downstairs, pushing through the door of the house. He emerged into the street to discover a small crowd outside the house.

Kyleth and Ghonik had followed him out of the door. Stepping past him, they shoved the inquisitive onlookers aside before bustling him back toward the palace.

Tarvek was not the only one surprised by the sudden recovery of Vehmina. The monk was equally taken aback by what had happened.

Almost from the time he became a monk he had been a healer, calling upon herbs, his ever-expanding medical knowledge, and his growing confidence in prayer to treat the sick. Ethen's miraculous recovery had been something entirely different. While never fully comprehending it, he concluded at the time that the Stone of Vitality had somehow boosted the potency of his prayers.

To all appearances, something similar had just happened again. The Stone of Vitality alone couldn't account for it. He'd been touching it when he first placed his hand on Vehmina, but the healing hadn't come until he prayed.

Brother Ander's own limitations as a healer had long been a source of frustration to him. Was it possible that his prayers, when supported by the stone, granted him access to a much more effective way of bringing relief to the sick and injured? He eagerly looked forward to further opportunities to find out.

BIG NEWS TRAVELED FAST throughout a city, but even Brother Ander was surprised by how quickly word of the woman's healing spread.

He rose the following morning to find himself besieged by requests for help.

The evident misery that lay behind the appeals stirred his compassion. Accordingly, he headed for the palace gates not long after the sun had risen.

Kyleth and Ghonik accompanied him as always, although they did not hide their reluctance. The remarkable recovery of Vehmina the previous day had left them no less wide-eyed than Tarvek. Yet both of them now seemed cautious and uncertain. Up to that point, their role as his guards had been relaxed and undemanding. Were they sensing that everything might be about to change?

Stepping through the gates, Brother Ander was greeted by a small crowd. Hope and despair warred within many petitioners, the tension evident on their faces.

Two people began to argue loudly about who had the right to be seen first. When a scuffle broke out, the two guards were forced to intervene. Quickly eyeballing those who had taken no part in the fight, Ghonik selected a woman holding a child who was clearly in pain.

Dispensing with his usual examination, Brother Ander immediately prayed for the child while grasping the Stone of Vitality. The gathered petitioners went quiet as they witnessed an immediate and remarkable transformation in the child's condition. Immediately a crowd of people pushed forward demanding attention. Chaos threatened.

Filled with confidence after witnessing the effectiveness of prayer supported by the stone, Brother Ander held up his arms for quiet. As soon as the noise abated, he addressed the crowd. "Please be patient!" he called. "I will try to see you all."

Having responded to the first couple of petitioners, he saw that a line had formed. It grew in length even as he watched, snaking back and forth as new people joined it. Taking a deep breath and exhaling slowly, he called forward the next person.

Weeping sores, broken limbs, blind eyes—almost every imaginable disorder confronted him. He refused to be daunted. Some conditions he recognized, some he did not, but every one of them yielded to his earnest entreaties augmented by the power of the stone.

The sensational recoveries might have appeared effortless, but for reasons he did not understand, they came at a cost. He barely noticed any impact from the first two or three healings, but after that he soon became profoundly weary. What he appeared to be achieving with little effort quickly drained him to the point of exhaustion. After every new healing he was forced to rest, and for longer each time.

The passing hours became a blur. People came and went until he was barely able to focus.

Eventually an authoritative voice rang out, calling an end to it. Looking up wearily Brother Ander found Tarvek and Vehmina facing the crowd.

"The monk needs to stop!" Tarvek called. "He is close to collapse! We will ask him to come tomorrow to Ugar's Repose. It is a well known landmark—the low hill to the southwest of the city. For now he needs to rest!"

Grumbling broke out at the suggested delay, but his condition must have been obvious to everyone, and the people accepted Tarvek's words. To Brother Ander's relief, the crowd slowly dispersed.

After agreeing to Tarvek's proposal and thanking him sincerely, the monk dragged himself back to the palace. Kyleth and Ghonik followed silently. He barely noticed them.

Reaching his rooms, he gulped down some water before collapsing onto his bed.

BROTHER ANDER WOKE before dawn to a dull pain throbbing in his head. He had barely eaten the previous day, and his stomach rumbled uncomfortably.

As usual, food had been delivered to his rooms, and he worked away at it steadily. Water had been provided as well, and after drinking freely his head began to clear.

Intending to set off for the palace gates, he left his rooms to find his guards waiting for him.

"You need to remain in the palace," Kyleth said bluntly.

The monk's eyebrows furrowed. "Why?" he asked, baffled at the thinly veiled hostility in the guard's tone.

Kyleth said nothing.

"It is safer here," Ghonik offered. His manner conveyed caution rather than antagonism.

"Thank you for your concern," said Brother Ander. "But unless the king insists I remain here, I will go. I made a promise to Tarvek and to the people."

With that, he set out determinedly for the gates. The guards followed close behind, Kyleth glowering at him and Ghonik looking concerned.

Tarvek was waiting for him. He seemed ill at ease.

"Is anything wrong?" asked the monk.

Tarvek lowered his voice. "We can expect trouble. Some of the priests have been stirring up the people. I have just come from Ugar's Repose. People began gathering there early this morning, but not everyone is sympathetic, and some of the sick have already been driven away."

Brother Ander wasn't entirely surprised. Bringing relief to suffering people wasn't likely to win over the priests of the dark gods if they perceived him as muscling in on their territory.

It made no difference. He had the means to help the afflicted, and he had no intention of ignoring them.

Tarvek led the way to Ugar's Repose, the guards following close behind. Ghonik wore a look of concern; Kyleth was scowling.

If Brother Ander had expected a sea of eager faces when he arrived, he would have been disappointed by the sullen glares that greeted him instead. A few in the crowd wore hopeful expressions, but the restless throng before him bore all the indicators of a mob. No priests stood nearby, although he spotted a couple of men wearing their distinctive black garb at the rear.

"You're not wanted here," a rough voice called.

"Go back to where you came from, foreign scum!" shouted another.

The hecklers were interrupted by an energetic woman who pushed her way to the front. She looked frail, but she was determined. "Let me through," she demanded.

Several of the bystanders jeered at her. "Go home, old woman," scoffed one.

"I ain't goin' nowhere!" she informed them tartly. "I waited in line for hours yesterday, and now it's my turn!"

With that, she approached Brother Ander boldly.

The monk greeted her with a gentle smile. Placing a hand on her head, he prayed for her.

"It's gone!" she shouted, a look of astonishment beaming from her face. "The pain is gone! Thank you! Thank you!" She bent low to him before capering about joyfully.

The reaction of the woman seemed to further rile the crowd.

"Think you're in charge around here, do you?" a voice snarled.

"Who are you to interfere with the will of Malzakh?"

"Keep your pretend god to yourself! We follow the dark gods of Rogand!"

Shouts of agreement followed this last statement. Clubs appeared, and men stepped forward menacingly.

"It's time to go, Brother Ander!" Tarvek called urgently, backing away in alarm.

The monk glanced instinctively at his guards. Ghonik began moving forward to defend him, but the crowd shoved him aside. Kyleth hung back out of harm's way.

Brother Ander didn't blame either of his guards. Two of them could not protect him against a mob.

He held his ground, facing the men who threatened him. "I bear you no ill will," he told them.

His calm demeanor seemed to enrage them further. Rushing forward, they began punching and shoving him. Pushed back and forth, he lost his footing and went down. Men surrounded him, kicking and beating him unmercifully. Curled up defenseless on the ground, he tried to protect his head with his arms.

Pain overwhelmed his senses. The frenzy continued unabated

until a voice dimly reached him through the agony, "Soldiers are coming!"

The blows ceased, but his suffering continued.

Darkness rose up to claim him. With his consciousness slipping away, his limbs slumped nervelessly. Sliding deeper into his robe, a hand came to rest upon the Stone of Vitality.

7

From the moment they arrived at Ugar's Repose, Ghonik could see there would be trouble. He had more than enough experience to recognize the signs.

This was not the crowd that had pressed in eagerly to the monk the day before, frantic in their enthusiasm to be released from their suffering. Today a sea of grim faces awaited the new arrivals, and the guard's unease grew the moment he spotted the dark-clad priests at the back of the mob.

It hadn't been difficult to predict what was coming. His own cousin was a priest of the dark gods, and Ghonik could readily imagine what he would have to say about foreign monks being permitted to roam the streets of Rog, stirring up the masses. Sooner or later the Arvenian would get what was coming to him, and loyal followers of the dark gods would surely applaud when it happened.

Kyleth had already made it obvious his sympathies lay with the priests. Given the way he despised foreigners, it was hardly surprising. When first assigned to the monk, he had accepted the duty with an oily smile. Around Ghonik, he made no attempt to hide his true feelings.

Yet this man was no ordinary foreigner. Who else healed the sick with a touch? Ghonik had always bowed without question to the dark gods. But he had never heard of their priests giving sight to a blind woman or mending a crippled leg.

He himself knew a soldier who witnessed the murder of the Arvenian commander's son. The soldier insisted that the boy had been dead, and that he returned to life after the monk lifted him into his arms and prayed.

The story hadn't convinced Ghonik. Not until he had seen the monk in action himself.

He doubted no longer. And he had never felt so conflicted.

Whatever his own uncertainties, his duty was to keep the foreigner out of harm's way. From the moment they arrived at Ugar's Repose, it was obvious to Ghonik that he should have done more to keep his charge from coming there. Passions had been roused, and the healing of the woman only inflamed the fury.

When the mob began to move in, Ghonik had stepped forward to do his duty. The crowd had muscled him aside. Tarvek would have tried to do something if Kyleth hadn't forcibly restrained him for his own safety. Kyleth himself made no attempt to intervene.

It took only moments before protecting the monk became impossible. There were simply too many assailants.

In the end Ghonik could only look on helplessly while the monk was brutally attacked.

The approach of a patrol of Lord Kulferan's soldiers brought an end to the assault, but it was too late for the victim. No one could survive such a savage beating.

Looking toward Kyleth, Ghonik caught his eye. The other guard shrugged apathetically, his manner conveying complete disinterest in the fate of their charge. Ghonik turned away with a scowl. His partner had the sensibility of a weasel.

Peering down at the victim once more, Ghonik wondered gloomily what they should do with the body. He couldn't begin to imagine what they were going to say to the king.

Then, impossibly, the monk stirred. His eyes blinked, and he drew in a shuddering breath. Then he sat up.

Ghonik stood open-mouthed with amazement. Kyleth had gone pale.

Apparently unaware of their reaction, Brother Ander stretched his limbs awkwardly before clambering to his feet.

Wincing, he smiled wryly. "I apparently didn't receive a warm welcome," he offered.

The magnitude of the understatement left Ghonik speechless.

Tarvek hurried to the monk. "Brother Ander, how is it possible? Your injuries!"

"I imagine it looked worse than it was," the big man returned. "I don't seem to have suffered any real harm."

The captain of the army patrol rode up, bringing their interaction to an end.

"What was the cause of the disturbance?" he demanded. "Is there a problem here?"

"No problem at all," said Kyleth brightly. "Just a minor misunderstanding. We were able to resolve the matter, so there's no cause for concern."

The captain looked less than convinced, but with no obvious need for his intervention, he soon wheeled his horse about. Signaling to his men, he led them away at a trot.

Kyleth sidled up to the monk. "Brother Ander," he said, "Congratulations on your magnificent recovery! I never doubted the outcome for a moment." He lowered his voice. "I think I might know someone who is very unwell and could benefit from your services, if you're willing."

"Of course. I'm happy to do whatever I can to help people," the monk replied. He seemed a little unsteady. "Perhaps tomorrow," he added tentatively.

Kyleth nodded with satisfaction. "Excellent! I'll set something up for tomorrow afternoon."

"We must return Brother Ander to the palace!" said Tarvek. Taking the big man in hand, he gently began steering him toward the city.

Kyleth fell in beside Ghonik. Leaning forward conspiratorially, he spoke in an undertone. "This could work out very well for us," he said. "I know a person with more coin than he knows how to spend. He has major health problems, and he'll pay handsomely for a bit of personal attention from our good friend here." He jerked his head toward the monk. He rubbed his hands. "Once he's sorted out, there'll be plenty of others."

Ghonik scowled at him. "What about the dark gods?"

"My loyalty hasn't changed," growled Kyleth. "But the priests will need to lie low for a while after what just happened. In the meantime, business is business!"

Ghonik made no attempt to hide his utter contempt for Kyleth and his proposal.

Kyleth rolled his eyes at his partner's reaction. "Suit yourself," he said with a shrug. Turning his back on Ghonik, he hurried forward to catch up with Tarvek and Brother Ander.

***

KYLETH WASTED no time before setting up a meeting with the sick acquaintance he had mentioned. The following afternoon was not far advanced before Brother Ander once more found himself leaving the palace with his guards.

This time they traveled in a covered wagon.

"You had an energetic day yesterday, Brother Ander," Kyleth explained. "It's only right that we spare your legs."

The monk suspected the mode of transport had more to do with keeping him out of sight than preserving his energy. Having already had more than enough excitement, he saw no reason to complain.

The wagon rumbled through the streets of Rog, carefully bypassing the seedier side of the city. Glancing out of the back, he noticed the dwellings becoming bigger and more pretentious. Eventually they came to a brief halt before being admitted through ornate gates into an expansive courtyard surrounded by high walls.

Climbing out of the wagon, he looked around. The mansion

before him surely belonged either to a member of the nobility or to a merchant of considerable means.

Hurrying to the entrance porch of the mansion, Kyleth announced himself to the pair of servants standing outside the large double doors.

Brother Ander turned to Ghonik. "Your partner seems to have overcome his reservations about this assignment," he observed.

Ghonik did not respond, rolling his eyes briefly before turning away.

The monk turned his attention once more to Kyleth, eyeing the guard thoughtfully for a long moment. It wasn't possible to hear what was being said, but to all appearances the guard was engaged in an animated negotiation with a senior servant of the household.

Kyleth's real agenda abruptly became clear. The monk wondered how he could have become so blind. A wry smile twisted his lips as he recalled that he had once been as cynical as the best of them.

They were soon ushered inside and led to a large room that overlooked an extensive garden. An elderly man lay sprawled awkwardly on an elaborately decorated recliner, flanked by a woman who appeared to be his wife. Their host greeted them distractedly, making no effort to get up.

A servant stood at the man's side, and he offered the visitors a tight bow.

"I welcome you on behalf of Roethen, the master of this house," he said.

Kyleth bowed in his turn. "Knowing as I do the difficult circumstances endured by your esteemed master," he replied, addressing the servant, "I have taken the trouble to bring here a healer of some renown. His name is Brother Ander." He indicated the monk before turning to the master and bowing again.

Roethen turned dull eyes upon the supposed healer. If the man harbored any hope of a cure, it was not apparent.

Throughout his years as a healer in Arvenon, the monk had occasionally found himself in similar situations. Knowing that payment would typically be withheld until some kind of treatment had been provided, he guessed that opportunity still remained to establish boundaries.

"I am very willing to pray for Master Roethen," he said, "although I need to make it clear that my services are not for sale."

The servant looked bemused at this statement, so he added, "I will not accept a fee. Not under any circumstances."

The astonishment on Kyleth's face was quickly replaced by a look of fury. Nevertheless, he said nothing.

The monk ignored him, approaching Roethen instead. "What are your symptoms?" he asked quietly.

"Chest pain. Shortness of breath. Extreme fatigue," the master wheezed.

"May I place my hand on your shoulder?" Brother Ander asked.

The servant looked doubtful, but Roethen nodded. Resting one hand on the sufferer while grasping the Stone of Vitality with the other, the monk spoke a brief prayer.

Roethen's eyes went wide in surprise. He sucked in a deep breath, then rose from the chair. "The pain has gone!" he exclaimed.

Ignoring the shocked faces around him, he began pacing jubilantly about the room. "Double the requested fee, and pay it immediately!" he commanded his senior servant.

Brother Ander shook his head stubbornly. "I found you in great need and with little hope for improvement. The same could be said of many others whose suffering has more to do with reduced circumstances than ill health. If you wish to express gratitude, use the fee to ease the burden of the disadvantaged."

"Gladly, if that is your desire," Roethen replied expansively. "See that it is done," he ordered his servant. "But first—refreshments for my honored guests!"

It didn't take long before the monk discovered that others among the master's family and servants also nursed significant ailments. He insisted on ministering to everyone who needed his help before returning to the palace. The result was that Roethen's household was buzzing by the time they left.

Roethen might have been delighted with the outcome of the visit, but not everyone shared his enthusiasm. Kyleth made no secret of his animosity toward Brother Ander, and the atmosphere in the covered wagon was thick with tension as it rumbled through the streets of Rog on its way back to the palace.

The guard's conflict of interest made it obvious to the monk that the time had come for change. It wasn't just that the current guard assignments were no longer workable. Brother Ander wanted to leave the city—to go where he could work among the poor and disadvantaged without attracting so much attention. He especially needed to avoid drawing a crowd.

Accordingly, Brother Ander decided he would apply for an audience with the king as soon as he rose the next morning.

***

KING KRASMIR RETIRED after a long and demanding day to find his wife waiting for him. It didn't come as a surprise.

"You were uncharacteristically silent during dinner this evening," he told her.

"I was recalling the time Rupert first joined us for a meal," Queen Deka replied. "He seemed to fit in so well! Everything went wrong so quickly after that." She brushed tears from her eyes. "I miss my Tasha so much. What has become of them both?"

Putting an arm around her, he held her close.

"No one has any idea. No one except the Grand Vizier." His face twisted into a scowl. "The day will come when I get my hands on that serpent!"

She gradually managed to calm herself. "What about this monk? I have been hearing such stories about him! Supposedly the Torbury boy—Ethen—was dead! The monk brought him back to life. One of my maids knows a soldier who witnessed it."

"I've heard the stories too," he acknowledged. "Brother Ander apparently has a remarkable gift for healing. He's been out and about in Rog putting it to use, and it's made him enemies. Some of the priests have apparently decided he's an abomination."

"Ha! It's a simple case of jealousy. I've never heard of the priests healing anyone!"

"Be careful what you say, my dear. The priesthood is an important institution in Rogand. Whatever the motivation of the priests, I can't simply wish them away. And neither can he. The priests stirred up a mob, and he was almost killed."

She stared at him in alarm. "You can't let that happen! This Brother Ander was on hand when he was needed last time. I want to know he'll be there when *we* need him!"

"I can't insist that he wait around in Rog on the off chance he's needed one day."

She opened her mouth to speak, but he got in first. "I will arrange for him to be properly protected. And I'll make sure he can get here quickly if we ever do need him."

* * *

"THANK you for being willing to speak with me, Your Majesty," said Brother Ander with a deep bow.

King Krasmir waved him to a seat.

"I hear you have become famous," the king observed evenly.

The monk winced. "That was never my intention," he replied. "I apologize for any disturbance I might have provoked."

The king brushed aside his apology with a wave of his hand. "I do not hold you responsible for what happened at Ugar's Repose." He sighed. "My men have tried without success to identify your attackers. I am just glad you avoided serious injury."

"You are well informed, Your Majesty," observed the monk, dipping his head respectfully.

"The abduction of Lord Torbury's son changed everything," replied the king soberly. "It became clear to me that the safety of foreign guests in Rog cannot be ensured without active effort. That is the reason I assigned guards to accompany you. Regrettably, I understand they have been of little value."

"I do not wish to criticize them," the monk assured him. "Two men could not be expected to hold back an angry crowd."

"Even if they wanted to," the king finished dryly.

When the monk said nothing, the king changed direction. "I'm sure you have a reason for wanting to speak with me."

Brother Ander nodded. "I do, Your Majesty. If you will grant your permission, I will leave Rog for less populous areas. Helping people is an important priority for me, but I would like to do it without attracting notoriety. That might be easier if I go where I am unknown and avoid staying in one place for too long."

"You will be a loss if you leave Rog," the king told him. He hesitated for a moment before continuing. "We intend to find our daughter, Brother Ander. But we can only guess at her condition when we do." His brows furrowed. "I will be frank with you. You have developed...a reputation. My wife takes considerable comfort from knowing you are near at hand." He peered at Brother Ander. "As do I," he acknowledged openly.

"I will come the moment Your Majesties call," the monk assured him.

The king returned a brief nod. "There is no certainty we will ever need your services, of course. It would be nothing more than self-indulgence to keep you here just in case, especially when many others could benefit from your gifts. I will gladly grant you permission to go."

Brother Ander bowed gratefully.

"There is still the matter of protecting you," the king said bluntly. "I will arrange for different guards to be assigned to you."

"Perhaps you could offer my current guards a choice. I suspect that one of them at least would be glad to be released. I cannot be certain about the other one."

The king grunted. "From everything I've been told, you are more generous than they deserve. Nevertheless, I will consider your suggestion."

A crisp nod from the king indicated that the interview was at an end. Brother Ander left after bowing deeply.

8

When Brother Ander emerged from his rooms the next morning, he found Ghonik waiting for him as usual. There was no sign of Kyleth.

A burly guard stood beside Ghonik, and the new arrival greeted the monk with a shallow bow. "I am your new guard," he said. "My name is Dannhur. Ghonik and I will be accompanying you wherever you choose to go."

"I am pleased to meet you," the monk replied with a smile. "I am Brother Ander."

At first appraisal, Dannhur appeared relaxed and confident. The new guard was in turn calmly appraising him, and Brother Ander couldn't help wondering what he was thinking. The monk stood slightly taller, but size didn't count for everything. Years of experience told him that Dannhur was not a fighter to be underestimated.

In contrast to his partner, Ghonik seemed uncomfortable. "We will protect you with our lives," he said. "The king personally made it clear what he expects of us."

"I am grateful to you both," the monk replied. "But I have no desire to see anyone put in harm's way on my account!"

"We volunteered for this assignment," Dannhur informed him.

"Why?" Brother Ander asked candidly.

"I have a sister," Dannhur replied. "Her son is the joy of her life, and he was dying. She tried everything, and no one could help him. Not until you appeared. You healed him."

When Brother Ander glanced at Ghonik, the guard shrugged. "I've made some bad choices in the past, and I didn't need this assignment to be my latest failure. I wanted a second chance. Besides, I owe it to you."

"You owe me nothing," Brother Ander assured him with a shake of his head. He faced them both. "Please do not burden yourselves unnecessarily. My times are in God's hands."

Neither of the guards responded. Perhaps they saw his views as strange. If so, it didn't trouble him, and he saw no need to try to convince them otherwise.

It was time to consider the future. "I am planning to leave Rog," he announced.

Dannhur nodded. "We were told to expect that. When do you plan to set out?"

"Right now. The weather seems perfect for wandering in the countryside." Glancing up into a blue sky interspersed with fluffy clouds, the monk could only smile with anticipation.

"We won't need to wander on foot," Dannhur informed him. "The king has arranged horses for us."

Seeing the monk's eyebrows raised quizzically, the guard added, "I believe he is hoping to be able to call us back to Rog quickly if the need arises."

The news came as no surprise to Brother Ander. "A mount could certainly prove useful at times," he acknowledged. "When there's no urgency, though, I'll be doing as much walking as the horse."

After a brief discussion the men decided to head west, away from the coast. Dannhur suggested they travel on horseback until well clear of Rog. He also suggested that Brother Ander conceal his features under a hood. Having no desire to revisit the recent turmoil, the monk readily agreed to the suggestions.

They were on their way before another hour had passed. Long before sunset, all traces of the city had disappeared behind them. With the guards now willing to slow the pace, Brother Ander dismounted and removed his hood. Then replacing the reins with a halter, he led his horse forward on foot, reveling in the late afternoon sunshine.

When darkness fell, the men gathered sticks and built a fire. After sharing a simple meal, they settled down for the night.

It had been far too long since Brother Ander last lay beneath a blanket gazing up at the stars. Luxurious beds in royal palaces might be well and good, but a setting of this kind seemed fitting for a man of his calling. Breathing out a sigh of satisfaction, he allowed his eyes to droop closed.

BROTHER ANDER'S small party had been walking through scrubland for most of the afternoon when Ghonik spotted a scrawny sheep. Glancing sharply around, he spotted two more. Instantly alert, he called a warning to Dannhur.

"We need to get away from here urgently!" he exclaimed, keeping his voice low and pointing to the sheep.

Dannhur understood at once. "Warn the monk!" he said.

Brother Ander had been striding ahead of the others. Ghonik looked up to see him disappearing over a small rise.

Ghonik hurried after him. Topping the ridge he saw that he was already too late.

Half a dozen shepherds were sitting around a small fire. Seeing the monk, they leaped to their feet.

Instead of fleeing while he could, he called a greeting and headed down to them.

What was he thinking? Brother Ander was probably unaware of their reputation of course, being a foreigner. Ghonik knew only too well. Even soldiers avoided shepherds unless they enjoyed over-whelming superiority in numbers.

From their earliest years, shepherds learned to be handy with a knife and deadly with a slingshot. It was therefore no surprise to see the men before them armed with long, wicked looking knives. Several had slingshots in their belts.

"Welcome!" called a rough voice.

Quickly surrounding the monk, the shepherds slapped him on the back, guffawing loudly. Their good cheer seemed forced to Ghonik.

Dannhur had joined him on the ridge. "They're well armed," the big soldier said grimly, "and there are a few too many of them for my liking. Stay close. We'll fight back to back if we need to. I'm not going to sell my life cheaply!"

With that, both guards headed down to join the gathering around the fire. Several of the shepherds moved to let them through, a couple of them eyeing the horses a little too obviously.

A wizened shepherd with gray hair and a game leg—clearly the leader of the group—was addressing the monk. "I am Yetvar, and I bid you welcome." He eyed the visitor closely. "You're a foreigner," he said bluntly. "What brings you to these parts?" The shepherd's tone suggested his genial demeanor could disappear in an instant if it suited him.

"I'm a healer," the monk said simply. "My name is Brother Ander. I'm wandering the countryside doing whatever I can to help people in the name of God."

"A healer, eh?" The man gave him a calculating look. "That might come in handy. And what about these two?" He jerked his head in the direction of the two guards. "Are they healers as well?"

A burst of mocking laughter from the shepherd's companions accompanied his question.

"This healer is under the personal protection of the king," growled Dannhur.

"Ooo. We'd better be careful then, boys," said one of the shepherds. His wide-eyed expression was greeted with a new round of laughter.

The leader bared his teeth in a crooked grin. "They're just having a bit of fun," he said gruffly. "Pay no mind to it. Me old mamma now, she could use a healer. She's back at our little village. The place might be humble, but it's what we call home. You'll all join us there. No arguments, mind—I won't take no for an answer!"

"We will gladly accept your invitation," said Brother Ander. "And I will do whatever I can for your mother."

Yetvar ordered two of the shepherds to remain with the sheep. Then he set off, hobbling determinedly toward the village with the monk and the two soldiers following close behind. The remaining shepherds trailed behind them, murmuring under their breath.

Both soldiers sidled up to Brother Ander. Dannhur leaned forward. "What do you think you're doing?" he whispered incredulously. "There won't be any mother at the village! All he wants is our horses. Shepherds lie from the moment they first open their mouths!"

Ghonik nodded emphatically.

"They'll put knives in our backs, and at their village they'll do it with the least risk to themselves," Dannhur hissed. "We're stepping into our own graves!"

"I'm sure we have no need for concern," the monk replied mildly. "It will all work out. God will protect us."

"That's well and good for you," growled Dannhur, "but our gods are not so considerate. I can already imagine Malzakh licking his lips."

At that moment the village came into sight, cutting short their conversation.

Children and a few old people appeared, along with more shepherds, all of them rough and unsmiling. Both of the soldiers eased closer to the monk. Dannhur looked every bit as uneasy as Ghonik felt.

Yetvar disappeared into a low hut, reappearing beside a stooped and wrinkled woman. It soon became obvious that she was Yetvar's mother, but it offered little comfort to them.

She began a tirade the moment she emerged.

"You're a cursed fool, Yetvar!" she spat. "I knew it from the moment you were born. Why bring soldiers here? It would have been tidier to slit their throats where you found them!"

Ghonik tensed further. His hand was itching to draw his sword, but he knew it would be seen as a provocation.

"The monk claims he's a healer," the shepherd snarled. "If he can't fix you, I'll carve him into little pieces myself."

"No one can fix me," she spat. "Certainly not this idiot. He must be soft in the head if he agreed to come here!"

The monk stepped forward. "I'm Brother Ander," he said with a smile. "I'm pleased to meet you."

"I'm pleased to meet you," she repeated in a mocking voice. Hobbling closer, she slapped him in the face, following it swiftly with a kick to his shins.

When she swung her arm to hit him again, he grabbed her wrist and held it firmly.

"You dare lay a finger on me?" she shouted in fury.

As Brother Ander muttered a hasty prayer, several shepherds moved in, knives in their hands. Ghonik and Dannhur drew their swords and prepared to fight for their lives.

"Wait!" the woman yelled. She turned to the monk. "What did you just do to me?" she asked, her voice catching in her throat.

"I did nothing," he told her forthrightly. "It was God who healed you."

She stretched her neck, twisting and turning energetically while bending her back. "The pain—it's gone! Completely!" she said in wonder.

The villagers looked on in bemusement, some with knives still raised.

Brother Ander turned to Yetvar. "What causes your limp?"

After a moment's uncertainty, the leader replied. "Gout. It's troubled me for years."

Tentatively stretching a hand toward Yetvar's shoulder, the monk asked, "May I?"

The shepherd eyed him suspiciously for a long moment before nodding.

As Brother Ander prayed, a look of astonishment came to Yetvar's face. "Put away your knives!" he ordered. "All of you! And bring out anyone who's sick."

The monk immediately became very busy. By the time the sun set, he had exhausted himself praying for each of those seeking relief.

The mood in the village had changed dramatically from the moment the old woman was healed. Even the two soldiers had become welcome guests, and it was a merry party that gathered around a huge communal fire to share a meal that night. After belated introductions by Yetvar, the shepherds brought out the best they had to share with their visitors. The preparations were overseen by his mother.

Ghonik watched, fascinated, as the old woman bustled cheerfully about. Her high spirits were clearly having an effect on others in the community.

Finding himself beside the monk, he nodded toward Yetvar's mother. "Is she the same person?" he asked dryly.

Brother Ander smiled, speaking a word that Ghonik did not recognize. Seeing the guard's blank expression, he said, "It's an Arvenian word. It means 'Vitality.' She's come alive again."

After a pause, he added, "She'd lost hope."

"Because of her ailments?" asked Ghonik.

"It's hard to say." The monk waved an arm around the settlement. "These people live hard lives. If she told us her story, I suspect we'd hear of disappointments and suffering beyond anything we could imagine."

Ghonik was struggling to make sense of it all. "And getting well has given her hope?"

Brother Ander shrugged. "I don't exactly understand how it works. Vitality and hope go together, although I can't say which follows the other. I do know that losing hope sometimes cripples more than just the spirit. It's difficult to be truly alive without hope of some kind."

The arrival of Yetvar cut short their conversation. "Stay with us," the shepherd urged. "For as long as you like!"

"Thank you," Brother Ander replied, "but we must leave in the morning. Others need our help."

"I won't let you go without a gift," Yetvar insisted.

Returning to his hut, he retrieved a woolen belt, made from thick strands of rough woven yarn. Metal clasps bearing a distinctive ram's horn pattern adorned the belt.

He presented it to Brother Ander. "Wear this prominently," he said. "No shepherd anywhere in these parts will give you trouble."

The monk thanked him, promising to wear the belt proudly in memory of the friendship of Yetvar and his fellow villagers.

GHONIK LAY down to sleep that night without fearing for his life or even for his horse.

The day had ended spectacularly, in spite of the earlier lurch from peaceful to ugly. After everything he had witnessed thus far, he had reason to expect the following day would end well too, whatever challenges it might bring.

He was under no illusions. Sooner or later the priests would catch up with them. Unless, of course, some nameless group of bandits killed them for their horses first.

He wasn't going to worry about the future though. For the first time in years he had no regrets about the choices he'd made.

9

Entering a small but well appointed cabin toward the stern of the ship, Thomas and Will accepted seats around an ornate wooden table, Bisri Ahuzza and Ronizah settling themselves in chairs facing their guests.

While drinks were being served, Thomas took the opportunity to study Bisri Ahuzza closely. As always, the stone revealed a treasure trove of information. He was able to witness the bisri's audiences with the emperor and his meetings with the Grand Vizier. Unfortunately, remembered conversations were of no value to him since he did not understand the Ahran language.

The process was far from straightforward, but Thomas was able to deduce a considerable amount of information from the interactions. To begin with, Thomas had enough experience with the stone to spot the difference between memories and imaginings. He soon saw that the bisri was no different from Arvenians or Rogandans. While Ahuzza conversed with someone, his imagination was hard at work. When he was speaking with the emperor, his mind pictures provided clues to the topics discussed. Importantly, nothing the bisri had imagined during conversations with the emperor offered any hint of armed conflict.

At one point Will glanced in his direction. Thomas made sure he maintained a calm and relaxed expression on his face.

The interaction began with a question from the bisri through the interpreter.

"Do you have any official status on behalf of your king, Lord Torbury?"

"I do," Will replied. "I am traveling to Rog as the representative of King Steffan."

The bisri's expressionless face revealed no sign of the surge of excitement he felt at this news. Thomas saw that Will's response had prompted the memory of one particular interaction with the emperor. At the time, the bisri had been picturing himself engaging gravely with a faceless foreign monarch.

"Are you on good terms with the Rogandan monarch—King Krasmir?" Ronizah asked on the bisri's behalf.

Will's eyes narrowed. "If you are looking for ways of driving a wedge between our kingdoms, Bisri Ahuzza, you are wasting your time," he replied curtly.

Hearing the translation, the bisri responded with energy.

"You misunderstand me! I was merely hoping that you might be able to help me gain access to King Krasmir."

"For what purpose?" demanded Will.

"To allow me to accurately convey to the emperor the views held by the rulers of this region."

"And what does the emperor propose to do with this information?" Will asked coolly.

The bisri appeared taken aback at Will's tone. "His Imperial Majesty wishes to be made aware of possible steps the Empire of Ahr could take to help resolve any...misunderstandings between our peoples."

"If your emperor truly wishes to resolve misunderstandings, he can begin by releasing King Rupert of Castel and Princess Teylee of Rogand—unharmed!"

"The Empire of Ahr had nothing to do with their disappearance," the bisri insisted.

"You speak out of ignorance, Bisri," Will replied grimly. "Either that or you are a blatant liar. Both Thomas and I are personally aware of the circumstances of their disappearance."

At a brief glance from Will in his direction, Thomas confirmed the statement with an emphatic nod.

"Their abduction was by no means the first such provocation. Ahran agents abducted my own son!" Will's voice had taken on a dangerous tone. "I was able to rescue him, but only after a protracted and debilitating search. The man who had taken my son responded to the rescue by attempting to murder him. King Rupert and Princess Teylee were present, and in the confusion they pursued him with one of their guards. They were surprised and captured by a group of your agents—led by this same man."

Thomas decided it was time for him to speak. "These agents killed the guard who accompanied the king and the princess," he said calmly. "I was present when King Krasmir found him. The guard was near death, but he lived long enough to confirm what Lord Torbury has told you."

Thomas saw that the bisri was not convinced by Will's claims. "And who is this supposed abductor?" he asked dismissively.

"His name is Bolnyk," Will replied. "He is one of your Grand Vizier's senior agents."

Will's response took the Ahran by surprise. The bisri knew of Bolnyk.

"If I ever encounter Bolnyk again," Will concluded stonily, "I will kill him myself."

Bisri Ahuzza's face hardened at Will's threat. "Since you wish to speak of abduction," he growled, "there is the matter of Her Imperial Highness Princess Neira."

"I have met with the princess personally," Will informed him. "She made no mention of abduction. She spoke of being left on an uninhabited island with her guard. If you doubt me, speak to the captain of the ship that carried Princess Neira and your Grand Vizier to this region. I believe his name is Captain Gharpin."

With no response from Ahuzza, Will continued. "She was abandoned by your Grand Vizier and left there to die. Fortunately for her, the island was inhabited. A hermit was living there, and he rescued her and her guard. They eventually made their way to Rog."

Pushing back his chair noisily, Ahuzza rose to his feet. "In sailing to this region, it was my sincere hope and belief that the empire could reach an understanding with your kingdoms. But it seems that these...fantasies of yours will be expected to form the basis of any conversation. I am beginning to see that I was deluding myself."

The bisri offered them a tight bow. "Ronizah will arrange for you to be returned to your ship."

Will got to his feet. "I was fortunate enough to recover my son, but the same cannot be said for King Krasmir. His Majesty personally heard the testimony of Princess Teylee's guard before the man died. If you or others from your empire desire a fruitful engagement with him, do not expect a warm welcome if you persist in describing the abduction and continuing captivity of his daughter as a fantasy." He left after a tight bow of his own.

As soon as the Nomad Lady's longboat had left Bisri Ahuzza's ship, the Ahrans hoisted sail and departed.

Thomas and Will climbed aboard the Lady to find Captain Yordin waiting for them.

"No idea what you said, M'Lord," Captain Yordin told Will as he watched the ships dwindling into the distance, "but looks like you scared 'em off." The old sailor peeled back his lips in a grin of satisfaction.

The commander's only response was a grunt.

Before long Will found an opportunity to draw Thomas aside for a private conversation.

"My diplomacy skills are getting worse, not better," he growled.

"You shouldn't blame yourself, Will," Thomas countered. "It's deeply personal to you. And to King Krasmir. Bisri Ahuzza doesn't have the same stake in the outcome."

Will wasn't willing to let himself off so easily. "I can't afford to let it be personal. We'll never beat them if emotion gets in the way."

"If it's any help, Bisri Ahuzza wasn't as totally dismissive as he might have seemed. You at least sowed seeds of doubt in his mind."

"What are the emperor's expectations?" asked Will.

"I can't say with any confidence. But I get the impression the emperor sent Bisri Ahuzza to Rogand so he doesn't have to rely solely on his Grand Vizier."

Will frowned in annoyance. "If that's true, I should have worked harder at building some kind of rapport with Ahuzza."

"He needed to hear the truth sooner or later," Thomas said. "And he had to know what to expect if he meets with King Krasmir. It wouldn't end well if he takes the same approach he used with you."

Will's brows drew together. "If the emperor wants diplomatic contact, it better not happen through his Grand Vizier. Not that he would ever be stupid enough to show his face in front of Krasmir. No, this Bisri Ahuzza will need to take the lead if anything's to be resolved. Next time I meet with him—if there is a next time—I'm going to be more measured."

***

"Which direction, Bisri?" asked the captain.

"Continue on a course for Rog," Bisri Ahuzza replied. "Find an anchorage where we can remain concealed."

After bowing low, the captain shouted an order to his helmsman.

Ahuzza gazed distractedly at the captain as he went about his work. He suspected that if the man had dared, he would have asked about the meeting with the Arvenians. Ahuzza wasn't sure himself how he would characterize it.

"Join me, Ronizah," he commanded, heading for his cabin.

The interpreter hurried after him.

As soon as they were seated, Ahuzza faced the other man. "Well, what did you make of them, Ronizah?"

"The Arvenian lord was all bluster!" The interpreter raised his hands in disgust.

"And the one called Thomas?"

Ronizah shrugged. "He gave almost nothing away."

"He was difficult to read," agreed Ahuzza.

"I thought you handled it well, Bisri!" the interpreter gushed.

"I'm not so convinced."

"You were clear and uncompromising! You called their stories what they were—fantasies."

Ahuzza frowned. "If I'm any judge of character, that Lord Torbury believed what he was saying."

"He might believe it, but that doesn't make it true, Bisri," insisted Ronizah.

The bisri remained silent, wrestling with his thoughts. He had now been directly exposed to the accusation that the Rogandan princess and Castelan king had been abducted by Ahrans, with the blame laid at the feet of Rheibas's senior agent. Yet Rheibas himself— before the emperor and in Ahuzza's hearing—had denied any such involvement.

"The Arvenian accused the chief minister of attempting to murder Her Imperial Highness Princess Neira!" Ronizah protested.

"Yes," mused Ahuzza. "He did."

An anxious look twisted Ronizah's features. "Please, Bisri! Do be careful!" he urged. "No one wants the chief minister as an enemy!"

Ahuzza's eyes narrowed. "I have no intention of making the chief minister an enemy," he said sharply. "Nor do I believe the monstrous claim involving Princess Neira."

The account had indeed been more than the bisri could stomach. The Arvenian nobleman had the audacity to assert that the chief minister tried to kill the emperor's daughter. Any such claim was not merely outrageous, it was a grave insult—not just to the chief minister, but to the empire he so energetically represented.

After eyeing the interpreter for a few moments, he said evenly, "Thank you for your insights, Ronizah. You are dismissed."

Rising and bowing low once more, Ronizah left the cabin.

Ahuzza watched his retreating back testily. Not for the first time, he wondered where Ronizah's loyalty lay. Pushing himself up from his chair, he paced restlessly about the small cabin.

When the emperor had set him the task of making independent contact with the Rogandans, he imagined that his biggest challenge would be to find an interpreter fluent in Rogandan. He had stumbled upon Ronizah the very next day. Ahuzza knew nothing of the man before they met, but a quick investigation confirmed that Ronizah's credentials were impressive.

Even at the time their chance meeting had seemed uncanny. Now Ahuzza wondered if chance played any part in it.

It wouldn't surprise him to discover that the man answered to Rheibas. The interpreter's caution about making an enemy of the chief minister sounded like the kind of thing Rheibas might say. It might almost have been a veiled threat.

The emperor had tasked Ahuzza with keeping an eye on Rheibas. Had Rheibas in turn tasked Ronizah with keeping an eye on him? There was an undeniable symmetry to it.

He frowned. Unsettling as these questions might be, there was more at stake here than Ronizah's loyalty. What was the truth about the shocking series of claims made by the Arvenian nobleman?

He was certain that Torbury believed what he was saying. But could Ahran agents really have been involved in the kidnapping of Torbury's son? And could they have abducted the Castelan king and the Rogandan princess as well?

Ahuzza could readily see the political potential from such actions —assuming the goal was to destabilize the local kingdoms. But why would Rheibas engage in activities of this kind? What was he hoping to achieve by it?

As for leaving Princess Neira to die on a remote island, it seemed too far fetched even to consider. Yet Lord Torbury had insisted he heard it from the mouth of the princess herself.

It was quickly becoming clear to Bisri Ahuzza that the emperor had done him no favors in assigning him this task. Political maneuvering had never appealed to him. He was much too straightforward for his own good. As for provoking the chief minister's wrath—the prospect was unnerving.

Nevertheless the emperor himself had charged him with making discreet contact with the Rogandans. He was not expected to make representations on the emperor's behalf, and it was not his responsibility to fix anything. But he had been told to actively monitor the situation.

He knew that Rheibas was unlikely to welcome his involvement, however hard he tried to avoid entanglement in whatever games were being played here. But like it or not, the emperor had given him a job, and he intended to do it.

10

At a nod from King Delmar a man was admitted to the small reception room in the royal castle at Varacellan. After bowing low, the new arrival stood silently before the king.

The king directed his gaze toward the other servants in the room. "Leave us," he commanded.

They quickly departed, closing the door behind them.

"What do you have to report, Maran?" Delmar asked his senior agent.

"Most of the Ahran agents have been dealt with, Your Majesty, including recent arrivals. We allowed a few to slip through as you ordered. They are now being watched closely."

"Have you learned anything useful?"

"Unfortunately our efforts have been hampered by language. Few of our agents are fluent in the Ahran tongue. However the agent I mentioned to you is now ready for assignment, and our plans are well advanced."

"I wish to meet with this agent."

"Of course, Your Majesty. It would be prudent to set up a meeting well away from prying eyes."

"Make it happen."

. . .

THE NIGHT WAS WELL advanced when the king was led toward a dark alley not far from the royal castle. Clad in a hooded cloak, he could have been just another wealthy merchant protecting himself from the evening chill.

A dozen guards led by Lord Karevis spread out protectively around the king as they went. All of them had been personally selected by Karevis, and by his orders they were cloaked and hooded like the king. The Varasan army commander was leaving nothing to chance.

Reaching the narrow alley, the group stretched out along it until they came to a broad common located almost directly below the castle. Delmar was familiar with the site. At most times during daylight hours it was frequented by townsfolk who strolled among the many trees that dotted the expanse or relaxed on the lush green turf.

After dark the setting could only be described as eerie. Bathed with thin light from a pale moon and devoid of any sign of life, the park was the perfect location for a clandestine meeting. The guards seemed on edge, and Delmar understood completely.

A man stepped out of the shadows behind the trunk of a large poplar, bowing to the king and whispering a previously agreed watchword. The king managed to recognize the voice of the agent who had met with him earlier.

Pointing to a small cluster of trees nearby, the agent murmured, "Over there, Your Majesty."

With a tight nod the king followed the agent into the trees, several guards shadowing them watchfully. Guards positioned themselves just inside the tree line. The agent stepped deeper into the trees, the king at his side.

A new figure appeared suddenly in front of them. Startled, Delmar reached for the hilt of his sword. Then the agent quietly greeted the newcomer, and the king willed himself to relax.

Delmar had not anticipated someone slight in build, and he

stared at the new agent curiously, trying without success in the dim light to get a glimpse of the hooded face.

"Your Majesty, I am honored."

The soft voice caught him entirely by surprise. He hadn't been expecting to meet a woman.

"Who am I speaking to?" he asked.

The woman chuckled—a melodious sound that seemed out of character for an agent. "Who would you like to be speaking to?"

Unsure how to respond, he said nothing.

"I mean no disrespect, Your Majesty," she offered. "I use different names, depending on the circumstances."

Her speech suggested she was noble by birth, but he couldn't place her accent. It must have been either Castelan or Arvenian.

Abruptly, her posture changed. "I be just a wee farmer's lass, ya see." She changed again. "Fresh mussels, Y'Worship? Octopus? Whateva y'r 'ungry for, I got it!" Her wheedling voice was coarse and guttural.

He gaped in astonishment at the transformation.

Without missing a beat she spoke a sentence in what he knew to be fluent Rogandan, before switching effortlessly to a language he didn't recognize at all.

"Were you just speaking Ahran?" he asked.

"I was, Your Majesty," she replied calmly, once again in the tones of a woman of noble birth. Her accent now clearly placed her as a native of Varas.

"I suddenly understand why you hesitated to supply a name!" he told her.

She laughed lightly, a cheerful sound in that dark place. "You may call me Maive."

"Very well, Maive." He hesitated. "Why are you doing this? Why become an agent?"

"My story would make a long and sorry tale, Your Majesty. It is enough to say that I have reason to do anything in my power to thwart the purposes of the man who clearly has designs on Varas and the kingdoms around it."

Unable in the darkness to catch the tiniest glimpse of Maive's face behind her hood, Delmar had no way of reading her. But he trusted Maran implicitly. She appeared capable of presenting herself as whoever she wanted to be, but his senior agent was not easily taken in. Before recommending her, he would have thoroughly investigated her character, her history, and her motivations. He would never have allowed her to meet with the king if any doubt remained about her reliability.

"Thank you, Maive. We are profoundly grateful that you have made your skills available in support of the well-being of Varas. Please be careful! Take no unnecessary risks. It will serve no one but our enemies if you come to any harm."

"I am grateful for your consideration, Your Majesty." She bowed. "Until next time."

Then she was gone.

She hadn't waited to be dismissed, but he was not offended. How could an agent thrive when constricted by convention?

As he headed back to the palace, it occurred to him that he applied a different standard to Maran and his other agents. Maive was different though.

He acknowledged wryly that she managed to be both mysterious and beguiling at the same time.

DELMAR STOOD with Maran on a castle balcony overlooking the city of Varacellan. To all appearances, nothing had changed. People were going about their business as always. Yet Delmar sensed that his kingdom was poised on the brink of a precipice.

However vigorously his agents rooted out Ahran infiltrators, others arrived to replace them. Most insidious of all, they came with gold—a seemingly unending supply of it. His own coffers had received a welcome boost from the small hoards seized already by his agents.

Gold shone with a sparkle all of its own, and there was no way of knowing how many of his subjects had been seduced by its glitter, agreeing to turn against their own people for the right price.

Seeking a more cheerful topic for rumination, Delmar's thoughts drifted in a different direction. The new agent had thoroughly roused his curiosity. The fact that he had never seen her face must surely be contributing to her mystique. He sometimes wondered if a single glance at her in the daylight might be enough to extinguish his fascination entirely.

He released a quiet sigh, at a loss to account for his own foolishness. Nevertheless, curiosity could not be denied. "How has your new agent been acquitting herself?" He hoped he didn't sound too interested.

"Her involvement has been invaluable, Your Majesty. We are preparing to take down what we believe to be the Ahran headquarters. Thanks to her we have considerable insight into their activities."

"What have they been doing?"

"They have been working hard at recruiting informants—and turning them into collaborators whenever they can. We have identified a number of people they have compromised. We'll be moving on them soon."

Delmar had the feeling something else was on Maran's mind. "Is there more?" he prodded.

The agent's brows drew together in frustration. "They seem to have an overriding goal, but we haven't been able to find out what it is. None of them speak of it directly."

"Keep me informed if you learn any more."

Maran bowed. "I will notify you the moment we uncover anything of significance."

***

THE HOUR before sunset saw King Delmar threading his way through the streets of Varacellan. A modest contingent of guards accompanied him, Lord Karevis among them.

Market day was drawing to a close; the sale of most wares had ended, and people were flocking around the ever-popular food stalls.

The king welcomed opportunities to mingle with his subjects, and people had learned to expect a brief visit from him at that time of the week. He had long since concluded there was no better time or place to quickly assess the mood of the populace.

"Your Majesty! Will you try one of my special fish cakes? Everyone agrees it's food worthy of a king!"

Delmar smiled, enjoying the vendor's enthusiasm. "Thank you, but I've eaten already. Perhaps next time."

"Over here, Your Majesty! I have a bracelet guaranteed to win the heart of any fair maiden."

The king smiled and waved, moving on without further acknowledgment. The vendor had touched on a delicate topic. Delmar would not produce an heir until he found himself a queen. It hadn't escaped him that the issue was a topic of animated conversation among his subjects.

As the light began to fail a sudden commotion shattered his musings. A runaway horse, with cart attached, was careering out of control, knocking over stalls and scattering vendors and customers in every direction. Delmar stood directly in its path.

Seeing the folly of any attempt at heroics, he threw himself aside with a shouted order to his men. "Stop that horse!"

Several guards grabbed at the traces as the horse passed, but all were thrown to the ground. None succeeded even in slowing the animal.

Sudden cries of alarm rang out from his scattered guards. Struggling to his feet he saw men with drawn swords setting upon his guards. None of those felled by the horse proved able to defend themselves. The rest were soon fighting for their lives.

He gaped in disbelief, unable to credit such a brazen attack in his own capital. Then five of the attackers broke away from the fight, heading straight for him.

Karevis, sword in hand, leaped into their path, furiously engaging two of them at once. The others ignored him, their full attention on Delmar.

"Run!" shouted Karevis.

With the attackers almost upon him, Delmar took the commander's advice and sprinted away. He'd been trained to fight from his boyhood, and he had no reason to doubt his capabilities. But he also possessed a cool head. Taking on three men with unknown fighting skills was risky at best.

Speedy and fit, he decided that running was a good strategy. Varacellan was routinely patrolled by his own soldiers. Provided he lived long enough he would stumble upon them eventually.

Turning the first corner that presented itself, he raced away from the market. The street bent away before intersecting with another broader street that led toward another heavily trafficked part of the city. Delmar didn't hesitate, dashing around the corner and flying down the middle of the broad avenue. A glance behind showed him gaining ground on his pursuers, but they were not giving up.

Townsfolk gaped open-mouthed as he sped past alone. Turning a corner, then another, he burst out onto a busy street. Frustratingly, no soldiers were anywhere to be seen.

As he glanced around, he realized that he would soon be recognized. Someone was sure to give him away by drawing attention to him with no awareness of the consequences. Accordingly he moved quickly to the side of a building that protruded into the street, hiding himself in the deepening shadows on the far side. Panting from his exertion, he peered out cautiously from his hiding place, waiting for the Ahrans to appear.

He had barely recovered his breath when a figure appeared before him, hemming him in. Reaching for his knife, he was startled by an urgent command.

"Take off your cloak! Quickly!"

The speaker was a woman. Although he couldn't place her, he removed his cloak, acting on instinct.

She grabbed it from him, tossing it aside into a pile of trash. Then she whisked off her own cloak—a thin garment colored a bold blue —and threw it across his shoulders. As Delmar's pursuers rounded the corner, she pulled him into an intimate embrace.

Choosing the same direction as Delmar, his pursuers headed toward the king. The men had sheathed their swords and hidden them below their cloaks, but all of them had their hands on the hilts. As they drew closer, he bent low, burying his face in her neck.

One of the passing Ahrans aimed a probing glance at them both, and she rounded on him, snarling. "Find a woman of your own!" Then, taking Delmar's head in her hands, she drew him close and kissed him on the lips.

Too startled to know how else to respond, he kissed her back.

His rescuer paid no attention to the Ahrans as they hurried past in search of their quarry. Even when they were surely long gone, she did not pull away. Nor did he.

Later, he was never sure precisely when it dawned on him who she was. Nor could he identify the exact moment when a clever diversion became a tender kiss. He only knew that something had shifted inside him.

He drew back at last, impatient to gaze upon the face of Maive.

She stared back at him uncertainly, her cheeks faintly flushed.

After a charged silence, she seemed to recover her poise. "Why were you alone, Your Majesty? And with Ahrans at your heels!"

"I hardly understand how it happened myself," he replied. He gazed at her in wonder. "How did you find me?"

"I noticed you when you hid. Then I saw the Ahrans. We've been watching them, so I knew who they were. When I realized they were searching for you, I decided to improvise."

"To great effect! Thank you for rescuing me!"

She looked up at him uncertainly. "Please pardon my forwardness. I'm sure you don't need me to say that the kiss meant nothing."

He tried to ignore the sinking feeling in his gut. "Of course! It's all in the line of duty. No doubt you often find yourself doing such things."

"Far from it, Your Majesty." Her tone was unexpectedly sharp. "There are lines I refuse to cross, even in the service of your kingdom."

"I didn't mean to suggest..." he stammered awkwardly. He took a breath. "What I meant was…"

Struggling to find the right words, he spotted Karevis, searching anxiously. The commander was trailed by one of the guards, other soldiers close behind them.

With a groan of frustration, he stepped into the open, reluctantly accepting that this conversation would need to wait.

Karevis spotted him at once. "Your Majesty!"

The relief on the commander's face was unmistakable. "I barely recognized you! What happened to the Ahrans?"

"They got away. I didn't need to defend myself though, thanks to my rescuer." He turned back to Maive with a grateful smile.

She was gone.

By the time he returned his attention to Karevis, the commander had retrieved his discarded cloak. "That's an impressive disguise," he said admiringly, pointing to Maive's blue substitute.

Delmar could find nothing to say.

It belatedly occurred to him that Maive might not have been the only one who recognized him. Had other townspeople seen him kissing her? He decided he didn't care.

Failing to notice his discomposure, Karevis surrounded him with soldiers and bustled him back toward the palace. The king went meekly, trying desperately to set his thoughts and emotions in order.

King Delmar sat in a small palace reception room with Maran and Karevis.

"How could such an attack happen?" he asked. "Right here, in the heart of my capital!"

Maran hung his head. "We were ready to move on the Ahrans. Clearly we waited too long. And they had considerably more men here than we realized."

"Were they responsible for the runaway horse?" asked the king. "Or were they simply taking advantage of it?"

The senior agent exchanged a glance with Karevis. "We can't be certain, but we think it was carefully planned."

The king raised an eyebrow inquiringly.

"You would have noticed they wasted no time in setting off after you," Karevis observed.

"We suspect that you were always the target," confirmed Maran. "You arrived as the markets were closing—as you almost always do—so they put their plan into action."

"Were they hoping to capture me? Or kill me?"

"We don't know."

The king met his commander's eyes. "What happened with the two men you were fighting?"

"I brought one of them down," Karevis replied. "One of your guards helped me deal with the other one."

"So the guards fought off the other Ahrans who attacked us?"

"Eventually. Three of the Ahrans left to chase you. That evened the odds. Even so, only one guard was still capable of fighting when it was over. It didn't matter. By then the place was swarming with soldiers alerted by the disturbance. I took a few of them and the remaining guard and we went looking for you. It was a while before we found you."

"Fortunately Maive reached you first," Maran observed.

"Yes, it was thanks to her that I escaped. How did she come to be there?"

"It was pure luck that she was there at all. And that she spotted you when she did," Maran replied.

Delmar couldn't help himself. "Where is she now?"

"She's left the kingdom."

"Why?" He couldn't hide his shock.

"It's possible that one of the missing Ahrans might put the pieces together. We couldn't take that chance—she's too valuable. We needed to get her away from Varacellan. She learned of a high risk mission outside the kingdom and had no hesitation in volunteering for it." Maran sighed. "I won't deny that she'll be a big loss."

Delmar opened his mouth to berate Maran for sending her away without consulting him first. He barely checked himself in time. He reminded himself that Maran didn't need his permission, and he was only seeking the best outcome both for Maive and for the kingdom.

All the same, it was frustrating. None of this would have happened if she hadn't needed to rescue him. It belatedly occurred to him that there might be more to her departure. Was it possible she was fleeing from him? He wasn't willing even to consider such a possibility.

He wanted to ask for details about her mission, but he knew it wasn't appropriate. Nevertheless, he wasn't going to give up. He would find a way to reach her.

THE DAYS PASSED, and Delmar could not get Maive out of his mind.

He knew almost nothing of substance about her. He didn't even know her real name.

At least he'd finally seen her face. She was no classic beauty, although there was something beguiling about her eyes as she gazed up at him. He longed to see her again, to properly appreciate and remember her. It occurred to him that he'd never seen her smile, never shared a lighthearted moment with her.

The more he dwelt on it, the more his sense of loss grew, until it came to feel like a crushing weight.

He winced whenever he thought of his ill-considered words to her. He hadn't intended to hurt her—he'd been thrown off balance by her assertion that their kiss meant nothing.

It was possible she had been telling the truth, but his heart told him otherwise.

He remembered how it felt as he nestled into her neck. His heart had raced as she drew his face closer. He sensed again her warm breath on his cheeks and the sensation of her lips exploring his own.

Everything had changed in that instant. Until then he had failed utterly to anticipate the raw power that lurked behind a simple kiss.

Now she was gone, far away, beyond his reach.

Would he ever see her again?

11

Steffan arrived in the queen's private chambers to find her overseeing the final preparations for her visit to Castel. Seeing the king arrive, the servants bowed and hurried from the room.

A troubled frown furrowed his brow. "This trip makes me nervous, Essanda!"

She smiled up at him. "Rufe will be riding with me, along with five hundred of your best soldiers." Seeing his reaction, she added, "We're not at war, and there isn't the faintest hint of internal dissent. The only possible threat is from the Ahrans, and I don't see what they could do. We'll be nowhere near the ocean at any point in the journey. How could they even get to me?"

Steffan grunted noncommittally.

Stretching up on tiptoes, she kissed him lightly on the lips before fixing him with a knowing grin. He could guess what she was thinking. She knew him well enough to know that it made no difference how many soldiers Rufe took—he wouldn't be satisfied until she was safe in the royal castle at Arnost again.

"Gordy will take good care of me," she said soothingly.

"Count Gordan is effective," Steffan conceded, before adding darkly, "Most of the time."

"You surely can't be referring to the morning I slipped away from him during the Battle of Torbury Scarp!" she protested. "That was years ago! And it was hardly his fault."

Steffan grunted again. "If it's any comfort to you, I agree he was a sensible choice as regent in the absence of your brother."

She raised an eyebrow ironically. "I'm greatly comforted."

He conceded a reluctant grin.

Her face became serious. "You said you had a dispatch from him this morning."

He nodded. "He's arranging for a detachment of his soldiers to meet you at Deadman's Pass. They'll accompany you to Castel Citadel."

"Wonderful! Then you have nothing to worry about," she said, leaning in to him.

He responded by pulling her into an embrace, wrapping his arms tightly about her.

After a few moments he released her with a sigh. "It won't be the same—for me or for the children—until you're back home again."

"I'll miss you all terribly!" she assured him. Then she added soberly, "This is an important opportunity to demonstrate our support for Castel. The kingdom has faced a great deal of upheaval in recent years. I can only imagine what the people must be feeling now they're facing even more uncertainty."

He nodded. "You're right of course. It's the only reason I'm willing to let you go." He glanced around at the chaos. "I'll leave you to your packing. There are things I need to attend to."

He left her with a smile, but inwardly he did not feel happy. A vague sense of unease had settled on him. He tried to tell himself it was mere foolishness, that there was no real reason to be concerned about her safety. Yet bitter experience had taught him just how unpredictable life could be.

With the border of Castel almost within reach, Rufe rode back down the column, checking on the men.

"We'll be crossing the border soon, men!" he called as he passed. "Never forget you are representing King Steffan and the Kingdom of Arvenon!"

Rufe had no doubt the soldiers would acquit themselves well, not least because he had selected their leaders himself.

When he reached the middle of the column, he came upon Queen Essanda.

"Why are we slowing down, Rufe?" she called inquisitively.

Her curiosity was understandable. For her own safety she had been placed far from any possible action. That also left her with little chance of seeing anything interesting.

"Deadman's Pass lies not far ahead, Your Majesty," he told her. "Our scouts are riding forward to make contact with the Castelan border guards."

"My thanks, Rufe, to you and your men for guiding me here safely. It's been far too long since I visited Castel." She concluded her words with a merry wave.

Rufe waved back, a grin on his face. In spite of long hours in the saddle and often primitive conditions when they camped at night, the cheerfulness and gratitude of the queen never wavered. When combined with her good-natured approachability, it came as no surprise that she was wildly popular among the men.

Having delivered his message to all of the men, Rufe turned his horse and rode forward at a canter until he reached the head of the column.

By the time he arrived, the column had come to a halt. Three of his captains were conferring to one side, and he rode over to them.

"What's the hold up?"

"The border post is deserted," one of them replied. "There's no sign of Castelan guards."

Rufe frowned. The Castelans had maintained a border post at the Arvenian end of Deadman's Pass for longer than anyone could remember. He knew that no Arvenian guards were stationed at the border, and he was aware of the reason. To begin with, King Steffan had inherited an almost uninterrupted history of peaceful relations between Arvenon and Castel. Having then married a native of Castel, the king was more than content to leave the pass in the hands of his allies.

"Did any of the scouts venture into the pass?" asked Rufe.

"No. They were reluctant to cross the border without approval from the Castelans."

Rufe nodded. "They did the right thing." He addressed two of the captains. "Choose fifty men and tell them to report to me. Make sure they're all capable archers. The rest should remain on high alert until we understand what's going on. Escort the queen to a position that's safe and defensible."

They nodded grimly, riding off immediately to carry out his orders.

He turned to the remaining captain. "You're with me, Hennis." He indicated the fifty men assembling nearby. "As soon as our preparations are in place, we'll head into the pass."

Almost half an hour had elapsed before the other captains reported back.

"I'm leaving you in charge of the column," Rufe told them. "Your priority is the queen. If anything happens, get her somewhere safe without delay."

They nodded. "What about you, Rufe?" one of them asked.

"Forget about me," he replied. "I'll have plenty of support."

He signaled to the men, and they moved out together, heading for the pass.

They came upon the border post almost immediately. It was indeed deserted. Dismounting, Rufe carefully examined the sturdy little building and its surrounds.

"There are food scraps here that are still fresh," he called to Hennis. "And the coals at the bottom of the fire pit outside the building are still warm. The post was occupied until quite recently."

Remounting, Rufe rode cautiously into the pass, trying to guess where enemies might have positioned themselves. Hennis rode beside him, tense and alert.

Rugged slopes stretched out before him as far as the eye could see. Rufe knew that the pass offered the only way of penetrating the mountain range that comprised almost the entire southern border of Castel.

From a military perspective, he could only admire the terrain. The mountain range with its solitary pass provided a formidable boundary between the kingdoms.

Readily defensible at many points, Deadman's Pass was aptly named. During the war with Rogand, the pass had been seized and held by a determined band of Rogandans. King Steffan's soldiers had eventually forced their way through, but they had paid a high price in human lives.

They had not ridden far before Hennis called softly, "Over there."

Following his pointing finger, Rufe saw two bodies. With no one else anywhere in view, Rufe dismounted again and examined them. "They haven't been dead for long," he said.

Once more they moved forward, more alert than ever. Rounding a bend in the pass they were challenged by a somewhat unsteady voice. "Are you Arvenians?"

"We are," Rufe confirmed. "Show yourself!"

Three men stepped into the open, raising a ragged cheer.

Signaling to Hennis to join him, Rufe dismounted and drew them aside. "Are you Castelan border guards?" he asked.

"We are."

"What happened here?"

"We were attacked. From Castel—from behind. Not long after dawn. We were taken completely by surprise."

A second man chipped in, "They killed our leader and another guard. We scattered and hid. For a while they tried to find us, but they soon gave up and left."

"Which way did they go?"

"Back down the pass toward Castel."

"How many of them?"

"Maybe six or seven. There wasn't any way to be certain."

Rufe scowled. "Do you know who they were?"

"No. But they were openly speaking another language."

Rufe exchanged a glance with Hennis. His captains had been briefed before they left Arnost; Hennis would be well able to guess the identity of the attackers.

"Count Gordan was planning to send an escort to meet Queen Essanda," Rufe told them. "Have you seen any sign of it?"

"No, but we've been expecting them. They can't get here soon enough!"

"Go and bury your friends," Rufe told them. "A couple of my men will help you. The rest of us will move forward to see if we can find any sign of your attackers."

The Castelans hurried away, relief evident on their faces. Rufe shook his head. Clearly they had not been well briefed on present realities.

The sound of their horses' hooves echoed from the hard rock as they rode forward. The pass was otherwise as silent as the grave. Rufe fully expected to find the way blocked and held against them, but they saw no sign of another living being until they reached the Castelan end of the pass.

They halted their horses and gazed out across the rolling green fields of Castel.

"Look, Rufe," called one of the men.

A body of men was riding toward the pass.

"It's probably Count Gordan's soldiers," Rufe suggested to Hennis. "But we can't afford to take any chances. Form up the men into defensive positions."

Something didn't seem right to Rufe. The incoming riders seemed too few in number to be Count Gordan's escort. Nevertheless he waited calmly until they came within hailing distance.

A rider separated himself from the column and called out, "Who are you?"

"We are Arvenians," he called back.

"Escorting Queen Essanda?"

"Yes."

"Excellent! I will join you." The speaker urged his horse forward, not bothering to wait for his men to catch up.

Rufe shook his head, unable to comprehend the heedless behavior of the Castelans he had met so far.

The new arrival rode up with a flourish. "Well met! I am Lord Thorsel. Count Gordan sent me to escort the queen to Castel Citadel."

"I am Rufe Sarjant."

Lord Thorsel's eyebrows went up, and he briefly dipped his head. "I am honored to meet you. King Steffan clearly places a high value on the safety of his wife!"

"How many men do you lead, My Lord?"

"One hundred. I thought it to be excessive, and told Count Gordan as much. He wanted to make it clear that the queen's safety is paramount. How many men have you brought with you?"

"Five hundred of King Steffan's best soldiers," Rufe replied evenly.

The Castelan was too surprised to respond.

Rufe saw no reason to indulge the nobleman. "You will need to reestablish your border post. The guards were attacked earlier today —from the Castelan side of the pass. Two of the five men were killed, including their leader."

Lord Thorsel was not unduly dismayed. "I am sorry to hear of their losses. Most likely it was robbers. I will order some of my scouts to look around for any sign of them." Seeing the look on Rufe's face, he added tersely, "Do you have a different explanation for the attack?"

"I have no proof, but I suspect that Ahran agents might have been responsible."

"Surely that's absurd! Why would you think that?"

"The guards reported that their attackers spoke a foreign language."

"They must have been Rogandans, then. If the guards were not imagining things. Why would Rogandans attack the pass? We're finally at peace with them."

"Have Ahrans been infiltrating Castel?" asked Rufe.

"There have been a few reports. But nothing worthy of undue alarm. Why?"

"Large numbers of them have entered Varas and Arvenon. Even more so Rogand."

"All of those kingdoms have major ports. Castel does not. That's undoubtedly the reason for the difference."

Rufe shook his head. "Ahran vessels foolish enough to dock in Rog are impounded and searched from stem to stern. Ahran agents are being put ashore on remote beaches."

"We have no evidence of any such activities in Castel. Perhaps our kingdom holds less appeal to them."

It was obvious that Lord Thorsel had no intention of taking the Ahran threat seriously, and Rufe saw no point in pursuing the issue further. He was confident Count Gordan would see it very differently.

"So you will entrust Queen Essanda to our care from here?" Thorsel asked.

Rufe was unyielding. "King Steffan made it clear we were to escort her to Castel Citadel, and remain there until she is ready to return."

Lord Thorsel's eyebrows had gone up again. "It's all a little irregular." He paused for a moment. "Arvenon is an ally, of course. I am sure Count Gordan will be willing to make your men welcome." Then he snorted. "As long as they behave themselves."

Rufe ignored the nobleman's ramblings. Queen Essanda would go to Castel Citadel accompanied by King Steffan's full escort, or she wouldn't be going at all.

The Castelan did at least follow through on his offer to have the area scouted. He also instructed his captains to meet with the surviving border guards. Having dealt with the practicalities, he asked to be presented to the queen.

Hennis's men escorted Lord Thorsel through the pass, Rufe at their head. When they reached the queen, Rufe introduced the Castelan nobleman.

"Your Majesty!" exclaimed Lord Thorsel, bowing low. "I bring the greetings of the regent, Count Gordan, and the entire Castelan court.

It is a great honor to welcome you back to the land of your birth. All of us are in shock after the appalling abduction of your brother, His Majesty King Rupert, and we are grateful for your consideration in our hour of distress."

"His Majesty King Steffan extends his greetings, as do I. He asked me to assure you that Arvenon will do anything it can to support Castel at this time. Securing the return of my brother to his throne is a high priority for our kingdom too."

Rufe excused himself and departed, more than willing to leave diplomacy to those better suited to it.

He headed first to Hennis. "Have the Castelan scouts discovered anything?"

Hennis shook his head. "No. But their captains are at least taking the attack on the border post more seriously than the nobleman."

"Are they blaming robbers?"

"Not at all. They questioned the survivors closely, and they've drawn the same conclusion as us."

Rufe nodded in satisfaction. "Brief some reliable messengers, and send them to King Steffan. He needs to know everything that happened here today."

THE REMAINDER of the journey to Castel Citadel proceeded without incident, and Rufe experienced considerable relief delivering the queen safely to Count Gordan. He had asked her to request a meeting with the Count, and she arranged it as a matter of urgency. Before the day of their arrival had ended, the regent led Rufe and Queen Essanda to a private reception room in the castle.

"I have been briefed on the events at Deadman's Pass," the count began. "I fully concur with your views, Rufe. I can only conclude that the Ahrans have a larger presence in Castel than any of us had realized. This is not the first occasion when events have gotten away from me. I intend to respond much more vigorously this time."

Rufe nodded in satisfaction. "I never doubted you would take the threat seriously, My Lord Regent."

Gordan's brows had drawn together. "One thing I cannot make sense of. Why attack the border post?"

"I have also given that a great deal of thought," Rufe replied. "Undoubtedly Will would grasp the purpose behind it in an instant, but he isn't here. Is it possible that the Ahrans planned to pose as border guards, and attack the queen as she passed?"

"It seems unlikely to me, Rufe," Queen Essanda replied. "What would they gain by it? They would only strengthen the resolve of the allied kingdoms in opposing them."

"Could they have been sending a message?" asked the count. "Issuing notice that no kingdom is beyond their reach?"

None of them were any wiser when they left the meeting. But the count had promised to spare no effort in hunting down Ahran infiltrators. He intended to begin the operation at dawn on the following day.

***

THAT NIGHT RUFE retired to his assigned room in the royal castle weary to the point of exhaustion. He had barely fallen asleep when he was roused by a servant. "The regent needs to meet with you urgently!"

Hurriedly throwing on his clothes, he followed the servant to a different section of the castle. Count Gordan and several senior nobles were seated around a large wooden table. He appeared to be the last arrival.

As soon as Rufe had been settled in his place, the count rose shakily to his feet, his face ashen.

"I have the most appalling news to report," he told the gathering. "I regret to say that Queen Essanda has been abducted!"

Chairs crashed to the floor as people leaped to their feet. Cries of dismay echoed around the chamber. Rufe sat with jaw agape, paralyzed with horror.

"Who has done this?" a voice cried.

The count ran a shaky hand across his brow. "It appears to be the work of Ahran agents. Our Arvenian friends warned me. I have been planning an operation to hunt them down—it was to begin tomorrow." His head sagged. "I have left it too late."

"What is known of the circumstances, and what is being done to retrieve the queen?"

Rufe eyed the speaker dully, grateful that at least someone appeared to have kept their head.

The regent recovered himself. "Her Majesty went for a walk in a secure private garden, accompanied by two guards," he replied. "Someone—presumably acting on behalf of the Ahrans—left a side gate unlocked. A small group of armed men somehow penetrated palace security. They overpowered the guards and took the queen. The guards were seriously injured, but they will survive. One of them reported that the abductors were speaking a language he didn't recognize."

Count Gordan clenched his fists. "None of this could have happened without active participation from our own people, undoubtedly compromised by Ahran gold. When we find those responsible—and we will find them!—they will be shown no mercy!"

He glanced around the table. "The city is being searched right now, and every access road will be strongly guarded. Soldiers are already spreading out across the countryside. All of us must use whatever means we have at our disposal to track down the perpetrators." He directed his attention to Rufe. "Under the circumstances, I doubly appreciate the strong force you have brought to Castel, Rufe. I would be grateful if you and your men would secure Deadman's Pass. It seems unlikely that the Ahrans would take the queen into Arvenon, but desperate men sometimes do surprising things."

Rufe pushed himself to his feet and bowed an acknowledgment. With a meaningful task assigned to him, his sense of purpose was returning. He would rouse his men and leave for the border the moment the gathering was dismissed.

Even a glance at Count Gordan made it obvious that the blow had hit the regent hard. Rufe knew that the count's affection for the queen dated from her childhood, and that he had been appointed her protector after her arranged marriage to King Steffan at barely fourteen years of age.

Rufe was no less devastated. Over the years he had watched in growing awe as she grew and matured, applying her energy and wisdom for the benefit of the kingdom she had so freely embraced. After assassins attacked both her and the king, he had witnessed her courage in the most harrowing of circumstances. Heavily pregnant, and with a gravely wounded husband at her side, she had endured with grace the seemingly endless retreat to the safety of Newhaven.

But Rufe had weightier reasons for his distress. He knew this would only be the beginning. Alone of those in the room, he had already endured the nightmare about to unfold. He had lived through the aftermath of Ethen's abduction, looking on helplessly as a frustrated and previously unshakable Will Prentis slowly fell apart.

The rejoicing at Ethen's eventual escape had quickly been muted by an even more devastating blow—the abduction of the ruling Castelan king and the Rogandan princess he was courting.

Now it was happening again. This latest masterstroke assaulted the very heart of Arvenon.

A single question haunted Rufe. What could he possibly say to King Steffan?

12

———

Will stood on the gangplank of the Nomad Lady, grateful to have reached Rog safely and eager to disembark. "Thank you, Captain Yordin. It has been a pleasure to sail with you, as always."

The captain bowed. "The pleasure is mine, Lord Torbury. You will always find a welcome on the Lady."

"Do you know who the king is sending to meet us?" asked Thomas as they stepped onto the dock.

Will shook his head. "The message didn't say."

While they were waiting, he walked toward the stern of the Lady, not pausing until the ship lay behind him. Gazing across the water, his attention was caught by a fishing boat returning home. The fishermen did not look happy. As they drew nearer, he heard them grumbling about their catch. At that moment, a large fish leaped from the water into the boat, followed immediately by another. The fishermen watched in astonishment as fish after fish launched themselves from the water and into their boat, flopping about at their feet.

Belatedly noticing what was happening, Thomas glanced at Will with an eyebrow arched.

"What?" asked Will innocently. "I'm sure you took the chance to practice in the early days."

Thomas rolled his eyes.

A group of soldiers in King Krasmir's livery found them before they could say more. The captain led Will and Thomas on foot through the docks to a place where horses were being held in readiness. As soon as they mounted, the soldiers took them through the streets of Rog to the royal palace. The captain ushered them into a reception room.

The king had already arrived. Nodding his thanks to the captain, he rose to greet them. "I am glad to welcome you once more to Rog, Lord Torbury. These are challenging times, and your wisdom will be greatly valued. You are welcome too, Thomas Stablehand."

Both men bowed. "We will willingly do whatever we can to help, Your Majesty," Will replied.

The king indicated the captain. "Your escort will show you to your rooms, Thomas. Please make yourself comfortable."

Thomas bowed again and left the room. The king waved Will to a seat.

It troubled Will to witness the state of his host. The face before him was drawn and haggard, as if the king had aged prematurely.

"Your arrival is timely, Lord Torbury. I have just received a request to meet with the Grand Vizier himself." The king scowled. "The man has a nerve coming here openly! I intend to meet with him though. I want to look my enemy in the eye."

Will nodded. "We had an encounter with three Ahran ships during our voyage, Your Majesty. We met with another Ahran, a man named Bisri Ahuzza. He claims to have been tasked with meeting you, with a view to conveying your views to the emperor."

The king snorted disdainfully. "His agents have abducted my daughter! What does he expect my views to be?"

"The bisri was dismissive when I told him the facts. If I am any judge of character though, this Bisri is not posturing. It may well be that neither he nor the emperor is aware of the truth."

"Then the emperor is a fool."

"Perhaps. It may also be that his Grand Vizier is deceiving him. He appears to have sent another envoy to form an independent assessment. That might suggest he has questions about the reports he's received from the Grand Vizier."

"What are you proposing?" growled the king.

"That we look for an opportunity to engage with the bisri. If the Grand Vizier is furthering an agenda of his own, it might be possible to drive a wedge between him and the emperor."

The king grunted again. He might not be entirely convinced, but he hadn't brushed aside Will's views either.

"Who will be meeting with the Grand Vizier?" asked Will.

"Apart from me? You, if you're willing!"

"Certainly, Your Majesty. I'm just as eager to see him face-to-face."

"The head of my security network will be there of course. Lady Tulinay—you would have met her briefly."

Will nodded. He did remember meeting her. He had also read the reports. Head of the security network meant she was tasked with oversight of the king's foreign and domestic agents. The Rogandan spy network was vast and sprawling, with a long-standing reputation of inefficiency. Tough as steel and a ferocious organizer, Lady Tulinay had made an immediate difference after her appointment.

"I'm also planning to include Lord Kulferan, Lord Boedwyk, and an interpreter. That will be more than enough participants."

Will's eyebrows went up involuntarily at the mention of the eccentric nobleman, but he chose not to comment.

The king had clearly settled on his attendee list already, and it came as no surprise that Thomas was not invited. Why would he include an Arvenian commoner? It made no difference though. There were other ways to expose the Grand Vizier to the Stone of Knowing. Will would ensure that Thomas was positioned where he could see the Ahran official as he entered the palace.

At a call from the king, an aide joined them in the room.

"You've had a long voyage, Lord Torbury," said King Krasmir. "I imagine you'll appreciate an opportunity to relax. The meeting with the Grand Vizier will take place mid-morning tomorrow. I'll send someone to collect you in good time."

Rising from his seat, Will bent at the waist. Then he followed the aide from the room.

He headed to his quarters with his mind already hard at work, churning through the best approaches to take in the coming meeting.

BISRI AHUZZA CLIMBED up a rope net toward the deck of a Rogandan warship, close behind the Grand Vizier and his translator. Ronizah clambered up after them.

The significance of the location was not lost on Ahuzza. Could there have been a more obvious way to say they were not welcome on Rogandan soil? He wondered what had prompted such hostility from their hosts. Could it truly be nothing more than a pretense, a cynical mixture of false accusations?

Not for the first time, he recalled the wild claims made by the Arvenian nobleman while visiting his ship. The problem was that Ahuzza had encountered many habitual liars, both at court and among the masses. The Arvenian showed none of the obvious signs.

Whatever the truth might be, he anticipated a frosty reception. A reception of any kind would be far more than Rheibas deserved if half of the nobleman's assertions were true.

The Arvenian had named Bolnyk. How did he know his name? What had Bolnyk been doing in Rogand? Ahuzza knew the agent to be ruthless. He had also long believed he was loyal to no one but Rheibas.

They emerged on deck to find five men and a woman waiting for them. Guards stood to attention on every side.

Ahuzza immediately recognized one of the men as the Arvenian who came aboard his ship. He had introduced himself as Lord Torbury. The man clearly recognized Ahuzza too, because he offered him a faint nod.

Clearly Torbury was on intimate terms with the Rogandan king. That much at least of his story was true.

King Krasmir's gaze passed briefly over Ahuzza before settling on the Grand Vizier. His glare offered no hint of welcome.

The woman addressed the Ahrans. "You have requested an audience with His Majesty King Krasmir," she announced coolly.

Ronizah deferred to his colleague, allowing him to translate her words on behalf of all the visitors.

The Grand Vizier glanced about him. "The Empire of Ahr is accustomed to receiving foreign emissaries with more respect," he said bluntly.

The king waited patiently for his own translator to relay the words. "The Kingdom of Rogand is accustomed to dealing with murderers and abductors as they deserve," he replied coldly. "Count yourself fortunate. You are only being received at all out of respect for your absent emperor."

"I am here for one reason only," the Grand Vizier stated. "I wish to secure the release of Her Imperial Highness Princess Neira."

"Then you are wasting your time," the king informed him. "The only topic I am willing to discuss is the safe return of Princess Teylee of Rogand and King Rupert of Castel."

"Why should I be blamed if two young lovers have absconded from under your noses?" sniffed Rheibas.

Fury twisted the features of the king.

Rheibas forestalled him. "I have information that the Arvenian queen—the sister of the missing king—knows where they are and is secretly planning to visit them. I have also more recently learned that some of my sailors stumbled by chance upon their hideaway," he said evenly.

Ahuzza saw anger and confusion on the faces before him. He studied King Krasmir in particular. If he could read people at all, the king was no more an actor than his Arvenian friend.

"If you have nothing to hide, then tell us the location of this supposed hideaway," said Lady Tulinay.

"Gladly," Rheibas replied. "As soon as you release to me Princess Neira."

"Are you hoping for an opportunity to finish her off properly this time?" asked Lord Torbury coolly.

"Ah. Lord Torbury, I presume. I've been hoping to meet you."

The Arvenian's face set hard. "And I've been interested to set eyes upon the man responsible for the abduction of my son. Did you order it yourself? Or did you simply take advantage of the grubby activities of your agents?"

Rheibas sneered at him. "Your ignorant insinuations do nothing to flatter you."

"I know more than you could possibly imagine," Lord Torbury replied, his lip curling in disdain. "Your senior agent, Bolnyk, abducted Princess Teylee and Prince Rupert. He did it immediately after he tried to murder my son."

The chief minister was a master at giving nothing away. Nevertheless, Ahuzza saw his eyebrows quirk momentarily. Was he surprised that Torbury knew Bolnyk's name and his role? Or was there something Rheibas hadn't already heard about Torbury's son?

The conversation was becoming uncomfortable for Ahuzza, and with a start he realized why. The polished manner of the chief minister, so familiar to the bisri, had never felt so false. The raw anger radiating from the Rogandan king and his Arvenian ally could not have been contrived. It was real. The contrast was marked, and it disturbed him.

Noticing Ronizah shooting occasional glances in his direction, he resolved to keep an impassive mask on his face.

He berated himself again for his naivety in hiring the man. It was too late to find an interpreter who owed nothing to the chief minister. With no alternative at hand, he was stuck with Ronizah.

Lord Torbury startled him out of his musing. "I am glad to see you again, Bisri Ahuzza."

Acutely aware that he'd said nothing to Rheibas about his meeting with Torbury, Ahuzza dipped his head to hide his momentary confusion. His reaction was unnecessary of course. The chief minister had undoubtedly received a full report from Ronizah.

And what reason did he have to be discomposed? The emperor himself had charged him with making independent contact with these people.

"I am glad to see you too, Lord Torbury," he returned.

"At our last meeting you questioned my description of Princess Neira's abandonment. I referred you to the man who captained the princess's ship. He spent time in Rog after the ship arrived, and his account was very enlightening. His name is Captain Gharpin. Have you spoken with him?"

The Grand Vizier interjected. "The captain you refer to has nothing of substance to offer on this matter," he said dismissively. "Sadly he was lost at sea."

Lord Torbury stared at him calmly. "Are you completely certain about that?"

The chief minister's eyes narrowed. He offered no response, but Ahuzza sensed what might have been unease. Did the Arvenian know something Rheibas didn't? Or was he bluffing?

The woman spoke quietly with the king before addressing herself to the chief minister. "King Krasmir has requested that I bring this meeting to an end. Do not expect to be received again, Chief Minister, unless you first return Princess Teylee and King Rupert safely to us." She concluded her words with a crisp bow.

Rheibas said nothing, but the bisri saw that he had gone white with anger.

She turned to Ahuzza and bowed again. "As the emperor's envoy, we would be glad to engage with you again on a mutually convenient occasion."

Returning a tight bow of his own, Ahuzza headed for the rope net, preparing to lower himself over the side. One of the Rogandan servants approached him to offer assistance. As the man helped him over the side, he surreptitiously slipped a small note into his hand.

Curious as he was about the content of the note, a single thought occupied his mind as he descended to the boat waiting below. A difficult conversation with the chief minister lay ahead. He wasn't looking forward to it.

***

WILL WATCHED SILENTLY with the others as the Ahrans were rowed away to their own ship. If only Thomas had been present. The king's decision to hold the meeting on a ship—not communicated to Will until they were leaving for the docks—had denied Thomas any opportunity to catch a glimpse of the Grand Vizier, even from afar.

When they were gone King Krasmir threw his hands into the air. "That wretch as good as admitted his people were holding Tasha and Rupert. How can we find out where they are?" Tension strained his face.

"I will send out ships to check islands in the region," Lord Kulferan said.

"Can I make a suggestion, My Lord?" Will asked the commander. "Order them to search out Ahran vessels and shadow them secretly. If we're fortunate, the Ahrans might lead us to wherever they're being held."

"Do it!" the king ordered Lord Kulferan.

The nobleman bowed an acknowledgment.

The king frowned. "What do you make of this claim about Queen Essanda?"

"It's absurd," replied Lady Tulinay.

"I found it alarming, Your Majesty," said Will soberly. "He might be planning to abduct her as well. I expect her to make a goodwill visit to Castel to offer them support. She would be especially vulnerable while traveling. I need to warn King Steffan. If I prepare a dispatch, would you be willing to send it to Arnost as a matter of priority, Your Majesty?"

The king nodded distractedly. "Of course."

Will bowed.

"The emperor must have questions about what's going on, or he wouldn't have sent an independent envoy," exclaimed the king. "What use can we make of this Bisri Ahuzza?"

Lady Tulinay did not hesitate. "I believe we need to build rapport with him, Your Majesty. It might weaken the Grand Vizier if we limit our communication to the bisri."

"It might also get Ahuzza killed," Will said grimly.

She frowned. "He's the emperor's envoy. Surely it wouldn't be easy to simply get rid of him."

"The Grand Vizier doesn't seem over-particular about who he eliminates," Will reminded her. "He was willing to kill the emperor's daughter. And apparently for no other reason than to create an incident he could use against us. The man has no scruples."

Will's brows drew together. "We must not underestimate him. He's accustomed to manipulating the truth to suit his own agenda, and he's extremely good at it. He had Ahuzza completely convinced when we first met. If the bisri is starting to have doubts, the Grand Vizier will see him as a liability."

"Then we've already put him in danger," said Lady Tulinay. "I was studying him carefully, and I had the clear impression he's becoming conflicted."

Will nodded. "I believe you're right. A change of heart will only work in our favor if Ahuzza manages to stay alive."

"There's little the emperor can do to save him," added Lady Tulinay. "He's too far away."

King Krasmir was frowning. "What *is* the emperor's attitude to all this? Surely he would be furious if he knew the games his chief minister has been playing!"

Will shrugged. "Without direct access to him, we can only guess, Your Majesty."

Lord Boedwyk gazed absently up at the mast, his brows drawn together thoughtfully. "Consulting directly with His Imperial Majesty could be...enlightening." He sighed deeply. "If only the voyage to Kat Ahket was not so long. Perhaps distance is emerging as our greatest enemy."

Lady Tulinay looked sharply at Boedwyk for a moment before

apparently deciding to ignore him entirely. "Bisri Ahuzza is the emperor's eyes and ears," she said, "so it's in our interests to have him report back. Since getting rid of him is likely to become a high priority for the Grand Vizier, preserving his life must be a high priority for us."

"We can try to warn him," said Lord Kulferan.

King Krasmir nodded. "Do it," he said. He turned to Will. "What were you saying about the Ahran captain, Lord Torbury? The one who brought the princess here. Is he still alive?"

Will shrugged. "We all know that the Grand Vizier is lying about what happened to Princess Neira. I decided to see how he would react if he thought we had solid evidence against him. I knew the princess mentioned Captain Gharpin by name. However, I need to make it clear there was no truth to anything I said, Your Majesty. As far as I know, while he was at Rog the captain never spoke about what happened with Princess Neira. And I have no grounds for believing he didn't perish at sea. I was baiting the Grand Vizier. I wanted to see how he would react when he wasn't the one controlling the information flow."

"He didn't like it," said Lady Tulinay decidedly.

"Maybe not," growled the king. "But how does that help us?"

"People make mistakes when they think they're losing control," said Will. He shook his head. "But we've done nothing to hurt him yet. He's as dangerous as ever."

"And we still don't know his agenda," said Lady Tulinay. "Even though I have my best agents working on it."

"To find a way forward we need the emperor involved," said Will. "Bisri Ahuzza is the key."

"Our priority is simple—to free Princess Teylee and King Rupert!" insisted the king. "Never lose sight of that!"

They made their way back to Rog without further comment.

Will returned more determined than ever. Having looked his enemy in the eye, he wanted only one thing: to see him brought down.

Bisri Ahuzza crouched wordlessly in the prow of the longboat as they glided away from the Rogandan vessel. The Grand Vizier sat facing him. The interpreters had found places of their own further back in the boat.

"So I have seen my celebrated adversary at last!" crowed Rheibas. He appeared to be in unusually high spirits. "I trust I appeared suitably shaken by Torbury's ridiculous assertions."

Too discomfited to speak, Ahuzza stared back at him.

"Already he will be composing a dispatch to his king. To no avail." He curled his lip. "The man is vastly overrated. It is beyond time for him to be humbled."

The boat pulled alongside the Grand Vizier's ship.

Rheibas prepared to climb aboard with his interpreter. "Return the bisri to his ship!" he ordered the sailors.

Then, bending low to Ahuzza's ear, he mouthed, "Be careful, Bisri. Be very, very careful."

13

———

Kahrlin shoved his captive forward roughly. In response the queen gave out a muffled cry, but she was wasting her time. The Ahran had tied her gag himself. No one would hear, however hard she tried to yell.

He smiled in grim satisfaction. Thus far the Castelan fools who accepted his money had done what he paid them to do.

Pulling the cloaked and hooded captive to an abrupt halt in the shadows of a building, he nodded to Akohlsa, the agent assisting in that night's extraction.

His confederate disappeared around the corner. The minutes dragged, and Kahrlin grew increasingly impatient. Before he could decide to do anything rash, Akohlsa reappeared leading a horse with a wagon. Empty barrels lay in the wagon beneath a thick waterproof covering. Akohlsa had already pulled back the covering, revealing a narrow space between the barrels.

The queen's arms had been tied in front of her. The two men now bound her legs and dumped her unceremoniously in the wagon, throwing the covering over the barrels and the prisoner.

Both men climbed onto the driver's bench, Kahrlin taking the reins. Clicking his tongue, he guided the horse toward the city gates.

It was imperative that they escaped the city before the regent's men locked it down.

One final hurdle remained. The guards at the gates had been bribed handsomely to keep the gates open and to ask no questions. There were never any guarantees though. Shifts could be changed, and the new guards at the gate might cause problems. There was little he could do about that. The guards he bribed would not receive the bulk of their payment until after the wagon was safely through the gates. That gave them an incentive to be on duty as expected.

The wagon rolled slowly away from the palace. Thus far there had been no hitch of any kind in Kahrlin's carefully laid plans. Faint cries sounded behind them as they approached the gates. The queen's fallen guards must have been discovered. The alarm had been raised. Time was now pressing.

Kahrlin's heart began to race. The temptation to goad the horses into a gallop grew as every minute passed. He resisted the urge, and they clip-clopped forward steadily as before.

To his relief, the gates lay wide open. If the guards had heard the distant cries, they were choosing to ignore them. Chatting casually to each other, they waved the wagon through.

Increasing the pace to a trot, Kahrlin crossed the bridge and swung the horses north. The hunt must surely be up now, but a safe house beckoned just clear of the city. He gave the horses their heads, and the wagon raced on into the night.

For the first time he allowed himself to enjoy a measure of satisfaction. He had every reason to be satisfied—this operation would be his crowning achievement. The groundwork had been laid slowly and patiently, the preparations meticulous at every stage. Arrangements were firmly in place well before the Arvenian queen arrived.

The single biggest challenge had been finding a way to lure the queen from the safety of her apartments into the open. Countless plans had been explored and discarded. In the end, Kahrlin had reluctantly concluded she would need to be extracted while she was sleeping. It was the highest risk solution, but he could see no alternative. Then, as the two of them lay hidden in readiness, she had decided to go for a walk—in the open, and with only two guards. He wanted to laugh out loud.

The horses were tiring when he finally guided them off the main road and down a narrow lane. Reaching the end of the lane, he steered the wagon toward a large barn beside a lonely farmhouse.

They had done it. The Arvenian queen had been plucked from the castle under the noses of her hosts.

The Castelan regent clearly had no idea what was taking place in his capital that night. The fool had no idea how thoroughly Kahrlin's agents had sidestepped his every attempt at security.

A wry smile came to his lips. He could only imagine the panic of the people he had bribed when they learned they had assisted in the abduction of their own former princess. He had spun them a yarn about pilfering barrels of wine from the over-stocked royal cellars. The fools had accepted the tale only too readily when they caught a glimpse of bags bulging with coins.

Their heads would roll once the regent's men ferreted them out. That suited Kahrlin perfectly. He had no interest in leaving behind loose ends.

<hr>

AFTER TWO WEEKS hiding out in a barn not far from the city, Kahrlin was more than ready to risk the next stage of the journey out of Castel. The queen had not proven especially difficult to manage, but he had already wearied of this assignment. He would never be able to relax until he had handed responsibility for her to someone else.

The mission held promise of becoming a huge success. If they were able to complete it as planned, he had every expectation of further promotion. At the very least he would be lavishly rewarded for his efforts. None of that would happen unless they made it to the coast undetected.

Assuming they reached the coast, a longboat would pull in to a remote beach and row the captive to an Ahran ship lying offshore.

Kahrlin and his small team would join them, remaining with the ship until they were handed their next assignment.

Getting to the coast undetected was easier to imagine than to achieve. The first problem was that the roads were swarming with soldiers. Ahran agents posing as merchants reported that access to the coast was regulated with unusual energy. Worse, people in every town and village in the kingdom had been asked to report abnormal activity or suspicious strangers. Under these circumstances it would be a remarkable achievement to make it halfway to the sea.

None of this came as a surprise to Kahrlin. From the beginning he had assumed a vigorous manhunt would be mounted. In response he and his confederates had come up with a simple, if unusual, plan.

The first step had been the preparation of a suitable mode of transport. A wagon with tall sides had been acquired and a false bottom installed, deep enough to accommodate a person lying prone. The ceiling and the base of the receptacle had been lined with thick wool, and pairs of metal brackets placed at one end. The false bottom had been cleverly designed to allow a section of it to be removed for easy access to the hidden space.

The intent was to place the queen inside the false bottom, lying on a layer of wool and with another woolen layer above her. Her ankles would be fastened to the metal brackets and her wrists tied. There would be enough space to wriggle around and turn her head, although movement of her body would be severely constrained. Sections of the wagon floor not covered by wool had sufficient gaps to permit adequate circulation of air.

One of Kahrlin's men tested the prison to ensure that the sound of any movement would be muffled effectively by the wool. He emerged unnerved after a few minutes in the confined space. Kahrlin sneered at his reaction, mocking him as nothing more than a baby.

Later that day the queen was forced to drink wine laced with crushed opium seeds. Dazed and disoriented, she was laid in her new quarters and secured in position. As soon as the false bottom was put in place, the wagon swung in behind a somber procession.

Leading the procession was an open wagon carrying nothing but a coffin. Immediately behind it was a carriage full of mourners. Their baggage had been collected earlier and placed on the false bottom of the wagon hiding the queen.

The genius of this solution to the Ahrans' dilemma was its simplicity. Several agents had searched the capital and the surrounding countryside until they identified a family with roots in a seaside village who had suffered a recent bereavement. The deceased was the patriarch of a small but tight-knit family, and his widow was surprised and touched to learn that an unknown benefactor had offered to pay all expenses associated with transporting the deceased to his home village and burying him there.

No reason existed for the procession to be secretive in any way. The corpse truly was that of a loved husband and father, and the mourners close relations who were genuinely grieved. None of them had any notion that the procession included several Ahran agents, nor that an abducted queen lay hidden beneath their baggage.

The procession inevitably attracted considerable attention. At the first town soldiers brought it to a halt, insisting on opening the coffin to check the corpse. They also briefly checked the baggage wagon without finding anything untoward.

At first distressed, the mourners were persuaded to be understanding. When the same thing happened at the next town, the widow became agitated. Emotions boiled over at the third enforced stop.

Quickly realizing that the situation was unsupportable, town officials arranged for soldiers to escort the mourners to their final destination. After that, neither the mourners nor their cargo were hindered in any way.

The journey took several days to complete, but thankfully the largesse of the benefactor extended to comfortable lodgings along the way.

Kahrlin's agents, all hand selected, looked like Castelans and spoke their language without noticeable accents. Posing as hired labor, they unloaded the baggage from the wagon at each overnight stop, reloading it the next morning.

Once it was fully dark, the queen was released and allowed to eat, drink, and stretch her legs. After long days spent in a confined space, the strain on the captive was extreme. More than once they removed the cover to find her unconscious. Whenever they returned her to her prison she resisted fiercely until they administered the drugged wine.

Kahrlin didn't care. In his eyes she was worth little more than another item of baggage. As long as he could deliver her alive and in one piece, he would be more than happy.

The last overnight stop was in a town not far from the coast. Local laborers were hired to take the place of the Ahran agents, both for the final leg of the journey to the coastal village and for the entire return trip to the homes of the mourners near the capital.

Kahrlin himself made sure the new laborers understood what was expected of them. While he was thus engaged, the queen was transferred to another wagon that other agents had prepared for their arrival. On this occasion she was bound and gagged but not otherwise confined.

Once the whole town was soundly asleep, the wagon rolled into the countryside, passing slowly in the dim moonlight over rough trails and rolling hillsides until it eventually came to a halt at the edge of a small beach.

Lifted from the wagon, the queen was carried bodily to a waiting longboat and dumped without ceremony into the bottom of it. Lying trussed at the feet of Kahrlin and his team, she was rowed to a waiting Ahran vessel.

A rope net was lowered from the deck, and the queen was placed within it. As soon as it was hauled aboard, the remaining passengers clambered up rope ladders onto the deck. The ship then raised anchor and departed.

Kahrlin finally allowed himself to relax. His efforts would be sure to attract the attention of the chief minister. And why not? His plan had been bold and imaginative, and he had executed it with his usual finesse. Unlike some of his fellow agents. His lips twisted into a smirk.

Bolnyk might be the chief minister's senior agent, but he could never be accused of finesse, much less of imagination. His recent successes looked impressive on the surface: capturing the Arvenian commander's boy, the Castelan king, and the Rogandan princess. But he deserved no credit for taking the boy. He only became aware of the abduction after it was done. Bolnyk's contribution had been to botch the boy's transfer. He had been forced to kill the child, ending any value he might have had as a hostage. As for capturing the king and the princess, that had been dumb luck and nothing more.

Bolnyk might be loyal, but he was also dull and uninspired. Sooner or later the chief minister would weary of him. When he did, Kahrlin intended to be seen as the obvious replacement.

As the shoreline slowly faded from view in the dim light, one of the sailors approached Kahrlin. "The captain invites you to join him."

Kahrlin followed the sailor to the captain's cabin and went inside.

"Welcome!" The captain greeted him enthusiastically, his face alight with satisfaction. "A job well done, Kahrlin! Well done indeed!" He handed the agent a goblet of wine. "A toast! In celebration of the perfect outcome to an extremely challenging mission!"

The two men sat together well into the night, laughing and drinking with increasing abandon.

THE FOLLOWING MORNING, a somewhat unsteady Kahrlin joined the captain at the mast. The queen, finally released from her bindings, stood nearby, silently staring out to sea. She made for a pitiful sight. With her cloak held close about her, and her face obscured almost completely by her hood, she seemed intent on hiding from the world.

The captain nodded in her direction. "From what you've told me, your queen showed considerable fortitude, considering everything she's been through in the last few weeks."

Kahrlin raised an eyebrow. "She can hear what you're saying."

The captain shrugged. "Hearing is one thing; understanding is another. I've been reliably informed she doesn't speak a word of our language."

"I was told the same thing, and I can confirm it. It became

intensely frustrating in the weeks she was with us. She doesn't even understand Rogandan. We had to lower ourselves to speaking Arvenian if we wanted a response." He spat onto the deck.

"Mentioning her fortitude was not intended as a compliment," the captain told him. "I just couldn't help wondering how our own Princess Neira might have handled similar conditions."

Kahrlin snorted before he could prevent himself. "I can well imagine!" He gazed at the forlorn figure. "What have you been ordered to do with her?"

"I've been instructed to drop her off at a remote island. I wouldn't be surprised if the chief minister himself decides to entertain her sooner or later."

Kahrlin grunted. "In that case, she'd better enjoy the voyage. If her last few weeks have been difficult, it's going to get a lot worse."

With some measure of freedom restored at last, the captive made her way onto the deck, avoiding the stares of the sailors. Some faces wore sneers, and a couple showed pity, but what did it matter? These sailors could do nothing to help her, even if they wanted to.

Swaying with the pitching of the deck, she headed for the rail. Grasping hold of it to steady herself, she stared off into the horizon.

The last few weeks had been a waking nightmare, coming to a head in the extreme conditions of her confinement in the wagon. The experience had been terrifying. She had heard tell of people with a crippling fear of confined spaces; she understood completely now.

It wasn't just the terror of being trapped. Her arms and legs had ached continuously from the forced inaction. Although her nose had never been deliberately blocked, at times she feared the gag would suffocate her. Constantly hungry, with only opium-laced wine to drink, and with her bladder full to bursting, even the release of crying out was denied her. Frequent lapses into unconsciousness had been the only reason she was able to endure the ordeal.

Whenever they were not traveling and she was released for a time, the only faces she saw were harsh and unyielding.

She had known times of suffering in the past, but this experience highlighted how fortunate her life had been. With the future dark and uncertain, she chose to revisit the past, savoring the many things she had to be grateful for.

It would have been easy to grieve what might have been, but she refused steadfastly to lose herself in daydreams. Fantasies could not prepare her for what lay ahead.

Only one thing mattered now. The chief minister would come to her.

She knew what she needed to do, and she was ready for it. Having so far played her role to perfection, she only needed to stay the course until she reached the end.

Maive leaned forward on the rail, dreaming of revenge.

14

Rufe sat in his tent, head buried in his hands, still unable to come to terms with what had happened at Castel Citadel.

Following the regent's shocking revelation, Rufe had led his men back to the border to seal up Deadman's Pass as he had agreed. It took no more than a moment to decide he would base his force on the Arvenian side. Castel held bitter associations for him now.

Before setting up camp, he had assigned guards to keep a watch over the pass from the Castelan end. A strong contingent of his men now stood on alert at the Arvenian end of the pass, near the Castelan border post.

Rufe's men had arrived to find the post abandoned. No doubt the Castelans would reestablish it at some point. In the meantime the regent had more pressing matters to deal with. He also knew the pass would be well guarded by Rufe and his men.

Late on the first day after they had arrived, one of his scouts sought him out. "A small group of riders is approaching from Castel, Rufe."

His heart leaped. Was it possible that the Ahrans truly were trying to escape into Arvenon with their captive?

Rufe called for Hennis. "Allow the riders to enter the pass. Then block their escape from both ends. Avoid fighting at all costs."

Hennis nodded and hurried away.

Much as Rufe longed for a chance to free the queen, he knew he needed to temper his enthusiasm. The reality was likely to be much less encouraging. The unknown riders would probably turn out to be nothing more than a new set of border guards.

Rufe moved to the mouth of the pass and sat on his horse waiting for word.

Almost half an hour had passed before Hennis reappeared. Approaching Rufe, he drew him aside. "Only one of them rode into the pass. He knew we were here, and he wants to speak with you."

"Who is he?"

Hennis raised his hands helplessly. "I have no idea. He won't talk to anyone except you."

"You're with me," Rufe told Hennis, heading his horse into the pass.

They had ridden all the way to the Castelan end before he caught sight of the rider, surrounded by Rufe's men.

"We've checked him, and he isn't armed," Hennis said quietly as they approached.

"What do you want?" Rufe asked.

"May I speak with you in private?" the stranger returned.

After a moment's hesitation, Rufe returned a tight nod. "We'll do it right here," he said, signaling his men to back off. The men moved out of earshot, remaining close enough to provide support if it should be needed.

The stranger wasted no time. "I have someone with me who would like to speak with you. The matter is highly confidential."

Rufe was not impressed. "I have no idea who you are or what your purpose is. You surely can't expect me to go anywhere alone with you."

"Would it be acceptable to you if the meeting takes place close to the mouth of the pass? My men will keep their distance if yours do the same."

Far too many things could go wrong with this arrangement. However, Rufe couldn't see how anyone apart from himself would be at risk. He nodded curtly. "The meeting can take place over there," he said, pointing.

The other man nodded his agreement.

"And I want all of you dismounted," Rufe said firmly.

After a brief nod, the other man rejoined his companions.

Calling Hennis to his side, Rufe issued instructions. "I've agreed to meet one of them over there. Be prepared to move quickly if there's any sign of treachery. If I raise my right arm, send me support, and round the others up. Don't let any of them get away." He gestured toward the group of riders.

Hennis nodded once before returning to the men to issue orders of his own.

Rufe moved to the agreed position and waited. A cloaked and hooded figure emerged from the group of dismounted riders and walked toward him. A strange sensation washed over him as the person approached.

He was greeted by a soft voice. "Please don't react in any way, Rufe. It's extremely important." The voice rendered him speechless. She continued, entirely unnecessarily, "It's me. Queen Essanda!"

"Your Majesty!" he finally stammered. Keeping his voice low required incredible restraint. All he wanted to do was shout in exhilaration at the top of his lungs.

"How is this possible?" he breathed, shaking his head in wonder.

"It's a long story. Don't worry, I'm planning to tell you everything. Do you have anyone with you who knows the way to Newhaven? It needs to be someone discreet and reliable."

He nodded. "Hennis, one of my captains, was with us in Newhaven. I trust him implicitly."

"Please get him. I'll ask Galvas, my new protector, to join us."

The small group assembled, and Rufe moved them to a location nearby that boasted a couple of fallen logs. They sat down, trying to make themselves comfortable.

"This is Galvas," the queen began. "He's a Varasan agent, and also the main reason I'm not currently in the hands of the Ahrans. It might be simplest if you provide some background, Galvas."

The Varasan nodded. "I need to make it clear that everything you will hear today is highly confidential. Do you understand?"

Rufe and Hennis both nodded. "Yes," they replied in unison.

"You may be aware that Ahran agents have become bolder and more determined in recent times. You probably don't know that King Delmar recently escaped an attempt to either kill or capture him—we can't be sure which. The Ahrans struck in Varacellan, in the open, while he was surrounded by guards. They very nearly succeeded. They were thwarted only thanks to quick thinking on the part of one of our agents."

He sighed. "King Steffan and King Krasmir both understand the full extent of the threat, and they are responding vigorously to Ahran infiltration in their own kingdoms. We tried to convey the danger to a number of the regent's people, but none of them were willing to be convinced that Castel is a target.

"As a result, we increased our presence in Castel with a view to limiting the damage the Ahrans could do. Some time ago, after the planned visit of Queen Essanda became public knowledge, we learned that the Ahrans intended to take advantage of the opportunity to move against her. We therefore stepped up our efforts to monitor their activities."

"Do you know why they attacked the border post here at Deadman's Pass just before we arrived with the queen?" asked Rufe.

"I can't be certain," Galvas replied, "but I can venture a guess. I suspect it was an attempt at misdirection."

Rufe frowned. "Misdirection?"

"They wanted you, and the Castelans, to believe that the queen was vulnerable in the countryside, outside the thick walls of a castle. They wanted you all to relax when she reached the safety of the capital, because that was always where they intended to strike."

Rufe nodded slowly. "So the attack on the border post was merely a diversion."

"Yes. The truth was that they couldn't hope to assemble a force large enough to seriously challenge her escort, so she was never in serious danger out here."

It all made sense. And the ruse had achieved exactly what the Ahrans intended.

"We learned that their agents were splashing money around. One of our people was able to connect with them. They paid him handsomely to supply a load of empty wine barrels. While he was with them he heard them speaking in their own language. He asked innocently if they were Rogandan, and they told him they were not, but that they had learned the language while trading with Rog. They said they used it when they didn't want others listening to their conversation. He got the point and said nothing further. Fortunately for us, he knows a little of the Ahran language. They continued to converse, and he was able to overhear a great deal of it. When we put the pieces together later, we were able to guess at both their intention and the approximate timing."

Queen Essanda took up the story. "I had barely arrived and settled in my apartments when a servant came to my room. She's a loyal Castelan who also works for the Varasans. She told me the Ahrans were planning to abduct me that night. I found it very difficult to believe at first. She brought in another woman who was about my height and with hair roughly the same color and length."

"The same woman responsible for rescuing King Delmar," interjected Galvas.

"This other woman wanted to dress up in my clothes and head out into the gardens adjoining my room. She said her goal was simply to lure the Ahrans into the open. I asked if Count Gordan was aware of this plot, and both of them insisted that no one could know. They were very persuasive, and my instincts told me I could trust them. I couldn't see what I had to lose, so I agreed to their plan."

She nodded to Galvas, and he continued. "Our guesses about the timing proved to be correct. We didn't expect them to be right there and ready to act immediately though. And our agent wasn't supposed to let them take her. We still don't know what went wrong, although we're starting to wonder if she had an agenda of her own. I understand she has reason to hate the Ahran Grand Vizier. It's possible she decided that posing as Queen Essanda would allow her access to him."

"I saw it from my rooms," the queen continued, "and it was terrifying. It happened so quickly. The two guards were overwhelmed and the agent was whisked away before I could fully understand what was going on. Galvas arrived immediately afterward." She turned to him. "I have no idea how you gained access to the castle, much less to my apartments."

"That isn't important," he told her. "What did matter was getting you to safety."

"Which also meant concealing the truth from the regent," she added.

"Why?" asked Rufe. "The poor man was completely devastated."

"He could never have been completely credible if he knew it wasn't true," said Galvas. "He was told what really happened the next day. He agreed to keep it secret, not just for the continuing safety of the queen, but especially for the safety of our agent."

Rufe nodded slowly. "If they found out the truth, they would kill your agent in a heartbeat and try again for the queen. What about the manhunt though?"

"The manhunt is real. Whatever our agent's reason for letting them take her, we desperately want to find and retrieve her." Galvas shook his head. "As you have heard, she looks remarkably similar to Queen Essanda. In her royal garments, anyone who hadn't already met the queen would almost certainly be taken in. There is one small but important discrepancy, though. Her eyes are not the same color as the queen's. If she meets an Ahran who is unusually well informed, it would be disastrous! We need to find a way to release her as soon as possible."

Rufe's head was spinning. There was little he could do about the agent's situation, but the queen was another matter. "What are your plans from here, Your Majesty? You asked about Newhaven."

"I think that's the safest place for me, at least for a while. Until the agent is freed—and until the Ahrans can be properly dealt with—it's important that no one knows I'm alive and free. I suspect that Anneka and Rellan might be willing to isolate Newhaven again, at least for a while."

"And what about King Steffan?"

Galvas responded. "It's painful, but he needs to be told the official story like everyone else. He won't need to pretend when he reacts to it. But we won't delay too long before telling him the truth."

"Even after he finds out I'm safe, he'll be furious at the Ahrans for trying to abduct me," said the queen. "He'll hunt them down with no less energy than if they'd succeeded. And at least he'll know I'm safe in the meantime."

"How can we get you to Newhaven?" asked Rufe. "Our soldiers will need to be kept in the dark as well."

"If you're agreeable," said the queen, addressing herself to both Rufe and Hennis, "Hennis can ride to Newhaven, with a couple of soldiers for his protection. The soldiers don't need to be told why they're going there. When you arrive, Hennis, you can ask Rellan to meet me in the same place he met us last time. I'm confident I can locate it again. Galvas and his men will deliver me there."

"You'll undoubtedly be concerned about the queen's safety with a small escort, Rufe," Galvas acknowledged. "But remember that no one believes that she is at large, so there's no reason for anyone to be looking for her."

"I can see the sense of the proposal," Rufe told him. "I also think it's wise to limit the number of people who know her exact location. So I appreciate your willingness to hand her over to Rellan before she reaches her destination."

Galvas bowed. "It seems we have an agreement. I hope Hennis can leave as soon as possible. We will follow immediately, but I expect we will travel more slowly. I would suggest that Hennis should be present at the handover to Rellan. He can then return here to report back to you, Rufe."

"I will choose a couple of men and leave at once," Hennis told them. "You can be assured of my complete silence on all these matters."

"All of our kingdoms are in your debt, Galvas," Rufe told him. "That applies to every one of King Delmar's agents, and not least the woman who willingly took the place of the queen."

RUFE WAITED IMPATIENTLY for the return of Hennis. Most especially he wanted confirmation that the queen had been safely delivered to Rellan.

The day after the queen had ridden through the pass, one of the regent's dispatch riders arrived, heading for Arnost. Unusually, he was accompanied by five armed guards. The following day a second dispatch rider passed through, heading for the same destination. He was similarly protected.

It wasn't difficult to guess what King Steffan would read in the two dispatches. He would be aghast when he read the first. The second would leave him both relieved and angry. Rufe was glad he wouldn't be there to witness it.

By the time Hennis finally returned, Rufe was becoming agitated.

"Did it go smoothly?" he demanded.

"Very smoothly," Hennis told him. "Anneka and Rellan were very willing to host the queen. They will cut off all contact with the outside world until we send word that it's safe for the queen to reemerge."

Rufe released a sigh. He could finally relax. "What happened with the Varasans? They didn't return this way."

"We rode with them for a short time," Hennis replied. "They asked us to guide them to Steffan's Citadel. They crossed into Erestor, heading for Maranelle. I believe they were planning to board a ship there. Perhaps they're planning to return to Varacellan. They didn't say."

"Wherever they're going, I hope they arrive safely," said Rufe. "We owe them an enormous debt."

15

The candle flickered and guttered, but Goultzar was not troubled by its tenuous glimmer. The Temple of the Dark Gods at Rog had always been a drafty place. Stepping forward unhurriedly, he reached a small door at the rear of the temple. After pausing long enough to snuff out the candle, he passed silently through into the cold night air beyond.

Moving confidently in spite of the darkness, he made his way to the outer wall of the temple compound. Peering back in the direction he had come, his eyes were drawn upward into the night sky, captured by the brilliance of the stars. He noted the empty section of sky where the temple buildings blotted out the twinkling lights. At first glance it almost appeared that the temple had reached hungrily into the heavens and consumed every star within its reach.

The mental image seemed symbolic. It brought to mind his Superior, the seemingly ageless High Priest, greedily snatching at years that did not belong to him.

Hearing a movement off to one side, he stiffened. Other movements followed, and softly murmured greetings reached his ears as several dark-clad forms loomed beside him. Even in the darkness he had no difficulty recognizing his agents. They were a diminished gathering—the lingering remnant of a once vigorous multitude.

"Worship of the dark gods is flagging in Rogand, and no one makes any attempt to arrest the slide," the Archprimus told them. "We have pledged ourselves to resist the decay with all our might. A new opportunity will soon arrive. Remain alert, and be ready to respond to my call at short notice."

Following a time-honored practice, Goultzar placed a clenched fist over his heart before flinging open all his fingers except the little one. After repeating the gesture, the others turned away and melted into the night.

GOULTZAR MARCHED THROUGH THE TEMPLE, ignoring the buzz that spread among the robed priests. He knew his appearance at that particular moment would distract them from their worship, but he didn't care.

An angry scowl came to his face as he saw the openly baleful expressions on many faces. Once his authority in this place had been unquestioned. He glared back at them. They could despise him all they liked—he had never been driven by a need for approval.

Some priests remained sympathetic, reduced though they might be in number. They kept their heads down and their opinions to themselves, and he encouraged them to do so. The tide had turned against him, and he saw no benefit in allowing his supporters to draw attention to themselves.

He found the priest he sought in an antechamber off the main worship area. "Ah, Zattu. Here you are."

From the way Zattu was backing away, Goultzar might have had the plague.

"I understand you were responsible for reassigning Atmek," the Archprimus offered mildly.

A wary look had come to Zattu's face. He nodded.

"You sent him to a small village near the border with Lestanor. Why that particular choice?"

Zattu's eyes narrowed. "I understand the worship of the dark gods has flagged in the region. I believed his talents would be appreciated there."

"And you did not consult with me before arranging the transfer?"

"I know you are a busy man, Archprimus."

"I see. I appreciate your thoughtfulness in sparing me such trivial details."

"I trust that I did not err."

"Not at all. I am grateful to you for alerting me to the need in that particular part of the kingdom. So much so that I have decided to transfer you there."

A shocked look covered Zattu's face.

"Atmek is needed for a special project, so I have recalled him. He is on his way back to Rog. But the credit must go to you for highlighting the need for a priest with organizational talents in the region. It seems appropriate that you take his place. You will leave immediately."

Zattu's eyes had gone wide.

"A cart is waiting outside for you now."

A sea of faces watched intently as Goultzar shepherded the horrified priest across the temple and outside into the open air. A cart stood ready as the Archprimus had promised. Goultzar stood with arms folded while Zattu climbed aboard. Then he nodded, and the cart rolled through the gates of the temple compound and joined the main road.

He reentered the temple, more than satisfied with his efforts.

Zattu had spoken the truth when he described Goultzar as a busy man. Overseeing the activities of priests throughout the kingdom was a monumental undertaking, and the Archprimus had long drawn upon assistance from a number of other priests, Zattu among them. However, the assignment of priests to vacant positions was a task he had rarely chosen to delegate.

More particularly, Atmek was one of Goultzar's most important supporters, and certainly not a man ever to be banished to the outer fringes of the kingdom. It seemed unlikely that the High Priest was directly involved. If he had been, such interference would have been unprecedented. Nevertheless, Goultzar had no doubt that Zattu had acted in what he believed were the High Priest's best interests.

In any event, justice had now been done, and Zattu's punishment fitted the crime perfectly.

A couple more days passed before Atmek reappeared. He sought out Goultzar the moment he arrived.

"My thanks to you for recalling me, Archprimus. I was beginning to think my life was over in that forsaken backwater."

"I am glad to have you back, Atmek. You are needed here more than ever. I am sure Zattu will do a fine job in your place."

Atmek's lips twisted into an ironic smile when he heard who was replacing him.

"Zattu has done me a favor," Goultzar conceded. "He has shown me the strategic potential of assignments. I acknowledge that I have failed to use them effectively in the past; however, I am already hard at work correcting that error."

"Is there any way I can be of assistance?" asked Atmek.

"Certainly. Draw up a list of names for me. Focus on priests who could most benefit from such an assignment."

THE TEMPLE soon witnessed a steady stream of departures as priests set out for uncelebrated destinations throughout the kingdom. The affected priests had not been selected randomly.

Even before a week had passed, a dramatic change had taken place in the tone within the temple. For the first time in many months, Goultzar's progress through the temple was not marked by hostile stares. The experience of receiving the respect due to his office had ceased to be a faded memory. His detractors had now become the priests anxious to remain out of sight.

Over the years his mission to foster devotion for his gods had become much more than an obligation—it had become a fervent obsession. All of that had been pushed aside by the tensions that simmered within the temple. Now he again worshiped freely with the acolytes, breathing in air heavy with incense and the sickly sweet smell of blood. Once more he invested energy in promoting devotion to the dark gods. In doing so, he was beginning to rediscover his earlier passion for his calling.

Then he received a summons to attend his Superior. He responded without enthusiasm. A considerable period of time had elapsed since he last visited the High Priest, and he had been more than content with the estrangement.

He arrived to find very little had changed in the High Priest's little chamber. The leathery skin of His Eminence appeared more stretched than ever, if such a thing was possible, but he still fixed Goultzar with the same unwavering stare.

Try as he might, Goultzar could not entirely ignore the protests of his aching body as the minutes dragged by. The stool opposite the High Priest felt as uncomfortable as ever, and waiting for him to speak was no less excruciating.

The stark reminder of his own mortality only served to emphasize his Superior's longevity. How did the High Priest achieve it? More importantly, if he'd discovered the key to long life, why was he so secretive about it? What right did he have to hoard such a prize for his own exclusive use?

His Eminence finally opened his mouth to speak. "You have been assigning men to every corner of the kingdom—men you do not like. Why have you yielded to favoritism?"

Goultzar said nothing in response, but anger began to well up within him. The High Priest should be happy that he'd been worshiping in the temple wholeheartedly for a change. That hadn't been possible until he removed the distractions.

His Superior apparently cared more about playing politics.

It didn't matter to Goultzar. Let the old man sit in his little room. Assignments were decided by the Archprimus, and he had no intention of backing away from what he had done.

The High Priest's eyes continued to bore into him. He had the feeling that His Eminence knew exactly what he was thinking, but it made no difference to him.

"There might be surprises in store for you," his Superior said dryly. He flicked a hand. "Leave me."

Goultzar left pondering the High Priest's comment about surprises. What might it mean?

He didn't have long to wait before finding out. As he exited the room, another priest was about to enter it. It was Zattu.

Normally he would have demanded to know why Zattu had abandoned his post. He didn't get a chance to ask.

"Archprimus," said Zattu, acknowledging him with a cool nod. "I have been recalled by His Eminence. It seems he has need of my services." With that he pushed through into the High Priest's room and closed the door.

The High Priest had blatantly undermined his Archprimus. And there was nothing Goultzar could do about it.

———

"You called for me, Your Majesty." Lord Boedwyk executed a clumsy bow, his bushy eyebrows bobbing up and down alarmingly.

King Krasmir waved him to a seat, trying not to wince as his guest swayed perilously close to a priceless vase on his way to the chair.

Settling into his seat with a deep sigh, the nobleman closed his eyes for a moment. Then, after opening his eyes again, his gaze traveled upward, his attention drawn to some feature of interest on the ceiling.

The king decided to open the conversation before the situation became even more awkward.

"I understand you have considerable knowledge of the Rogandan priesthood, My Lord."

Boedwyk nodded modestly. "It is true that I have made a thorough study of the priests of the dark gods and their various rituals," he acknowledged. "Indeed at one time I briefly considered a vocation as a priest myself."

The king's eyebrows rose in surprise.

"When I was a child I occasionally painted my face and clothed myself in priestly garb, precisely imitating their practices. Purely for my own amusement, you understand. I also memorized their various chants." He steepled his fingers thoughtfully. "I once led a group of stray cats in the Call to Fear. My feline apprentices were incapable of delivering the usual responses, but they nevertheless entered in with considerable enthusiasm. The caterwauling soon attracted a large and animated audience. Sadly, not all of the bystanders were equally able to appreciate the solemnity of the occasion. The incident prompted my parents to confiscate my robes and ban any further development of my budding talent for religious expression."

A mad laugh escaped the king's lips, in mockery of his best attempts to restrain it. He quickly smothered the outburst with a throaty cough.

Wasting no time before moving to safer ground, he observed, "I have heard whispers of tensions within the temple at Rog. Are you aware of the mechanics of leadership succession within the priesthood?"

"I can shed light on the historical precedents, Your Majesty. I must make my appeal to history since no High Priest has been inducted in living memory. The current incumbent is notoriously long-lived."

Similar reports had reached the king. He wondered if the High Priest's successor was becoming impatient.

"And the second in command is the Archprimus?"

"Yes, Your Majesty. Normally the High Priest serves until his death, at which point the Archprimus succeeds him."

"Who chooses the new Archprimus?"

"The outgoing Archprimus chooses his own successor. It is thought that such an approach is best suited to promoting harmony, at least for a while."

"What happens if conflict arises between the High Priest and the Archprimus?"

"A documented history of such conflict exists, of course. The outcome has invariably been the death of one, or occasionally both, of the men."

The king did not hide his surprise. "Are you suggesting the priests murder each other?"

Lord Boedwyk chortled appreciatively. "Your Majesty is unusually candid given the delicacy of such matters. One of the benefits of your station, I imagine." He looked suddenly mortified. "I meant no offense, of course!"

He quickly recovered himself. "The records speak of Nehrvina the Awful escorting the departed to Paradise. No mention is made of the circumstances of their passing."

"I have been wondering if anything is expected of the crown at such times," said the king.

"Nothing is expected at all, Your Majesty. Any attempt to involve yourself would be viewed as unwelcome interference."

"So I should simply sit back and let them battle it out?"

The nobleman nodded happily. "Your wisdom does you great credit, Your Majesty." He instantly looked horrified. "Please pardon my wayward tongue! I did not mean to be condescending!"

"Get over yourself, My Lord," growled the king. He softened his words with a genial smile. "It seems it is my turn to ask for pardon. Please remember that being candid is a benefit of my station."

Lord Boedwyk rewarded him with a laugh of delight.

The king returned a genuine smile. "I am grateful to you, My Lord. Please consider yourself released."

The nobleman departed with a bow and a cheery wave, leaving the king shaking his head and chuckling with amusement.

16

———

Kamash stood forlornly on the beach of his little island. It was hard to believe he must leave it again, and so soon after returning.

Gharpin had already climbed aboard the little boat, but he seemed content to allow Kamash whatever time he needed to say his goodbyes. Perhaps the Ahran was beginning to understand. Perhaps he, too, had learned to treasure a haven from the restless confusion of humankind.

Wondering if he might be turning his back on the island for the last time, Kamash released a quiet sigh as he pushed the little craft away from the sand and stepped in. Before long the boat was skipping over the water in a steady breeze.

Noticing the easy familiarity with which Gharpin steered the boat and managed the sail, the old man sat quietly and watched as the island slowly dwindled in size. His former home had long vanished from sight before Kamash finally found the resolve to direct his thoughts to the future. Catching the eye of his shipmate, he silently dipped his head in gratitude for his help. Then he directed his full attention to the boat.

. . .

IF THE ELEMENTS had united in saluting Kamash's return to the island, he could hardly be surprised if they took exception to his departure. In any event, the steady breeze that carried them from the island quickly deteriorated into a gale, and dark clouds gathered ominously on the horizon.

Gharpin did not seem perturbed in the least. Turning the boat westward, he handed the tiller to Kamash and reefed the sail. He then rummaged in the bottom of the boat until he found a storm jib, celebrating his discovery with a whoop of glee. Raising the jib, he took the tiller back from Kamash and settled into place once more with a grunt of satisfaction.

Kamash observed the process with considerable fascination. Having almost always sailed alone, he had been forced to rely entirely on his own skills. Sharing the boat with a competent seaman made for a refreshing change.

He soon discovered that Gharpin had an uncanny instinct for the weather. Using only the storm jib to propel the little craft through the heavy swell, the Ahran initiated a series of unlikely course corrections that saw them skirting around the worst of the storm front.

Simply watching Gharpin at work left Kamash feeling exhausted. Nevertheless he readily accepted the tiller when it became obvious his companion was too weary to continue.

Lying down in the bottom of the boat, the Ahran was soon soundly asleep.

THE STORM HAD BLOWN itself out, but only after blowing them far off course.

Their voyage would now be much longer than planned, but Kamash was not concerned. They had brought aboard an abundant supply of provisions, and one or other of the numerous islands dotted around these waters would provide them with fresh water if they needed it.

Turning the boat about, he headed once more in the direction of Rogand.

Calm seas and favorable winds had driven them forward for several hours when Gharpin called a sharp warning. Looking up, Kamash spotted a sail on the horizon. A ship was approaching from the southeast and moving steadily in their direction. They could never match its speed, but there might still be time for them to avoid it if they decided it was necessary.

A small island lay off the port bow, and after a few hurried words and much waving of hands, they swung about and set a course toward it. Their boat was a tiny speck on a vast ocean, and Kamash was hopeful that the island would shield them from view before the sailors on the ship became aware of them. If the ship was Rogandan or Varasan, their caution was unnecessary. The look on Gharpin's face suggested otherwise.

Sailing to the far side of the island, they reefed the sail and waited. Kamash watched tensely as the minutes passed.

Eventually the ship came into view again. The look on Gharpin's face left no doubt about its origins. After passing the island, it continued on the same course as previously. There was no sign that their little craft had been spotted.

Finally able to relax, Kamash hoisted the sail while Gharpin took the tiller. To the amazement of Kamash, his companion pointed the boat in the direction of the disappearing Ahran vessel instead of resuming their course toward Rogand.

"What are you doing?" he demanded.

Gharpin pointed toward the Ahran ship with a frown. "Where?" he growled.

The old man threw up his hands. "I have no idea where they're going, and I don't want to know!"

If Gharpin understood his meaning, he gave no indication of it. He held his course, a determined look on his face.

Kamash shook his head in exasperation. The language barrier prevented discussion, reasoned or otherwise. What could he do? Wrestling for control of the tiller was not an option he would even consider.

He sighed in resignation. It seemed they would be chasing the Ahran ship.

The ship's masts were already disappearing below the horizon when he looked up. "You do realize we can't keep pace with them."

With no response from Gharpin, he shrugged. What did it matter? The Ahrans might hold to their current course, but without visual contact there was no chance Gharpin could steer in exactly the same direction. In the vastness of the ocean, the smallest deviation would guarantee a wide divergence in the courses of the two vessels. Even if the final destination of the larger vessel was within reach, they would probably never discover it.

Gharpin must have been equally aware of these realities, yet he appeared undismayed. He sat at the tiller, staring grimly ahead, betraying no sign of tiredness.

Kamash decided to leave his companion to it. After sailing around searching for a couple of days they would be forced to give up anyway, and he could see no real harm in another detour. If they ran short of food they would just go hungry for a while.

With the conditions unusually good and his eyes drooping uncontrollably, there would never be a better time to take a nap. Stretching out in the bottom of the boat, he closed his eyes.

THE LITTLE BOAT glided through the water, Kamash at the tiller. When Gharpin had finally succumbed to exhaustion, he raised his eyebrows questioningly before relinquishing his seat. The Ahran had yielded control only after the old man had answered the unspoken question with a firm nod, accompanied by a sigh of resignation. When he awoke, he sat peering forward intently.

Open sea lay before them with no sign of ships. Islands were dotted about throughout these seas, but none of those nearby were large enough to support habitation. Kamash eyed his companion hopefully. Surely even Gharpin must be ready to admit defeat soon.

Then the tiniest hint of a mast appeared, far ahead. Kamash immediately swung the boat about, steering for the nearest island. To the old man's relief, they reached its shelter long before they could have been seen.

The vessel was unmistakably Ahran. Even Kamash felt certain it was the same vessel they had been following.

Gharpin moved to the tiller, waving at Kamash to move aside. The old man complied, rolling his eyes in mute protest. His companion ignored him.

As soon as the ship had disappeared entirely, Gharpin resumed their journey, continuing in the same direction as before. Kamash understood. The Ahran ship had probably stopped somewhere—almost certainly at an island—before heading back the way it had come. If they were fortunate, sailing back along its wake might lead them to the island it had visited.

They had not sailed for long before several islands came into view.

As they drew closer, Kamash spotted a thin plume of smoke rising lazily into the air from one of them. Surprised to find such a small island inhabited, he pointed to it at once. Gharpin immediately changed tack, steering instead for a closer island that was even smaller.

"Will they be able to see us?" asked Kamash, pointing to the island with the smoke.

Gharpin clearly understood the question. He responded with a shrug.

They soon reached the smaller island. Anchoring the boat in the sheltered waters behind a promontory, they quickly removed the sail.

Swimming to the rocks and clambering out of the water, they peered out toward the larger island. It was too far away to draw firm conclusions, but it seemed almost certain that the island was inhabited. Having chosen a not dissimilar setting for his self-imposed exile, Kamash understood why someone might choose to live in such isolation. But he also knew how unusual such behavior was. Who was living there, and why? And, more importantly, why had they received a visit from an Ahran ship?

Such questions were better answered by the Varasans or the

Rogandans. They could send a warship with armed sailors to explore the island. Kamash and Gharpin merely needed to ensure they could provide details of its location.

"We can leave after dark," Kamash suggested.

His companion shook his head. "Dark is good. Good for quiet visit."

Just the suggestion of spying was enough to flood Kamash with alarm again.

"You can't be serious!" he said.

"Serious?" Gharpin seemed to consider. He finally returned a determined nod. "Serious," he said, poking at his own chest.

He swept an arm across the vastness of the ocean before pointing at the island. "Why Ahrans? Why here?" He shook his head. "No good, no good."

Kamash readily understood these concerns, but he had no desire to go anywhere near the island, in the dark or not. He could well believe that Ahran captains would be expected to gather intelligence for the empire while traveling abroad, but he saw no reason to suppose they were trained as spies. Even if Gharpin had received such coaching, he himself was certainly not equipped to do it.

The sun set without any resolution to Kamash's concerns. Frustrated at his inability to sustain the simplest of conversations with Gharpin, he eyed his companion uneasily. The two men had been sharing a simple meal using supplies from their boat, and they were almost finished. What was Gharpin planning to do next? Did he expect Kamash to help him?

It occurred to him to wonder what his companion might do if he found himself among his countrymen once more. Would he grasp the opportunity to put the past behind him and make common cause with the Ahrans, in spite of everything that had happened?

He quickly saw he had no reason for doubt. Even in the failing light, a glance at the former captain showed his face rigid with determination.

Gharpin was a man on a mission. He would never rest until it was accomplished.

THE BOAT GLIDED SILENTLY FORWARD, Gharpin sitting keen-eyed at the tiller. In the moonlight, the sail would surely be visible from the island. Thankfully the moon had not yet risen.

The island was little more than a smudge against the brightly twinkling stars, but it stood out enough to show them where they needed to go. Landing on a beach was out of the question—they would need to find a suitable place to anchor nearby.

The island loomed larger, and Kamash's heart began to pound. As Gharpin steered them in close to the beach they saw fires flickering brightly among the trees. Figures were briefly outlined as they moved in front of them. It wasn't possible to guess anything about the identity of the people or why they were there.

Turning the boat about, Gharpin swung into a rocky bay not far from the beach. Low hills overlooked the sea, with a gully emptying into the little bay. For anyone willing to grope over rocks in the dark, the gully might provide a path onto the island.

The thought held no appeal for Kamash. Drawing close to his companion, he hissed, "This is a bad idea!"

If Gharpin understood the warning, he ignored it. "I go," he said softly. "Sun comes, you go." His hand flicked away from the island, out to sea.

He didn't pause for a reply. Slipping over the side, he struck out for the shore.

Kamash saw him reach the rocks. He pulled himself out of the water and stood dripping for a while. Then, slowly and carefully, he climbed toward the gully. A moment later he was lost in the darkness.

The old man sat alone in the boat, tense and unhappy. How long would his companion be gone? Gharpin would be careful, wouldn't he? Surely he would do nothing worse than sneak around for a while. When he discovered nothing sinister, he'd return. He should be back well before dawn.

The night had scarcely begun, though, and he didn't find the waiting easy. Anxious and jumpy, he flinched at the slightest sound.

Each time, concluding there was no reason for concern, he would peer into the darkness, hoping for his friend's return.

The hours wore by without any sign of Gharpin. Perhaps he had been forced to hide. It was also possible that he had been caught. What if he had injured himself climbing in the darkness? Kamash steadfastly pushed the more morbid possibilities from his mind.

At some point he realized that he was at risk as well. If Gharpin was spotted, it would be obvious that a boat had reached the island. Enemies might be searching for him at that very moment.

Was there another boat on the island? They might be in trouble if there was.

Clammy palms and a pounding heart told him he was becoming overwrought. Closing his eyes, he took in a deep breath and tried to calm himself.

KAMASH COULD DENY it no longer. The sky was showing clear signs of brightening.

What should he do? If he left now, Gharpin might arrive to find himself stranded. If he waited much longer, he might be seen from the island as he was leaving.

Eventually he decided to take Gharpin's words seriously. "Sun comes, you go." He would return as soon as it was dark. If Gharpin had been forced to hide for some reason, he would reappear under the cover of darkness.

Rowing clear of the rocks, he hoisted the sail and made for the nearby smaller island.

A sleepless night lay behind him, with the prospect of another to come. As soon as the boat was safely hidden, he threw out the anchor and lay down to rest.

The afternoon was wearing away by the time he woke. He helped himself to food and drink and waited restlessly for the sun to set again.

Gharpin might find his way back to the boat that night, but

Kamash was no longer hopeful about it. He couldn't continue to avoid the question that had been nagging at him. What should he do?

He could take the risk of doing a search of his own. Or he could resume the journey to Rog, and lead a rescue team back to the island. The sun set without him reaching a decision.

Sailing back to the island, he anchored the boat and sat wrestling with his thoughts.

A full hour passed before he decided. He could never live with himself if he made no attempt to discover the fate of the Ahran. Gharpin might be lying injured nearby. Sailing away might be condemning him to a slow and painful death.

With a sigh of resignation he lowered himself into the sea, swam to the rocks, and struggled ashore. Having committed himself, he took a deep breath and followed Gharpin into the gully.

17

Kamash reached the top of the gully without seeing Gharpin or anyone else. All activity seemed to be centered around the beach. Moving as noiselessly as he could, he crept forward in that direction.

He continued until he reached the edge of a large clearing. People were moving about, their shapes revealed in the dim light from a couple of large fires. He could also make out the outlines of a number of huts within the clearing.

None of the people seemed especially alert. That gave him hope. If Gharpin had been found, or even seen, surely the coastline would be swarming with people searching for his boat.

With no way to resolve the mystery of the Ahran's disappearance, he took the only option available to him. Positioning himself well out of the range of any firelight, he settled down to watch and wait.

A couple of hours had passed with nothing to show for it, when he felt a hand settle firmly on his shoulder. Leaping to his feet and spinning around in alarm, he barely managed to restrain himself from crying out.

Kamash found himself confronted with the familiar visage of

Gharpin. Still trying to calm his racing heart, he gaped in wide-eyed amazement. Finally he threw up his hands in exasperation.

Apparently surprised at the reaction he had provoked, the Ahran responded with a dispassionate shrug. Pointing across the clearing at two small buildings, he began speaking animatedly in a low voice.

Kamash could not understand a word of it. "Stop! I don't understand you," he said. He was forced to repeat it with increasing intensity before Gharpin's flow of words eventually came to an end.

His companion pointed into the clearing, then touched his ears.

"You heard them talking. And they speak your language."

Pointing once more at the buildings, Gharpin held up his arms, tightly connecting them immediately below his wrists.

"Bound at the wrists," murmured Kamash. "Prisoners!"

Gharpin held up three fingers.

"Three people," said Kamash.

The Ahran nodded. He held both hands wide, palms facing. Then he lifted them high, bringing them down slowly on either side of his head.

A couple of minutes went by before the old man made sense of the action. "A crown!" he said. "One of the three people is royal."

Gharpin cupped a hand on each side of his chest and looked at his companion expectantly.

Kamash frowned. "A woman?"

The Ahran grinned in triumph. Holding up one finger, he repeated first the crown movement and then the woman movement. He then held up two fingers, repeating the crown movement before cupping a hand between his legs.

The old man frowned. "A woman and a man, both of them royal?"

He stared at Gharpin in astonishment. "King Rupert and Princess Teylee? You mean they're here?"

Ignoring the question, Gharpin held up three fingers. Then he repeated the movements indicating a crown and a woman.

"A third captive? Also royal?" Kamash shook his head in confusion.

It didn't make sense. For one glorious moment he felt certain they'd found the abducted king and princess. But a third royal? That couldn't be right. He must have misunderstood what Gharpin was trying to communicate.

A rough voice called out words Kamash did not understand.

Gharpin froze. Grabbing Kamash's arm, he pulled him away from the clearing.

A second voice was shouting now. The two men ran through the trees, heading for the boat.

Throwing a glance over his shoulder, Kamash saw torches bobbing in their direction. Too many torches. He raced after Gharpin, desperate to keep up.

As the sounds of the sea grew louder, he tripped on a root. Falling headlong, his head hit the ground hard. He lay stunned, blinded by pain and unable to orient himself.

An arm reached down. He was dragged to his feet. Head throbbing, the old man took a stumbling step, then another. Gharpin urged him to greater efforts.

They were in the gully now. Angry shouts rang in his ears. Their pursuers were gaining on them.

Dragging him across the rocks, Gharpin propelled him into the water. He gasped a breath as he went under. Buoyed up by Gharpin, he splashed out feebly for the boat.

Then he was alone. Gharpin reached the boat in a few hurried strokes and hauled himself aboard. Freeing the anchor with a mighty tug, he hurriedly released the sail. An oar appeared in front of Kamash, and he clutched hold of it.

Loud splashes sounded behind them. Time was running out.

Kamash reached the boat. Abandoning his attempts to clamber aboard, he hung on grimly as the boat began to drift away from the rocks.

They were moving too slowly. With swimmers almost upon them, Gharpin reached again for the oar. Kamash felt a hand grab at him, trying to pull him away from the boat. Then abruptly the hand went slack as Gharpin landed a heavy blow on the man's head.

A breeze began to fill the sail, and they picked up speed. Gharpin sat at the tiller, leaving the old man to hang on as best he could. The effort and the pain were too much. As his hold on the boat began to slip, the Ahran appeared and hauled him aboard.

Kamash began to mumble. "Do...they have...a boat?"

Then everything went black.

His eyes opened on thin clouds skidding across a blue sky. The boat lurched suddenly, setting his head pounding. He closed his eyes, waiting for the aching to ease.

After a while he rolled onto one side. Propping himself up on one arm, he peered toward the stern. Gharpin sat calmly at the tiller. Seeing the old man awake, he gave him a wink.

The effort was too much for Kamash. Lying back again, he closed his eyes and drifted off to the slap of the boat plowing through the waves.

When he woke again the sky was ablaze with stars. The pounding in his head had subsided at last.

Sitting up cautiously, he looked around. The boat was racing through a moderate swell, driven by a stiff breeze. They appeared to be sailing almost due east.

Clearly Gharpin had not left the tiller. Moving to his side, Kamash found him barely able to function. Gently wresting the tiller from the Ahran's hands, he waved him forward. Gharpin was asleep almost before he collapsed into the bottom of the boat.

There was so much to ponder. They had been fortunate indeed to escape from the island. He wished he could speak with Gharpin. Had they been pursued?

He wondered again about the prisoners. Who were they?

The priority now was to pass on what they had discovered.

It would be too late of course. With outsiders discovering the island, the Ahrans would move the prisoners as soon as another ship arrived. By the time they returned with Varasan or Rogandan warships, there would probably be no one there.

He wondered if it might have been possible to rescue the prisoners, but he quickly discarded the idea. With so many guards about, any attempt to spirit away three prisoners would have been a recipe for disaster.

In the end they had done well to escape themselves.

He felt sure Gharpin had an important story to tell. Getting him safely to Rog would be enough of an achievement.

RUPERT AND TASHA watched warily as the latest Ahran ship appeared around the end of the island and anchored offshore. Longboats were soon making their way to the little beach.

Rupert tried not to imagine what the Ahrans might do next. Anticipating a fresh round of violations would not help anyone.

A group of guards were soon heading their way. To his surprise they had another captive in tow.

Tasha aimed a puzzled glance in his direction. He returned a shrug.

The Ahran leader approached, dragging the captive in front of Rupert. "I'm sure you weren't expecting a visit from your sister," he gloated.

Rupert stared in alarm at the captive. Her head was bowed, but even without a clear glimpse at her face he knew it was not Essanda. Opening his mouth to contradict the leader, he caught a momentary glimpse of the woman's eyes. His mouth snapped shut, his mocking smile melting away even before it appeared on his lips.

"Essanda! How do you come to be here?" he asked, loading as much dismay into his voice as he could muster.

Once more her head hung low, and she offered no reply.

The horror on Tasha's face almost undid him. With an effort he restrained the impulse to blurt out the truth.

The leader remained oblivious. "There's work to be done," he barked, waving his guards back toward the beach. All of them followed him except two. It wasn't hard to guess why they had been left behind.

"You're the last person I expected to see here," he told the newcomer, speaking loudly in Arvenian. "I have no words for my dismay when I saw you."

The sentiment was not entirely feigned. It must have been a terrible misfortune for the woman to find herself in these circumstances. And he was beginning to wonder if impersonating Essanda might have been a deliberate ploy to save her.

"Thank you!" she said, speaking quietly but with great intensity. Then, more loudly. "I never expected to see you either, Rupert. Not in these circumstances." She covered her face with her hands. "All I can think about is Steffan. He will be so distraught!"

Tasha was beginning to look confused, and Rupert drew both of them into an embrace.

"Thank you for not exposing my pretense!" the woman whispered again.

"You mean this is not your sister?" hissed Tasha.

"We need to talk," murmured Rupert. "Let's see if we can shake off these guards."

He led them swiftly toward the hut he was now sharing with Tasha. The guards trailed behind at a distance.

"We have a couple of minutes at best," said Rupert.

"They think they kidnapped Queen Essanda," the woman told them hurriedly. "They would have succeeded, too, if I hadn't taken her place."

Tasha stared at her in alarm. "They'll kill you at once if they find out the truth!"

The woman nodded. "I'd be dead already if you hadn't played along."

The guards were drawing closer.

Rupert managed one last question. "So who are you?"

"You can call me Essanda," she replied with a wink.

SHULKAHR, the Ahran responsible for the guards and the captives on the island, watched in irritation as the final boatload was ferried across from the supply ship. The vessel had arrived as expected. The surprise package among its cargo was another matter entirely.

It made no difference to him how many prisoners were delivered to the island. Not if he had warning. On this occasion he'd received none. He hated surprises.

Further, the Arvenian queen had been delivered in very poor condition—exactly what he might have expected of a clumsy fool like Kahrlin. Shulkahr cared nothing for her welfare, but powerful people, like Bolnyk, who had appointed him, or even the Grand Vizier himself, almost certainly had plans for her. He would be held accountable whenever it was his turn to hand over.

TWENTY-FOUR HOURS HAD PASSED before he was able to properly establish a new routine. At last he could relax.

"Intruders! Spying on us!"

Startled, he looked up to see one of his men pointing off into the trees.

"Get after them!" he shouted.

Leaping into action, he hastily rounded up a half dozen men. After passing around lighted torches, he sent them after the intruders. Then he found several others and instructed them to guard the prisoners with extra vigilance.

Restless and impatient, he waited for the searchers' return.

Eventually he spotted one of the pursuers returning. Several others straggled behind him.

The look on the men's faces was not promising.

"Well?" Shulkahr demanded.

"There were two men. It's impossible to know how long they'd been observing us."

"Where are they now?" he growled.

"We chased them. But they had too much of a head start. They got away. They had a small boat anchored nearby."

Other stragglers joined the conversation as they arrived.

"It wasn't a longboat, so they didn't come from a ship."

"They must have been fishermen."

"Yeah. A bit too inquisitive for their own good."

"They couldn't be Rogandan. Rogand is too far away."

"Nah. Varasans or Castelans for sure."

"That's enough!" Shulkahr shouted. "I'm tired of your wild guesses!"

He glared at them. "There's no way to find out how much they heard—not now you've let them escape!"

"Even if they overheard us talking, they wouldn't have understood a word. None of the people in this region understand Ahran."

"It isn't just how much they heard, you idiot!" he retorted. "It's how much they saw!"

He shook his head in annoyance. "How did they find the island? It's nowhere near any trading routes. It has to be one of the smallest pimples of rock in this part of the ocean."

"Perhaps they were blown off course in the recent storm," someone suggested.

"It makes no difference!" he snarled. "You all know what this means. We'll have to abandon the settlement. We have no choice now it's been compromised. You've got a lot of work ahead of you."

A howl of protest greeted his words.

"Silence, you fools!" he roared. "You've got no one to blame but yourselves!"

He paused until he had calmed down enough to think. "The next supply ship is due in another week. When it leaves we'll leave with it. All of us, including the three prisoners."

None of them said a word.

Gazing moodily out to sea, Shulkahr faced his real dilemma. Leaving the island wasn't the worst difficulty confronting him. Where would he take the prisoners? Without any way of consulting with Bolnyk, he'd be forced to make it up as he went along.

He faced his men grimly. This was their fault, and he wasn't going to let them off lightly.

"In the meantime you will remove every trace of our presence."

They instantly found their voices again. "That's impossible!"

"What's impossible is two intruders escaping from a crowd of armed guards! Somehow you let it happen."

He scowled at them. "I've been far too easy on you. As of now, someone will be positioned at the highest point of the island throughout daylight hours. We won't be caught by surprise again. And the coastline will be patrolled constantly, day and night. The entire length of it!"

Shulkahr ignored the groans. They'd let the intruders escape, but they wouldn't be the ones who wore the consequences.

When Bolnyk had first appointed him in Dessue's place, Shulkahr couldn't believe his luck. It was a high profile assignment, one that was certain to attract the attention of the chief minister. How had everything managed to unravel so spectacularly?

A huge amount of effort had gone into establishing and maintaining this prison hideaway. Now he had to tear it all down.

He refused to let himself dwell on what would happen when the Grand Vizier found out.

18

"Ship ahead!"

Perched high in the rigging of the Rogandan warship, the lookout was pointing west.

"How many masts?" bellowed the captain.

"Three, Cap'n!"

"Is it Ahran?"

The reply drifted faintly down. "Can't tell! We need to get closer."

Captain Pultek turned to the helmsman. Jerking his head toward the lookout, he ordered, "Follow his directions."

"Set more sail!" he bellowed, looking on with satisfaction as sailors hurried to scramble aloft.

Glancing behind, he saw the two accompanying vessels altering course as well. Keeping up would be their problem. He wouldn't be waiting for them.

Lord Kulferan himself had tasked Pultek with finding and following Ahran ships. The commander seemed to think the best hope of locating Princess Teylee and the Castelan king was to tail the Ahrans.

It would be easier if the Ahran ships weren't so fast. Most Rogandan vessels, including his own, were two masters. Almost every

Ahran ship he'd spotted in recent times had three masts. The empire seemed intent on sending its best ships to Rogand. That didn't bode well.

He'd asked Lord Kulferan directly if they were at war with the empire. The commander had replied that King Krasmir was not likely to declare war while any hope remained of recovering his daughter. When Pultek left the meeting, he had been authorized to use force only in self defense or if it meant the princess and her betrothed could be safely rescued.

He made his way to the wheel.

"Think we'll catch 'em?" asked the helmsman.

The captain frowned into the distance. "Not if they spot us."

He shouted up at the lookout. "If we're getting too close I want to know!"

"Aye, Cap'n!"

As the pursuit dragged on, the three ships in his squadron became strung out. The nearest one was still within reach, but it was slowly slipping behind. The mast was all that could be seen of the other.

Standing beside the helmsman, Pultek scowled back at the other vessels. "What are those idiots about?"

The helmsman grinned, exposing yellowing teeth with dark gaps between them. "Their problem is they don't 'ave you as cap'n."

A call from aloft dragged their attention back to the Ahran ship.

"They're turning!" The lookout was pointing to the northwest.

The helmsman swung the wheel, and the ship slowly came around.

Only a few minutes passed before the lookout called again. "We're gaining on 'em."

The captain reacted immediately. "Reef some sail!"

Sailors sprang into action.

"Make sure we keep our distance!" he called to the lookout.

The man waved an acknowledgment.

Tiny splotches began to appear on the horizon. Islands lay ahead.

"They're slowing down!" called the lookout. Moments later he shouted, "I can see the island they're heading for." Then, "I think they've seen us!"

Pultek yelled up to the sailors still aloft. "Prepare to reef the sails!"

He swung around to face the bosun. "Break out the weapons!" he ordered.

The bosun immediately sent men below.

The Ahran vessel had anchored off a small beach. They were still several minutes away from the island, but they were beginning to close on it. The captain saw three longboats in the water. One of them was already pulling in to the beach. Quickly loaded with passengers, it was ready to return before the other boats had even arrived.

A line of people stood ready to board the moment the other two boats drew in to the sand.

Pultek's gaze flicked back to the Ahran ship. Armed men lined its side. He snorted. His men could handle them.

His own ship began to slow as they drew closer. Archers stood expectantly on his deck, bows at the ready. "Hold your fire, men!" he called. "Wait for my orders."

The Ahran ship was already beginning to move, its anchors barely clear of the water. His helmsman spun the wheel, and they slowly drew alongside it.

As they were passing the stern of the other vessel, he caught a brief glimpse of the activity on its landward side. All three longboats had reached the ship and disgorged their passengers. People were scrambling up rope nets, desperate to reach the deck. The first boat was being frantically hauled aboard. The other two longboats were already drifting away from the ship, abandoned by the Ahran sailors in their haste.

Any opportunity to board the other vessel was fast disappearing. Although his ship was moving faster, he was slowing while they were gaining speed. If he could force the Ahrans toward the island while he still had forward momentum, it might be possible to board their ship.

"Cut them off!" he ordered the helmsman.

Slowly, painfully slowly, the ship began to turn.

The island lay on one side, with Pultek's vessel on the other. And the gap was closing. Nevertheless, the Ahrans were picking up speed. They might still slip through.

"Hoist more sail!" he shouted.

As his sailors responded, a stream of arrows flew from the other ship. Pultek saw at a glance that the Ahrans were targeting his men in the rigging.

"Return fire!" he yelled.

Chaos soon reigned on the decks of both vessels. Picked out by Ahran shafts, several Rogandan sailors aloft were sent crashing to the deck. His own archers struck the Ahran helmsman, causing momentary confusion as the other captain hurried to replace him.

The volley from their opponents proved only too effective. Hindered in their attempts to set more sail, the Rogandans had failed to pick up speed quickly enough. They watched helplessly as the Ahran vessel slipped neatly through the gap, its stern missing their bowsprit by a matter of yards.

People were still clinging to rope nets on the other side of the Ahran vessel. It occurred to him to wonder if Princess Teylee and King Rupert might be among them. With stray arrows flying everywhere, the risk of hitting them was too great.

"Hold your fire!" the captain bellowed.

His men managed to hoist the sails, but too late to make a difference.

Their reduced speed had allowed both of the other ships in his squadron to draw closer.

Calling for the signalman, he pointed toward the nearest of the two. "Signal them to join the pursuit," he ordered.

Then he pointed toward the other ship. "Signal them to search the island."

As the signalman set to work, the captain returned his attention to the chase.

The Ahran ship was proving to be the faster vessel. He could only glare after it in impotent fury as it slowly diminished in size.

A GUARD CAME RUNNING into the Ahran encampment, calling excitedly. Immediately the Ahran leader began shouting instructions. Guards raced around frantically, gathering items and dumping them on the beach.

Rupert saw at a glance that the so-called Essanda had been listening intently to the shouting. Once more he envied the agent's fluency in the Ahran language.

"A ship has been sighted," she said. "It's heading for the island. The guard thinks it's Ahran."

"Sounds like we'll be leaving soon," said Rupert.

She held up a hand for silence. "There's more! Another ship is trailing it. And it isn't Ahran."

Tasha's eyes had gone wide. "They're searching for us!"

Guards were hurrying in their direction. "Try to stay together!" hissed Rupert.

The guards were in no mood to be patient. "To the beach! Move!"

Shoved forward roughly, Rupert hardly noticed that he was being manhandled with unnecessary force. One question alone occupied his thoughts. Was it possible they would be rescued at last?

THE SUPPLY SHIP was arriving two days early, but a foreign vessel was not far behind it. It might barely be possible to evacuate in time. They would need to be ready to leave the moment the ship arrived.

At least they had some warning. Placing a guard at the highest point of the island was proving to be a canny move.

Even before his lookout finished shouting the news, Shulkahr realized he'd been thrown a lifeline. Until that moment, the island was being evacuated solely due to a major security lapse, one for which he was responsible. The appearance of a foreign vessel in hot pursuit of the supply ship changed everything. Evacuation had now become essential.

It would go a long way toward rehabilitating him in the eyes of Bolnyk and his master if he oversaw a successful extraction. Incredibly, he found himself thoroughly prepared for just that.

It was possible that the pursuit came as a direct result of the earlier incursion by two unidentified intruders, but no one would ever know for certain.

Whatever the reason for this latest exposure, the settlement was a secret no longer. Attempting to remove all evidence of their presence was now a waste of time. He grunted in satisfaction. It was one less thing to think about.

The prisoners arrived, hustled along by a group of guards. Nothing mattered to Shulkahr now except extracting the prisoners.

They stood with heads bowed, saying nothing. They seemed more than usually submissive, but he was not deceived. The subtle signs were there. They were dreaming of escape, of rescue.

Let them dream. "I'm not letting you out of my sight," he growled. Hope was a fickle mistress.

The supply ship glided around the island, anchors thrown overboard before it had properly slowed. The captain was in a hurry.

The first longboat was quickly in the water. Shulkahr noted with satisfaction that it was empty apart from rowers.

Moving forward onto the beach with the prisoners, he saw a brawl breaking out behind him. The idiots couldn't be left unsupervised for a minute. Leaving the prisoners with other guards, he hurried back.

"What are you fools arguing about?" he roared.

They stared at him sullenly. No one answered.

There was no time to get to the bottom of it. "Get onto the beach! Now! The next person I see fighting will stay here."

They moved off without a word.

Returning to the beach, he was annoyed to see the first longboat already full and ready to return to the ship. It didn't matter though. Two more longboats had been lowered, and they were already on their way.

Then the foreign ship appeared around the edge of the island. It had arrived more quickly than he could possibly have imagined.

Getting the prisoners to the ship had now become critical. As the first of the boats arrived, men pressed forward insistently, trying to force their way into it.

"Move aside," he shouted.

Either they didn't hear or they ignored him. Physically dragging two guards from the boat, he drew his sword. "The prisoners are getting into the boat. I'm getting in with them." He waved his sword. "Anyone who tries to board without my permission will get a taste of this."

As he clambered aboard, the other longboat arrived. The remaining guards raced for it, pushing and shoving in their eagerness to secure a place.

"Go!" he shouted. The rowers bent their backs, and the boat pulled away from the beach.

The foreign ship was nearing the island. He could see men with bows stretched out along its deck. Another vessel had appeared behind it too. The situation was becoming critical.

The Ahran ship lay immediately ahead. They were barely going to reach it in time.

Nets had been thrown over the side of the vessel, and men were clinging to them, waiting for those above them to climb onto the deck.

They reached the ship at last.

"Start climbing!" Shulkahr ordered the prisoners. When they didn't move, he drew a knife and held it to the throat of the princess. "Unless you want me to carve her pretty neck, you'll do as I say."

That got them moving. All of them grabbed the net, with him behind them. But the men above were not moving. When a succession of stray arrows whizzed overhead he realized why. The Ahran ship was under attack, and the decks were exposed. It was apparently safer on the net.

The ship was moving now. The two longboats drifted away, empty.

Shulkahr was becoming impatient. "Get moving!" he yelled to the people higher on the net. He was wasting his breath. Climbing upward as far as he could, he began haranguing the men above him, trying to stir them to action.

The ship was moving faster, and he saw that their pursuers had fallen behind. The flow of arrows appeared to have stopped as well. They were surely going to escape.

A second ship was swinging in behind them too, but it was going no faster than the first vessel.

Then he caught sight of a third ship, clearly heading for the island. They could search all they liked. They would find little of interest there.

He shook his head, astonished at how close it had been. They had barely made it out in time.

Glancing up he saw movement at last on the net above. It was time to get the prisoners onto the deck.

Looking down, he was baffled to find no sign of them. He swung his head around and then peered upward. They were nowhere to be found.

His heart skipped a beat. Where could they possibly have gone? He tried to remember the last time he had seen them. It was immediately before he climbed up to get people moving again.

He hadn't been gone for long. Yet in that short period of time they had somehow disappeared.

They could only have jumped into the sea. He peered back along the ship's wake, but he saw no sign of heads bobbing in the water. If they had been spotted from the pursuing ship, some attempt would have been made to pick them up. But the other ship had not turned aside or lowered a boat.

That meant they must have jumped while the other ship was still alongside. They would have been noticed otherwise.

He looked back at the island, disappearing in their wake. The prisoners must have been a lot closer to it when they jumped in, but they would still be hard pressed to swim to it, even with the tides on their side. If they were lucky enough to reach it, and if they got there before the foreign ship had left, they would soon be on their way back to their kingdoms.

He shook his head in denial.

He thought about the guards beside them on the ropes. If the prisoners leaped into the water from the net, they must have seen it.

He noticed for the first time that he was alone on the lower section of the net. All the guards had climbed above him. The last of them was about to disappear over the top onto the deck.

He shouted at the top of his voice, venting his frustration. He was wasting his breath. No one on deck would even hear him.

That was the moment when he realized all was lost. Of course the guards had seen the prisoners jumping from the ship. They couldn't possibly have failed to notice it. None of them would ever admit it though.

He understood why none of the guards had taken the risk of following them into the water. Why should they? They weren't ultimately responsible for the prisoners.

The blame would fall squarely on Shulkahr.

Returning without the captives did not bear thinking about. Taking a deep breath he leaped away from the net. He hit the water hard, disappearing briefly below the waves. When he surfaced, he looked up to find his ship already distant. If anyone had spotted him jumping, there was no indication of it.

Even before the first of the pursuing ships sailed past, his sword had begun to weigh him down. Treading water determinedly, he released the belt and let the weapon sink into the depths.

Left with only a knife in his belt, for a moment he wondered if he might live to regret being almost defenseless. He quickly dismissed the thought. It would be enough of a challenge to make it to the island without the extra burden. With it, his chances would be greatly diminished.

He squinted toward the island. It seemed so far away. But it was too late for regret.

Taking a deep breath, he started to swim.

19

———————

Moody and unsettled, Bisri Ahuzza stood at the stern of the ship staring into the darkness. More than three hours had passed since the sun disappeared. Almost all of the sailors had gone below decks, away from the cold breeze that tirelessly brushed the hair from his face.

His ship lay at anchor not far from a secluded shoreline dimly visible in the moonlight. Rog was somewhere to the northwest, distant enough for Ahuzza to feel confident of their privacy.

He had no idea where the other Ahran ships were located. They had split up to avoid detection, and he was not sorry about it. The greater the distance between him and Rheibas, the better he liked it.

Even with Rheibas out of sight, the presence of Ronizah provided a constant reminder that the chief minister's eyes and ears were everywhere. The interpreter was beginning to weigh him down, like a millstone around his neck.

In appointing Ahuzza as envoy, had the emperor fully realized the potential for friction with the chief minister? Unforgiving and ruthless with his enemies, Rheibas was not a man any rational person wanted to cross.

A dull splash sounded below him. He stared down vacantly, half expecting to catch a glimpse of silver as a fish leaped from the water. With nothing visible in the darkness, he redirected his gaze to the shoreline.

Little as he desired company, he was beginning to wonder if he should go below decks when he was startled by a soft voice from below.

"Bisri Ahuzza?"

He stared down in astonishment. A dark figure dangled from a rope apparently attached to the stern of the ship.

"Who is it?" he demanded, speaking in a whisper.

"I was sent by King Krasmir. Is it safe to talk?"

Whoever it was spoke fluent Ahran.

"How do I know King Krasmir sent you?" For all he knew, it was one of Rheibas's men sent to trap him.

"The note you received after meeting with King Krasmir. I can tell you its contents."

His eyes went wide. He had read the note eagerly the moment he was alone. It made no sense. Perhaps it was coded. If so, he had no way to unlock it. At the first opportunity, he tore it into little pieces and tossed it into the sea. Then he had promptly forgotten about it.

"What did it say?" Ahuzza demanded breathlessly.

"Sightless fish dwell in deep waters," came the response.

So it was a pass phrase. The message had been intentionally cryptic.

"Why are you here?" he asked.

"You need to come with me, Bisri," the agent said insistently. "We believe your Grand Vizier wishes to prevent you from engaging directly with us. We think it likely that an attempt will be made on your life."

Disconcerting as the warning was, Ahuzza was not at all inclined to take it seriously. However unhappy Rheibas might be, surely he wasn't about to murder him. He had done nothing to warrant such an extreme reaction.

The agent spoke into the silence. "King Krasmir wanted to warn you, and to protect you in any way he can."

"How does he propose to protect me?" Ahuzza made no attempt to keep the skepticism from his voice.

"A Rogandan ship will return you to Kat Ahket whenever you are ready. In the meantime, King Krasmir wants to meet with you. His desire is to be frank and clear in what he communicates to the emperor."

So the Rogandan king expected him to simply slide down a rope and leave with this man? He stared at the dark figure, shivering in his wet garments. Did these people seriously think he would throw himself into their hands? What grounds did he have for trusting King Krasmir? And who was this agent anyway? How had he managed to elude the guards?

He had no doubt what his countrymen would conclude if they learned he had gone over to the Rogandans. They would certainly label him a traitor.

He couldn't possibly take the offer seriously. Nevertheless, it was alarming how tempting it felt.

He shook his head stubbornly. "Please thank the king for his offer. But I could never retain the trust and respect of my countrymen if I slipped away in secret and threw my lot in with a foreign ruler."

The agent didn't seem surprised. "Are you certain?"

"I am."

"Then I wish you all the best, Bisri," he murmured.

He left as silently as he had come.

Hurrying away from the stern Bisri Ahuzza hid himself in his cabin. He hoped desperately that the conversation had not been witnessed by anyone.

As he lay in his hammock trying to sleep, he pondered the agent's warning. Surely his life could not truly be in danger. The Rogandans were undoubtedly exaggerating, and why wouldn't they? They had an agenda of their own.

He sternly reminded himself that the emperor had given him an important task. He was determined to see it through.

BOLNYK BOWED as he entered the cabin on board the chief minister's ship the following day. "I have just received news, Your Eminence. A Rogandan agent has met with Bisri Ahuzza."

Rheibas raised his eyebrows. "Where and when?"

"The agent went to the bisri's ship late last night."

"What did they discuss?" asked Rheibas.

"Our agents were not able to overhear the conversation."

"Have you questioned Ronizah, Ahuzza's interpreter?"

"He was not involved, Your Eminence."

The chief minister scowled. "I warned Ahuzza. I told him to be careful."

Bolnyk found it hard to understand why someone as well informed as the bisri should need such a warning. If he was fool enough to ignore it, he deserved whatever he got.

"Unfortunate accidents can happen so easily at sea. Arrange one for the bisri."

Bolnyk bowed once more and departed.

As he emerged onto the deck he spotted the bosun. "I will need a longboat. Have it ready two hours before dawn. I will provide the crew."

The bosun hurried away to arrange it.

Bolnyk did not wait around for confirmation. He had work to do.

THE FOLLOWING night Bisri Ahuzza found himself standing at the stern once more. He didn't know for certain why he was there. Was some part of him hoping the agent would appear again and renew the offer to spirit him away?

"Bisri, what are you doing out here in this cold air?"

Taken completely by surprise, Ahuzza spun around to find Ronizah before him. After a quick bow, the interpreter stood staring at him quizzically.

"Why are you here if it's so cold, Ronizah?" asked Ahuzza testily.

"I have been asked to pass on a message. The chief minister

wishes to meet with you. He is planning to send a boat in the morning."

The bisri contented himself with a tight nod of acknowledgment.

After a deep bow, the interpreter departed, soon disappearing below decks.

Ahuzza was left in turmoil. A seemingly endless succession of questions flooded through his mind. What was the chief minister planning? Why had the message been delivered to Ronizah instead of to him directly? Could a sinister purpose lie behind the meeting? It was especially unnerving coming so soon after the agent's warning.

Restless and uneasy, he stood shivering, trying to convince himself it was due to the cold.

Eventually he made his way below decks. The irregular rocking of his hammock did nothing to soothe his jangled nerves. Desperate for the release of sleep, he closed his eyes. Yet the oblivion he craved refused to come. Long hours dragged by before he finally succumbed.

AHUZZA WOKE to a pounding on his cabin door. He groaned, opening his eyes reluctantly.

The muffled voice of his interpreter called, "Bisri! Are you awake?" How had he failed to notice the whining tone of the man's voice?

Stumbling out of his hammock, he called back, "What is it, Ronizah?"

"The chief minister's longboat has arrived. His senior agent is waiting for you."

His senior agent? Rheibas had sent Bolnyk to collect him? The name banished every trace of sleepiness. He was fully alert.

Of all people, why did it have to be Bolnyk? Dismissive though he had been of Lord Torbury's allegations, Ahuzza was well aware of the man's reputation.

As he opened the door, he reminded himself sternly that the emperor himself had appointed him to his mission. He would not shrink from carrying it out. And what reason did he have to worry anyway? He'd done nothing to oppose Rheibas.

He would say as much to the chief minister's face if it proved necessary. Everyone knew the man had an uncanny knack for detecting falsehood. It would be obvious to him that Ahuzza was telling the truth.

Nevertheless, it seemed wise to take a couple of guards with him. It might seem little more than symbolic, but it would be making a statement. Passing a group of them as he moved toward the hatch, he selected two of their number and ordered them to accompany him. They immediately swung in behind him.

As he and his guards followed Ronizah onto the deck, he caught sight of Bolnyk at the side of the ship. Walking boldly to the agent, he glanced over the side. A longboat waited below. Rowers occupied all of the available seats apart from one at the stern.

He frowned at Bolnyk. "There isn't room for me and my guards."

"There is room for you in the prow, Bisri," Bolnyk replied coldly. "My orders referred to you alone. You will not require guards."

Ahuzza bristled. The agent showed none of the deference due a bisri, much less the handpicked envoy of the emperor. He glared disdainfully at the agent. "Either my guards travel with me, or I arrange my own transport to the chief minister's ship."

It must have been apparent to Bolnyk that Ahuzza had no intention of yielding. "There's space for them," he growled, waving the two guards irritably down to the boat. Ahuzza climbed down after them.

Ahuzza sat glowering in the prow as the longboat pulled away from his ship. His two guards crouched awkwardly in the middle of the boat, trying to keep out of the way of the rowers. Seated comfortably at the stern, Bolnyk ignored them all.

The rowers faced away from Ahuzza, but he felt certain he recognized one of the men immediately in front of him. The missing chunk of his left ear made him unmistakable. The bisri felt sure he had once seen the man in the company of Bolnyk.

Was it possible that these men were not sailors at all? Had Bolnyk chosen a crew from among his own henchmen? He began to wonder if he should have insisted on making his own way to Rheibas's ship.

He reminded himself once more of his status and his mission, but it didn't prevent a cold sweat from prickling his skin.

Long minutes passed, and the boat moved around a point into a narrow bay enclosed by rocky promontories on both sides. Waves splashed onto a lonely beach. The shoreline and the hills beyond it were deserted.

Bolnyk held up a hand, and the rowers ceased their labor. Getting up, he walked purposefully between the rowers, heading for the prow. Ahuzza watched his progress with wide eyes and pounding heart. As he reached the bisri, the agent thrust a hand into the bottom of the boat and retrieved an anchor.

"Bisri Ahuzza, the emperor finds you guilty of treason," he snapped.

At these words, the man with the missing ear spun around and pinned the bisri's arms to his side. Crying out for his guards, Ahuzza struggled to free himself. His guards could do nothing to help. Set on from every side, they were fighting for their lives.

In spite of the bisri's desperate thrashing, Bolnyk succeeded in looping the anchor rope three times around his neck. After knotting it tightly, the agent seemed to glimpse something over Ahuzza's shoulder. "Move!" he shouted to his men.

As the rowers bent to their task, both men threw him from the boat, sending the anchor in after him. As he went in he caught sight of his guards being thrown overboard as well.

Sucking in a huge breath as he hit the water, Ahuzza wrestled with the rope, frantic to remove it from his neck. But the weight of the anchor pulled it tight, dragging him relentlessly toward the bottom.

He carried a knife in his belt, and it was still in place. Retrieving it with trembling hands, he almost dropped it in his haste. Frantic, and struggling to grasp it firmly, he attacked the rope, sawing fiercely at it in a desperate attempt to free himself.

The knife was sharp. Severing the final strand, he felt the rope go slack. But he could hold his breath no longer. With the surface far above him, his despairing upward kick was nowhere near enough.

His lungs filled with water, panic sweeping away all coherent thought.

CONSCIOUSNESS RETURNED GRUDGINGLY. He dimly heard a peculiar sequence of noises: labored gasp, haunting wail, gasp, wail, gasp— endlessly repeated. Confused and disoriented, he struggled to comprehend how the sounds coincided so exactly with his breathing.

He finally registered that the noises were coming from him.

A quiet voice spoke words he did not recognize.

Closing his eyes, he abandoned any attempt to make sense of the world around him.

He slept.

AHUZZA WOKE TO A POUNDING HEAD. He felt as if he had been beneath the waves, tumbling helplessly on the sand, his body pummeled by a relentless succession of breakers.

Fluid was pressed to his lips, and he drank submissively, grimacing at the taste. Then he closed his eyes again.

The pounding slowly eased, and he became aware he was lying on a comfortable bed.

"Where...am I?" He barely recognized his own voice.

"You are in the royal castle at Rog."

With an effort, Ahuzza propped himself up on one elbow and looked around. He decided he vaguely recognized the speaker.

The man saw it and nodded. "Yes, we have met already. On your ship."

Of course. He remembered water dripping from a dark figure. The agent.

"How?"

"We knew they would try to kill you. We arrived in a sloop as they were throwing you overboard. When they saw us they didn't wait around. We ignored them. Time was short—critically short. We barely reached you in time."

He paused. When Ahuzza said nothing, he continued.

"Fortunately for you, a healer had arrived just before we set out. A monk with rare skills. We brought him with us." The agent's lips twisted into a smile. "I thought you were done for. But he doesn't seem to know how to give up."

"And my guards?"

"They'd been brutally stabbed, but he got to them in time as well. You'll be able to see them later."

Ahuzza slumped with relief. "Can I meet this monk? To thank him?"

"Certainly. He isn't far away. But he speaks no Ahran."

The agent called out in a language Ahuzza didn't recognize.

A burly figure clad in the robes of a monk appeared in the doorway and approached the bed. A rare serenity encompassed the monk, and a gentleness that seemed incongruous for a man of his size.

The stranger gazed down at him, his eyes filled with compassion.

"Bisri Ahuzza," said the agent. "This is Brother Ander."

VOLUME 2—SEEDS OF HOPE

20

———

Bolnyk approached the emperor's throne, five steps behind the Grand Vizier. Not one to be easily daunted, he had told himself that the might of the emperor could never intimidate him. Now, admitted to this place for the first time, he was overawed in spite of himself. The menacing ranks of guards, the boastful grandeur of the chamber and its furnishings—everything about the imperial throne room reeked of power. The slightest whim of the emperor could end the life of any one of his subjects in a moment.

Rheibas did not seem at all intimidated, and Bolnyk took courage from that.

The emperor's greeting was blunt and to the point. "Where is Bisri Ahuzza?"

"I have grim news, Your Imperial Majesty. Even before I reached Rog the bisri had made independent contact with the Rogandans and their allies. After a recent conference with me, he set off to meet with them again at their invitation. I urged him to be careful, but he insisted on going alone. He has not been seen since. I regret to say there is every indication that he was murdered by the Rogandans."

The emperor glowered at him. "Why? How could such behavior benefit them?"

"Their motives are difficult to comprehend, Your Majesty. Why have they captured your daughter and refused to release her? They seem to think they can act with impunity where the empire is concerned. Perhaps the vastness of our physical separation convinces them they have nothing to fear by way of consequence."

"What do you propose?" demanded the emperor.

"The most effective response would be to return with an army."

The emperor scowled. "I have come to rely on your skills as a negotiator, Chief Minister. Those skills appear to have entirely deserted you!"

The Grand Vizier bent humbly. "I have been negotiating from a position of weakness, Your Majesty. I have become a tame lion. I can roar as fiercely as any wild animal, but without teeth I am little more than a carnival curiosity."

The emperor glared at him for a few moments. Finally he said, "Very well. You wish to catch the attention of the Rogandans. I will assign ten warships to the task, and as many soldiers as they will accommodate."

"So few, Your Majesty!"

"You will get no more!" the emperor snapped. "I am approving a show of force, not authorizing you to start a war. General Vholahr will command them. He will receive his orders directly from me, and he will not answer to you."

Rheibas bowed low.

The emperor's brows bristled. "My patience is wearing thin, Chief Minister. I have enough complications within my own empire—as you well know! Get my daughter back, and do it without embroiling me in a new catastrophe. You are dismissed!"

Ushered into the emperor's private audience chamber, General Vholahr bowed low.

"Come in, General." The emperor waved him irritably to a seat. "Rheibas has so far failed to retrieve my daughter from the Rogandans, and I fail to understand the reasons. I sent Bisri Ahuzza to monitor the situation on my behalf, and somehow he has disappeared. I am sending you to Rogand with a force of ten ships. You will carry on where he left off."

"Will the chief minister have authority over me and my men, Your Majesty?"

"He will not. I am sending you in a supporting role, and I certainly expect you to make contact with him when you arrive in the region. Nevertheless, you are to operate with complete independence. Under no circumstances are you to receive orders from anyone other than me."

The general dipped his head.

"Ensure that at least some of your soldiers speak Rogandan. If it is safe to do so, make contact with the Rogandan king. I want to be informed of whatever you learn."

"Under what circumstances am I authorized to use force?"

"I expect you to defend yourself vigorously if attacked. Beyond that, avoid even the appearance of aggression. I wish to retrieve my daughter without starting a war."

"So my men are largely intended as a show of force?"

"Precisely. The situation is volatile and confusing. I have chosen you because you combine military competence with unusual diplomatic subtlety. Do you understand what I require of you?"

"Yes, Your Majesty."

"Then you are dismissed."

General Vholahr bent low and departed.

Bolnyk scurried after the Grand Vizier, eager to be gone from the throne room. Only when it was behind him was he able to relax.

There had been moments when he felt almost afraid. The emperor seemed far from satisfied with his chief minister's handling of the Rogandan situation. Bolnyk had never before seen Rheibas bow to anyone, and it was alarming to witness the Grand Vizier being called to account. After humbly pleading for provisions, his master had stooped submissively when the emperor threw him crumbs. It had been a stark reminder that, powerful as his master was, ultimate authority in the empire did not rest in his hands.

Curiously, Rheibas did not seem at all taken aback. In fact he seemed remarkably buoyant.

"How did you enjoy your first taste of the emperor's throne room, Bolnyk?"

"I was disappointed at his lack of support for your proposal, Your Eminence."

"For more troops?" Rheibas waved a hand indifferently. "Ten ships will be more than enough. I would have been satisfied with five."

The agent stared back at him in surprise.

Rheibas laughed. "I have access to more than enough men, Bolnyk. You of all people should know that. I lack one thing only. None of my men bear the imperial insignia on their uniforms." He grew serious. "The Rogandans have hunted down and killed our agents with impunity. They will think twice when they're facing the emperor's soldiers. If they kill just one of them, they'll have a war on their hands."

The strategy could not be simpler. Ever a master manipulator, Rheibas would have no difficulty steering the situation in whichever direction he chose.

"Leave me now," the chief minister said brusquely. "I have matters to attend to."

Bowing low, Bolnyk hurried away.

Disconcerting as the audience in the throne room had been, the impact quickly dissipated.

As time passed, he found the contrast between the emperor and his master more and more striking. Richly cloaked with every trapping of limitless power, His Imperial Majesty seemed hesitant to exercise it. Rheibas could not have been more different. To every outward appearance he was weak and insignificant. Yet he routinely surprised friends and enemies alike with his swift and decisive action.

Everything he did was carried out in the emperor's name. Credit for his successes was deflected to the emperor, with Rheibas deferring unfailingly to His Majesty in private as well as in public. Nevertheless, Bolnyk knew better than anyone how crafty his master was.

In practice, the chief minister had almost unrestricted access to the emperor's power. And he benefited more than anyone. The agent found it all very instructive.

Beyond all that, he could not ignore his own glow of satisfaction. Given his humble beginnings, he could never have dared to imagine being admitted to the emperor's presence. It said a great deal about the way Rheibas regarded him.

Having begun life as a nobody, he had found purpose, usefulness, and increasing authority under Rheibas. Over time he had been granted greater insight into his master's designs. Rheibas told him only what he needed to know, but Bolnyk felt sure that vastly more had been entrusted to him than to anyone else.

That thought brought to mind Rheibas's mysterious prisoner. After a bemusing introduction, Bolnyk had learned nothing further about who the man was or what Rheibas wanted from him. He had no idea what had become of him. Perhaps he was being held somewhere in Rogand.

The whole situation was beyond unusual. It was baffling, too. While normally very willing to include his senior agent in his plans, Rheibas had clearly decided to treat this case very differently. The implied lack of trust smarted. It also made the matter highly intriguing.

Bolnyk reminded himself to stay focused. He had more than enough to deal with. He couldn't afford to allow himself to become distracted.

Bolnyk approached the chief minister's reception room apprehensively, the afterglow from his visit to the emperor no more than a memory. A servant announced his presence, and he was ushered inside.

"The captain of one of our supply ships has just arrived in Kat Ahket, Your Eminence. He has brought alarming news."

Rheibas frowned at him. "Well?"

"Our royal prisoners have gone missing."

The frown instantly became a scowl. "How is that possible?! Where is this captain?"

"Waiting outside."

"Then bring him in!"

Hurrying to the door, Bolnyk waved the captain into the room.

The new arrival entered the room and bent low. He looked harried.

"How has this happened?" demanded the chief minister. "I want to know every detail! From the beginning. And do not dare to mislead me! I'll have your head if I discover you've gilded the truth even slightly."

The captain had gone pale. "Of course, Your Eminence." He blinked nervously, then began. "I was tasked with taking supplies to the island where the prisoners were being held. As we approached the island, our lookout spotted a foreign ship coming in behind us. Until that moment he had seen no sign of another ship."

"The fool is clearly blind!" spat Rheibas.

"We were surprised to find the guards ready to evacuate the island, with the prisoners. As soon as they saw us, they lined up on the beach, waiting to be collected."

"Why were they ready to leave?"

"I questioned the guards later, Your Eminence. A few days earlier a couple of fisherman were discovered on the island, watching the guards from the trees. They escaped in a small boat. The leader of the guards, Shulkahr, concluded that the island's location had been compromised. He decided they all needed to leave on the next supply vessel."

"Where is he? I want him here!"

"He is missing, Your Eminence."

The chief minister opened his mouth—most likely to yell. Apparently thinking better of it, he abruptly snapped his mouth shut again. "Go on," he finally managed.

"I launched three longboats as soon as it was possible, and we got everyone off the island. By then the foreign boat was almost on top of us. We retrieved the longboat crews, but had to abandon two of the longboats before we could haul them aboard. The people we rescued were hanging on to ropes on the side of the ship when we pulled the anchor. They couldn't climb onto the deck at first because of arrow fire. The foreigners tried to steer across our bow to cut off our escape. Some of our archers slowed them down, and we managed to slip past them. Once we were under way, we quickly outpaced them."

He paused, but the chief minister waved at him to continue.

"The foreign ship was not alone. Two others followed it in. One joined the chase, and the other headed to the island. As soon as I could, I sought out the leader of the guards. His name was Shulkahr. I discovered that Shulkahr never reached the deck. Nor did any of the three prisoners."

"Did you question the guards?"

"I did. I questioned them vigorously. All of them, including the guards who climbed the net last, denied any knowledge of what happened to the missing people."

"Where are these guards?" Rheibas's voice had gone quiet. Bolnyk recognized it as a dangerous sign.

"They dispersed as soon as we docked."

"Find them and bring them to me," Rheibas told Bolnyk curtly.

The agent bowed, saying nothing.

"What do you believe happened to the prisoners and to Shulkahr?" Rheibas asked the captain.

"If they were weakened by their captivity, they might have fallen into the water. Or perhaps they jumped, in an effort to escape. Shulkahr probably followed them in."

"On his own?"

"He might have felt responsible for them."

"Could they have swum to the island?"

"They would have had a considerable distance to swim. It would depend largely on the currents, but I think it unlikely."

The chief minister asked a few more questions before dismissing the captain. "Don't go anywhere. I might have other questions for you."

After bowing clumsily, the captain almost tripped over himself in his haste to leave the room.

Rheibas turned to his senior agent. "Shulkahr is known to me. Who appointed him to this position?" he asked.

Bolnyk's heart sank. "I did, Your Eminence."

His master's eyes narrowed. "I seem to recall another man—his name was Dessue—being placed in charge on the island. On the recommendation of Kahrlin, I believe. What became of him?"

Rheibas missed nothing. And his memory for detail was terrifying.

"I felt concerned that Dessue might be too soft. I replaced him with someone I expected to get the job done more effectively."

"So your action had nothing to do with your rivalry with Kahrlin?"

"Not at all, Your Eminence. I believed I was appointing the best man for the job. I apologize if I erred."

Rheibas said nothing for a long minute. Then he turned away from Bolnyk. "You are dismissed," he said coldly.

The senior agent left almost as hastily as the captain.

His master had chosen not to linger on the issue of Shulkahr's appointment, but as usual he had seen to the heart of it. Rheibas had guessed correctly. In spite of Bolnyk's bold denial, replacing Dessue had everything to do with Bolnyk's determination to undermine the man who recommended the appointment.

Kahrlin might be clever, but he was boastful and arrogant. More importantly, he lacked respect. He lusted after Bolnyk's position and status, and he made no secret of it. Bolnyk had witnessed first hand how the chief minister outmaneuvered his own challengers. Surely he could not be expected to behave any differently.

None of it would have mattered if it hadn't been for his own appointee's monumental blunders. Lax security had exposed the island to unfriendly eyes. That was bad enough. But Shulkahr's negligence in failing to effectively guard and restrain the prisoners during the evacuation was unforgivable.

Throwing himself into the water after them might have been the only sensible thing Shulkahr had done.

IT TOOK TWO WEEKS, but Bolnyk rounded up every one of the missing agents. He was relentless, sparing no energy in tracking them down.

By the time they were dragged before Rheibas, one at a time, they were justifiably terrified. After a lengthy interrogation, each of them was led away to be executed.

"Wringing the truth from them presented no challenges," observed Rheibas.

Bolnyk nodded stiffly. "Men are unusually pliable when they're frightened enough."

"It seems our captain told us the truth."

"It appears so, Your Eminence."

"On this occasion he has saved his life by doing so."

The senior agent dipped his head. "I will have him released."

Rheibas stared at him pointedly. "None of this should have been necessary, Bolnyk. Don't imagine I've failed to notice your contributions toward this debacle. Do not continue to test my patience."

The blood drained from the agent's face. To him the Grand Vizier's master plan remained a mystery. But clearly the stakes had never been higher. Why did it all have to unravel now?

The chief minister's brows drew together. He appeared to have forgotten his rebuke already. "Only one question matters now. Do our enemies realize that we no longer have the prisoners?"

With nothing to offer except guesses, Bolnyk decided to keep his mouth shut.

After musing for a few moments, Rheibas reached his conclusion. "We will act as though nothing has changed. If the prisoners are dead or still at large, the Rogandans will be none the wiser. A bluff will be as effective as the truth." He shrugged. "We will only be exposed if they have recovered the prisoners themselves. That could only have happened if they swam as far as the island. And if they did so before the foreign ship left."

Unsettled and tentative, Bolnyk felt adrift in uncharted waters. Knowing his master despised passivity, he decided to risk an observation. "The captain seems to think they drowned."

The chief minister treated the comment with disdain. "Guesswork holds no interest for me," he said coldly. "I will send a ship to the island and find out."

"Would you like me to arrange it, Your Eminence?" He hoped he didn't sound like he was pleading.

Rheibas directed an indifferent gaze toward him. "That will not be necessary. I understand that Kahrlin is ready for an assignment. His operation to abduct the Arvenian queen was masterful. I'm sure he would be interested to know what's become of her."

21

Will hurried after a servant on his way to King Krasmir's reception room. In response to his request for an urgent meeting, the king had agreed to receive him immediately.

The king was waiting for him when he arrived.

He bowed hastily. "I have just received a dispatch, Your Majesty. It has taken a while to reach us." He ran an unsteady hand across his brow. "I hardly know how to say this. Queen Essanda has been abducted by Ahran agents!"

The king appeared thunderstruck. "How is that possible?"

"She had traveled to Castel on a goodwill visit. King Steffan made sure she was well protected on the journey. She was abducted from a small garden adjoining her rooms in the palace."

King Krasmir's eyes narrowed in anger. "The Grand Vizier had already planned this when he met with us. I see no other way to interpret his remarks about the queen."

Will nodded. "I agree. And there is more. The Ahrans attempted to abduct King Delmar in his own capital. He escaped only thanks to the quick thinking of one of his agents."

This latest report came as no surprise to the king. "I recently received a dispatch with similar information. I have doubled the guards around my palace as a result. And I have given orders that I should be informed immediately if strangers are seen anywhere in the vicinity of the palace."

Will dipped his head in acknowledgment. "I am faced with a difficult decision. Should I remain here, or return to Arvenon? The dispatch offered no guidance."

"I will understand, whatever you decide," the king told him. He shook his head grimly. "The Grand Vizier has achieved one useful thing at least. By presenting our kingdoms with a common enemy he has succeeded in mightily reinforcing the alliance between us."

THE FOLLOWING day Will made his way back to the king's conference room. He arrived to find the king engaged in animated conversation with Lord Kulferan and Lady Tulinay.

"Welcome, Lord Torbury. I am aware that you requested a meeting with me, but unless your matters are urgent, I will meet with you later. We have news to share with you."

If the look on the king's face offered any indication, the king's news was mixed. Will decided to speak out immediately.

"I have good news for a change, Your Majesty. It is quickly conveyed, and very appropriate for this audience. But I am more than willing to leave the timing to you."

"Please proceed, Lord Torbury. We could all use some good news."

"I received a dispatch today that supersedes yesterday's news. Queen Essanda has not been abducted at all! The Ahrans made off with an agent impersonating her. As you might imagine, this information is extremely sensitive. The Ahrans are not aware they have the wrong person, and for her sake it is important that we maintain the deception. King Steffan apologizes for sending misleading information. He was himself subjected to the same false report, to ensure that his initial shock and outrage were real."

The king nodded in satisfaction. "That is a great relief, Lord Torbury. It is gratifying to know that the Ahrans don't have it all their own way. Is there a reason why this agent allowed herself to be abducted?"

"It was not part of the plan. I know no more than that."

"It might yet work in our favor." The king nodded to Lord Kulferan. "Please update Lord Torbury with our news."

Lord Kulferan was happy to oblige. "I followed your suggestion, Lord Torbury, and ordered our warships to tail Ahran vessels. A small squadron of three ships under a captain known as Pultek managed to do exactly that. They followed a ship to an island. The island was being hastily evacuated, presumably in response to their arrival. They were unable to prevent the ship from escaping—Ahran archers managed to slow them down enough to allow the ship to slip past them."

"Where was this island?" asked Will.

"West of Varacellan. It lies north of Savage Strait, not far from Baron Island. A cluster of tiny islands surrounds it, so it isn't close to any shipping lanes."

"Do they know why the Ahrans were on the island?"

"One of the ships landed a couple of boatloads of soldiers. They searched the island thoroughly. The Ahrans left in a hurry, so they took very little with them. It isn't possible to be certain of anything, but from their description it could well have been the place where the captives were being held."

"Was anyone still on the island?"

"No one. It was completely abandoned."

Lady Tulinay shook her head in disgust. "They could be anywhere now."

At that moment a knock sounded on the door.

"Enter," called the king.

An aide stepped into the room and bowed. "A man wishes to see you, Your Majesty. He is most insistent. I told him you were busy. I am aware you have met with him before, but I did not assume you would want to make a priority of meeting him again. Especially since he has an Ahran with him."

"Who is this man?" demanded the king.

"He says his name is Kamash."

"And who is the Ahran?" asked Will.

"Supposedly his name is Gharpin."

Will stared back at him in astonishment. The others were no less surprised.

"Show them in immediately!" ordered the king. "Then find my Ahran interpreter and bring him here."

"Bisri Ahuzza?" asked Will.

The king did not hesitate. "Have Bisri Ahuzza brought to us as well! Hurry!"

After a quick bow, the aide scampered from the room.

Will was struggling to contain his excitement. Could it be possible? Was this the missing captain who sailed with the princess? The one who the Grand Vizier claimed was lost at sea?

Kamash and the Ahran were shown into the room before anything further could be said.

The old man bent low, the foreigner copying him.

"Welcome, Kamash. I did not expect to see you again," the king said candidly.

"Thank you, Your Majesty. I no more expected it than you."

"I understand you have been asking to meet with me."

Kamash nodded. "We arrived in Rog a couple of days ago, Your Majesty. I have been trying to get an audience with you since that time."

The king glowered at this news. "I am sorry to hear of the delay."

Kamash shrugged, apparently satisfied at having achieved his goal. "May I introduce my companion, Gharpin? He is Ahran. Our communication has been very limited, but I believe he captained an Ahran ship. He is certainly a skilled sailor. He also seems to have a connection to Princess Neira."

Gharpin bowed. "Your Majesty," he said. He spoke the words in Rogandan, with a heavy accent.

"You speak Rogandan?" asked the king in surprise.

"Little Rogandan," replied Gharpin, his lips drawing back in a smile. He pointed at Kamash. "He teach."

The king nodded. "I bid you welcome, Gharpin."

He turned his attention to Kamash. "While we are waiting for an interpreter, perhaps you can tell us your news."

Agreeing without hesitation, Kamash proceeded to outline all that had happened since he returned to his island. He gradually unveiled his meeting with the shipwrecked Ahran, the painstaking process of teaching him Rogandan, their departure for Rog, the storm that blew them to the west, their visit to the island.

"I am impressed with your determination to follow and find the Ahran ship," Lord Kulferan told him.

"I was very reluctant," Kamash told him honestly. "We did so only at Gharpin's insistence. He was suspicious about their reason for being in the area."

"With good reason, it seems," concluded the king. "Do you know what he saw and heard on the island?"

The old man shook his head. "I have been waiting eagerly for an opportunity to find that out. Along with many other things, of course. Gharpin's history in particular."

They did not need to wait much longer before the king's interpreter arrived, Bisri Ahuzza with him.

A new round of introductions was carried out. When the bisri heard the name of the other Ahran, his eyes went wide.

Once the formalities were concluded, the king addressed Gharpin.

"All of us are eager to hear what you have to say, Gharpin. Please speak freely."

Once his words were translated, the Ahran began without hesitation.

"Thank you, Your Majesty. Determined as I was to survive, a part of me doubted that my story would ever be heard. It is therefore both surprising and satisfying to be able to speak to you now. Above all, I want the emperor to know the truth. I would be grateful beyond words if you can help me find a way to speak to him."

"If you are truly committed to speaking the truth, I will do whatever is in my power to help you," King Krasmir assured him.

Gharpin bowed. "I was privileged to captain the vessel that bore Her Imperial Highness Princess Neira to this region." He scowled. "I regret to say that Rheibas, the Grand Vizier of the Empire of Ahr, was also aboard my ship."

If he was aware of the consternation that greeted his words, Will saw no sign of it.

All of them listened intently as he spoke of the abandonment of the princess, the return trip to Kat Ahket, and the sabotage carried out by Rheibas and his men. He made it clear that daring to challenge the Grand Vizier had led to him paying a heavy price along with his entire crew.

After being washed ashore barely alive, against the odds, he spoke of his amazement when Kamash arrived. He could scarcely believe it when he realized that Kamash had access to a sturdy little boat. When they set out for Rog, he had never been so happy. Then the Ahran ship appeared.

The questions multiplied when he began to relate his experiences on the island.

"What was their reason for being there?" asked the king.

"I hid as close to them as I dared. They were speaking Ahran, and I listened to them for hours. Their purpose for being there was to guard three royals—two women and one man. One of the women hadn't been there for long. They never mentioned their names. I only heard them use disparaging nicknames I won't mention."

"Who did these guards report to?" asked Lady Tulinay.

"A man called Shulkahr had been placed in charge on the island. I don't know who he reported to. But they understood themselves to be working for the Grand Vizier."

"Was the emperor aware of their mission?"

"Not as far as I could tell, although they believed they were working for the benefit of the empire." He snorted. "With Rheibas directing their efforts?" He shook his head in disbelief.

"What were they planning to do with the prisoners?"

"They didn't seem to know anything about such plans."

The captain shrugged. "Then Kamash arrived. Not long after that they discovered us, and we ran for the boat. We barely escaped with our lives."

King Krasmir had been listening intently to the translation. When the captain finished, he nodded gratefully to him. Then he shook his head with wonder. "Once more we find ourselves greatly indebted to you, Kamash!" he said. "My only regret is that the solitude you long for has been denied once more."

Kamash bowed in response.

With a moment's pause at last, Bisri Ahuzza took the opportunity to ask Gharpin a rapid-fire series of questions. After a brief but heroic attempt at translation, the interpreter accepted defeat. All of them watched patiently as the two men engaged in a spirited interaction.

When they finally came to an end, Bisri Ahuzza spoke briefly to the interpreter.

"He wants me to tell you that he believes Captain Gharpin's account," the interpreter told them. "He especially asked me to apologize to you, Lord Torbury."

Hearing Lord Torbury's name, the bisri bowed formally to Will.

"He says it would have been much simpler for him, and for everyone, if he had believed you from the beginning."

Will bowed in his turn. "Please convey my compliments to the bisri. I can only imagine how difficult it must be to discover he has been so deceived."

Catching the attention of the interpreter, Gharpin spoke rapidly to him.

"The captain wishes to know how you are proposing to contact the emperor."

"We need to be sensible," warned Lady Tulinay. "We can't just put the captain and the bisri on one of our ships and send them to Kat

Ahket. If they were intercepted, no one would benefit except the Grand Vizier."

Lord Kulferan nodded soberly. "I agree. The voyage is long and perilous. And apart from that, the design of Rogandan and Ahran ships is noticeably different. A Rogandan ship would become increasingly conspicuous the closer it came to Ahr-chitani. I could not guarantee their safety."

Captain Gharpin leaped to his feet when their words were translated. "We cannot sit here and do nothing!"

An animated conversation followed. After watching it silently for many minutes, Will decided to intervene.

"May I speak?"

King Krasmir seized upon the request. "By all means, Lord Torbury! You have the floor."

Will began at once. "I would like to offer a suggestion."

Every eye was upon him.

"The Grand Vizier's position gives him access to considerable resources, and he has not been sparing with those resources. He has been freely moving ships and men wherever he chooses, almost without hindrance. However, from what Bisri Ahuzza has told us about the emperor's attitude, it seems evident that the Grand Vizier is furthering his own interests rather than the cause of the Empire of Ahr. It isn't clear what those interests are. Even his closest associates might not be aware of exactly what he is trying to achieve."

With no immediate comment, Will continued. "We are faced with a number of pressing challenges. We need to limit the Grand Vizier's freedom of movement, we need to make the emperor aware of the true situation, and we need to do it quickly. So far we have seen Ahran agents rather than the emperor's soldiers. That is likely to change. Sooner or later the Grand Vizier will find a way to escalate tensions."

A number of heads nodded.

"Here is what I believe we should do..."

22

Along with the other evacuees from the island, Maive clung to a net on the side of the Ahran ship, Rupert and Tasha at her side.

Sudden hope sprang up within her as another vessel, most likely Rogandan, appeared unexpectedly, heading straight toward them.

The Ahrans hastily raised anchors, and the ship slowly began to pick up speed as it fled from the oncoming vessel. The Rogandans pulled level on the opposite side of the ship, apparently trying to cut off their escape.

No one was moving on the net above them. Given the stray arrows flying about, Maive well understood their hesitation. The leader of the guards was less sympathetic. Clearly annoyed, he climbed upward to prod them into action.

Maive turned to her companions. "This is our chance!" she hissed, jerking her head downward. "We have to go now!"

Rupert and Tasha peered uncertainly down at the water.

They apparently needed some encouragement. Launching herself away from the side of the ship, she hit the water hard. To her immense relief, she resurfaced to see Rupert and Tasha following her in. They submerged briefly, then their heads reappeared nearby.

Maive glanced up at the net, already some distance away. A couple of heads were turned in their direction.

So their escape had been noticed. Yet none of the guards had followed them into the water. She smiled grimly to herself. Sooner or later they would have reason to regret it.

Incredibly, the leader of the guards must still be distracted. Knowing that every moment was vital, Maive began swimming strongly toward the island. The others swam behind her. Her sole focus was to get as far away from the ship as possible before the leader realized they were missing.

The Rogandans would not have seen them when they jumped—the position of their ship prevented it. But a second vessel, presumably also Rogandan, had joined the chase. Seeing it heading right for them, they hastily swam to one side, waving and calling as it passed. All attention must have been fixed on the Ahran vessel ahead, because no one noticed them.

The leader of the guards must surely know they were missing by now. The ship was steadily receding into the distance, and Maive could see no sign of heads in the water behind them. But they could not afford to lessen their efforts.

She returned her attention to the island. Already she felt herself tiring, and it was so far away. Then to her amazement she spotted a new ship heading for the island.

The others had seen it too. "Could it be Rogandan?" asked Tasha.

Rupert was squinting toward it. "It doesn't look Ahran."

They watched as a longboat made its way to the beach and men spread out to search the island.

"Let's get closer," suggested Maive. "We'll stay out of sight if they're Ahrans."

Even the hint of a rescue was enough to drive them forward with renewed energy.

Many weary minutes dragged by before Rupert voiced her unspoken fear. "The island isn't getting any closer."

"I've been thinking the same thing," Tasha confessed.

Maive paused and began to tread water. "We must be in a current. I've swum in currents before. We need to swim to one side."

"But that won't get us to the beach," protested Tasha.

Maive shook her head. "No, it won't. But we don't have a choice. If we keep this up we'll wear ourselves out going nowhere."

The others nodded reluctantly. They began swimming along the shoreline instead of toward it, hoping to approach the island from the side.

At first Maive thought the strategy was working. The beach began to disappear from sight as they moved around the island. At the same time, though, she saw that the current was pulling them away from the land. In mockery of their best efforts, the island, and the ship anchored beside it, was steadily moving out of reach. Any hope of rescue was disappearing with it.

"I'm not sure how much longer I can keep this up." Tasha sounded weary and a little desperate.

Maive felt tired too, but she was determined not to give up. "Don't fight the current. Let it carry you for a couple of minutes. Just while we decide what to do."

She spun around in the water, eventually pointing in the opposite direction. "The current's taking us toward that little island. Maybe we can go ashore there." It was their best chance—maybe their only chance—of survival.

Rupert was squinting toward the island. "Won't the current just sweep us past it?"

"Not if we get out of it in time."

Tasha nodded. She seemed too weary to speak.

All talk ended as they refocused their energies on the new target.

Swimming with the current made a huge difference. The island drew closer surprisingly quickly. Reaching it wasn't straightforward though. Maive began heading out of the current sooner than the others. It was immediately apparent that she had made the right decision.

It was also clear that Tasha was in trouble.

"Rupert!" Maive pointed to Tasha, who was moving sluggishly at a time when she needed to put in extra energy.

Seeing what was happening, Rupert began calling encouragement to Tasha. "Swim to me!" he urged. When she didn't respond, he called, "I'm coming to you!"

Maive couldn't leave them to struggle alone. Striking out strongly toward Tasha, she reached her side not long after Rupert.

"Grab one of Rupert's ankles and one of mine, Tasha. We'll do some swimming for you."

Towing someone for more than a couple of minutes would have been challenging for Maive at any time. She was attempting it when almost spent, and Rupert was no better off. All three of them were flirting with disaster.

But Maive had underestimated Tasha's spirit. Rallying, the princess let go of their ankles. Propelling herself forward with new energy, she steered herself out of the current.

The island drew ever closer. Maive dared to believe they were going to make it. The last strokes felt almost out of reach, but she gritted her teeth and pushed on. Then her kicking feet brushed against a rock.

No sandy beach awaited them. Embracing the only available option, they dragged themselves out of the sea onto some rocks. Somehow they had survived. They were free.

For many minutes they lay exhausted, too weary to celebrate. Maive was the first to stir. Getting to her feet, she looked around, assessing their situation. Their new refuge appeared to be small and covered with trees.

Peering back in the direction they had come, she saw the other island. It seemed such a short distance away. She almost felt like she could reach out and touch it.

As she watched, a ship detached itself from the land. In the vastness of the ocean it seemed so close to them—heartbreakingly so. She stood helplessly as it sailed slowly away, heading in the direction the other ships had taken.

"I suppose they had no reason to stay."

It was Rupert who had spoken. Swiveling her head, she saw he had positioned himself beside her.

"No," she replied. "They waited longer than I expected."

"At least we're alive. We have you to thank for that. And for our freedom."

She shrugged. "Freedom isn't going to mean much if we're stranded here."

Tasha joined them. "I'm thirsty. Do you think there's fresh water on this island?"

"We might be lucky," Maive replied. "Let's do some exploring."

They set off together, heading for the trees.

To her relief, the island boasted at least one spring, and it didn't take long to find it. Scooping the crystal clear liquid into their cupped hands, they sipped it cautiously. Then, delighted at its freshness, they eagerly slaked their thirst.

"Food is going to be more of a challenge," said Rupert.

Maive nodded. "There might be seabird eggs among the rocks. But we'll need a lot more than that to keep us alive."

"There are plenty of fish in the sea of course," said Tasha. "I've caught fish before. But never with my bare hands." She glanced at them self-consciously.

Rupert shrugged. "I haven't either." He glanced around at the trees. "The guards left plenty of supplies on the island. We can't swim there, but could we build a raft? If we had some kind of sail, the current shouldn't be an issue."

"I'm not sure how we could build a raft without any tools. We don't even have a knife."

Tasha was staring out to sea. "What's that?" she asked, pointing into the water just offshore.

All of them stared in the direction she was indicating. At first Maive saw nothing, then she spotted something bobbing in the water. Was it a seal?

"It's a head!" said Rupert.

She narrowed her eyes, peering intently. "You're right!" she exclaimed in surprise.

"Is it one of the guards?" asked Tasha anxiously.

Rupert's face had gone hard. "If it is, he deserves to drown."

"We can't just leave him to die," Tasha protested.

"What do you want to do?" asked Maive.

Rupert released a heavy sigh. "I suppose we should at least try to rescue him."

He made to head back to the water, but Maive forestalled him.

"I'll do it. Agents are trained for situations like this."

Leaving the trees, she headed back across the rocks and eased herself into the water.

Rupert and Tasha stood watching from the water's edge.

"Tell me if I'm going in the wrong direction," she shouted. Then, calling upon her weary limbs to make a new effort, she headed out to sea.

Outward progress wasn't hard to achieve. But she knew once she was caught in the current, it would be extremely difficult to break free. She could never have achieved her purpose if the unknown swimmer hadn't been carried almost to her.

She realized as she reached him that it was the leader of the guards. He was nearly done for. Hope rose in his eyes when he realized someone was coming for him. The hope immediately died away when he saw who it was.

It would have been so easy to leave him to the ocean. After the way he had treated his captives, his end would have been fitting.

Ignoring her uncertainties, she approached him from behind. "Don't fight me," she said, only just remembering to limit herself to Arvenian. "I'm here to help."

He was too far gone to struggle. Grasping hold of him around his chest as she had been taught, she began kicking her legs vigorously, desperate to break free of the current once more. There would be no hope for either of them if they were swept past the island.

Just when she began to think all was lost, the rocks drew within reach at last. With the final residue of her failing strength, she propelled them to safety. Hands reached down and pulled them from the water.

While clutching the guard tightly to herself, she had noticed a dagger in his belt. The guard now lay prostrate on the ground, too weak to move. Retrieving it, she handed it to Rupert.

"Keep this safe," she told him, before whispering, "Remember that I'm supposed to speak only Arvenian."

Nodding, he secured the knife in his belt. Then he leaned toward Tasha, passing on the message to her as well.

Between them, Rupert and Tasha dragged the guard away from the rocks and into a clearing among the trees. She followed on wobbly legs.

Stretching him out on the ground, they sat on a fallen log nearby to watch him.

They could manage without her. With a sigh of relief, she permitted herself to collapse on the ground.

MAIVE WOKE to find stars twinkling above her. She sat up and looked around.

The guard she had rescued was lying nearby. He hadn't moved, and he appeared to still be asleep.

Rupert had managed to light a fire, presumably using the knife. He had positioned himself not far from the guard, and he was keeping a watchful eye on him. Tasha was resting on the opposite side of the fire.

Feeling surprisingly refreshed after such a short rest, Maive got up. As she moved closer to the fire to examine the guard, she caught him snapping his eyelids shut.

She laughed scornfully. "Everything has changed," she told him frankly. "The sooner you accept that the better." She spoke in Arvenian, confident he understood the language. "King Rupert now has your knife. He's a trained fighter, and he's in the best condition of any of us. I wouldn't suggest testing him."

Giving up the pretense, the guard opened his eyes. He didn't try to get up.

She crossed her arms and stared down at him. "We haven't been introduced. My name is Essanda. You may call me 'Your Majesty.'"

He studied her quietly for a few moments. "I am Shulkahr. Why did you save me?"

Her lip curled in an ironic grin. "During my brief time as your guest, you won me over with your charm and your generous spirit." Then she willed her face to relax. "Not all of us show the same contempt for human life and dignity as you Ahrans."

He glared back at her. "I am what I am. Not all of us have been born to a life of ease and privilege."

She shrugged. "I am no stranger to hardship."

"I know all about you. And I am well aware of your history. You were betrayed and attacked by your own countrymen. Men in the pay of the king of Rogand, whose armies invaded your kingdom."

When she did not respond, he added, "Ahrans do not seem to have a monopoly on contempt for human life and dignity." He shook his head in scorn. "How quickly you have forgotten. These same Rogandans are now your treasured allies."

"It is true that human nature is not determined by our place of birth," she acknowledged. "Our values and priorities are shaped first by our parents and our community. But our leaders have great influence—for good or for ill. The previous king of Rogand proved that, as you said. His successor has indeed become our ally—because he has chosen a different path." She eyed him calmly. "Perhaps the Empire of Ahr is not so fortunate in its leaders."

"The empire might seem unfortunate if you value weakness," he sneered.

"So I should have left you to drown?" she asked.

He went silent. "I owe you my life," he admitted reluctantly. "I do not forget my debts."

It was a concession of sorts. But she was no fool. She harbored no illusions about how much they could expect from him.

One last thing needed to be said. "Some believe that cruelty demonstrates strength, and mercy exposes weakness. But things aren't always as they appear. Cruelty is the first refuge of the insecure. True strength deals out mercy as freely as judgment."

She didn't wait around for him to disagree.

23

Shulkahr's rescue had shaken him almost as much as the ordeal that prompted it. He was alive, but at what cost? Not only had the roles been reversed, he now found himself indebted to a former captive. The humiliation was unbearable.

The island had been far away when he went into the water. Nevertheless, believing himself to be a strong swimmer, he expected that with perseverance he would reach the island. The Rogandan ship anchored off the beach would present a problem, but he decided to face that when the time came.

His confidence proved to be wildly misplaced and his best attempts futile. Swept helplessly away by the current, he had abandoned hope before the Arvenian queen appeared and towed him to shore. Without her he would have drowned. He owed his life to a captive, and a foreign queen at that. It was mortifying.

As if that wasn't enough, while lying exhausted beside the fire he had overheard another of his former captives, King Rupert, talking to the princess.

"You've been sitting there so long!" the king had said. "You should take a break."

"He might need my help," she replied simply.

"He doesn't deserve it," the king had growled.

"No, he doesn't. But if we treat him the way he treated us, how are we any better?"

He didn't respond, and after a moment she added, "What's troubling you, Rupert?"

"You mean apart from the fact that we're stranded on a tiny island with no food and no prospect of rescue?"

She laughed, a cheerful sound that seemed incongruous in light of their situation. "We've made it this far."

"And we've done it together," he replied. The angst was gone from his voice. He sounded almost content.

The king must have moved away, because their conversation did not continue.

Shulkahr was left restless and unsettled. Something about the princess's laugh evoked memories of his childhood, of carefree times before his mother's untimely death soured his life. A forgotten ache gnawed at him, seeking release. Unwilling to allow it to surface, he shoved it back down, determined to push it away.

As he lay wrestling with his thoughts, the unsavory truth about his current condition slowly penetrated his defenses. The princess had been watching at his side solely because she was concerned about him.

The situation was unendurable. Being beholden to one person was more than he could stomach. He refused to be further obligated to these people.

He could see only one way forward. For the moment he would work with them. Stranded on a tiny island as they were, any pooling of resources would benefit them all. After that he would consider any debt repaid.

Cooperating did not mean he would soften his attitude toward them. As soon as an opportunity arose, he would reverse the roles again. Next time it would be final.

T HE HIGHER UP THE tree Shulkahr climbed, the more it began to sway. As it started to bend, he tied a vine to it and threw the other end to the ground. Rupert grabbed it and pulled tight. Shulkahr then began bouncing up and down vigorously. Before long the tree began to creak ominously.

"That's enough!" shouted Rupert. "It's about to break!"

His warning came too late. With an almighty crack, the trunk of the tree split. Shulkahr rode it to the ground, tumbling off as he landed.

Both Rupert and Essanda hurried over, staring down at him in alarm.

Shulkahr lay stunned for a moment. After carefully testing each of his limbs, he announced, "I don't seem to have broken anything."

"Your dedication is admirable," Rupert told him. "But there's no need to kill yourself."

The former guard slowly clambered to his feet. Although he would never have admitted it, he couldn't remember when he'd last enjoyed himself so much.

He'd allowed himself to go to seed on the island. Leading a group of guards had not played to his strengths. He much preferred hands-on pursuits—the higher the energy the better.

The arrival of the princess cut across his thoughts. She'd been gone for some time, foraging for anything safe to eat.

A few small eggs lay in her hands. "Food is served," she announced brightly.

Borrowing the knife from Rupert, Essanda took one of the eggs and poked a small hole in each end. Then she lifted the egg to her mouth and sucked out its contents. Poking holes in one egg at a time, she handed them around.

"I only found eleven," Tasha said ruefully.

"Don't worry," Essanda told her as she handed Tasha the last of the eggs. "I'm satisfied with two. All of you have been working harder than me anyway."

Rupert and Tasha protested, but Shulkahr remained silent. He saw no reason to complain as long as he wasn't the one missing out. Nevertheless, the irony of the situation was not lost on him. His former prisoners were freely sharing what little they had with him. In spite of his harshness toward them, they were treating him as an equal.

It was hard to believe they were all royal. They seemed so normal, quite unlike any royals he had ever heard of. He'd never met Her Imperial Highness Princess Neira, but from everything he knew of her, she differed from these three in almost every possible way. The idea that commoners could warm to their sovereigns had never occurred to him. Yet it wouldn't surprise him to hear that the subjects of these royals both loved and admired them.

He frowned, shaking his head. Maybe he was getting soft.

"Time to get back to work," Rupert said to Shulkahr.

He nodded absently, following the youthful king back to where they had been building the raft. After gathering a collection of tree trunks, they were binding them together as best they could with vines. Tasha and Essanda were weaving palm fronds together to make a crude sail.

The biggest challenge would be the mast. They had acquired a suitable tree trunk. None of them were quite sure how to secure it to the raft.

He glanced across at Essanda, hard at work on the sail. She might be slender, but she was tough. He remembered the confident ease with which she towed him to the island. She must have already been exhausted, but she found the strength to do it.

Nothing about her was what he would have expected from a queen, much less the mother of three children. Something about her didn't add up, although he couldn't identify it.

He frowned in bemusement, trying to make sense of it.

Rupert's voice cut across his thoughts. "I think I know how we might secure the mast."

He looked up to see the king lashing a long branch to one corner of the raft using vines. Then he secured the other end to the mast, most of the way to the top.

"That might work," agreed Shulkahr.

The two of them repeated the exercise until the mast was supported on four sides.

"It only has to stay upright long enough for us to reach the island," Rupert observed.

Shulkahr held up a makeshift tiller. "We can use this to steer the raft. It shouldn't be hard to attach it."

"How is the sail?" asked Rupert.

"As good as it's likely to get," Essanda replied. She didn't look overly confident, but after looking at it closely, Shulkahr doubted he could have done any better.

Rupert eyed the weather. "The conditions look good, but the sun will be setting soon. Should we chance it now, or leave it until the morning?"

"We leave in the morning," asserted Shulkahr. "And that's final!"

Rupert stared at him. "Thank you for your *opinion*, Shulkahr," he said pointedly. He turned to the others. "What do you think?"

"I'm hungry," said Tasha wistfully.

"I am too," agreed Essanda. "But it might be wise to wait until daylight. What do you think, Rupert?"

The king shrugged. "I'm of two minds. I'm looking forward to eating a proper meal, but I'm also weary. I suspect I'll be better prepared in the morning."

"Very well," said Tasha with a sigh. "If the rest of you can wait, I can too."

ALL FOUR OF them stood glumly at the water's edge, staring at the other island. The sun had barely risen, but they didn't need its light to tell them they should have set out the previous day.

The strong wind that sprang up in the night had whipped the waves into a frenzy. They didn't have far to go, but in these conditions it would be dangerous folly to attempt any kind of journey on their makeshift raft.

Shulkahr knew he was being irrational, but he felt annoyed. "It shouldn't have taken a whole day to build the raft," he spat. "It was just my luck to be stranded with royal incompetents."

The others glanced in his direction, but none of them chose to bite. That made him angrier.

He raised his hands heavenward. "Without me and my knife you'd be stranded here. I should have left you to starve!"

Rupert's face had gone hard. "No one forced you to jump in after us."

"If you'd had the sense to stay on the ship I wouldn't have needed to."

Stepping forward, the king planted himself in front of Shulkahr, glaring at him coldly. "Wherever this island is located, it's well within the territorial waters of Castel. You're in my kingdom now! You've given me more than enough reason to execute you. As king, it's my right and privilege. Don't push your luck."

Shulkahr snorted. The fool had just admitted he was soft.

He'd heard more than enough. A sneer on his lips, he brought up both arms and lunged forward suddenly with all his strength.

He wasn't nearly fast enough. Twisting lightly aside, the king thrust out a leg, using Shulkahr's momentum against him.

The Ahran crashed to the ground. Before he could blink, a foot landed heavily on his neck, pinning him helplessly.

The foot ground his face into the dirt. "Give me one reason why I shouldn't kill you."

With his life on the line, Shulkahr realized he'd seriously misjudged this man. He'd mistaken restraint for weakness. He wouldn't do it again.

It was his turn to exercise restraint. His opportunity would come if he was patient.

Forcing his body to relax, he quit struggling. "No reason," he sputtered, barely able to speak with his face in the dirt.

Abruptly the foot was gone. Rupert stood back and let him get up.

He clambered to his feet, his face burning red.

The queen mistook his blush for anger. She stared at him with narrowed eyes. "Next time, if he doesn't kill you, I will."

He stared back at her. She meant it, and he didn't doubt she would follow through on her threat.

His brows furrowed. Something about her wasn't right—he was sure of it.

"Do you doubt me?" she growled.

He hastily broke eye contact, shifting his gaze to the ground. She soon moved away, ignoring him completely.

The rest of the day passed miserably for all of them. Fresh water was plentiful, but they had nothing to eat. And the hours wore away with no sign of the weather improving.

All of them were avoiding Shulkahr now. Improbable as it might have seemed, he had established a fragile bond with his former captives. That bond had been shattered.

He told himself only a fool would care what a group of captives thought.

They lay down around a fire that night, but Shulkahr couldn't settle. He had the impression that none of the others were sleeping any better than he did.

As the hours dragged on, he tried to make sense of his inner churning. He knew the others saw him as behaving badly. What he couldn't understand was why that bothered him. He concluded that he was being weak. It had been folly to allow circumstances to influence his thinking and behavior. For a brief time he had treated them as if they mattered. His fellow agents would mock him unmercifully if they knew. And he deserved it. He didn't allow himself to think about what Bolnyk would have to say.

He managed to get some sleep in the end. It wasn't restful.

In the morning the wind had eased, but the waves remained choppy. Noon came and went with only a minor improvement in the conditions. All of them were becoming impatient.

The king chose a moment when they were all together. "Are you willing to risk it?"

The princess and the queen both nodded.

He turned to Shulkahr. "Are you coming?"

A sharp retort rose to his tongue, but he bit it back. He nodded. "I'll take the risk."

The four of them carried the raft to the water's edge and put it in. The princess held it while the queen retrieved the sail. Shulkahr attached the rudder. Then they climbed aboard.

Raising the sail was a tense moment, but it held together as the wind caught it. The raft rocked alarmingly, and they hastily sat down to improve its stability. Shulkahr had taken the rudder, and he steered in the general direction of the other island.

The further they ventured into open water, the heavier the swell became. A bigger than usual wave rolled toward them, and Shulkahr swung the rudder desperately, trying to steer into it. He was only partly successful. Smashing into the raft side on, the wave twisted it violently, almost swamping them. One of the four supports holding up the mast broke free, but the others held. The mast was now leaning to one side, but the sail continued to catch the wind. Somehow the logs were holding together.

"I'm not sure how many more like that we can survive," said the king grimly.

No one else spoke.

Shulkahr peered ahead intently, trying to anticipate the next threat. He didn't have long to wait.

It came in the form of a series of three huge waves, rolling inexorably toward them. This time he managed to swing the raft around before they arrived. The flimsy craft rose, creaking and groaning as the first wave swept beneath them. Then the second reached them. Tilting ominously, the raft twisted enough to leave it exposed to the full force of the third wave.

A giant wall of water smashed into the fragile platform. The vines that bound it together were torn loose, allowing several logs to separate from the rest of the raft. Two of the remaining mast supports broke free, bringing the mast crashing down. The sail fell onto the princess, almost launching her into the water. The impact broke the sail apart. Pieces of it began drifting away with the tide.

Huddled with the other passengers on what remained of the raft,

Shulkahr stared longingly toward their goal. The island seemed so close. But it was beyond their reach.

Then the queen picked up a piece of the sail, and held it aloft. The king quickly followed her lead. The princess grabbed a third piece before it floated out of reach. All three of them knelt on the raft, using their bodies as masts.

Somehow the rudder had remained connected. Positioning himself beside it, Shulkahr fought the elements to steer them in the right direction. Slowly, sluggishly, the raft responded.

No further giant waves appeared to assault them. It was as if the ocean, having pummeled the little craft almost to oblivion, had lost interest in them.

Incredibly, the island drew closer. Shulkahr hardly dared to breathe. He had the sense to hold his course until they had passed the little beach. Then he turned toward the island.

The change of direction proved too much for the crippled vessel. Struck by a larger than usual wave as it came around, it broke apart.

Nevertheless, the raft had carried them most of the way. The vines binding it together had done their job for long enough. Pitched into the water, the fugitives struck out for the beach, swimming with the tide.

Shulkahr emerged as the laggard. By the time he pulled himself from the water, the others were already wandering among the pile of supplies abandoned beside the beach, searching for food.

The princess called out in excitement. "Over here! I've found some bread."

He arrived in time to hear the queen's response. "Well done, Tasha! I'm so hungry I don't care how stale it is." Both of them were biting hungrily into the food.

His eyes went wide. The conversation had been in Rogandan. Yet he had been reliably informed that the Arvenian queen spoke her own language, and nothing more.

It all came together in a rush. He'd known something wasn't right about her, but he hadn't been able to put the pieces together. Now the truth had been laid bare. Whoever she was, she wasn't Queen Essanda. She'd been masquerading the whole time.

The operation to abduct the Arvenian queen had been master-minded by Kahrlin. He'd captured an impostor. The arrogant fool thought he was so clever. He'd be in for a very big surprise.

The fake queen was staring at him. From the look on her face, she knew she'd been exposed.

"Was it my eyes?" she asked.

He looked at her blankly. "What about your eyes?"

She didn't enlighten him.

"If you're asking what gave you away, it started with your heroic rescue." His lip curled into a sneer. "You were far too strong and too clever for your own good. You should have left me to drown."

The other two had ceased their search and joined them.

"He knows." The impostor sounded tired.

The king frowned. "What are we going to do with him?"

The princess was staring out to sea. "I think we might have bigger things to worry about."

Shulkahr followed her gaze. A ship was gliding around the edge of the island. He saw at a glance that it was Ahran.

The mock queen grabbed the arm of the king. "Is there anywhere we can hide?"

Shulkahr snorted. "Save your energy. This island was chosen for a reason."

A boat was lowered from the ship and set out for the shore. All four of them stood watching as if mesmerized.

As it approached the beach, Shulkahr saw a face he recognized. The man poised in the prow of the boat was Kahrlin.

24

———————

Commodore Pultek stood at the helm as the Princess Teylee plowed through another wave. He smiled in satisfaction at the creaking of the ship's timbers. It was good to be back at sea.

The ship that interrupted the Ahran evacuation of the island was now a memory. Frustrating as that engagement had been, his energy and initiative had gained him favorable attention from Lord Kulferan. As a reward, he had been promoted and given command of a newly commissioned ship, named for the missing princess.

The Princess Teylee was one of a kind. Sporting three masts, she was the fastest ship in the Rogandan navy. And Lord Kulferan had sent the Princess off laden with a full complement of fighting men. Pultek was itching to put the Ahrans to the test. He had no doubt that the outcome would be very different next time.

Commodore Pultek's squadron had also grown as a result of his promotion. Five ships now sailed under his command. It was true that the other four were older and less nimble than his flagship, but they would play their part.

A great deal of responsibility had been placed on his shoulders, and he was more than ready to embrace it. His squadron would no longer search for the princess. The hunt would continue, but that task had been assigned to other ships. He had been given a new strategy.

Sailing conditions were ideal—fine weather coupled with steady winds. Having sent his orders to the other captains in his squadron, Pultek set off in search of his quarry.

Steering north of Rog, he continued until he was well clear of the islands that dotted the ocean near the mainland. Then he turned west, heading toward Varas, and Castel beyond it. He had positioned two ships on either side of the Princess and instructed their captains to hold a steady course. Between them, the ships now covered a broad sweep of ocean. If any of them sighted an Ahran vessel, they would signal the nearest vessel, which would in turn notify the Princess. Pultek intended to waste no time before pursuing any ship unlucky enough to come in sight.

Nothing was predictable at sea. Conditions could change in a moment, and only the unexpected was inevitable. Nevertheless, on this occasion fate seemed determined to smile upon the commodore and his newly commissioned flagship.

Having cleared the islands and turned west, they sailed for only a few hours before the lookout called, "A signal, Cap'n!"

None of the men had adopted his new title, but Pultek didn't care.

The signalman relayed the message. "A ship sighted to the northwest, Cap'n."

"Is it Ahran?"

"No indication yet."

"West by northwest!" Pultek ordered the helmsman. "Steer a course to intercept them."

"Set full sail!" he bellowed.

Sailors immediately scrambled aloft.

Pultek grunted with satisfaction as the Princess responded. He had never experienced such speed and responsiveness.

"Sail ahead!"

The call from the lookout came much sooner than he expected.

"How many masts?"

"Three, Cap'n!"

He turned to the bosun. "Get the soldiers onto the deck! Make sure the archers are ready for action!"

By the time everyone was positioned, the sails could be clearly seen from the helm.

"Are they changing course?" he shouted to the lookout.

"No, Cap'n."

Pultek smirked at his helmsman. "They think we're Ahrans. They're not used to being chased by ships with three masts." He stared at his quarry. "Everything is about to change," he promised.

They were upon the other ship before the Ahrans realized anything was wrong. By the time sailors scurried into the rigging to set more sail, it was too late.

The commander of the soldiers had positioned himself beside Pultek.

"Tell me as soon as we're in arrow range," Pultek ordered.

The commander nodded, but no advice was necessary. The Ahrans hadn't waited to get into range to begin firing at the Princess. As soon as shafts were whizzing over the deck, Pultek gave the order.

"Target the men in the rigging!" he ordered.

A volley of arrows shot upward, and sailors crashed to the deck.

Pultek watched in grim satisfaction. "I learned that trick from you," he growled.

"Bring her alongside!" he ordered the helmsman.

"It's your job now," he told the soldier.

Hurrying down to the deck, the commander shouted orders to his men. As soon as the two ships were close enough, grappling hooks were thrown onto the other vessel. Ahran sailors retrieved axes and began hacking desperately at the ropes. But archers targeted them mercilessly, and more grappling hooks were thrown for every one they severed.

Soldiers were soon leaping across the gap onto the Ahran ship. As hand-to-hand fighting raged across the deck, men began assaulting the forecastle.

Taken by surprise and heavily outnumbered, the Ahran

defenders found that bravery was not enough. The Ahran captain had no choice but to surrender.

The commander reported back to Pultek. "The ship is yours, Commodore! My men have disarmed the survivors and have them under guard. No Ahrans remain below decks."

"Your casualties?"

"Relatively light, I am pleased to say."

"Well done, Commander. What is their cargo?"

"Supplies, mostly."

"Any clues as to their intentions?"

"Their captain tried to destroy his papers, but my men prevented him from completing the task. Unfortunately his orders are written in the Ahran language. I have no one who can translate them."

"They will be sent to Rog. Your men performed admirably today, Commander. Please convey my compliments to them."

The papers seized from the Ahran captain, along with the captured sailors and agents, were transferred by Pultek to the slowest of his ships, along with a strong contingent of guards. A skeleton crew took over the vessel and set a course for Rog.

As previously directed by Lord Kulferan, Pultek renamed the captured Ahran vessel the King Rupert. He transferred to it the remainder of the crew from the ship now on its way to Rog. Their numbers were bolstered with sailors from the other vessels in his squadron, along with soldiers drawn from all of his ships.

Communicating effectively while transferring personnel at sea proved challenging. However the seas remained calm, and his men performed admirably.

With the transfers almost complete, Pultek arranged for the most capable of his captains to join him. "Captain Bezai, I'm placing you in command of the King Rupert. I am sure you will work tirelessly to deliver on my expectations."

Captain Bezai made no effort to hide his delight, and he wasted no time in transferring to his new vessel.

As the afternoon wore on, Pultek had begun to wonder if urgent matters requiring his attention would never end. With the tasks finally behind him, he had every reason to be satisfied.

His flagship had performed magnificently. As he cast his eyes across the ships clustered around him, his gaze lingered on the newest addition to his squadron. The captain and the men he placed on the captured ship had more than fulfilled his expectations, and they well deserved a vessel better suited to their skills.

The three remaining crews were now dissatisfied and grumbling. Their complaints didn't bother Pultek at all. That day's efforts were only the beginning.

Signaling his orders to the squadron, he led the ships on a course westward, the new three-master close by on his starboard side. From now on the Princess Teylee and the King Rupert would be hunting together.

PULTEK LED his squadron as far as Baron Island without encountering another Ahran vessel. At that point he could have sailed south toward Maranelle after either rounding Baron Island or traversing Savage Strait. He chose instead to bring his ships about and head back toward the east.

Winds were light, and progress slow. In the afternoon of their second day, a lookout on the King Rupert signaled the Princess Teylee. Positioning the Princess near the other vessel, he invited Captain Bezai to join him. A boat was duly launched, and the captain came aboard.

"Welcome, Captain," Pultek told him, leading him to his cabin. "I am eager to hear your news."

The captain bowed. "Thank you, Commodore. About an hour ago we came upon a fishing boat. As soon as they were certain we were not Ahrans, they made obvious efforts to catch our attention. We sent a boat to investigate, and they told us they had chanced upon two Ahran ships anchored off an island beside their fishing grounds. They wanted us to send the Ahrans away."

Pultek's eyebrows rose. "I wonder what they're up to on the island."

"Could they be holding the princess there?"

"It doesn't seem likely. I'm guessing they would search for a location well away from prying eyes." Pultek paused for a moment, musing. "Did the fishermen say how many masts these ships had?"

"Three, Commodore. They were very definite about that."

Pultek grinned. "This might be just the opportunity we've been searching for. If it ends well, Captain, a couple of your disgruntled fellow captains might find themselves with a three-master of their own."

THE ROGANDAN ARMY commander called a quiet command, and eight longboats from the Princess Teylee and the King Rupert glided silently through the moderate swell, heading for two tall ships sitting at anchor off a small island. A bonfire twinkled on the beach, faintly illuminating a number of dark shapes clustered around it.

The army commander watched tensely from the forecastle of one of the smaller Rogandan ships in Pultek's squadron.

He noted with satisfaction that the moon had not yet risen. The conditions perfectly suited the soldiers crammed into the boats even now approaching their targets.

Abruptly the boats separated, four moving alongside each of the vessels. It was too dark to see the action, but the commander could imagine grappling hooks flying high into the air, dull thunks sounding as they gripped the side of the ship. He knew that men would already be shimmying up the ropes.

Sentries must have been posted, because loud shouts of warning were soon echoing across the water.

Lanterns threw light onto the deck of each ship. On the ship anchored furthest from the island, he saw armed Ahran sailors reaching the side of the ship just as the first attackers climbed onto the deck. Shouting ferociously, the two groups assaulted their enemies. The deck quickly degenerated into a confused mass of men struggling back and forth. He could see more defenders emerging from the hatch with every minute that passed, but in the chaos they seemed to be having difficulty reaching the ship's side quickly enough to stem the tide of Rogandans climbing aboard. He had the clear impression that most of the attackers had reached the deck and joined the fight.

The Ahran sailors showed they were not frightened of combat, and they fought with reckless bravery. He knew that Rheibas's agents would be battling beside them. By reputation the agents were self-reliant, and many of them boasted unusual fighting skills.

But he had confidence in the Rogandan soldiers facing the Ahrans. They were experienced fighters, handpicked for this assignment.

As the fighting intensified, he sensed that the discipline of the soldiers was beginning to have an impact. He didn't doubt the courage of the Ahran crew, but they were sailors, not soldiers.

As for the Ahran agents, they were almost certainly too few in number to decide the outcome. And in spite of their prowess, they were accustomed to relying on themselves. His men had been trained to fight as a company.

It quickly became evident that on the other ship the assault was not going so well. Only a few attackers made it onto the deck before the defenders reached the ship's side. Ahran sailors hacked through some of the ropes attached to grappling hooks. Men were sent plunging into the sea, and in one case, directly onto a longboat still disgorging soldiers. The longboat capsized, pitching its occupants into the water.

The Rogandans on the deck fought ferociously to protect a space for others to clamber up behind them. They achieved their goal at the cost of their lives.

The attackers had gained a precarious foothold. Greatly outnumbered and under constant pressure, they ran the risk of being overwhelmed at any moment.

The commander had not failed to notice that additional pressure was about to be applied from a different direction.

As soon as the alarm sounded, the men on shore had left their bonfire and hurried to their longboats. They rowed frantically toward the nearest ship where the Rogandans were hanging on by a thread.

The army commander had been holding in reserve four longboats from the other ships in the squadron, all of them loaded with soldiers. He now ordered them forward urgently.

The longboats from the island were racing toward the Rogandan boats still sending men aloft. Most likely the Ahrans did not carry grappling hooks as a matter of course in their longboats. With no way of climbing aloft themselves, they must have decided to disrupt the flow of attackers onto the deck. Eventually they might be able to use the attackers' ropes to climb to the deck themselves.

Two of the Rogandan reserve longboats arrived at the same time as the Ahrans. The resulting melee was so chaotic the commander could not determine who was winning.

The other two longboats held in reserve rowed to the other side of the Ahran ship. The commander lost sight of them once they rounded the stern, but he knew they would climb aboard and attack the defenders from behind. He could only wait impatiently for the first of them to appear.

At that moment he saw that his men had taken control of the first ship. A few Ahran defenders had been rounded up and disarmed. They now sat on the deck under heavy guard.

As he watched, men descended the ropes to one of the longboats below. Rowing hastily to the ship that was still in dispute, they too disappeared from sight as they rounded the stern.

His reserves appeared to have prevented the Ahrans from the island from reinforcing the defenders. It was impossible to know exactly what was happening, but a lot of men seemed to be in the water.

He saw at last Rogandans soldiers clambering onto the deck from the far side. By the time the defenders moved to respond, the new arrivals had established a foothold.

With the defenders surrounded and under pressure from both sides, the initiative began to tilt in favor of the attackers. Before another thirty minutes had passed, the second ship was also firmly under the control of the commander's soldiers. The Ahrans had all been killed or captured.

"Notify Commodore Pultek that the Ahran ships are his," the commander ordered.

PERHAPS IT SHOULD HAVE BEEN SIMPLER the second time, but taking command of two captured vessels in the dark complicated Pultek's task enormously. His first action was to spread the surviving Ahrans across two of his older ships. Both ships set off for Rog well before dawn, manned by skeleton crews supported by soldiers. Men wounded in the recent battle returned with them.

With three of his original ships now on their way to Rog, Pultek was well short of the required complement both of sailors and of soldiers. Three-masted ships carried more crew, and his command now included four of the vessels. It was becoming increasingly obvious that he could not continue his operation without correcting these shortfalls.

In the meantime, his men desperately needed to rest. After ensuring that every ship was well defended, he ordered his captains to lower anchors and wait for the dawn.

As soon as the sun rose, the whole squadron set sail for Rog.

Pultek had managed barely two hours of sleep. Bone-weary as he was, he was nevertheless ecstatic. He had been tasked with disrupting the Grand Vizier's activities by capturing or disabling his ships, and within days he had succeeded in doing precisely that. His squadron must surely have dealt a significant blow to the Ahran operation. He could only guess at the bemusement of the Grand Vizier when he learned that three of his vessels had simply vanished.

Best of all, the Rogandan navy had received an important boost. Having set out with a single three-master, Pultek was returning with four.

He couldn't wait to see the expression on Lord Kulferan's face.

25

As Kahrlin's longboat approached the beach, the impostor leaned toward the Castelan king. "Give me the knife," she urged.

The king handed it to her without hesitation, and she hid it beneath her clothing.

Shulkahr scowled at the woman. Her short-lived masquerade was coming to an end. Captives didn't carry knives. And the knife belonged to him anyway.

He would disarm her the moment Kahrlin's men landed.

She must have read his thoughts, because she murmured, "You owe me this much, at least."

A wave of irritation rose in him at the reminder of his debt. Nevertheless, he would not allow her to keep the knife. The situation had changed, and she was a fool if she couldn't see that.

The longboat slid onto the sand, and Kahrlin leaped out. The gloating look on the agent's face made Shulkahr sick to his stomach.

Abruptly changing his mind about the knife, he decided to let the situation play out. For the moment, the woman could keep it. Perhaps she might do him a favor and dispose of Kahrlin.

The self-satisfied fool was smirking at him. "You can relax now,

Shulkahr. A competent agent has finally arrived." He waved lazily toward the other three. "Seize them! Tie their hands and get them into the boat."

Stung by Kahrlin's contempt, Shulkahr opened his mouth to deliver his own barb. Then, on the brink of exposing the impostor, he realized that to do so at that moment would play into Kahrlin's hands. He needed to choose his timing. Kahrlin would be the one reporting on the mission when they returned. Why give him the information now? Knowing him, he'd find a way to rationalize his mistake and take credit for uncovering the truth.

No, the revelation about the Arvenian queen was better saved for a more appropriate audience. Satisfying himself reluctantly with a contemptuous glance at Kahrlin, he followed the captives into the boat.

When they reached the ship, Kahrlin herded the captives below decks, accompanied by four guards. "You can come, too," he told Shulkahr.

He led the way to a storeroom below the waterline. Entering it, he held a candle high. "This will be your new quarters," he told them. "I hope you find it to your liking."

He handed the candle to Shulkahr. "I can't spare anyone to guard them," he sniffed. "You can do it. It might give you a chance to redeem yourself."

Without waiting for an answer, he left the room and bolted the door. The sound of laughter faded as Kahrlin walked away with his guards.

Furious and humiliated, Shulkahr glared at the captives. "This is your fault!" he spat.

The king glared back at him. "It's true that you wouldn't be in this position if not for us. You'd be floating face down somewhere out at sea!"

Shulkahr suddenly noticed that all three of them were unbound. And the king once again had the knife. The princess had retrieved the blade from the other woman while he was distracted and used it to cut their bonds.

Slumping to the floor with an angry growl, Shulkahr grudgingly accepted that once more he was in the weaker position. For the moment.

"Why didn't you tell him?" The woman was peering at him suspiciously.

"That you're not Queen Essanda?" A mocking smile came to his face. "Don't imagine I was holding back for your sake. It's purely a matter of timing. In case you weren't aware, the man who originally brought you in is the same idiot who just collected us. He's known as Kahrlin. Taking him down in front of the right audience will be well worth the wait."

She regarded him seriously. "When will we be taken before the Grand Vizier?"

He frowned at her. Something about her tone wasn't right. Not only did she not sound terrified, there was a suppressed eagerness in her tone.

He peered at her suspiciously. "Why would you want to see him?"

"I want to know why he had us abducted." She sounded casual. A bit too casual.

It all came to him in a rush. He gaped at her open-mouthed. "That's why you wanted a knife! You think you're going to assassinate him!" He laughed mockingly. "Do you really imagine he'd let you get close enough to do that?"

A flush of anger passed across her face, but she quickly mastered herself.

"That *is* what you were planning, isn't it?" He looked at her in open amazement. "So you took the place of the queen, not to save her, but because you wanted to take down the chief minister?" He stared stupidly at her, shaking his head in unbelief. Finally a mad laugh burst out of him. "It's too much!"

The woman was watching him with narrowed eyes, but she didn't speak.

Finally he mastered himself. "I'm sorry to disappoint you, 'Your Majesty.' But I've seen enough of the way His Eminence works to know that none of you should ever expect to set eyes on him. Much less get anywhere near him. He's far too smart for that."

"Why?" The king's skepticism was obvious.

"Because if he ever met with you directly, it would be as good as admitting he knew you were abducted. He'd have to kill you. Don't misunderstand me! You'll be killed in a heartbeat if he decides you're no longer useful. But if he ever decides it would be more profitable to work with you, he might want to reinstate you."

"How could he possibly expect us to work with him?" scoffed the king. "No one would be that stupid after what he's done."

"How certain are you that he's responsible for anything that's happened to you?"

All three of them were staring at him as if he were a carnival curiosity. "How can you even ask such a question?" asked the princess.

"What proof do you have?"

"Bolnyk abducted us," retorted the king. "And he's the Grand Vizier's right hand man."

"What if Bolnyk was working on his own, without the chief minister's knowledge? From everything I heard, Bolnyk took you when an unexpected opportunity presented itself. No one planned it— certainly not the chief minister."

The king scoffed at him once more. "Your chief minister is Bolnyk's master, and he's done nothing to set the situation right. Any reasonable person would hold him equally responsible."

"As far as the chief minister is concerned, only one person's opinion counts. That person is the emperor. If the emperor accepts his version of events, nothing else matters."

None of them knew what to say.

"The chief minister is the smartest man alive. You might as well accept that now. It might give you a faint hope of extending your pitiful lives."

"He isn't smarter than Lord Torbury," the king said stubbornly.

"The Arvenian army commander? The one whose son went missing? He might be a clever strategist where armies are involved.

Matching wits with someone like the chief minister is a different matter entirely."

"I wouldn't bet against Lord Torbury."

Shulkahr's lip curled into a condescending sneer. "We will see."

"The chief minister will see you now."

Kahrlin followed the servant into the chief minister's cabin. It was unpretentious and simply appointed. Rheibas had never been overly concerned with appearances.

"I hear you have retrieved the captives," Rheibas began.

The agent bowed modestly. "They had made their way back to the island, Your Eminence. Fortunately I was able to extract them without incident."

"You have done well. What of Shulkahr?"

"He was with them on the island."

Rheibas cocked an eyebrow.

"They seemed to be on friendly terms," offered Kahrlin.

"Where is he now?"

"I brought him back with the captives, Your Eminence."

"Dispose of him. I have no tolerance for failure."

Kahrlin bowed.

"Don't go anywhere, Kahrlin. I might have further need of you. You are dismissed."

The agent bent once more and left the cabin, struggling to conceal his elation.

On his way out, he noticed Bolnyk waiting outside the door.

The man was rapidly becoming irrelevant. Kahrlin wondered if he was aware of it. After a brief comment, he ignored his rival and made his way onto the deck.

"Fetch Shulkahr," he told one of his men imperiously.

The bosun was nearby. "Arrange for a longboat to be launched immediately," Kahrlin said. "I'll need an extra anchor." After a moment's reflection, he added, "Make that two. I'll provide the crew."

By the time Shulkahr arrived, his crew were climbing down to the longboat.

"Come with me," he told Shulkahr.

"Where are we going? I need to see Bolnyk. And the chief minister."

"You'll have to see them later. We have work to do for the chief minister."

Shulkahr glowered, but subsided. He followed Kahrlin down to the boat.

Kahrlin sat at the back of the boat, facing the rowers. He positioned Shulkahr in the bow.

As they rowed away from the chief minister's ship, Kahrlin stole an occasional glance toward the other man. He looked anxious and distracted. He had every reason to be.

The chief minister's ship disappeared from sight as the longboat rounded a head. Kahrlin glanced down into the water. It was too deep for the bottom to be visible.

He nodded to the two rowers closest to the bow. Turning swiftly, they each wound an anchor rope around the startled Shulkahr. Then they threw him overboard, tossing the anchors in after him.

It was done in a moment.

The doomed man managed to shout, "Wait! There's something you don't—"

Then he was gone.

Kahrlin nodded again, and the longboat came about, heading back to the ship.

HAVING ENJOYED unprecedented access to the chief minister for so long, it was a major adjustment for Bolnyk to find himself waiting. It had become a consistent experience of late. He tried to remind himself that his master juggled many priorities and had every reason to be preoccupied.

He had positioned himself near Rheibas's cabin, ready to seize an opportunity as soon as one emerged.

The door opened and Kahrlin emerged. If the look on his face offered any indication, he was currently basking in the favor of his master.

"I imagine he will see you now," Kahrlin offered indifferently as he breezed past.

Bolnyk ignored him. His rival might think he was very clever, but he was not aware that some of his most trusted men were loyal to Bolnyk.

Consequently, Bolnyk already knew what had happened to Shulkahr. The fool had deserved his fate. He had not repaid Bolnyk's faith in him.

Nevertheless, it was galling that Rheibas had given the task to another person. Perhaps it was his way of showing consideration to the man who had appointed Shulkahr, but somehow Bolnyk doubted it.

Approaching the chief minister's door, he knocked, willing himself to remain calm. He couldn't afford the luxury of dwelling on Kahrlin. He was bearing news that would not please his master. More than ever he needed to steer a careful course.

"Enter," growled the voice of Rheibas.

Bowing low, he pushed his way into the cabin.

"Bolnyk," intoned his master indifferently. "What bad tidings are you bringing this time?"

Had Rheibas caught wind of what he was about to say?

"Our agents at Rog report that a Rogandan squadron just sailed into the harbor, Your Eminence. The squadron consisted of five ships. Three were of Ahran design, all of them with three masts."

"Impossible!" spat Rheibas.

"That is not all. Three other Rogandan vessels have docked in recent days bearing prisoners. Our agents are certain the prisoners were Ahran."

He had Rheibas's full attention now. "Is there more?"

Bolnyk nodded soberly. "Three ships bearing our agents appear to have gone missing. No reports have been received of their where-abouts, and there have been no sightings for many days."

The chief minister was scowling. "What is your conclusion from all this?"

"That the Rogandans are attacking and seizing our ships. Any survivors are taken prisoner. The ships are then repurposed for use in their own navy."

"Utterly detestable, if clever. Three ships, you say."

Bolnyk nodded.

"Who is responsible for the dispatch of our ships?"

"I am, Your Eminence."

The chief minister's voice became a growl. "Then how have you allowed this to happen?"

The question was monstrously unfair. Bolnyk offered no response.

Rheibas seemed uninterested in a reply. "I want to know which ships are missing. Exactly—get me details. And find out if more have gone missing since. While you're at it, confirm that the prisoners are Ahran. Don't keep me waiting!"

Bolnyk stooped low in acknowledgment.

"And circulate an order for all ships in the region to maintain high alert at all times. You are dismissed!"

THE CHIEF MINISTER'S next summons to Kahrlin was not long in coming. The agent entered the cabin and bowed low.

"I have a task for you, Kahrlin. An extremely sensitive one. I am relying on your utmost discretion. And I need you to carry it out quickly and effectively."

Kahrlin bowed once more. "I am at your disposal, Your Eminence."

"I need you to hire enough competent sailors to man three ships. Make sure all of your sailors know how to fight. The ships need teeth —fill them with mercenaries. A high proportion of your mercenaries need to be capable archers. Hire only Rogandans. Is that clear?"

"Perfectly, Your Eminence. Are there limits on the funding?"

"Money is no object."

"Should I hire captains for these ships?"

The chief minister shook his head firmly. "I will identify people of our own to carry out that role." He bared his teeth. "Our enemies think they are very clever. They will discover they are nowhere near clever enough."

The agent stood waiting to be dismissed.

"You have one week. I have high hopes for you, Kahrlin. Do not disappoint me! You are dismissed."

After bowing low, Kahrlin hurried away. A monumental task lay ahead of him, but he couldn't have been more jubilant.

As he entered Rheibas's cabin, Bolnyk's heart was pounding uncomfortably. Never had he felt more uncertain in the presence of his master.

A few days previously, Kahrlin had disappeared with the most capable of the agents. It was whispered that he was engaged in a highly sensitive and critically important mission on behalf of the chief minister. The situation was unusually galling, not least because most of the agents now assisting Kahrlin had originally been selected and trained by Bolnyk.

A lifetime must surely have passed since his master led Bolnyk into the emperor's throne room. Such honors were faded memories. People looked away now when he approached. He had not been summoned by Rheibas for days, and everyone knew it. Once more in the chief minister's cabin, he felt only apprehension.

His master seemed to notice him at last. "Ah. Bolnyk."

He stood awkwardly at attention, restless under the cold scrutiny of the chief minister.

For years he had drawn from a seemingly boundless reserve of confidence, never doubting his ability to achieve whatever his master demanded of him. In recent days that self-assurance had deserted him completely. He understood why—his master had lost faith in him. Nevertheless, the suddenness and completeness of the change remained as mystifying as it was alarming.

His entire adult life had been consumed in a tireless effort to further the interests of the man before him. That same man had become a stranger. Every night Bolnyk lay awake, desperate for the numbing oblivion of sleep. But its release was denied him. His mind, constantly churning with the injustice of his plight, refused to set him free.

A simmering anger had begun to bubble, close to the surface. Difficult as it was to ignore, he forced it down. He could not afford for Rheibas to sense it.

"You have served me faithfully for many years, Bolnyk."

His brows drew together. Whatever he might have been expecting, it wasn't that.

"You deserve a chance. A proper chance. An opportunity to demonstrate again the capabilities that made you so valuable to me."

The ice in his heart began to thaw. His master had his full attention.

"I have been planning an operation. A highly sensitive and very special operation. I assigned the legwork to Kahrlin, but he is not the right person to lead it. I need someone who is dependable beyond doubt. Someone whose loyalty goes beyond self-interest."

He stared at Bolnyk forthrightly. "Are you that man, Bolnyk?"

"I am, Your Eminence." He tried not to sound too desperate.

"Excellent." Rheibas was actually smiling. "Then here is what I need you to do..."

26

General Vholahr peered distastefully across the endless succession of rolling waves. He had participated in many amphibious operations, but this operation was different. Never before had he spent so many days stranded on a ship with nothing to do.

He was there to provide bargaining support to the chief minister, yet there had been no contact from him since arriving in the region.

The emperor had also charged Vholahr with making contact with the Rogandans, but the situation harbored enough uncertainty that he was unwilling to risk any kind of connection before the chief minister briefed him on the current state of negotiations.

Much as his men needed time on dry land, it was out of the question. Any landing would only risk inflaming tensions with the Rogandans. All they could do was circle endlessly outside of Rogandan territorial waters.

That left them at the mercy of wind and wave. Thankfully conditions had improved over the previous couple of days. Prior to that, storms had battered them relentlessly, tossing them about on mountainous seas. Sea sickness had incapacitated many of his soldiers, and at times he himself had barely been able to stand.

None of it would have mattered if he was making forward progress on the emperor's mission. He shook his head in frustration.

As if in mockery of his thoughts, he looked up to see the ship's captain hurrying toward him, a grave look on his face. "We have just received a signal, General! Two of our ships are under attack."

"What?! We will move to their support immediately." He pointed to the other ships in sight. "Signal them to join us!"

The captain hurried to the helm, shouting orders as he went.

As the ship slowly began to come about, the general called for his captains. "Get the men armed and on deck. It appears we will see action at last!"

Men began scurrying about, heading for their assigned stations. Everyone was in place long before they saw any sign of fighting. The men were becoming restless when five ships came into sight. Their design showed that the vessels were all Ahran.

As they drew closer he saw two ships on either side of a third ship, attacking it from both directions. Two other ships nearby were engaged in close fighting. It made no sense. Why would Ahrans be attacking Ahrans?

As they approached, the three attackers disengaged. Setting full sail, they were soon disappearing in the direction of Rog.

The captain approached. "Should we pursue them, General?"

The general shook his head. "We can't know where they might lead us. No, this attack needs to be investigated, and it needs to be done immediately. We can't afford to be caught unprepared a second time."

A couple of hours passed before men from every ship had gathered in response to his orders. In the absence of a large enough room, and with the weather moderate, they clustered on the forecastle.

"I want to know what happened," the general began. "In order."

An army captain, heavily bandaged from multiple wounds, responded first. "Two of our ships were in the same vicinity when three other ships appeared. They were clearly Ahran, so we did nothing to prevent them coming alongside. As soon as they were close enough, bowmen appeared and opened fire. We were not expecting an attack, and they caught us unprepared. As you know, we have few archers among our ranks. We could not prevent them from sweeping the decks with arrows before they boarded."

"How many men did you lose?"

"Fifty at least. They pulled us close with grappling hooks, then they boarded from both sides. Most of our men had sheltered below decks. Once hand-to-hand fighting started, they poured out of the hatch, and it turned into a real fight. We were outnumbered, but we gave a good account of ourselves. When they saw you approaching, they took their wounded and jumped back onto their own ships."

Another captain reported in. "We had a similar experience, although we were only facing one attacker. Their archers also took out a lot of our men. They lost plenty of men themselves when they boarded. If they hadn't withdrawn when they did, we might have been able to board them. When they saw you coming, they ran like rabbits. They only left their dead behind."

"Who were they?"

"It's hard to be certain, but they weren't speaking Ahran," the first captain said. "One of the crew recognized a few Rogandan words."

"Rogandan navy or pirates?"

The captain shrugged. "It's impossible to say. They showed discipline in removing their wounded, but they didn't fight like regular soldiers."

The second captain nodded. "I agree. The real mystery is how they came to be sailing Ahran ships. Those ships were definitely Ahran-built."

The general frowned. "There are too many unanswered questions for my liking. Nevertheless, you've acquitted yourselves well under difficult circumstances. Convey my appreciation to your men." He eyed them grimly. "As of now, all of our ships will stay in formation. And we clearly need archers. If we're lacking bows, find a way to manufacture some."

He dismissed them, and they returned to their ships.

"What do you make of all that?" the general asked his aide. "Who were the attackers, and what was their purpose? And how did they gain possession of three of our ships?"

"I can only guess, General," the aide replied. "I'm wondering if they knew they were attacking army transports. It's possible they thought we were merchants."

"They know nothing about Ahran ship design if they think we're merchants."

"But why would they attack army ships, General? Is it in retaliation for us having supposedly abducted their princess?"

The general snorted. "They could begin by explaining why they abducted our princess!" He shook his head. "If they want a war, they'll get one."

He glared out across the water. "It's past time we heard from the chief minister. His negotiations appear to have achieved nothing. I am planning to ask the emperor to assemble a serious force, and the chief minister will not find it easy to dissuade me."

AFTER ABANDONING THE ATTACK, Bolnyk led his little squadron back to the island where they had first taken on board the Rogandan fighters.

The mercenaries had been transported to the island as they were hired by Kahrlin. After a few days, when a sufficient number had assembled, three of the chief minister's newest ships arrived and disembarked their crews. The ships had been turned over to the mercenaries under the command of Bolnyk.

Two other trusted agents joined him—one to captain each of the vessels. Once they were all aboard, the ships set sail and departed. Surrounded by men of dubious character, Bolnyk had made it clear that none of them would receive payment unless all of them promptly carried out his every command.

The original Ahran crews had settled down on the island to wait for the return of their ships.

When the fighting was over, Bolnyk returned the mercenaries to the island and ferried them ashore. As the original crews boarded the ships once more, he gathered the mercenaries and addressed them.

"You have fulfilled the terms of your agreement," he told them. "You will shortly be collected and returned to Rogand. In the meantime, supplies have been laid out for you. Eat and drink your fill!"

"What about our pay?" a rough voice demanded.

"A worthy question!" he replied. "Your payment has been buried for safekeeping. You will find the full amount over there, beneath those spades." He pointed. "Dig it up at your leisure." He surveyed them with a humorless smile. "I am sure you will make every effort to share it fairly."

A group of mercenaries gathered threateningly around him and his men. "Don't think you're going anywhere! Not until we see our payment."

He folded his arms indifferently.

None of the mercenaries showed any interest in feasting. All eyes were on the digging. The first of the treasure was exposed within a few minutes. It was clearly a sizable hoard. Every one of the mercenaries abandoned Bolnyk, racing to claim their share.

A single longboat remained for Bolnyk's use. Climbing aboard with his men, he set off for one of the ships. As they climbed onto the deck, they saw that fighting had broken out between the mercenaries at the diggings.

Bolnyk had no interest in waiting around for the outcome. He gave the order, and the three ships weighed anchor and sailed away. He didn't even spare a backward glance at the island.

As soon as they were underway, he was joined by the agents who had captained the other two ships during the attack. Their faces were strained.

"What happened?" one of them asked, not trying to hide his consternation. "We were supposed to be taking ships back from Rogandans! Rogandans who'd captured them from our own people!"

The other was nodding vigorously. "We were attacking Ahran navy ships! I only realized it when we boarded them, and I found myself fighting men in imperial uniforms! I called off the attack immediately."

"You did the right thing," grunted Bolnyk, his brows furrowed.

Nothing about the operation had been as he expected. "I have no idea what went wrong. We were in the location where the ships were supposedly last seen."

Both men began speaking animatedly. "If anyone finds out we led an attack on the emperor's soldiers, we'll be dead men!"

"It was the chief minister's operation. We were just following his orders!"

"That's right! He'll protect us. Won't he?"

"Why did Kahrlin bury the mercenaries' pay? They're normally paid individually."

"I have no idea. Making them divide the spoils makes no sense. It's a recipe for conflict."

The flow of words continued uninterrupted as they glanced back toward the island.

Bolnyk didn't interrupt them. What could he say? He was no longer sure about anything.

Throughout the journey his mind churned uneasily, trying to make sense of all that had happened. His thoughts moved well beyond that operation. A seismic shift had taken place in his standing with Rheibas, and he was struggling to understand what had precipitated it.

Important questions had been raised by the operation he had just led on Rheibas's behalf. Had a careful plan somehow gone terribly wrong? Or, more alarmingly, was he merely an unwitting dupe in the most recent of the chief minister's devious schemes?

Having worked with Rheibas for a very long time, he was confident he could read him as well as anyone. He would know the truth when he stood before his master.

He would also know if he had any kind of a future.

"Enter," growled Rheibas.

Pushing into the cabin, Bolnyk bowed low, trying to calm his racing heart. So much hung on this interaction.

For a long moment, the chief minister stared at him, his features expressionless. "I have been briefed on your mission," he finally announced with an angry scowl.

Bolnyk kept his own face impassive. "We sailed to the location you described, Your Eminence," he said. "The ships we found there were not manned by Rogandans."

The chief minister's eyes flashed. "I warned you! I told you this mission was extremely sensitive! Yet you dared to attack the emperor's soldiers! Are you trying to destroy me?"

Bolnyk gazed calmly back at him. "The emperor's soldiers were attacked by a group of Rogandan mercenaries. The emperor has no need to know who was behind the attack."

Rheibas was incredulous. "You want me to lie to the emperor? Just to cover your mistake?"

A flush rose involuntarily to Bolnyk's face. It was indignation rather than embarrassment—he knew Rheibas well enough to recognize his posturing for what it was.

Deception was integral to the way the chief minister operated—Bolnyk had seen ample evidence of that throughout his life. Not much time had passed since he personally witnessed the chief minister lying brazenly to the emperor.

Rheibas hadn't finished. "I've protected you, Bolnyk—elevated you. I took you into the emperor's throne room! But even I have my limits. Don't expect me to constantly be available to rescue you from your own stupidity."

He waved a hand dismissively. "I'll decide what to do with you later. In the meantime don't leave this ship. You are dismissed!"

Bowing tightly, Bolnyk left the chief minister's cabin.

His worst fears had been confirmed. He was being cast aside like a worn out rag.

It wasn't difficult to guess who would be brought in to take his place. No doubt Kahrlin was already celebrating his predecessor's demise. He shrugged. Let his rival enjoy his moment in the sun—in time he would be discarded too.

His thoughts returned to the recent operation. Rheibas had said nothing of substance about it. Nevertheless, Bolnyk felt able to make a few intelligent guesses.

In spite of the chief minister's bluster, Bolnyk felt sure imperial soldiers had always been the target of the attack. Perhaps Rheibas was looking for an incident—a spark to ignite a war against the Rogandans.

Whatever his schemes, he would undoubtedly make sure his former senior agent was on hand to take the blame. He shook his head in disgust.

He wondered what had become of his mercenaries. Were they being returned to Rogand as promised? He didn't believe it for a minute.

Burying their payment was unprecedented. It must surely have been done for a reason. It wasn't hard to guess that the mercenaries would fight bitterly over the loot. Bolnyk had himself encouraged them to eat and drink their fill. It wasn't until after he left that he learned the supplies laid out for them consisted mainly of alcohol. Getting drunk wasn't going to help them stay calm.

At that moment, whoever had survived would be waiting anxiously on the island, wondering why they hadn't been collected. They would be facing starvation.

No doubt Rheibas would eventually send a team back—probably under Kahrlin—to finish off any survivors. Their bodies would be buried in the mass grave they had so helpfully dug for themselves. With no mercenaries left to claim their payment, it would be gathered together and returned to the chief minister.

Ingenious as the whole thing was, the sheer cynicism of it was breathtaking. The scale of the brutality was unusual, even for Rheibas.

Bolnyk had served Rheibas devotedly for years. Yet until his master turned on him, he never thought to question whether the man was worthy of such devotion. Recent events had answered the question emphatically.

Curiously, with all hope gone for any future of his own, he felt more calm and composed than he had for a very long time.

Abruptly it occurred to him to wonder again about the mysterious prisoner that Rheibas had shipped with him to Rogand. Who was he, and what did Rheibas want with him?

For that matter, where was he being hidden?

King Krasmir had aggressively hunted down many of the Ahran agents operating within his kingdom. Individuals continued to operate, but Krasmir had somehow succeeded in rooting out every Ahran base on Rogandan soil. How he had done it baffled Bolnyk, although it was no longer his concern.

It did mean that the prisoner was not likely to be located anywhere in Rogand. He might be confined on an island somewhere. It seemed unlikely though. Bolnyk had the impression that Rheibas wanted him close at hand. Why else would he have brought him aboard when he sailed from Kat Ahket?

The more he thought about it, the more likely it seemed that the man was locked away in the hold of that very ship.

With no longer anything to lose, Bolnyk headed for the hatch, hungry for answers.

27

Since displacing Bolnyk, Kahrlin had been spending a great deal of time with the chief minister. He could still scarcely believe how much of his day was spent sitting across from the second most powerful person in the empire. He had no doubt about one thing: power was intoxicating.

The ship that Rheibas used as a base was the scene of seemingly endless activity, with people and messages arriving and departing constantly. His private cabin was the central hub of it all.

The latest visitor was a servant. Handing a dispatch to the chief minister, the man bowed low and scurried away.

Rheibas watched his departing back thoughtfully before breaking open the seal and unrolling the parchment. As he read, his lips curled slowly into a satisfied smirk.

He glanced toward Kahrlin. "I understand that General Vholahr is anchored nearby with his squadron. He wishes to meet with me. Arrange a boat to take me to him."

Kahrlin got up and departed.

It wasn't difficult for the agent to guess what had prompted the general's communication. Nevertheless he didn't doubt that Rheibas would manage to appear suitably shocked when informed about the recent attack.

He knew that the chief minister had been avoiding contact with the general. It seemed that the time was finally right for them to meet. He didn't blame Rheibas for his aloofness. If he understood the situation correctly, the general was only there to provide support anyway.

He smiled to himself. The Rogandans must have thought they were so clever capturing three of the chief minister's ships. The unwitting fools had no idea they were furthering his purposes marvelously. They were clearly ill equipped to face an adversary like him.

No more than a couple of hours passed before Kahrlin delivered the chief minister to the general's ship. They boarded together, and Rheibas waved him forward, indicating he should remain to hear the conversation.

"Welcome to my ship, Chief Minister. You have proven difficult to track down."

"I can only apologize, General Vholahr! I have been much occupied of late. Three of my ships disappeared several days ago. I am at a loss to know what happened, but all the evidence points to the Rogandans. They apparently attacked and captured the ships and imprisoned the crews. For what purpose I cannot say."

"I can enlighten you as to their purpose," growled the general. "Two of the ships in my squadron recently suffered an unprovoked attack. That attack was carried out by Rogandans, and in three Ahran ships."

"You astonish me, General! My attempts to negotiate with the Rogandans and their allies have been frustrated at every turn. I have learned to expect nothing worthwhile from them. But as far as I know we are not at war. Such an attack is contemptible, even by their standards."

"I intend to ask the emperor to dispatch a credible force. Our current display is nothing more than a token."

"I urge you to show moderation, General! We must do everything in our power to avoid embroiling the empire in a war, especially one so far from home."

"May I remind you, Chief Minister, that I am not the one provoking a war!"

"I understand your frustration. I truly do! Perhaps there is a middle course."

"What do you suggest?"

"The emperor authorized ten ships. Perhaps he would be willing to release thirty more. A total of forty ships should be more than enough to show we cannot be trifled with. I doubt that too many others could be provisioned in any reasonable time frame anyway."

The general's eyebrows had gone up. "I was planning to request half that number. Nevertheless, in view of what has happened you have my support."

"Can I leave this matter in your hands, General? I have more than enough to occupy my attention already."

The general bowed stiffly. "Leave it to me. Now, please join me for refreshments, Chief Minister. I am eager to hear your assessment of the local situation."

A HOODED FIGURE stepped quietly up to the chief minister's empty cabin. His arrival was not met with a challenge of any kind.

Two guards normally stood at attention outside the door. That day they lay sprawled on the floor, sleeping soundly beside another guard.

The guards had not succumbed to weariness—they were incapacitated. Not long after Kahrlin had left with the chief minister, a fellow guard had brought them wine. An unexpected break from the constant demands of their master offered a perfect excuse for a small celebration, and all three settled down to enjoy themselves. None of them, including the guard who had brought the wineskins, were aware that the wine had been drugged.

After eyeing the motionless forms for a moment, the cloaked

figure stepped carefully over them, opened the door, and slipped inside the cabin.

Finding an unused parchment, the intruder brought it to the chief minister's desk. Dipping a quill into an exquisite ink pot, he scratched away patiently until words had almost filled the page. As soon as the ink was dry, he rolled up the document.

A candle stood at one side of the desk. Lighting it, he melted some wax and dribbled several large blobs across the edge of the rolled parchment. Finally, he wrote a single word on the outside of the document.

The visitor seemed to know where to find everything he needed. Retrieving a hidden key, he unlocked a drawer and removed the chief minister's official seal. After pressing the seal firmly onto the soft wax, he returned it to its hiding place. Then he tidied the desk, snuffed out the candle, and left the cabin.

Knowing that the guards would soon begin to stir, he stepped carefully over their prone figures and stole away as silently as he had come.

ONE OF THE many nameless servants of the chief minister scurried about his master's ship, looking for a particular agent. The man he sought was leaning over the rail staring at the horizon.

"This is for you," said the servant importantly, handing him a document bearing the seal of the chief minister.

"Why is it for me?" demanded the agent skeptically. "It isn't addressed to me."

The servant shrugged. "I was told to give it to Zhukha. That's you."

"Who told you that?"

"He didn't say who he was. But Kahrlin instructed him to give the document to you. It's sensitive. It's something His Eminence wants done urgently."

The agent eyed the servant loftily. "Kahrlin told me nothing about it. And he isn't here—he left with the chief minister a while ago. This isn't my responsibility. It can wait until they get back."

The servant shook his head obstinately. "I was told it has to be done now. His Eminence will not be happy if you ignore his orders."

"*Who* told you?" Zhukha repeated.

"I already said! I don't know!"

Rolling the document over in his hand, Zhukha fingered the seal absently. As he did, a barely legible word on one side caught his eye. Pulling it closer, he squinted at the writing. "It does have my name on it! But it's so badly smudged I can barely read it. You put your hand on the ink, you idiot!"

"I did not! It was like that already!" retorted the servant, hurrying away before the agent could say anything further.

Zhukha rolled his eyes. Then he turned his full attention to the parchment, ignoring the servant.

Breaking the seal, he unrolled the document and scrutinized its message carefully. The orders were simple enough. He was directed to two large crates in the hold and instructed to take them ashore. The destination was a deserted beach. It lay to the southeast, just beyond a headland with a large dead tree standing alone at the end of it. No one would be there to meet him. He should leave the boxes above the waterline. They would be collected later. He should destroy the document once the task was completed. When he returned to the ship he was to tell no one of the mission.

He hesitated for a moment when he saw that the document wasn't signed. It was, of course, sealed with the chief minister's seal. After a moment's thought, he realized he wouldn't know the chief minister's signature even if he saw it. He had no idea how His Eminence signed documents. Did he use one of his titles, or simply sign it with his name?

Zhukha shrugged. Most likely the chief minister didn't sign documents at all. The seal was signature enough.

Searching out the bosun, he requested a longboat and a crew, explaining that he had urgent business on behalf of the chief minister. Seeing uncertainty on the bosun's face, he allowed him a glimpse of the document and its seal. He was careful to conceal the contents.

The boat was duly prepared, and Zhukha led a group of sailors to the location of the crates in the hold. The crates were large and unusually heavy. It took four sailors to lug them onto the deck. Maneuvering them down into the longboat was a considerable achievement.

The beach referred to in the parchment proved to be considerably further away than Zhukha expected. Eventually the crates were manhandled ashore and left above the waterline as instructed. Several hours had passed by the time the boat returned to the ship.

HALF AN HOUR HAD PASSED since the crates came to a final halt and the last sounds ceased from the departing sailors. It was time to move. Reaching for a long metal tool, Bolnyk levered off the top of his crate and climbed out of it.

Moving to the other crate, he pried off its top as well.

"You can come out now. We're free, at least for the moment," said Bolnyk, speaking in Rogandan.

He handed over a bag. "I packed a few supplies. We need to leave. It's impossible to know how long we have before they'll begin chasing us."

The other man stretched uncomfortably. "I've been confined to small rooms for a very long time. I'm not too confident about my ability to walk long distances."

"Just do the best you can."

He nodded. "I suppose I should thank you for breaking me out. Except that he'll probably kill both of us if we're caught."

"I know how to shake off pursuers," growled Bolnyk. "Just stick to me." He studied his companion closely. "I still don't know who you are, or what the chief minister wants with you, but you can keep your little secrets, at least for the moment. You'd better be clear about one thing though. I'll kill you myself if you try to head off on your own."

The other man shrugged. "We may as well get going."

One final thing needed to be done before they left. Replacing the lids on the crates, Bolnyk used the metal tool to bash a large hole in each lid. After dragging the crates back into the water, both men piled rocks in through the holes until the crates were barely afloat. Bolnyk then towed them out into deeper water. Once the waves were lapping around his neck, he allowed the crates to fill with water and sink.

Returning to the shore, Bolnyk did his best to smooth away the drag marks. With the obvious traces of their location removed, they set off inland, moving as quickly as they were able.

THE LIGHT WAS FADING from the sky when Kahrlin finally returned to the ship with the chief minister. Rheibas did not immediately release Kahrlin. A number of pressing issues demanded attention, and the night was well advanced before either of them retired to their beds. Kahrlin was weary enough for sleep to claim him almost immediately.

He was awakened before dawn by a commotion. Instantly alert, he armed himself and threw on a nightgown. Pushing through the door, he headed for the chief minister's quarters. Two men had been stopped by the guards at the door. The men were extremely agitated, seemingly incapable of calming down.

Rheibas appeared and took in the scene. Ordering the entire group to follow him, he led them to the deck.

He faced the men. "Speak to me," he growled.

Both of the guards were trembling with fear. One of them began talking, but he wasn't even vaguely coherent.

Finally Rheibas lost his temper. "If one of you doesn't start talking sense, I'll have both of you tied to the mast and whipped senseless."

That got their attention. The second guard managed to calm down enough to make himself understood. "We were drugged, Your Eminence!"

The chief minister's eyes narrowed. "How were you drugged?"

The guard shifted nervously. "Someone brought us wine."

"So you were having a little celebration while you were on guard duty?"

Neither of the men spoke.

"And the man you were guarding?"

"W...when we came to, he was...gone."

Rheibas had gone deathly quiet, and Kahrlin saw that the blood had drained from his face.

"He is...GONE?!" The chief minister's voice might have been calm, but Kahrlin saw the rage in his eyes. "If he is not back by dawn, both of you will pay with your lives!"

He turned his back on the men. "Find Bolnyk and bring him here," he spat.

Although Rheibas had not specifically directed the order to him, Kahrlin set off at once in search of his predecessor. Whenever he saw agents he recognized, he pressed them into service.

He didn't return until they had searched the ship thoroughly.

"There is no sign of Bolnyk, Your Eminence."

The chief minister stood silently with his eyes half closed. He appeared to be struggling to master himself. Finally he spoke, addressing himself to Kahrlin. "Whatever happened here could not have been achieved without help. I want to know who was involved, and what they did. I don't care what it takes to extract the truth. I expect a full report in two hours."

Kahrlin hurried away. He knew what to do. The first fifteen minutes he spent among the crew—he told them enough to terrify anyone with something to hide. Then he sat down to wait.

The news raced through the ship like wildfire. When he deemed the time was ripe, he called people onto the deck in groups. Some of them were exhibiting obvious signs of anxiety. After extracting them, Kahrlin began applying pressure.

Within half an hour he knew about the drugged guards outside the chief minister's cabin as well as outside the prisoner's cell below decks. It took him another hour to find out about the parchment and the crates. He had to threaten to drag Zhukha in front of the chief minister before the agent was willing to reveal the contents of the parchment.

Before two hours had elapsed, Kahrlin had assembled everyone with even the vaguest role in what had taken place. Most, if not all of them, had been unwitting dupes, but he suspected that Rheibas wasn't likely to concern himself with fine distinctions.

As soon as he was able to piece together a full outline of what had happened, he reported to the chief minister. Rheibas regarded him with narrowed eyes as he spoke.

"Most of those involved did not understand the implications of their actions, Your Eminence," Kahrlin concluded. "Apart from Bolnyk, I've seen no clear evidence that anyone was intentionally disloyal."

"What actions have you taken?" demanded Rheibas.

"Since time was critical, I sent three boats filled with armed men to the place where the crates were delivered. They left as dawn was breaking. The men have been ordered to follow the fugitives."

The chief minister nodded tightly. "You have done well, Kahrlin."

He gazed darkly toward a group of men huddling restlessly off to one side of the deck. "Regardless of the final outcome, there will be consequences for what has happened today."

He turned to Kahrlin. "Take another boat and go after them. Do not..." He paused, frowning. "Do not fail me, Kahrlin," he finally growled.

Kahrlin set off the moment a boat was ready. He had sent Zhukha to direct the earlier party, but he knew roughly where to go, and he expected to find three longboats beached at the right location.

It took longer than he had hoped to find the beach. His boat soon joined the others drawn up on the sand. The crates were nowhere in sight.

Many footprints led away from the beach, and he followed them with his men. The tracks led up and over a series of low hills, then directly across a broad plain toward a stand of trees. A wide stream flowed beside the trees, and at that point the tracks became confused.

Wading along the stream, he eventually found a place where a large group had left the stream. Following the new tracks, they came to another stream. Another hour passed before any of his men found tracks again.

Leaving the stream, he set off again with his men. The tracks wound through the trees, eventually leading over another hill and down onto a new plain. A dense forest covered the plain.

Kahrlin came upon the earlier group of searchers just before he reached a broad river.

An agent he recognized saw him coming and moved to join him.

"We have men searching both sides of the river, but they haven't seen any sign of Bolnyk."

"How long have you been here?"

"A couple of hours." The agent shrugged. "It isn't surprising. Bolnyk is probably the best tracker we have."

"We don't *have* him!" spat Kahrlin. "He's working against us, not for us. We're *hunting* him! Enough talking—get back to your search."

After two more hours had passed with no sign of the fugitives' tracks, Kahrlin sent a couple of men ahead to scout. They returned within an hour.

"We crossed a series of streams," one of them told him. "Beyond that, the forest becomes almost impassable." He shook his head. "Bolnyk chose a perfect place to lose us. And he knows how to cover his tracks. There's no way we'll ever find him."

Kahrlin refused to accept it. As the sun was setting, he called the men together. "Build fires. We'll camp here overnight and carry on the search in the morning."

Reluctance showed on every face, but none of them argued.

The following day brought no better success. When the sun began to approach the western horizon, Kahrlin finally accepted that they were not going to find Bolnyk, or Rheibas's prisoner. The fugitives had gotten clean away.

Rheibas would be furious. Kahrlin remembered his final words. *"Do not...Do not fail me, Kahrlin."*

He had the impression that Rheibas had caught himself on the brink of saying something else. Had he been about to order Kahrlin not to return at all if he didn't come back with the fugitives?

He'd been the one who figured out what had happened, and he wasn't responsible for any of it. Rheibas surely wouldn't blame him. Would he?

Having taken Bolnyk's place at the chief minister's side with restless enthusiasm, Kahrlin had held nothing but contempt for his displaced rival. It now occurred to him to wonder if Bolnyk had actually been set free.

For the first time, he felt a tiny flash of envy for his predecessor.

28

____

One of King Krasmir's servants located Will as he sat in the gardens outside his rooms in the palace. He had been enjoying a relaxed conversation with Thomas and Brother Ander.

The servant addressed himself to Will. "King Krasmir wishes to meet with you urgently, My Lord." As if to emphasize the seriousness, he hurried away without waiting for a response.

Will exchanged an intrigued glance with the others. As he was getting up to go, the king himself appeared.

"Please pardon the intrusion, Lord Torbury," he said, sparing a nod for Thomas and Brother Ander. "I have received a request for an audience, and I would be glad if you would join me."

"I would be honored to do so, Your Majesty. Who is this man?"

"His name is Kahrlin. He claims to represent the Grand Vizier of Ahr."

Will's eyebrows went up in surprise. There must surely be a great deal to learn from someone with access to the Grand Vizier. A glance at Thomas suggested the possibilities were clear to him as well.

"Would you be willing to allow my companions to attend the interview, Your Majesty?"

After a moment's hesitation, the king shrugged. "I don't see why not. It can't hurt for Arvenon to be well represented."

The three men followed the king back into the palace.

It struck Will that the presence of Brother Ander had been especially fortuitous. Asking for his friends to be included was asking a lot, and he felt certain he had the monk to thank for the king's positive response.

There was no real reason for Brother Ander to be present at the coming interview of course. The person who needed to be there was Thomas. But the king had no awareness of the Stone of Knowing.

The king was, however, one of the few people aware of Brother Ander's role in the recovery of Bisri Ahuzza. The incident had only served to boost Brother Ander's already formidable reputation. Will had the feeling the king was eager to do anything he could to keep the monk close at hand, just in case his services might one day be required.

They settled themselves in one of the king's reception rooms, along with Lady Tulinay and Lord Kulferan. After a brief conversation about how to approach the interaction, the king issued instructions for Kahrlin to be admitted to the room.

Kahrlin entered the room, and offered a small bow. An aide to the king offered brief introductions, then left.

The agent didn't seem overawed by the situation, nor did he seem troubled by the frosty reception he encountered.

Will studied the stranger carefully before permitting himself a brief glance at Thomas. He was gratified to see his friend fully focused on the Ahran.

"You requested an audience on behalf of the Grand Vizier," the king observed coolly.

"Yes, Your Majesty. His Eminence wanted to make another attempt to reach an understanding with Rogand. He regrets your decision to take three of his ships by force. Using those vessels to carry out an unprovoked attack on two vessels of the Imperial Navy— on the high seas, and without a declaration of war—is a disappointing move that has prompted the emperor to strengthen his presence in the region."

Will exchanged bemused glances with the king and his nobles. Choosing to ignore their confusion, Kahrlin continued.

"We expect significant reinforcements any day. Once they arrive, the potential for escalation must surely increase. The Grand Vizier wishes to avoid any further deterioration in relations. He therefore proposes a summit conference with you as a matter of urgency."

He paused, surveying their faces. Then he added, "I understand you are still searching for three missing members of the royalty. He believes he might be in a position to provide information about them, should you be interested."

"We are open to any information you might care to offer," the king observed darkly.

"I regret that I am not privy to particulars. No one apart from the Grand Vizier is in a position to provide details."

The king was clearly unimpressed with this answer. He nevertheless responded diplomatically. "We will discuss the Grand Vizier's proposal. Should we wish to pursue a further meeting, we will need to know how to contact him. My aide will discuss practicalities with you as you leave."

With a cursory bow, Kahrlin left the room.

Animated conversation broke out the moment he was gone.

"What do you make of this purported attack on the emperor's ships?" asked the king, frowning.

Will didn't hesitate. "I suspect that when the Grand Vizier learned that we had taken three of his ships, he saw an opportunity. He used three of his own ships to launch an attack on the imperial navy, and blamed that attack on us."

The king looked dubious. "His own men attacked their countrymen?"

Will shook his head. "He would almost certainly have used mercenaries."

The notion made sense to Lady Tulinay. "A while ago I received persistent reports of people looking for mercenaries to hire," she said.

"It wasn't clear at the time who was doing the recruiting, or for what purpose. It seems we have our answer."

"The Grand Vizier is a devious man," offered Lord Kulferan, "if not quite as clever as he imagines."

"He is certainly devious," agreed Lady Tulinay. "There is some mystery surrounding these mercenaries. From all reports, they vanished entirely after signing up. I wonder what other purposes he is planning to use them for."

"He may not have plans for them at all," said Will. "He doesn't strike me as a man who likes loose ends. It wouldn't surprise me to discover he found a way to dispose of them after their raid on the emperor's navy."

Others were raising eyebrows, but Thomas inclined his head slightly, apparently confirming Will's guesses.

"I have a more immediate concern," said Lord Kulferan. "I was not aware that the emperor had naval ships close to our shores. If he is increasing that force, we need to urgently consider the possibility of an escalation into armed conflict, not least because the Grand Vizier seems intent on provoking a war for reasons known only to himself. Based on hints from both Princess Neira and Bisri Ahuzza, it seems unlikely that our navy is as strong as theirs. If they send enough ships, we may not be able to prevent them from landing a force."

"The key uncertainty is how many ships the emperor will send," offered Will. "We know he sent three ships with Bisri Ahuzza, but we have no way of knowing how many ships are currently in the region, nor how many more he will send in response to any request from the Grand Vizier."

Lady Tulinay responded quickly. "Our best intelligence suggests the emperor has no more desire for a war than we do. He will want to limit the size of any force he sends. It will also take time to fit out and send a fleet of any size."

Lord Kulferan shook his head impatiently. "All we can do is guess at the emperor's response, and we cannot base our preparations on guesswork. We must take measures to strengthen our army, and we must do it now! It will take time for the nobles to assemble and dispatch local levies."

"I sincerely hope you are right, My Lady," the king told Lady Tulinay. "Until we can be certain, it seems prudent to have too many troops on hand rather than too few."

He turned to his commander. "Do what you need to do, My Lord. You have my full support."

The meeting seemed almost at an end.

"Would either of you like to offer any thoughts?" the king asked Brother Ander and Thomas.

Both men shook their heads.

In spite of their response, Will didn't doubt that Thomas had a great deal to say, and he was impatient for the meeting to end.

As they were leaving the king's reception room, a man approached Will and handed him a dispatch. Will recognized the courier as Varasan. Without opening the document, Will returned with Thomas and Brother Ander to their rooms in the palace.

When the monk excused himself for a few minutes, Will seized his opportunity. "I'm eager to hear what you can tell me, Thomas. Let me read this message first, though, in case it needs urgent attention."

Opening the dispatch, he saw that it was a message from King Delmar. Since one of Delmar's agents had taken the place of Queen Essanda, it came as no surprise that the king was eager for any update on the search for her, King Rupert, and Princess Teylee.

Will threw it aside with a sigh as he settled into a chair. "It's from King Delmar. He wants to know if we've made any progress on finding the missing royals."

"I might be able to help with that," said Thomas.

Will surged to his feet, trying to contain his excitement. "So this Kahrlin knows their whereabouts?"

Thomas nodded. "They managed to jump into the sea as the Ahran ship was taking them from the island where they had been held. They returned to the same island."

Will grimaced, passing a hand across his face. "Do you mean that if we'd returned to the island ourselves, they would be free now?"

"So it seems," Thomas confirmed. "The Grand Vizier sent a ship back to find them. Kahrlin was in charge of the mission. After he had recaptured them, he deposited them on another island."

"Do you know where?"

"I have a general idea. The landmarks were clear in his mind."

"We have to alert King Krasmir immediately! We mustn't fail this time!"

Thomas looked alarmed. "The king will want to know how we discovered the location."

Will waved a hand dismissively. "I'll simply tell him I've just received the information from a confidential source. He saw that courier hand me a dispatch. He'll assume the Varasans have uncovered the location and passed it on."

"Will he know that the man is Varasan?"

"You can be sure the king knows everything that goes on in his palace!" Will found a parchment and a quill. "Describe the location as well as you can."

Writing swiftly, Will documented everything Thomas was able to tell him. "I need to get this to the king urgently. Is there anything else important you learned from the Ahran?"

"I learned a lot," Thomas assured him. "But nothing that can't wait until you've notified the king. The sooner he sends someone to the island, the better."

Will hurried away. After seeking an urgent meeting with King Krasmir, he passed on the news, handing over the information about the island's location.

The king did not hesitate. A fire had come to his eyes, and he hastened away to organize a force to be sent to the island.

With nothing useful to contribute to the operation, Will returned to find Thomas in conversation with the monk.

Brother Ander got to his feet as soon as Will walked in the door. "Would you like me to leave, Will?" he asked.

"Not at all! Please stay. You're as deeply invested as any of us."

The monk nodded and sat down again.

Something was bothering Thomas. The look on his face said he was feeling extremely uncomfortable.

"I hope you don't mind, Will, but I decided it was time Brother Ander knew about the Stone of Knowing."

After an initial wave of alarm had passed over him, Will shrugged. "Have you told him about the scroll?"

Thomas shook his head.

"Then it's time we did. I suspect we can trust him." Will gazed at Brother Ander with a wry smile.

Beginning at once, Will launched into a brief description of the scroll and what it had revealed about the three stones. Finally he retrieved the Stone of Authority and handed it to Brother Ander.

The monk shook his head in amazement. "A number of mysteries are starting to become clear." His face became serious. "You have given me a great deal to think about. One thing is clear to me: it is a great privilege, as well as a responsibility, to be the stewards of such resources. God must have placed these stones in our hands for a reason."

Will locked eyes with him. "I hardly need to say that we must keep the existence of all three stones a closely guarded secret. I am trusting you to honor that."

"Most certainly," Brother Ander replied, nodding slowly as if to emphasize his words. "Please be assured that I will never reveal the existence of any of these stones, or that you are their guardians."

With a grunt of satisfaction, Will turned back to Thomas. "What else did you learn from the Ahran?"

"He appears to be the Grand Vizier's senior agent right now. Bolnyk has been displaced, and he's gone missing, along with a mysterious prisoner that the Grand Vizier was holding."

Will's eyebrows had gone up. "Gone missing?"

"Yes. He found a way to leave the Grand Vizier's ship undetected. He went ashore."

"You mean he's wandering around somewhere in Rogand?"

"That's what Kahrlin believes. He led a large group of men on a man hunt. They never found Bolnyk."

Will was almost licking his lips. "I'd give a lot to get hold of that man! I have a score to settle with him."

"Bolnyk was involved in the attack on the imperial navy too," continued Thomas. "He led the operation."

"Is that why the Grand Vizier displaced him?" asked Brother Ander.

Thomas shook his head. "The attack was ordered by the Grand Vizier. Kahrlin hired the mercenaries and delivered them to a location where Bolnyk collected them for the raid."

Will's brows were furrowed. "Casting him aside is undoubtedly another example of the Grand Vizier's devious mind at work. Given that Bolnyk has been the key player in everything from the abductions to the recent naval attack, the Grand Vizier might have decided to shift the blame onto him. He could simply claim that his senior agent acted without his authority or knowledge, undermining his best attempts to negotiate."

"There's even a grain of truth in it," said Thomas. "The Grand Vizier might have taken full advantage of the capture of King Rupert and Princess Teylee, but we know that Bolnyk acted on his own initiative when he first took them."

"And it was Bolnyk who oversaw the drowning of Bisri Ahuzza," added Brother Ander.

"What you're saying is we have no hard evidence of the Grand Vizier's direct involvement," growled Will. "He's been very clever. It can't hurt to get access to Bolnyk though. Can you identify where he went ashore?"

"Only roughly. It was southeast of Rog, but I can't be too specific."

Will nodded. "It's a start. I'll speak to the king and Lord Kulferan. I'm sure they'll be willing to send patrols into the area."

KAHRLIN REPORTED to the chief minister's cabin as soon as he returned to his ship.

"Well?" demanded Rheibas.

"They seem willing to meet with you, Your Eminence."

"Who was present at this meeting?"

"King Krasmir, a noblewoman called Lady Tulinay, the head of his security, which I presume means his spy network, and Lord Kulferan, his army commander. No other Rogandans. There were three Arvenians present: Lord Torbury, the army commander, a Thomas Stablehand, and a monk, Brother Ander."

The chief minister cocked an eyebrow. "Did these last two contribute anything?"

"Nothing at all."

"The Arvenians have sunk low indeed if such men are representing them," snorted Rheibas.

He paused thoughtfully. To Kahrlin's eye, he had a gloating look on his face.

"Move the royal captives to a different island immediately," he ordered. "And don't allow them to get settled. I won't risk them being discovered a second time."

He stared coolly at Kahrlin. "If they've agreed to meet, I have preparation to do. You have your orders. You are dismissed!"

THE AHRAN GUARD could not decide whether to be gratified at being chosen or irritated at being left on the island by Kahrlin. The three royal captives had already been transferred to the ship and secured in the hold, and the final group of guards were waiting for Kahrlin in a longboat. Once they left, he would be alone on the island.

"You have enough supplies?" asked Kahrlin.

He nodded. "Yes. Buried out of sight."

"Are you confident you can remain hidden if anyone lands on this island?"

"Yes. There's a cave near the beach. I have hidden the entrance. No one will ever find it."

Kahrlin seemed satisfied. "Watch for ships throughout the

daylight hours. I want to know if anyone even passes by. Do you understand?"

He nodded again.

"Good. I'll expect a full briefing when you're collected in a few days."

The guard watched as Kahrlin climbed into the boat, returned to his ship, and sailed away.

The vessel slowly dwindled to nothing.

Settling down with a sigh and peering out across an empty sea, he commenced his lonely vigil.

UNDER FULL SAIL in a three-masted ship on a special mission for Lord Kulferan, Captain Bezai led a small squadron of two-masted Rogandan vessels in a search for the island where the captive Castelan king, Rogandan princess, and Arvenian queen were supposedly being held. With Commodore Pultek otherwise occupied, he had been granted the honor of leading this mission.

It had been impressed on him that speed was critical, and after Rogandan rescuers had previously missed out so narrowly on reaching the captives in time, he was not willing to wait for slower ships in his squadron.

Although his vessel soon outpaced the others, it didn't concern him. His ship had a full complement of soldiers, many of them capable archers.

The directions had been less than specific. He knew the general vicinity, and he knew he needed to find a small island, positioned between two larger islands each with tall rocky peaks. With islands aplenty in the region, he had no alternative but to carry out a careful search. He was accordingly planning to order the other ships in his squadron to spread out once all of them arrived in the right area.

A protracted search proved unnecessary. His ship located the island surprisingly quickly. With no sign of Ahran vessels anywhere nearby, he put ashore several longboats filled with soldiers. They spread out over the island, searching thoroughly. In the end they found clear indications of recent habitation, including a number of buildings that had been hastily abandoned. They also dug up buried supplies. But they found no sign of people. Returning to the ship, their leader declared the island deserted.

Bezai had been instructed to return immediately if he found the island abandoned. He waited only until the rest of his squadron reached him, then he set sail once more for Rog.

29

Bisri Ahuzza stared moodily ahead as the island of Ahrchitani slowly came into view. The beating heart of the empire lay before him, dazzling in its glory. For the bisri, drawing close to it had always stirred pride, along with a deep sense of belonging. For the first time it felt strangely alien.

He wondered why he had never noticed the brooding menace of the mountain that overlooked the capital of Kat Ahket. Nothing remained of its towering peak except a jagged crater. The vista whispered of the frailty of humankind. If the mountain ever erupted again, no city dweller would be safe, from the emperor to the most wretched. The power of nature was a great leveler.

He allowed his eyes to be drawn lower, across the bustling harbor of Kat Ahket to the glittering palace that lay beyond it. He could only guess at what awaited him there.

Gharpin stood at his side. The former captain seemed unusually taciturn, and Ahuzza wondered what might be on his mind. Perhaps his thoughts were with his crew, every one of them lost at sea thanks to the sabotage instigated by the chief minister. So many men who would never return to their families.

Ahuzza's two guards were standing nearby. They at least had

survived. He had brought them because they had also witnessed the chief minister's treachery, and it was possible that the emperor might wish to question them.

A familiar voice broke across his thoughts. "What are you anticipating most, Bisri? The surprise and delight of the emperor at your unexpected return, or the consternation of the chief minister's people at your impossible escape from a watery grave?"

The question drew a grim smile from Ahuzza as he turned his attention to the speaker. "I'm more interested in their reaction when they discover that I've sailed to Kat Ahket with the infamous Shallam —one of King Krasmir's most capable agents."

"Hardly infamous. My goal is to be invisible, although I'm willing to settle for inconspicuous. In any event, I certainly won't be at your side when you meet the emperor."

Shallam's dry humor was one of many things Ahuzza appreciated about him. After risking his life climbing aboard Ahuzza's ship to warn him, the agent had played a key role in rescuing him from drowning. It was hardly surprising that the bisri was predisposed to like him. But Shallam had proven to be unexpectedly good company on the voyage to Kat Ahket, and Ahuzza had come to consider him a friend.

There was one question he had never put to Shallam. "I know your parents are responsible for your fluency in both Rogandan and Ahran. But how did you end up working for King Krasmir?"

Shallam smiled. "You want the truth? I found myself with a choice between working for King Krasmir or for Rheibas, your chief minister. What I knew about Rheibas made it an easy choice."

"It took me far too long to see the truth about Rheibas!"

"You shouldn't berate yourself. He's exceptionally good at hiding his true nature."

"He didn't manage to hide it from you!"

"That's because I think like a spy. Spies find ways to ferret out other people's secrets. You're a diplomat. You're more interested in finding ways of working with other people."

There might have been truth in what Shallam was saying, but

Ahuzza wasn't prepared to let himself off that easily. He would be approaching things very differently in future.

"Have you decided how to approach the palace?" Shallam asked. "Are you aiming for bold or subtle?"

"Subtle is much more my style. I also think I'll have a better chance of reaching there alive if no one recognizes me."

Shallam nodded approvingly. "I think you're wise. While you're there, I'll do my best to mingle with the crowd. With any luck I might learn something useful."

"What about me?" asked Gharpin. "We never decided whether I should go to the palace with you immediately or wait until you've made contact with the emperor."

"Now that we're almost there, I'm inclined to think you and my two guards should wait," Ahuzza replied. "All of us have important testimony that implicates the chief minister. It might be wise to avoid any possibility that we could be eliminated at one stroke. If my meeting with the emperor proceeds without incident, I will ask his permission to call for you all. I have no doubt that the emperor will be eager to hear what you have to say."

"That seems prudent," agreed Shallam.

Gharpin nodded his agreement.

As they drew closer to the harbor, Commodore Pultek approached. "Lord Torbury seems to have been right about sailing here in one of our newly acquired Ahran ships rather than my Rogandan-designed three-master. I admit I wasn't enthusiastic about exchanging vessels with Captain Bezai for this mission, but now I'm glad I did. We don't appear to have attracted any attention at all. I'll be taking no risks, though. I'll anchor in the bay rather than pulling in to one of the docks. I'll make a boat available for shore visits. Hopefully that will allow us to avoid attention, at least for a while."

Ahuzza and Shallam disappeared below to prepare for the trip. Ahuzza returned to the deck clad in an unremarkable cloak with a hood to hide his face. Shallam was similarly attired.

A boat was lowered, and after climbing down to it, they were rowed to the shore. Before returning to the ship, the sailors agreed to watch for a prearranged signal, and to send a boat whenever they received it.

The men knew that the quickest way to the palace would be to hire a carriage. However, to avoid drawing attention to themselves they set off walking instead. With the morning not yet spent, they felt they could afford the time.

"How are you planning to arrange an audience with the emperor?" asked Shallam as their destination drew closer.

"I made some preparations before we left the ship," Ahuzza replied. "I'll need your help though."

"Whatever you need," Shallam assured him.

Ahuzza retrieved a parchment from his robe. "This document states that the imperial envoy, Bisri Ahuzza, urgently requests a private audience with the emperor. You'll need to give it to a particular servant. I can tell you his name and how to locate him."

"What about a reply?" asked Shallam.

"You'll need to wait for it. It could take hours, depending on how busy the servant is. The timing of the interview will depend on the emperor's schedule. I imagine that His Majesty has been told I was lost at sea though, so I expect my message will get his attention. I'll be surprised if I need to wait long for an audience."

After sending Shallam away with detailed instructions, Ahuzza settled down to wait.

The afternoon dragged away with no sign of his friend returning, and Ahuzza began to wonder if something had gone wrong. Becoming ever more restless, he decided he would go to the palace to investigate if the sun set before Shallam appeared.

Ahuzza was still hesitating well after the sun sank below the horizon. Unsettled as he was, he knew that leaving the agreed location meant that Shallam would not be able to find him. He briefly contemplated hiring someone to search on his behalf, but the risks were too great to ignore.

In the end he acknowledged that the only sensible course was to continue waiting.

Several hours of darkness had gone by before Shallam eventually returned.

"What happened?" demanded the bisri, trying unsuccessfully to master his agitation.

"It didn't take long to find the servant," Shallam replied, "but he didn't seem in any hurry. He questioned me closely about who I was, and especially why you didn't deliver the message yourself if you were present in the city."

"What did you tell him?"

"What we agreed. That I was your servant, and that you were keeping out of sight due to the sensitive nature of your business. But he'd never seen me before, and I think I roused his suspicions. He asked me a lot of questions."

"What did you do?"

"I answered them. I didn't see I had any choice."

"Do you think he realized you weren't who you were claiming to be?"

Shallam grinned. "I doubt it. I like to think I'm good at what I do. When he eventually decided to give up the questioning, he left without telling me what he was going to do or how long it would take. He only returned two hours ago."

"Two hours ago! Why did it take you so long to get here?"

"It quickly became obvious that I was being followed, so I decided to provide them with some exercise. Once I was confident I'd shaken them, I returned here. I don't think it would be wise to remain here though. It would be safer to return to the ship. I can tell you the outcome while we're signaling the boat."

Ahuzza made to head for the road.

"Not that way!" Shallam called softly. "Follow me! I suspect I know the back alleys of this city as well as you know the major roads."

Even with Shallam wanting to be followed, Ahuzza barely managed to keep up with him. It wasn't difficult to see how the agent had succeeded in losing his pursuers. Shallam wended his way rapidly through streets and alleys, keeping out of sight and avoiding anyone loitering suspiciously in the dark.

Arriving breathless at the designated location on the shore, Ahuzza saw that Shallam had somehow acquired a burning torch. After he had waved the agreed signal, they settled down to wait.

By then, Ahuzza was almost bursting with impatience. "Do I have an audience with the emperor?" he demanded.

"You do," confirmed the agent. "Although it's with the imperial crown prince rather than the emperor."

"Why?" He could make no sense of it. Why wouldn't the emperor want to speak with him?

Shallam could only shrug. "He didn't say. You have an audience the day after tomorrow at noon."

"The day after tomorrow? My note said it was urgent!"

Shallam gave the bisri a wry smile before looking away. "I have a feeling it's going to be a long two days," he muttered.

ARRIVING at the palace at the appointed time, Bisri Ahuzza was ushered into the emperor's reception room. His request for a private audience had been honored, although it was indeed Crown Prince Ahreitas who greeted him rather than the emperor.

"Bisri Ahuzza! Welcome! I am most gratified to see that reports of your death were exaggerated."

"Thank you, Your Imperial Highness," the bisri replied, bowing low. "I am grateful to be received by you. I trust that His Imperial Majesty is not unwell."

"Ah, so you are not aware," the crown prince replied. "Rheibas requested reinforcements. His negotiations with the Rogandans have apparently stalled. My father decided to do more than simply dispatch the requested soldiers—he sailed with them. He is deter-mined to find out what is going so badly wrong. He appointed me regent in his absence."

The news filled Ahuzza with alarm. "I fear for His Majesty's safe-ty!" he exclaimed.

The crown prince frowned. "You believe the Rogandans will try to harm him? I have no doubt he will be well protected by his men."

"No, Your Highness. My concern lies solely with the intentions of the chief minister."

"Be careful what you say, Bisri," growled the crown prince. "It is no small matter to slander the chief minister of the empire!"

"This is not slander, Your Highness!" retorted Ahuzza. "After appointing me as his envoy, the emperor sent me to make independent contact with the Rogandans. In doing so I was able to uncover what the chief minister has been doing there. To prevent me from reporting back to the emperor, he ordered my execution, on the pretext that the emperor had found me guilty of treason! My rescuers barely reached me in time. I was fortunate to survive."

"You were present when the chief minister ordered your execution?"

"I did not personally witness him giving the order," Ahuzza admitted. "The accusation against me was delivered by Bolnyk, the chief minister's senior agent. His men restrained me while he knotted an anchor rope around my neck and threw me overboard with the anchor. The chief minister might not have been directly involved, but Bolnyk only ever carries out the wishes of his master."

The crown prince frowned. "I've never understood what possessed Rheibas to drag Bolnyk from the gutter."

He considered Ahuzza gravely. "These are weighty charges, Bisri, and they must be properly investigated. I also wish to hear whatever you have learned in Rogand. All in good time. I have many responsibilities to attend to. While a formal inquiry is being set up, I will arrange accommodation for you. I will also ensure that you are properly guarded—purely for your own safety of course. You seem to have been making powerful enemies."

"But I must warn the emperor, Your Highness!"

The crown prince eyed him condescendingly. "My father's safety is not your concern, Ahuzza," he said haughtily. "His men are well able to ensure his security."

Calling for the imperial guards, he nodded toward Ahuzza.

"Escort the bisri to a secure apartment. Make sure that he is well provided for, but ensure that he remains safely under your protection until I notify you."

With that, the crown prince appeared to lose interest in the bisri entirely. Accompanied by his aides, he left the room without a backward glance.

Dismayed and downcast, Ahuzza allowed himself to be led away by the imperial guards. He wondered if he should have mentioned Gharpin, but he found it hard to imagine that the captain's testimony would have swayed the crown prince.

After a long delay, he was taken to a small palace apartment overlooking the city and ushered inside. The guards left with a promise of refreshments, locking the door behind them.

A brief inspection revealed that the apartment was comfortable, well appointed, and entirely self contained. It also confirmed that the door to the apartment provided the only access to the room. The outer wall featured a single large window, its shutters thrown wide to reveal an impressive outlook across the city. Unfortunately the window was perched several stories above the ground, offering no opportunity for escape.

Ahuzza groaned in frustration. It was now apparent that he had sailed past the emperor without realizing it. If only they could have met at sea. The emperor had personally appointed Ahuzza—he surely would not have ignored the warnings of his own envoy.

As regent, Crown Prince Ahreitas should have taken the threat to his father more seriously. A new and deeply disturbing possibility now occurred to him. Why had the crown prince sidelined Ahuzza and dismissed his concerns? Was it possible he was in league with Rheibas? Or was he simply willing to benefit by turning a blind eye to Rheibas's treachery? It wouldn't be the first time an heir to the throne had become weary of waiting his turn.

In any event, there could be no doubt that the emperor was sailing into deadly peril. Worse, the men charged with protecting him would be looking in the wrong direction. Alert to any threat from the

Rogandans, they would see no reason to guard their master against his own people.

The more Ahuzza's mind churned through the possible scenarios, the more alarmed he became. But there was nothing he could do. He was a prisoner in all but name.

30

The first full day of Ahuzza's confinement dragged by with nothing more remarkable than a brief social call from a winged visitor. Flying into the room through the open window, a bird fluttered about for a few moments before flying out again.

The freedom of the bird provoked considerable envy from the bisri. Had he been fortunate enough to possess wings, he would have fled the room in an instant.

He thought about Shallam and Gharpin, and Pultek and the ship, hoping they hadn't encountered trouble while waiting to hear from him. If they had decided to wait, it was likely they wouldn't be going anywhere for a very long time.

If only he had a way of getting a message to them. There was nothing preventing them from setting out to warn the emperor. Gharpin's testimony needed to be heard no less than his own. But who could he trust with a message? He knew plenty of people in Kat Ahket, including a number who were worthy of his trust. None of them had any idea he was in the city though, and he had no way of reaching them even if they did.

He had slept poorly the previous night. It had nothing to do with the bed—his mind simply refused to quit. With the crown prince unwilling to take his concerns seriously, it wasn't clear to him who else might be in a position to safeguard the interests of the emperor. The sovereign's personal bodyguards were sworn to defend him with their lives, but how could they be effective without a proper awareness of the threats they were facing?

The more he thought about the emperor sailing off in support of Rheibas, the more it alarmed him. The chief minister's agenda was a mystery, but two things were clear—his behavior was neither open nor transparent, and he was acting in his own interests, not in the interests of the emperor.

How far might Rheibas be willing to go? Was the life of the emperor at risk? In the absence of clear answers, Ahuzza could only guess. He was left with nothing to do but agonize helplessly.

Consequently, he waited until he was drooping with weariness before retiring for a second time. Closing the shutters, he lay down and waited for exhaustion to claim him. It was not until the early hours of the morning that he succumbed at last.

The release of sleep came at a price. Caught up in the distorted reality of a dream, Ahuzza found himself afloat in the sea, not far from the ship that bore the emperor. Standing on deck, the emperor seemed unaware that the vessel was sailing directly toward a massive whirlpool. No one on board showed any awareness of the peril, the helmsman maintaining his course steadfastly until the ship was almost in the grip of the maelstrom.

Below them in the water, Ahuzza began swimming frantically in the direction of the ship, shouting at the top of his lungs in a desperate attempt to deliver a warning. His efforts proved futile. Along with the ship, he was swept into the whirlpool, spinning helplessly as he sank lower and lower into the vortex.

A giant crab suddenly surfaced beside the circling ship, tapping a claw rhythmically against the hull. Before he could make any sense of the bizarre experience, Ahuzza woke with a start. Someone was tapping on the shutters of his window.

Rising blearily from his bed, he stumbled to the window and

opened the shutters a crack. The tapping ceased abruptly, and he dimly glimpsed a dark figure hanging from a rope outside his window. He drew back in alarm. A hood covered the head of the intruder, but a voice he recognized said softly, "Is it safe to come in?"

After staring wide-eyed for a moment, he grasped the rope and swung the interloper into the room. "What are you doing here, Shallam?" he breathed incredulously as the agent released the rope and removed his hood.

"I came to find out what your situation was," the agent replied quietly, a smile on his face. "It occurred to me you might not want to remain stuck in here."

"You certainly got that right!" Ahuzza assured him. "How do you propose to get me out though? There are guards stationed permanently outside the door."

"Are you any good with ropes?" asked Shallam calmly.

Seeing the astonishment on Ahuzza's face, he added, "It's only five floors to the ground. I'm confident you can manage the descent."

After hesitating for a long moment, Ahuzza nodded reluctantly. "I'll try. Being stranded here indefinitely is not something I'm willing to consider. Not for any reason."

"I'll show you how to do it," Shallam assured him. "I'll make sure you've got it right before I let you attempt a descent."

First he instructed Ahuzza to put on a sturdy cloak. "You'll need that to avoid rope burn," he said. Then he handed him a thick pair of gloves and told him to put them on.

Pulling in plenty of slack, Shallam ran the rope between his legs, pulling it around his left leg and up over his right shoulder. Running it across the back of his neck, he brought it under his left arm, stretching out his arm to grasp it firmly below his waist. Then he reached up with his right hand and grasped the rope at head height.

"You'll use your left hand to control the speed of your descent," he said. "When you relax your grip on the rope, it will slide through your hand and you'll slide downward. Place your feet on the wall of the building and allow your body to lean outward. Then push away from the wall with your feet and slide down a short distance before letting your feet come back onto the wall again. It works best if you use a hopping motion. You simply repeat that until you reach the ground. When you want to descend, your left hand should be away from your body. To stop, draw your left hand across your body and grasp the rope tightly."

Shallam stepped out of the rope and helped Ahuzza wrap it around his own body in the correct way. Then he repeated his instructions.

"Do you understand?" he asked.

Ahuzza nodded. He pointed to a second rope hanging outside the window. "What's that for?"

"That rope is for me," Shallam told him, reaching for it. "I'll be descending beside you. If you need help, I'll be right there."

Once he was satisfied that they were both ready, Shallam stepped onto the window sill. "Don't look down!" he warned Ahuzza. "Focus on the wall in front of you." Then with a little hop, he lowered himself a short distance.

As Ahuzza took his place on the window sill, he broke out in a cold sweat. With his hands suddenly clammy, he was grateful for the gloves. He stood trembling for a couple of long minutes, hanging out over the void.

"You can do it!" whispered Shallam.

With a little hop, Ahuzza lowered himself a tiny distance. To his amazement, it worked. Repeating the movement, he landed beside Shallam.

"The rope is starting to burn my shoulder," he whispered, grimacing.

"The best way to end that is to reach the bottom," the agent told him, hopping downward a little further.

Ignoring the discomfort, Ahuzza followed him down. The descent was going surprisingly well until they reached a shuttered window on the floor below.

"We need a bigger hop this time," Shallam whispered, nodding his head toward the window below. "If we land on the shutters, it might wake whoever's in that room."

He demonstrated by lowering himself the entire length of the window in one smooth motion.

Ahuzza's attempt at the same maneuver yielded a very different outcome. Managing to descend just half the distance, he landed on the shutters with the whole weight of his body. The noise sounded deafening in the stillness. Remarkably, the shutters remained closed. Ahuzza hung there helplessly, barely able to control his shaking.

"Once more!" Shallam urged.

Closing his eyes, Ahuzza forced himself to do another hop. This time he cleared the shutters.

"Well done!" whispered Shallam. "Let's not wait around to see if that room was occupied." So saying, he hopped downward once more, resting while he waited for the bisri.

The rest of the descent felt to Ahuzza like a waking nightmare. Somehow both of them reached the ground in safety. Incredibly, no one appeared to have been roused in the process. Leaving the ropes, Shallam led them to the shelter of some trees nearby.

"Wait here," he said. "There's a simple way to get onto the roof where I tied the ropes. I'll climb up and untie them."

After he had reached the ground, Ahuzza's limbs had begun shaking uncontrollably. He sat down in an attempt to master his trembling, watching distractedly as the agent disappeared once more on his way back up to the top of the building.

After a few minutes, he untied the ropes and they fell to the ground. Climbing back down from the roof, Shallam retrieved the ropes. Coiling them swiftly, he put one over each shoulder.

By then Ahuzza felt able to move. Setting off after Shallam, he wound his way back through the darkened streets of the city. They reached the shore without incident. Signaling the ship, they settled down to wait for a boat to arrive.

Less than two hours passed from the time Shallam arrived at Ahuzza's window to the moment Commodore Pultek and Gharpin welcomed them aboard.

"When can we leave?" the bisri asked, waiting impatiently for Shallam to translate the question for Pultek.

"The tide should turn in about an hour," Pultek replied. "I expect we can be well clear of the bay before dawn." His brows furrowed. "Not a moment too soon, either. We were beginning to attract attention. Just before sunset I spotted a couple of port officials pointing in our direction. I don't think we could have avoided a visit if we were still here at sunrise."

Pultek excused himself to oversee preparations for their departure. As soon as they were underway, Ahuzza, Shallam, and Gharpin joined the commodore in his cabin.

Pressure had slowly been building inside the bisri since his escape from the palace, and now the dam burst at last. Everything poured out—his conversation with the crown prince, the decision to confine him under guard, his frustration about being denied an opportunity to warn the emperor.

Apart from Shallam's translation for the benefit of Pultek, all of them listened in silence, and when he came to an end, they politely gave him time to recover himself.

Needing to deflect attention elsewhere, Ahuzza asked Shallam, "How did you find me?"

"It took a while. It cost me some coin too. But eventually I was able to discover exactly where you were being held. Getting you out proved a lot easier than I feared. You did well with the rope." Seeing the look on Ahuzza's face, he chuckled. "I'll be happy to help you perfect your technique any time you like."

The bisri shuddered. "I won't be sorry if I never touch another rope again."

The agent jerked his head back in the direction of Kat Ahket. "It won't be too long before the guards discover you're missing. They'll be wondering how you managed to disappear without trace. I imagine the crown prince won't be too pleased."

"He certainly won't," said Ahuzza emphatically. After hesitating for a moment, he revealed his fears about the crown prince and his possible motives.

"We need to warn the emperor as a matter of urgency," he concluded. "How quickly can you get us back to Rogand?" he asked the commodore.

"This ship is fast, and while you were gone Captain Gharpin familiarized me with a few aspects of its design I was unfamiliar with," Pultek told him. "I also took the opportunity to drill my men. Bad weather aside, we'll be there sooner than you could possibly imagine."

Dawn found them plowing swiftly through a moderate swell, favorable winds filling their sails. Ahr-chitani had already dwindled to a tiny dot behind them.

The breeze whipped the hair from Bisri Ahuzza's face as he stood leaning against the rail, gazing at a horizon that revealed nothing apart from the endless wave crests rolling toward them.

A single question dominated his thoughts—would they reach the emperor in time?

31

Will sat in conference with King Krasmir and Lord Kulferan, waiting for Lady Tulinay to join them. The spy chief arrived breathless and unsettled.

"I have news—a lot of news! Most importantly, an Ahran fleet has been sighted!"

Lord Kulferan frowned. "How many ships?"

"The report came from a merchant, so it's difficult to be certain. He counted fifteen, but he was sure there were more."

"Where did he see them?" asked Will.

"About two days out from Rogand. They were heading in this direction. They didn't appear to be in a hurry."

"We could use some bad weather right now," Will muttered, shaking his head.

His own attempts at using the Stone of Authority to influence the weather had been far from encouraging. Not for the first time, he wished that Amyra had traveled with him to Rogand. If it came to an invasion, they would be forced to rely on more conventional methods to overcome the Ahrans.

A grim look had come over the king's face. "So the threatened reinforcements are almost here." He turned to his commander. "How advanced are your preparations?"

Lord Kulferan was already on his feet, anxious to leave. "The first levies have arrived, Your Majesty. I have men searching out landing points that might be suitable for a large force." He shook his head. "There are far too many possible locations for the Ahrans to use. Before we can be confident of our defenses, there is a great deal that needs to be done."

"Go!" the king told him. "I won't be far behind you. I intend to notify the nobles within the hour."

The commander hurried away.

King Krasmir had turned to face Will. "Will Arvenon stand with us, Lord Torbury?"

The king's voice was calm, but with the moment of truth upon him at last, the tension in his face betrayed his uncertainty. Will wasn't surprised. Not many years had passed since Rogand invaded the neighboring kingdoms, inflicting great suffering and distress, and neither the king nor anyone else could magically undo the damage.

"Arvenon will stand with you, Your Majesty. Letting go of the past is difficult for many, but King Steffan understands what is at stake here."

The king was clearly relieved. "Please express my gratitude to your sovereign, My Lord."

Will bowed.

"You suggested there is other news," the king told Lady Tulinay.

"Yes!" the spy chief confirmed. "A patrol has brought in two men from the region where Bolnyk and his companion went missing."

Will's heart began to race at the prospect of confronting the man who had murdered his son.

"Do you think you would recognize Bolnyk if you saw him again?" Lady Tulinay asked Will.

He did not hesitate. "Most certainly!"

The king was eager to be gone. "Please find out if he has any useful information. We need any help we can get."

· · ·

THE DUNGEONS under the royal castle at Rog were largely vacant under King Krasmir. Nevertheless, guards stood alert as Will followed Lady Tulinay into an occupied section. She came to a halt before an iron door that offered a square viewing hole at eye level. Peering in, Will saw that the prisoner was Bolnyk.

Will glanced at Lady Tulinay. "It's him."

"You're certain?"

He nodded.

"Then I'll have him restrained. I didn't want to do it before we were confident of his identity."

She waved forward a group of guards. "We need to talk to the prisoner. Secure him!"

Unlocking the door, four guards went inside. Three of them stood watchfully by as the fourth attached leg irons to the prisoner's ankles. He did not resist.

The guards left the cell and stood aside to allow Will to enter. Lady Tulinay followed him in.

The appearance of the Ahran agent suggested he had been through hard times since last Will had seen him. His eyes seemed sunken, and his clothes were torn and ragged.

Bolnyk gazed at them indifferently for a moment, then a frown came to his face. "I know you," he said, eyeing Will.

Will stared back at him coldly. "I'm the man whose son you murdered."

The prisoner's eyes narrowed. "I was following orders."

"And you think that absolves you? You were the one who killed my son! Your Grand Vizier didn't do it!"

"It wasn't personal," Bolnyk returned indifferently.

An icy calm had settled over Will. Approaching the agent, he leaned forward aggressively until he was inches from Bolnyk's face. "Maybe I'll kill you now," he purred. "And just so there's no misunderstanding, it will certainly be personal."

Lady Tulinay apparently decided the time had come to intervene. Dragging Will back, she positioned herself between him and the prisoner. "Give me one reason why we shouldn't execute you."

"You want to bring down the chief minister. I'm the only one who can do that."

Will scoffed at the claim. "You're the only one who's going to be brought down! You've been very busy on your Grand Vizier's behalf, and he's going to blame you for all of it. He'll say you acted independently. It will be your word against his. It isn't hard to guess who the emperor's going to believe."

"Unless I provide proof," Bolnyk returned quietly.

Will glared at him. "What proof?"

The prisoner refused to say another word.

Glowering at him in frustration, Will berated himself for not bringing Thomas.

Lady Tulinay jostled Will from the room. As soon as they were out of earshot she rounded furiously on him. "What game do you think you were playing? You don't get to decide about his execution! If he is executed, it won't be purely to satisfy your need for revenge!"

Will glared back at her. "It's personal for me, and I won't pretend otherwise."

"Then in future you won't be going anywhere near him."

His fury abated as they walked away. As soon as he had mastered himself, she asked, "Do you think he has proof?"

Will snorted. "I doubt it. Notice he didn't actually say that he has! It's probably no more than a ploy. He's lived by deceit and manipulation—he wants to keep us hanging so we'll let him live for a while longer."

She didn't seem convinced. "If there's any truth to his claim, we can't afford to ignore it. There's far too much at stake. I'll explore it with him later." She glowered at Will. "Sometime when you're not around."

THOMAS SAT WITH BROTHER ANDER. Will had joined them as they were discussing the arrival of the emperor's ships. The news had spread rapidly through the palace, and the tension in the air was almost palpable.

"What do you think about the ships, Will?" Thomas asked anxiously.

Will waved a hand dismissively. "Bolnyk is being held in the dungeons right now! That's of much more interest to me."

Will's mind was clearly buzzing, and they eyed him uneasily as he paced restlessly back and forth.

"I need you to get a look at him, Thomas! I want to know if he has proof of the Grand Vizier's involvement, or if he's just lying."

Thomas nodded. "Of course. I'll go if you can arrange it."

The appearance of Bolnyk had clearly reawakened the trauma of Ethen's captivity. It was obvious that Will was not himself.

Will's intensity brought back uncomfortable memories for Thomas. No one but the Grand Vizier would benefit if he remained in this state. "You can't let Bolnyk get to you, Will! All of us are relying on you. We need you more than ever right now."

Will offered nothing more than a grunt in response.

"You're going to have to forgive him, Will," Brother Ander said calmly.

"Forgive him?! Never! He doesn't deserve it!"

The monk was not deterred. "No, he doesn't," he agreed. "I don't deserve forgiveness either. Not after some of the things I've done. But if God is willing to extend mercy to me, how can I do less to others?"

He paused, gazing at Will in concern. "Your anger will consume you if you don't let it go."

Will grunted again, although he seemed less agitated than before.

"You're right. Both of you," he conceded. "It isn't going to be easy, but I'll do my best to be calm and measured where Bolnyk is concerned." A wry smile came to his lips. "It isn't actually an option. Until I can manage to do that, Lady Tulinay isn't going to let me anywhere near him."

With the threat of war uppermost in every mind, it was clear to Will that access to Bolnyk would soon be viewed as a low priority. He wasted no time in meeting with Lady Tulinay.

"Have you learned anything useful from Bolnyk?" asked Will.

The spy chief scowled. "He has a few things to say—when it suits him. But he's short on details."

"Would you allow me to meet with him one more time?"

Her lips twisted in an ironic grin. "So you can carve him up into little pieces?"

"No. You can expect a different approach from me. I won't pretend my feelings have changed, and you'll never convince me he doesn't richly deserve anything I might do to him. But I'm no fool. None of us can afford the luxury of personal vendettas. Especially now. I'm willing to let King Krasmir decide whether and when Bolnyk's life should come to an end."

She eyed him suspiciously. "How do I know you're telling the truth?"

He sighed. "Because I make a habit of telling the truth. Ask anyone. You'll soon discover that I'm a man of my word."

"And where are these people who can vouch for you?"

"Arvenon, Castel, Varas," he said mildly. "Aen-irac, too, if you're looking for somewhere closer to home."

She scowled at him. "Your answers are about as useful as Bolnyk's."

Cocking an eyebrow, he gazed at her knowingly. "I'm not trying to be glib. I've heard reports of the spy network you oversee, Lady Tulinay. Even the Varasans and Castelans envy its reach! I know your agents have compiled a detailed profile on me. There's no point in denying it! The most cursory examination of that information will quickly confirm what I'm saying."

She rolled her eyes. "The report you refer to certainly exists, and you can be assured that I have studied it carefully. I might add that it also warns you're a smooth talker."

He executed a little bow.

"Why should I make it a priority for you to meet with Bolnyk again?" she demanded.

"I want to ask him some questions in the presence of my friend and countryman, Thomas Stablehand. The reason for including Thomas is that he is unusually adept at discerning falsehood and deceit. Bolnyk claims to have evidence that implicates the Grand Vizier. We need to know if there's anything worth pursuing, and we need to know now. We might not have a lot of time."

The spy chief was studying him closely through narrowed eyes. "Very well," she said finally. "Don't come armed. You'll be sitting across a table from Bolnyk. It will be a wide table. I will decide when the interview is over, but you can certainly expect it to end the moment personal feelings make an appearance."

"And what about the other man? Can we meet with him too?"

"No," she said flatly. "I'm letting you meet with Bolnyk because there's an outside chance he might prove useful. But we have a foreign army on our doorstep! I'm not setting up interviews for you with every prisoner that catches your fancy. There's no point anyway —he refuses to answer questions."

He wouldn't need to answer questions if Thomas was present in the room. But Will couldn't say that. In the face of her stubborn resistance, there was no point in pursuing it further.

He bowed. "You have my thanks, My Lady. I promise there will be no surprises from my end when we meet with Bolnyk."

* * *

Will led Thomas into a room dominated by a very large table. On one side of the table sat Lady Tulinay with an aide at her side. Across from her sat Bolnyk, his wrists chained and secured to the table.

"Lord Torbury," said the spy chief with a welcoming nod. "You have already met Bolnyk." She ignored Thomas, probably in a considerate attempt to preserve his anonymity.

Having been waved to seats located on the same side of the table as Lady Tulinay, Will and Thomas made themselves comfortable. Both of them immediately turned their full attention to Bolnyk.

Will addressed the agent. "Are you aware of the Grand Vizier's purpose in coming here?"

Bolnyk gazed back at him dispassionately. "Your question would be better directed to the man who escaped with me from the chief minister's ship."

"Who is he, and why was he being held captive? And how is he aware of the Grand Vizier's intentions?"

"If I knew the answers to any of those questions, I wouldn't need to direct you to him."

"You spoke of evidence of the Grand Vizier's duplicity. What is the nature of this evidence?"

"The evidence is for the eyes of the emperor alone."

"If you expect us to put you in front of the emperor you'll need to do better than that."

Bolnyk's mouth clamped shut.

Glancing at Thomas, Will saw his friend blink twice. By prior agreement, blinking twice meant that Bolnyk did indeed have evidence.

Will headed in a different direction. "What do you know of reinforcements from the emperor?"

Bolnyk offered no response. His body language made it clear they would get nothing further from him.

Aiming a grateful nod at Lady Tulinay, Will got to his feet and headed for the door, closely followed by Thomas.

The spy chief followed them outside.

"Well?" she asked.

"I am satisfied that he has evidence," Will told her. "That means his life is worth preserving, and it also means we need to find a way to get him in front of the emperor."

She eyed him curiously. "Why the sudden change in your attitude?"

Will shrugged. "When he first arrived I found it very hard to be objective. I'm sure that won't surprise you given our history."

"And what convinced you about the evidence? He didn't say a word about it."

"That's what convinced me. If he was lying to save his life, I would have expected him to have plenty to say."

She didn't seem satisfied. "Why say nothing, though? How does that benefit him?"

Thomas finally decided to help. "Perhaps he's conflicted. He's angry with the Grand Vizier, but even so, it can't be easy to turn against someone he's served for so long. Some part of him might still be hoping the Grand Vizier will decide it was a mistake to have cast him aside."

The spy chief was looking at Thomas as if she was noticing him for the first time. Thomas didn't seem to be enjoying the attention.

"Do you believe you can convince Bolnyk to work with us?" Will asked her.

She shrugged. "If your friend here is right, Bolnyk might never fully cooperate until it's obvious his master has abandoned him completely."

Will nodded. After thanking her once more for setting up the interview, he left with Thomas.

The moment they returned to their rooms, Will turned eagerly to Thomas.

"What did you discover?"

"I was shocked when I saw Bolnyk. He's a different man from the one I saw previously. The Grand Vizier's betrayal is something he never thought possible, and it's scarred him deeply. Some part of him is still hoping that things will return to normal, even though deep down he knows that isn't going to happen."

"If he's conflicted, he hasn't completely changed sides. We can't lose sight of who he is. He might be wounded, but he's still dangerous."

Thomas nodded. "He's capable of doing a lot of damage if given the chance."

"What about the former prisoner he escaped with?"

"Bolnyk was telling the truth. He doesn't know who the prisoner is, and he has no idea what the Grand Vizier wants with the man. The time they spent together after landing in Rogand left him none the wiser."

"Why did they escape together?"

"Bolnyk was entirely responsible for that. He wanted a simple and effective way to hit back at the Grand Vizier."

"And what about Bolnyk's evidence?"

"The evidence exists. It's a document."

"What's in it?"

"I can't be certain." Seeing Will's surprise, he added, "Bolnyk has handled a lot of documents over the years he's served the Grand Vizier, all of them written in Ahran. You're aware that I can't read. Even if I could, I don't understand Ahran. That means I can't make a lot of sense of Bolnyk's memories of the contents. I was able to identify which document is relevant, but it doesn't help."

Will threw up his hands in frustration.

"And there's another complication. Bolnyk thinks there might be a problem if he uses this document against the Grand Vizier. The problem is somehow connected with Princess Neira, but I can't tell you any more than that."

Will buried his head in his hands.

Thomas wasn't finished. "There's something else going on as well. It involves the priests of the dark gods, although I can't tell if the main contact is the Archprimus—the second in charge—or the High Priest himself."

"Why can't you tell?"

"The Ahrans have a title that means nothing to me, and that's how Bolnyk thinks about him. There have been meetings with priests, but they've always been hooded and unrecognizable."

"What's the purpose of the connection?"

"Bolnyk doesn't know. He believes there's some kind of power struggle going on within the priesthood, but he doesn't know what the priests want from the Grand Vizier."

"What's in it for the Grand Vizier?"

"Bolnyk has absolutely no idea."

32

———

Roused from sleep long before she was ready, Princess Teylee opened her eyes to find herself staring into the unyielding face of an Ahran guard.

"Get up!" he growled. "You're being moved!"

Throwing a small lump of hard bread at her feet, he turned on his heel and strode away.

A glance to one side showed her that her fellow captives had been woken as well.

Pulling herself to her feet, Tasha stretched uncomfortably. Her back was aching, but that was hardly surprising after another night sleeping on the ground.

"The early days of our captivity feel like a distant memory," she told Rupert wistfully.

He nodded. "Remember Dessue, the first guard in charge of us? He was impossibly benevolent, although I probably didn't see it that way at the time."

"It's been a continual downward slide since then," she agreed.

"They've come down especially hard on us since our escape," the pretend queen observed. "It seems they've been told to keep us alive and to keep their hands off us. Beyond that, they clearly have unlimited discretion to do as they see fit."

Tasha shrugged. "It wouldn't matter so much if they didn't keep changing our location."

Leaving them in one location for any length of time was apparently considered a security risk. The problem was that the guards had no interest in constantly building new shelters for the prisoners. If the prisoners wanted shelter, they had to build it themselves.

"Are we going to sleep under the stars again at the new location?" she asked, screwing up her nose.

"I imagine it will depend on the weather," Rupert replied.

Their companion gazed up at the sky. "We should be able to do it a while longer. At least until the rainy season starts."

"More delightful hours spent with the hard earth at my back," said Tasha with a sigh.

Rupert stared at the guards, busy preparing for another departure. "I wonder how much longer this will go on. They can't keep holding us forever."

Neither of the women responded. It was a topic they preferred not to dwell on.

He gazed at the Varasan agent. "What will you do if we never get to see the Grand Vizier?"

She shrugged. "One way or another I'll find him. And when I do I'll kill him."

"Why do you hate him so much?" he asked.

She gazed off into the distance without speaking. When she finally replied, her mouth was tight. "I had an Ahran father and a Varasan mother. We were living on the island of Ahr-shesan. There was a revolt there, and he came to put it down. My parents were good people. They'd done nothing wrong, and he well knew it. He had them executed anyway, along with five hundred others. He wanted to make a statement." After a pause, she added tersely, "I don't like to talk about it."

Her voice trailed off, and she continued staring at nothing.

Reaching out, Tasha placed a tentative hand on her shoulder. She couldn't find words. Maybe it was another subject better left alone.

Soon they were bustled into a boat and rowed to a ship. The guards didn't let up on them until they were locked in the hold without food or water or light.

The day was rapidly turning into one of those times when Tasha wondered if she could bear it for another minute. Closing her eyes, she released a shuddering sigh.

In response Rupert groped his way over and threw an arm around her shoulder, drawing her close. She gazed up at him in the darkness, appreciating afresh his warmth, his solidity, and his determination to win through in spite of everything. She had lived through the worst of times with him at her side. Always he had treated her with respect and consideration.

"We'll make it through this, and we'll do it together," he said determinedly.

"Together," she echoed, returning a tender smile she knew he couldn't see.

***

KAHRLIN FOUND himself summoned to Rheibas's cabin.

His master looked up from his desk when Kahrlin arrived. "Send a message to our contact among the priests. Tell him that the moment has arrived."

The agent bowed an acknowledgment.

Rheibas got to his feet and stretched himself to his full height. "The time has come to meet with Krasmir and his ragtag band. Are you prepared?"

"I am, Your Eminence."

"Are there any hindrances?"

"None that I am aware of."

"Then summon them to the meeting!"

The chief minister's lip peeled back to reveal his teeth. "It's time the Rogandans did some dancing, and to our tune."

WILL SAT in his usual seat conferring with King Krasmir, Lady Tulinay, and Lord Kulferan. The group had developed into an informal council of war, meeting early each morning before the main business of the day began.

The irony of his current role was not lost on Will, given his reputation as the architect of the Rogandan defeat in Agon's war. He guessed that his inclusion gave tangible expression to the alliance King Steffan had promised in the event of an attack. He also hoped that the king appreciated his strategic insights. Above all, he felt humbled by the trust the king placed in him.

What Krasmir's other nobles thought of his involvement was another matter entirely. He didn't know and had no desire to find out. That said, it wasn't hard to guess. The locals referred to Will as the Lash of the Devil—King Krasmir himself had told him as much.

His musing was interrupted by a servant who hurried in with a dispatch for the spy chief. She quickly scanned it.

"It's finally come. The Grand Vizier proposes that we follow through on the summit discussed with his senior agent Kahrlin. He points to the risks associated with any continuation of the 'current misunderstandings.' He urges us to meet with him as a matter of great urgency."

"Where does the snake propose to meet?" growled the king.

"On board his ship," she replied.

Lord Kulferan gave a mocking laugh. "We cannot possibly agree to that! It would pose an unacceptable risk. The man's history of treachery is far too well established."

The king was scowling. "We'd be doing his emperor a favor if we engaged in some treachery of our own and rid the world of him entirely."

Will nodded gravely. "Satisfying as that would be, Your Majesty, it might better serve the cause of international harmony if we let the emperor dispose of him—after we get the captives back. In the meantime, our own plans are in motion. They need time to come to full fruition."

The king sputtered, but he accepted the change in tone.

The others shot Will a grateful look.

Will had every sympathy for the king. He understood better than anyone the impact of a beloved child's abduction. Whenever the king's simmering anger threatened to bubble over, Will recognized the signs and worked deftly to steer the king in a more helpful direction.

There could be no doubt that King Krasmir understood perfectly well what Will was doing. Thus far at least he had tolerated it with good grace.

"We could provide a ship of our own," Lord Kulferan suggested.

"Or we could suggest a suitable location ashore," Lady Tulinay offered.

Will wasn't convinced. "Allowing them to land on Rogandan soil might be sending the wrong message."

The king grunted his agreement. "It took far too much effort to root out their previous footholds—I'm not letting them back in. Besides, I can't imagine them agreeing. For all they know we could have an army waiting over the hill."

"I believe a Varasan diplomatic vessel recently docked in Rog Harbor," observed Will. "As far as we're aware, the Ahrans still believe they abducted Queen Essanda rather than a Varasan impostor. From their perspective, that leaves Varas as the one kingdom in the region with no active grievance against them. In view of that, perhaps we could prevail upon the Varasans to offer their ship as a neutral location."

"A suggestion worth considering. Lady Tulinay, please explore it with the Varasans on my behalf."

As the meeting broke up, Will leaned toward the king. "I would like to propose that Brother Ander be present on board, Your Majesty."

The king frowned back at him. "You want him to attend the conference?" he asked in disbelief.

"Not at all. My request is prompted by his unusual healing gift. I see it as a precautionary measure to have him available."

"It's hard to believe that it might be necessary. But I will concede that the Grand Vizier is unpredictable. I suppose it is acceptable, provided he stays out of the way."

Will contented himself with a grateful nod.

The king was eyeing him shrewdly. "If I know you at all, Lord Torbury, your next request will be for Thomas Stablehand to be allowed to keep Brother Ander company."

"An excellent suggestion, Your Majesty! I'm glad you thought of it."

The king rolled his eyes, but he didn't seem to have strong objections to the notion.

So much about the Grand Vizier was unknown, and the pressing need for insight into his plans and motives made it crucial that Thomas was present with the Stone of Knowing. Not for the first time, Will had traded on the king's respect for Brother Ander to achieve the result they needed.

THE IMPERIAL ADMIRAL sought out the emperor. "We have reached Rogandan waters, Your Majesty. I am keeping our ships well away from land, as you instructed."

The emperor nodded gravely. "Search out the chief minister, and General Vholahr. I want their reports as a matter of urgency. Make the request in your name, not in mine."

"At once, Your Majesty."

The admiral withdrew with a bow and began rapidly issuing orders. Four ships soon separated from the fleet and set off in search of the other Ahrans.

Two full days passed before the admiral again appeared before the emperor. "I have received two dispatches, Your Majesty."

Taking the dispatches, the emperor opened and carefully scanned the first of them. He turned to the admiral. "General Vholahr acknowledges your arrival. There has been no further change in his situation. He will hold his squadron at its current location until he receives new orders."

The second dispatch appeared to be more consequential. "The chief minister is about to join a summit meeting with the Rogandans, and he urgently requests your presence," the emperor told the admiral. "I will join him at the indicated location. Bring three additional ships for close support. The rest can follow at a distance."

After hastily signaling the rest of the fleet, the admiral set a course for the location of the meeting.

BISRI AHUZZA WAS RESTING below decks when he received an invitation to join Commodore Pultek at the helm. Shallam was included in the invitation.

"My lookout has spotted a number of ships ahead. All of them have three masts. It is possible we have reached the emperor's fleet."

Barely able to contain his excitement, Ahuzza asked, "Can we contact them?"

"Of course," Pultek replied. "They might regard us as hostile when they find out who we are, though."

"I will speak to them," Ahuzza assured him.

The ships ahead were traveling slowly, and before long Pultek was able to reach them. A boat was lowered, and Ahuzza was rowed to the nearest ship. A net was lowered for him, and he climbed aboard.

Several soldiers surrounded him as soon as he stepped onto the deck.

"I am Bisri Ahuzza, envoy to the emperor," Ahuzza told them confidently. "I need to speak with your captain."

The soldiers appeared suspicious, but they nevertheless led him to the captain who was standing at the helm. Ahuzza thought he vaguely recognized the captain, but he couldn't be certain.

"I need to speak with you privately—on a matter of considerable urgency, Captain," the bisri told him.

After considering him for a moment, the captain nodded. "I know who you are, Bisri. Follow me." Setting off toward his cabin, he waved Ahuzza to his side.

As soon as they were alone, Ahuzza said, "I need to reach the emperor on a pressing matter. His Highness the Crown Prince informed me that the emperor had joined the fleet in sailing to Rogand. Can you please direct me to His Majesty urgently?"

It proved significant that the captain knew Ahuzza to be genuine. He said without hesitation, "Several ships have gone on ahead. The emperor is with the admiral on the flagship." He then described the location.

"Thank you, Captain! Please excuse me. I must do everything in my power to reach the emperor before his meeting."

None of the soldiers hindered Ahuzza as he climbed down to the boat. After being returned to the ship, he climbed aboard and gave the location to Commodore Pultek.

Soon the ship was plowing through the waves under full sail, racing for the emperor's destination.

Thus far everything had gone as well as it possibly could. The most important question remained. Would they reach the emperor in time?

33

____

The ship bearing the Grand Vizier of the Empire of Ahr and his senior agent sailed north before turning east. Avoiding the harbor at Rog, it sailed into a quiet bay nestled among the cliffs of a rugged coastline. Rheibas had agreed to the rendezvous location and also to the proposal that the Varasans host the conference. The conference vessel was sitting at anchor in the bay. No other ships were nearby, apart from a small Rogandan vessel anchored within signaling range.

After a boat was lowered, Rheibas and Kahrlin climbed down to it. By prior arrangement, once they were delivered to the conference vessel, the boat would return to their ship, and the ship would withdraw.

A rope net had been lowered for them, and Kahrlin climbed aboard the Varasan ship ahead of Rheibas. The four guards who followed offered no more than token security, but Kahrlin knew his master was not expecting to need protection.

They were offered a muted greeting once they reached the deck, then without further comment the Grand Vizier was ushered to a seat at a large table positioned in the middle of the main deck.

Kahrlin stared at the arrangement curiously. An ornate wooden table seemed out of place positioned in the middle of an open deck. He could only imagine the difficulty of maneuvering such a heavy item of furniture onto the ship. Nevertheless, with the vessel lying at anchor in the shelter of a quiet bay, the deck felt surprisingly steady, its gentle rocking barely noticeable.

The other delegates had already arrived. The man at the head of the table rose to his feet. "I am Lord Talmon. As the envoy of the Kingdom of Varas, I am your host today." He nodded toward each of the other seated participants. "Seated around the table are King Krasmir of Rogand, Lord Torbury of Arvenon, Lord Giddel of Castel, and the Grand Vizier of the Empire of Ahr. I believe the Grand Vizier proposed this summit. I will therefore offer him the opportunity to speak first."

As the Varasan's words were translated into Rogandan, Kahrlin scanned the audience. Most of the people present on the deck were not known to him. He was not surprised to see Lady Tulinay and Lord Kulferan hovering near their king. More interesting was the presence of Thomas Stablehand and Brother Ander, both of them at pains to stay in the background.

Rheibas did not immediately respond to Lord Talmon's invitation. He had been slowly surveying every person on the deck, by no means limiting himself to those seated at the table, and he clearly intended to complete his observations before saying anything. When he had finished, he glanced briefly at his senior agent, his eyebrows raised questioningly. Kahrlin responded with a tight nod.

Satisfied with the outcome, Rheibas directed his attention at last to the representatives of the local kingdoms. "I have informed you that the emperor has seen fit to increase the size of his force in this region. His action is in direct response to the unprovoked aggression directed at ships belonging to the imperial navy."

He paused, studying the faces opposite him. He received nothing in return except a stony silence.

Kahrlin was not surprised. The Rogandans and their allies had nothing to do with the attack on the Ahran navy ships, and none of them were stupid. They would undoubtedly have guessed that the attack had been staged by the Grand Vizier in retaliation for the Rogandans capturing three of his ships.

Kahrlin could only marvel once more at the masterful simplicity of Rheibas's counterstroke. If the chief minister's enemies had not fully appreciated his shrewdness before, perhaps they were beginning to grasp it now.

"Very little time remains to us to reach an understanding," Rheibas continued. "For my part, my sole desire is to see the honor of the empire upheld. Beyond that, I am willing to put the past behind me."

"What is it you want?" asked King Krasmir bluntly, his voice a growl.

"Let us begin instead with what you want," Rheibas replied boldly. "Am I right in supposing that the missing royals weigh most heavily on your minds?" He didn't wait for an answer. "Unfortunate as their absconding might be, I believe it is within my power to arrange their safe return."

King Krasmir's eyes narrowed. "And what would you be expecting in exchange?"

It was a key question, and Kahrlin didn't know the answer to it.

"My expectations are modest and reasonable. To begin with, the Princess Neira must be released from her current imprisonment. Once that is done, I wish to negotiate a trade agreement that places the empire on an equal footing with the kingdoms in this region. Beyond that, there are a few...minor matters I wish to explore with the Arvenian delegation."

Every face around the table wore a frown once his words were translated. It was clear to Kahrlin that they were not willing to trust a word he said.

King Krasmir was the first to respond. "If you wish to be taken seriously, release the hostages."

Rheibas sighed loudly. "I will try to be patient with your posturing. At best, any claim that I am holding hostages demonstrates a profound ignorance of me and of my intentions. At worst, it reveals an unjustified animosity that does not flatter you."

Even as he was speaking, a lookout called out a warning. "Four ships approaching! All bearing three masts!"

The Rogandan king was on his feet in an instant. "So you propose to attack us during a peace conference?" he bellowed. "Or are you hoping to take us hostage as well?"

"Please!" Rheibas replied calmly. "You misunderstand entirely. I no more expected ships to arrive than you did. It is most likely the vanguard of the reinforcements I warned you about."

The ships could now be seen from the deck, and Kahrlin soon saw that Rheibas was right. They were clearly of Ahran design. He worked hard at suppressing a smirk. The timing of their arrival could not have been more perfect.

Rheibas's words were translated, but if the others heard it, they gave no indication. The Rogandans had clustered together, flanked by Lord Torbury and the Varasan and Castelan envoys. Prompted by King Krasmir, the captain of the Varasan vessel began issuing orders frantically, and signals were sent to the smaller ship stationed nearby. That ship in turn seemed to be relaying the signals to other ships not visible from the deck.

Within minutes, other sails began to appear from the direction of Rog. A standoff between the Ahran and Rogandan navies appeared imminent.

In the midst of the confusion, Thomas Stablehand approached Lord Torbury and whispered in his ear. Torbury responded by speaking quietly but forcefully to his huddled allies. They slowly seemed to calm down. Glancing around, Kahrlin saw that Thomas had made himself inconspicuous once more.

Rheibas watched it all with an inscrutable smile.

A boat was launched from one of the newly arrived Ahran vessels. All eyes were upon it, and Kahrlin saw at once that the conference would not proceed until it reached them.

Throughout the excitement, Rheibas had been sitting calmly, an indulgent look on his face. He looked for all the world like a tolerant uncle, unruffled as he watched an unruly group of nephews and nieces run amok. He showed no apparent interest in the Ahran boat as it drew ever closer.

The boat disappeared from sight as it pulled in alongside the Varasan ship, but Kahrlin watched with great interest as a rope net was lowered over the side to allow its occupants to climb aboard. Two sailors appeared and were greeted by the Varasan envoy, Lord Talmon. After a brief conversation with the sailors, Lord Talmon called over King Krasmir, Lord Torbury, and Lord Giddel. The group huddled for a few minutes, then the sailors disappeared back down the rope. Their boat was soon being rowed away.

Not many minutes passed before another boat arrived alongside. Kahrlin watched with interest to see who would be joining them. He guessed it would be an Ahran admiral.

The first person to appear was an Ahran imperial guard. He was followed by the emperor himself.

Kahrlin looked on with mouth agape. Shooting a glance at Rheibas, he saw that his master had gone pale. He otherwise gave nothing away.

Lord Talmon greeted the emperor with great deference, as did the representatives of the other kingdoms.

The Grand Vizier had pushed himself to his feet the moment the emperor appeared. He now stooped low. "It is both unexpected and gratifying that you have chosen to join us, Your Imperial Majesty. Your august presence is a balm to our spirits, and access to your ineffable wisdom is more than we could have hoped for."

The emperor offered his chief minister no more than a curt nod before he took the offered seat.

"Thank you for coming so swiftly in response to our invitation, Your Imperial Majesty," said King Krasmir.

Another swift glance at Rheibas showed his eyes narrowed. The Rogandan king seemed to have taken him by surprise.

The emperor did not look happy. "Invitation or not, I needed little inducement to come, in spite of the hazards of the journey. It is beyond time I saw for myself what is going on here. Where is my daughter, King Krasmir, and why has she not been returned to her people?"

"It will give me great pleasure to reunite you with your daughter, Your Majesty," the Rogandan king replied. "For her own safety we were unwilling to entrust her to your Grand Vizier, given that he had previously left her to die on a remote island. I would only ask in return that you prevail upon him to release the people he has abducted and held captive. I am referring to my daughter, Princess Teylee, as well as King Rupert of Castel and Queen Essanda of Arvenon."

Rheibas bristled. "These are monstrous falsehoods, Your Majesty! I have already explained the true situation to you regarding your daughter. Her Highness was abducted from my ship by Rogandan pirates, almost certainly acting on behalf of their king." He aimed a poisonous glare in Krasmir's direction. "As for these so-called abductions, it is beneath me to involve myself in such atrocities. My understanding is that the princess and the king absconded, presumably for the purpose of eloping. I can hardly be held responsible for that. Nor is it my fault if the Arvenian queen later chose to visit her brother in their romantic hideaway."

The Rogandan king turned to the emperor, fury on his face. "This despicable attempt by Your Majesty's servant to explain away his provocative outrages does no credit to him, nor to the empire whose interests he claims to represent."

"Do you have proof of your assertions, King Krasmir?" the emperor asked calmly.

"We do," the king replied. He nodded to an aide, who disappeared below decks.

While he was gone, Krasmir continued. "I must also mention the son of Lord Torbury, who was abducted by Bolnyk, the Grand Vizier's senior agent. The boy was murdered at the hands of Bolnyk. Lord Torbury endured the horror of witnessing it personally."

As his words were being translated, the aide returned with a man in chains. Kahrlin recognized the new arrival at once. It was Bolnyk.

Rheibas seized the initiative. "I see that the Rogandans have

Bolnyk in their custody, and I can only express my delight that he has been apprehended. He deserves great censure for his behavior. In recent times it became evident to me that he was operating on his own initiative, carrying out actions I could never condone. The moment I discovered this, I removed him from any position of responsibility. Until recently he was being held on my ship, but he managed to escape while I was absent. He escaped using a letter he wrote in my name and stamped with my seal. He has done all of us a service by turning himself in to the Rogandans."

The emperor frowned at Bolnyk. "What do you have to say for yourself?" he demanded.

Bolnyk had been watching Rheibas closely. He appeared hesitant when he first arrived, but the chief minister's words seemed to have decided him. "For many years I have been acting as the chief minister's senior agent, Your Majesty. He placed me in that position in large measure because of my willingness to carry out his orders without question, however unprincipled those orders might be. I have done things in his service that would generally be regarded as contemptible. Murder is not the worst of them."

In spite of his admission, Bolnyk did not appear repentant. "It is true that I was responsible for the abduction of Lord Torbury's son," he continued. "I also later took advantage of an opportunity to abduct Princess Teylee and King Rupert. None of those abductions were carried out on the chief minister's orders. Far from disowning them though, he immediately proceeded to take full advantage of them. I murdered Lord Torbury's son on the explicit orders of the chief minister. As for the abduction of Queen Essanda, that was planned and carried out by the chief minister's new favorite, Kahrlin." He pointed an accusing finger at Kahrlin. "The operation was ordered by the chief minister. The chief minister also masterminded the attack by Rogandan mercenaries on three imperial navy ships. Kahrlin hired the mercenaries, and I led the attack, in the mistaken belief that we were attacking ships seized by the Rogandans. I called the attack off as soon as I realized the true situation."

The emperor was scowling at Bolnyk with barely controlled rage.

"And were you also responsible for abandoning my daughter on a deserted island?" he demanded.

"I was involved, Your Majesty, but I was following the orders of the chief minister. He invented the pirate story for the benefit of the Rogandans, and for the benefit of Your Majesty. He gave a different explanation to Princess Neira. Her Imperial Highness was told that she had been abandoned by Captain Gharpin without the knowledge of the chief minister. The chief minister is skilled at twisting the facts to suit his purposes."

Rheibas waved a hand contemptuously. "We are listening to the ravings of a dangerous and desperate man. By his own assessment he is unprincipled and contemptible. He admits to being a murderer and an abductor. Nothing he says can be believed."

He turned to Krasmir. "You appear to have embraced the fantasies peddled by this renegade. Has he offered you a single shred of proof?"

Almost as if the question was a signal, a Rogandan servant approached Bolnyk and pressed a parchment into his hand. Bolnyk's eyes went wide when he examined it.

"How did you come by this?" he demanded.

The servant offered no response, but his eyes flicked momentarily to Thomas Stablehand. Other eyes followed his glance, to the obvious discomfort of the Arvenian.

Bolnyk held the document out to the emperor, who hesitated for a moment before taking it.

He frowned when he read it. "This is stamped with your seal," he growled, staring at Rheibas.

"What is it?" Rheibas asked innocently.

The emperor scowled at him. "It is a letter from you to my daughter. It proves that you have lied to me!"

34

———

Kahrlin watched wide-eyed as the emperor waved the parchment in Rheibas's face. "This letter you wrote to the princess acknowledges that she was indeed abandoned on a deserted island, and it confirms Bolnyk's claim that you gave different explanations to different people. It also concedes that you lied to the Rogandans about the supposed pirate incident."

Rheibas glared at Bolnyk with narrowed eyes. He had gone pale with anger, but he didn't speak.

The emperor turned to Bolnyk. "The letter orders you to destroy it. Why did you choose to disobey those orders?"

Bolnyk shook his head. "I cannot explain my own behavior, Your Majesty. I initially intended to destroy it as soon as the princess had read it. When the time came, I hesitated. Something told me it might prove significant. So I hid it instead."

The emperor waved the document at Rheibas. "I demand an explanation!"

"The explanation is very simple, Your Majesty. This document that I supposedly authored is nothing more than a fabrication."

"It is stamped with your seal!"

Rheibas was not perturbed. "Bolnyk had access to my seal. He clearly wrote the letter in an attempt to implicate me. As I have already told you, he recently used the same trick to escape from my ship! After writing a letter in my name and sealing it with my seal, he hid himself in a crate. The letter ordered one of my men to transfer that crate to the shore. Witnesses on my ship can confirm these facts!"

He raised his hands heavenward in frustration. "Bolnyk claims I ordered him to destroy the document before you. By his own account he disobeyed a direct order to further his own interests. I have found such behavior to be consistent with his attitude. The man was once useful to me, and to the empire. In recent times he became dangerous and unreliable to the point where I was forced to stand him down." Rheibas shook his head regretfully.

"The truth about this document is more straightforward," he continued. "I have never seen it, but the details Your Majesty has revealed suggest it was written solely for the purpose of discrediting me."

The emperor had thrown up his hands in irritation. "What am I expected to believe?" he demanded.

As they had been speaking, another ship of Ahran design had appeared. After drawing alongside one of the imperial navy ships, presumably for the sake of communication, Kahrlin saw the new arrival separate itself and launch a boat. The boat was at that moment pulling in alongside the Varasan vessel hosting the summit.

Others noticed it too, one of them approaching the emperor and whispering in his ear. All conversation ceased while the gathering waited for the arrival of whoever was climbing the rope net.

<hr>

AHUZZA CLAMBERED onto the deck of the ship, his two guards and Captain Gharpin close behind him.

The first face Ahuzza recognized was that of the emperor. He at once bowed deeply. "Your Majesty!"

"You are welcome, Bisri Ahuzza!" the emperor exclaimed gladly. "I am gratified to see you alive and well."

Almost immediately the bisri noticed the chief minister sitting across from His Majesty. The sight of Rheibas openly engaged in conference with the emperor, free and unrestrained, filled the bisri with unease.

Rheibas had clearly been taken by surprise at Ahuzza's appearance, for all that he tried to mask it. As soon as he spotted Gharpin though, his face burned red. Distracted by the new arrivals, no one appeared to have noticed apart from Ahuzza.

Belatedly the bisri noticed Bolnyk—in chains, which brought Ahuzza at least some satisfaction. The agent was standing wide-eyed, staring at him as if he were seeing a ghost. Ahuzza snorted. His would-be murderer had good reason to be shocked.

"I see the man who tried to murder me and my guards has been apprehended," he said tightly, staring at Bolnyk.

Rheibas wasted no time responding. "We now have further confirmation of Bolnyk's treason from the lips of Bisri Ahuzza, a reliable witness. It seems the perfidy of my former associate runs deeper than I had imagined," he said grimly. "I sincerely regret having raised him from the gutter. He has not repaid the confidence I placed in him."

"He acted on your orders!" cried Ahuzza.

"Do you have evidence of that, Bisri, or did you simply assume it?" demanded Rheibas reasonably. "I know the answer, of course. No evidence exists, because I gave no such order."

The same reasoning had been used by the crown prince, and hearing it from the chief minister only heightened Ahuzza's frustration. He himself would never again be taken in by Rheibas's lies. Disappearing into the depths with an anchor tied around his neck had seen to that. But the emperor was the one who needed to be convinced.

Rheibas faced his sovereign. "Have I ever failed you before, Your Majesty? It is true that I have been unable to resolve the Rogandan crisis, but I hope the reasons are becoming clear. I have been undermined at every turn, and by a man who owed his position of power and privilege solely to me." He shook his head sadly.

Ahuzza was not impressed by the chief minister's attempts at deception, but he eyed his sovereign anxiously, not at all certain what he might be thinking.

The emperor did not immediately respond to Rheibas's assertions. "Who is this accompanying you, Bisri?" he asked with a frown, nodding toward the Ahran captain.

Gharpin bowed low. "I am Captain Gharpin, Your Majesty. I captained the ship that carried Her Highness Princess Neira from Kat Ahket."

The emperor's eyes went wide. "I have been told that you were lost at sea!"

"That is very close to the truth, Your Majesty. My ship went down in a storm after being sabotaged. When we took to the boats, we found that the timbers had been staved in. It was a miracle that I survived. Sadly, my crew were not so fortunate. I was washed ashore on a remote island and rescued there."

"Your ship was sabotaged, Captain? Who was responsible for such an outrage?" demanded the emperor.

Gharpin pointed to Rheibas. "The chief minister. His men inflicted the damage immediately before they transferred to another ship with their master."

"Ridiculous!" scoffed Rheibas. "What possible motive could I have for such a heinous act?"

Gharpin's face twisted with anger. "That question, at least, is easy to answer," he growled. "You wished to make certain that none of my crew lived to tell the emperor that you had abandoned his daughter and her personal guard to die on a remote island."

Heartened that Gharpin had at last found the ear of the emperor, Ahuzza aimed a glance at the chief minister.

In no way abashed, the chief minister waded immediately into the attack.

"By your own admission you oversaw the loss of one of the finest ships in the emperor's fleet, Gharpin. And you assure us that the ship went down with the loss of all hands. Such a disaster is unimaginable! We can only ask how it is that you survived, when every other life was lost? In my naivety, I believed that a captain put the safety of his crew ahead of his own." He glared at Gharpin. "The results of your negligence have been catastrophic, and yet you have the temerity to blame me for sabotage?"

Facing the emperor once more, Rheibas sighed deeply. "Although the honor of Your Majesty has suffered greatly due to a series of misdeeds, the perpetrators now stand before you." His finger flicked first to Bolnyk then to Gharpin. "Each of them is bent on shifting the blame, and it seems I have become their favored target. I am beginning to wonder if they are part of a conspiracy."

Ahuzza listened to his words with growing agitation. The emperor had been presented with Gharpin's testimony as well as his own, and undoubtedly King Krasmir and his allies had already made statements of their own, yet there was no clear sign that any of it had stuck. Was it possible that, in spite of all the evil he had instigated, Rheibas might yet slither away?

Glancing around, he saw that others shared his frustration. King Krasmir and his allies knew the truth, whatever lies Rheibas might spout. But they risked a war with the empire if they took matters into their own hands. The emperor needed an opportunity to reach his own conclusion.

"I am aware that Your Majesty has received wildly different accounts from different people," Rheibas continued, "accounts that are impossible to reconcile. Even though a great deal of slander has been directed at me, I am prepared to disregard it, knowing that such opinions were formed in ignorance of the true situation. To demonstrate that I bear no animosity, I would like to offer a gesture of goodwill. I believe that much of the misunderstanding with the Rogandans and their allies lies around the prolonged absence of the Rogandan princess, the Castelan king, and the Arvenian queen. I well understand the discomfort associated with their disappearance. I confess to similar discomfort in connection with our own Princess Neira. Having stumbled upon the location of their hideaway, I am in a unique position to restore the missing royals, and I propose to do so immediately. It need hardly be said that they could have returned home of their own accord at any time, but I will speak no more of that. I should forewarn you that they were not pleased about being extracted from their retreat against their will. I ask you to overlook that. I saw it as a necessary price for them to pay to bring this quarrel to an end."

It was a masterful performance. Even though Ahuzza understood the true character of the chief minister, it was hard to remain untouched by the force of his words, and the apparent sincerity with which they were expressed.

"What exactly are you proposing?" asked the emperor.

"If you will allow me, I will return to my ship to make arrangements for the three royals to be delivered here. King Krasmir has promised to return Princess Neira to the care of Your Majesty. If he delivers on his promise, all of us can return to this ship tomorrow afternoon for the handover. With those steps completed, it is my hope we can begin negotiations around less contentious matters, such as a mutual trade agreement."

"You are wasting your time protesting your innocence," Lord Torbury said coldly. "Nevertheless, you are right in suggesting that the return of the three missing royals is of primary concern to the allied kingdoms, just as the return of his daughter is, I am sure, the primary concern of the emperor. By all means let us settle those issues before addressing the matter of your duplicity."

Rheibas contented himself with an indulgent smile.

"You mentioned matters you wanted to explore with the Arvenian delegation," Torbury added. "What is the nature of those matters?"

"Perhaps you could join me as I return to my ship," suggested Rheibas. "That will give us an opportunity to discuss them freely."

"Why not discuss them here?" demanded Torbury.

"Are you afraid of me, Lord Torbury?" asked Rheibas mildly.

Torbury's reply was caustic. "You mistake me entirely. I do not fear you. But I will never be fool enough to trust you. You delude yourself if you think you can induce me to voluntarily place myself in your power."

"I think you underestimate us both, Lord Torbury. Nevertheless, I am willing to defer our discussions until tomorrow."

The emperor had not offered any clear indication of his position, and all eyes turned to him.

"The return of my daughter and the three other royals is a necessary precondition for any further discussion," he stated flatly. "I am willing to reconvene when that has taken place." Turning to Rheibas, he glared at him with narrowed eyes. "I must warn you that I am far from satisfied with the account you have given. I will make a final judgment tomorrow."

Lord Talmon bowed. "I pronounce this conference closed for today," he declared formally. "Thank you all for your participation."

It took time for boats to be summoned for the emperor and for Rheibas. While they were waiting, King Krasmir approached Bisri Ahuzza and Gharpin.

"You are welcome to remain with us if you wish," he said.

Both of them bowed when his words were translated. However Ahuzza shook his head. "Your offer is gracious, Your Majesty, but the emperor has invited us to join him on his ship. The captain and I are hoping for further opportunity to interact with him, and he has yet to hear the testimony of my guards."

"Of course," the king replied. "We are grateful to you all. The timing of your arrival was uncanny! I trust you did not encounter difficulties when you arrived in Kat Ahket. The emperor must have already left."

"I was detained by the crown prince," Ahuzza told him frankly. "Fortunately Shallam was able to extract me from the palace."

Krasmir lowered his voice. "Are you suggesting that the crown prince is implicated in the Grand Vizier's schemes?" he asked with a frown.

The bisri shrugged. "It is difficult to say. He said he was confining me for my own protection, and it's possible he was sincere." He paused. "A more immediate issue is occupying my mind. I set out to warn the emperor. He now has most of the facts at his disposal, but he has also been subjected to the full force of Rheibas's lies. Thankfully, he seems to have reservations about what Rheibas has told him. We will do what we can to help him see the truth."

"I wish you both good success," King Krasmir told them.

No further interaction took place between the various parties. Rheibas was rowed away, soon followed by the emperor. Ahuzza, Gharpin, and the bisri's two guards traveled with the emperor in his boat. Only after they had boarded his ship did Ahuzza allow himself to relax.

THE MOMENT the guests were being returned to their ships, Will took Thomas aside. He was barely able to contain his eagerness.

"You finally got your chance to see him, Thomas!" he hissed. "What did you learn?"

Thomas grimaced. "Almost nothing useful."

Will stared at him incredulously. "How is that possible?"

"I'll explain later," Thomas murmured uncomfortably, flicking his eyes back over Will's shoulder.

Will turned to see King Krasmir approaching.

The king looked grim. "The emperor has now been presented with the best evidence available, but he still hasn't made it clear where he stands."

"His position isn't entirely clear," agreed Will dryly. He shook his head. "Seeing the Grand Vizier in action was certainly enlightening. The man is devious beyond belief! Without doubt he's the most accomplished liar I have encountered. I shudder to think how many people he has trampled on to reach his current exalted position. I don't doubt he's proven useful to the emperor, but I wonder how well the emperor—who appears to be a reasonable person—understands him."

A snort sounded from Bolnyk who was standing nearby. "I served him for years, and even I don't understand him. I do know what he's capable of though. He's more than devious enough to conceal his true character from the emperor."

All of them fell to musing silently.

Will was the first to speak. "Whatever we have learned about him, we haven't answered the question that troubles me most: what is his agenda in all this maneuvering?"

Bolnyk had one final piece of advice. "That question should be directed to the person I brought from his ship. I've told you that already."

With that, the former agent turned away, making it plain that he had nothing further to say.

Will turned to Lady Tulinay. "I need to interview your other prisoner, as a matter of urgency. Please do not refuse me! He might hold the key to all of this."

"Very well," she replied. "I will write a letter for you to give the guards in the dungeon. If you leave now though, you might miss the start of tomorrow's conference. You might also miss the return of the hostages."

"I don't care," he assured her. "To me this seems more important."

"If you're returning to Rog," King Krasmir told him, "Lord Kulferan can accompany you and bring back Princess Neira. Commodore Pultek can take you as far as Rog. Captain Bezai is currently at Rog—he can bring you back. I will send a couple of other ships as well for security."

"Thank you, Your Majesty."

It wasn't difficult for Will to guess why the king wanted to send Pultek back to Rog. The commodore was currently commanding a ship seized from the Ahrans, and it made no sense to flaunt that fact in front of them.

"May I offer a suggestion?" Will asked, his face grim.

"By all means, Lord Torbury."

"It might be wise if everyone involved in this conference spends the night in another location. Somewhere very well guarded."

35

Will and Lord Kulferan were soon plowing through the waves on their way to Rog. Thomas and Brother Ander sailed with them.

As soon as an opportunity presented itself, Will called Thomas and Brother Ander to his side.

"Why weren't you able to learn anything useful, Thomas?"

Thomas winced. "The Grand Vizier is unlike anyone I have encountered. My worst nightmare cannot compare with a few minutes probing his thoughts and memories. I've never attempted anything so difficult or so taxing."

"But you must surely have discovered something!"

"Astonishingly little, I'm sorry to say. To begin with, the only language he understands is Ahran. He was thinking hard and drawing a lot on memories while responding to the accusations against him, but I didn't understand any of it. The same was true for his memories of spoken interactions. Images weren't hidden from me, but that's what made it so traumatic. His thoughts were filled with horrific images from his past—torture, brutal executions, and worse —most of them perpetrated directly or indirectly by him. He kept working them over and over in his mind, to the point where I couldn't bear to look. His mind truly is a cesspit."

"Did you get any idea at all of what he's up to?"

"Two things did emerge through the confusion. The first involves a prisoner. I suspect it's the man we're going to meet—as soon as I see him I'll know. The prisoner is at the very forefront of the Grand Vizier's mind, but I couldn't make any sense of why. The other thing was more of an impression than anything. He's planning something big—something to do with the conference. But I don't know exactly what."

Having set high hopes on Thomas's insights through the stone, Will couldn't help but be bitterly disappointed. Nevertheless, he held his peace. Although he held a stone himself that might seem almost limitless in its potential, his personal experience had featured frustrating limitations as often as great power.

In any event, a visit to the prisoner might well provide the answers they were seeking.

"What about the emperor?"

"He's a very different kind of person. He has his flaws, but for the most part he's straightforward and honorable."

That at least was something to celebrate.

DARKNESS FELL before they reached Rog, and the night was well advanced by the time they docked. They parted from Lord Kulferan after agreeing to return to the ship at dawn.

Late as the hour was, Will was not willing to delay the meeting with the prisoner even for a moment. Accordingly Thomas and Brother Ander trailed after him to the dungeons. Lady Tulinay's letter provided them the access she had promised, and a guard led them to the cell where the prisoner was being held.

"Can we go inside to talk with him?" asked Will.

The guard shrugged. "If you want to. He's shown no hint of violent tendencies."

Retrieving a large key, he unlocked the iron door and pushed it open before handing Will a burning torch. Then without a backward glance he returned to the meager comforts of his guard station.

Will pushed his way into the cell to find a bleary-eyed man of late middle-age stretched out upon a low bed. Thomas and the monk followed him in.

A brief glance at Thomas yielded a barely perceptible nod. So this was indeed the man on the mind of the Grand Vizier.

The man didn't get up from his bed. "Welcome," he said. "I don't often receive visitors, particularly at this time of night." He glanced at Thomas, eyed Brother Ander curiously, then turned his full attention to Will. The sword at Will's side briefly caught his eye, but he seemed fixated on his visitor's face. Will guessed his scarred visage was the reason.

"What brings you here at such an hour?" To Will the prisoner's cheerful tone seemed forced.

"I am Lord Torbury, and my companions are Thomas Stablehand and Brother Ander. We have some questions for you. The first is simple. Who are you?"

The prisoner couldn't seem to decide whether to be intrigued or terrified. When he finally spoke, he seemed surprisingly bold.

"I haven't heard of any of you. I am Rogandan by birth. I have lived most of my life in or around Rog, although a few years ago I made the mistake of traveling to Kat Ahket. I was eventually unfortunate enough to capture the attention of the Grand Vizier. He brought me here as a prisoner on his ship. A fellow prisoner decided to escape and brought me with him."

He waved a hand around his cell tragically. "As you can see, I have merely exchanged one jail for another. I am not entirely complaining, though. I prefer King Krasmir's dungeon over the finest cabin the Grand Vizier's ship has to offer." He paused. "I must say the food is only marginally better though."

"You have plenty to say," Will told him.

"I rarely have the pleasure of company," the prisoner replied. "The Grand Vizier refused to let anyone speak with me, and although I spent a lot of time with Bolnyk after we escaped, he was no conversationalist. When I first arrived I decided to hold my tongue, and since then none of King Krasmir's people have shown any interest in me. I've been starved of human contact." He gazed at Will thoughtfully. "You might look fierce, but I get a feeling none of you are especially vicious. So I decided to take a chance."

"You still haven't told us who you are," Will reminded him.

"No, I seem to be easily distracted. After being silent for so long, it's intoxicating to have an opportunity to speak." He sighed. "I'm still straying from the point, aren't I? Who am I? I've been many things, a mystic among them, but the truth is I'm a nobody. I do have the dubious distinction of being a nobody who briefly advised the late King Agon on the topic of living forever, if you can believe that. Unfortunately for me it happened to be a topic close to his heart."

Getting to his feet, he gave a little bow. "My name is Chalno."

<hr>

CHALNO LOOKED at the blank faces of his visitors and smiled.

"I see you have never heard of me. The tiny part of me that desires fame and recognition is tempted to be dismayed by that, but anonymity is a much more useful achievement, at least in my case."

"What does the Grand Vizier want with you?" asked Lord Scarface. He was clearly the one in charge. The other two hadn't uttered a word.

"Ah the Grand Vizier. I haven't been missing him in the slightest. He was my host for far too long." He sighed noisily. "I left Rogand just before the death of King Agon, may Malzakh gnaw his bones! I had good reason to get as far away from him as I could. My wanderings eventually led me to the empire, and in time I became acquainted with the sleaziest corners of Kat Ahket. I might have done a little too much boasting about some topics better left alone. Sadly for me, I caught the attention of the ravenous monster known as Rheibas—the Grand Vizier."

"What topics was he so interested in?"

Chalno shook his head, wagging a finger reprovingly. "Now, now,

My Lord. That is not a safe question to ask. Not safe for me, that is. You will learn nothing from me on that topic. Not unless you happen to possess the fabled Stone of Knowing, of course."

Laughing heartily at his own witticism, he failed at first to notice their faces. When he did, it filled him with dread.

"Surely not you as well!" The blood drained from his face. "That *is* what you're here about, *isn't* it?" he asked incredulously.

They gave no reply, but they didn't need to.

He shook his head in stubborn denial. "You won't get another word out of me. Even if you torture me! I already know how to endure torture, thanks to the Grand Vizier."

"You misunderstand us," asserted the nobleman. "We only want to know what the Grand Vizier is planning."

They were wasting their time. Climbing onto his bed, he curled into a protective ball, waiting for the blows to begin.

Nothing happened. Nothing at all. After a few minutes he dared to take a peek. The room was dark and empty. A moment later the guard appeared and locked his door.

He was alone once more.

THE MOMENT they were clear of the dungeon, Will turned to Thomas.

"Well?" he asked.

"Chalno has given us plenty to think about," Thomas replied. "He was overflowing with information."

Will sighed with relief.

"I'll try to give you the important pieces, although I'm still working to sort it all out in my mind."

"There's no hurry. We have until dawn," Will assured him.

Thomas returned a wry smile. "I guessed that none of us would be getting any sleep tonight."

He shrugged in resignation. "I might as well make a start. Apparently it all began when King Agon discovered a scroll among the effects of Lord Drettroth after his death. The scroll apparently outlined a ritual to buy unending life from the dark gods. The beneficiary had to be willing to pay, of course."

"What was the price?" asked Brother Ander curiously.

"Blood. For someone like Agon, rivers of it! Agon couldn't make sense of Drettroth's document, so he turned to a mystic for help. That mystic was Chalno. He tried to be clever with the king, and it nearly cost him his life. In the end he managed to convince Agon that he had unraveled the mysteries of the scroll, and even that he had performed the ritual and acquired unending life himself, although at a much more modest cost given his lowly estate. It was mostly bluff, although to this day he isn't sure whether the ritual had any effect or not. Agon left after Chalno explained to him what he needed to do to achieve the same result."

Will smiled grimly. "Agon didn't achieve unending life. I can personally vouch for that."

"Chalno wasn't willing to wait around for Agon to try it out. He realized he would never be safe in Rogand while Agon was alive, so he booked passage on a merchant ship. He eventually made his way to Kat Ahket. He arrived with no money and no understanding of the language. He eked out an existence telling stories in taverns to anyone who would listen—mostly merchants who understood a little Rogandan. Not surprisingly, his most impressive tale involved his consultations with the Rogandan king regarding unending life. As he told us, word of his stories eventually reached the Grand Vizier. That's where our problems began.

"Chalno later discovered that Rheibas, the Grand Vizier, had assembled an extensive collection of ancient documents from other lands. Collecting them and studying them used to be his favorite hobby—back in the days when he still had time for a hobby. He liked to read of ancient kings—how they became powerful and what brought them down. But he especially enjoyed imaginative tales. Rheibas knew about the scroll that talks about the stones. He'd somehow gotten hold of a copy and had it translated. He later told Chalno he didn't believe a word of it, but it fascinated him, and he never stopped imagining what his life would be like if he possessed the stones."

"It's no wonder Chalno caught his attention, with all his talk about King Agon and unending life," said Will.

"Exactly. Rheibas wanted Chalno's opinion on the scroll, so he gave him a Rogandan translation to read. By then Chalno had realized that Rheibas was at least as dangerous as Agon. He needed to give Rheibas something. He didn't want to talk about Drettroth's ritual, because he guessed Rheibas would want it enacted immediately. That might soon lead to him concluding that Chalno was a fraud. Rogand seemed a very long way away, so he talked instead about the great age of the High Priest at the Temple of the Dark Gods at Rog. He wondered aloud if the High Priest had the Stone of Vitality, or had perhaps discovered some other way of extending his life."

Will groaned. "So he got the Grand Vizier's hopes up."

Thomas nodded.

"How did they communicate?" asked Brother Ander. "Does he speak Ahran?"

Thomas grimaced. "At first Rheibas brought in an interpreter. After using his services, he confined him until the next time he was needed. Eventually he instructed him to teach Chalno the Ahran language. It took a long time, but Chalno eventually became reasonably fluent. By then he and the interpreter had become friends. Rheibas ordered the interpreter's execution, making sure it was done in front of Chalno. The result was predictable—Chalno became terrified of Rheibas."

The monk shook his head in dismay.

"After that Rheibas was able to speak with him in private. Their conversations were just the beginning. Rheibas sent agents to Rogand, and eventually to the other kingdoms as well. He began to hear tales about a commander able to inspire incredible devotion from his men—a commander who had never been defeated. He even heard about Lord Drettroth invading Arvenon so he could pursue a youth who had something he wanted.

"He questioned Chalno closely about these things. Chalno had the impression that he gradually came to the conclusion that the stones described by the scroll were not only real, but available to be seized by someone with sufficient determination and resources. After that he didn't meet with Chalno as often. But he kept him close, and refused to let anyone speak with him. He also threatened Chalno with dire consequences if he dared to speak to anyone."

"So the Grand Vizier is after the stones!" exclaimed Will.

Thomas nodded sadly. "It seems to be the reason behind everything he's done—his schemes, his infiltration, his abductions, his threats about war."

"He's been trying to flush out the stones," said Will. "And he's done an admirable job. He manufactured a threat significant enough to bring us into the open to counter it. He's probably guessed that I have the Stone of Authority, even if he's drawn that conclusion for the wrong reasons. And he won't find it hard to guess who has the Stone of Vitality once he hears of a monk who performs miraculous healings and even resurrections. Assuming he doesn't still think the High Priest has it. With that in mind, I'll tell Lord Kulferan I've heard vague whispers of a threat to the High Priest, and ask him to send a warning to the temple before we leave."

"I think I can guess why Rheibas filled his mind with horrific memories during the conference," said Thomas morosely. "He wanted to distract and confuse anyone with the Stone of Knowing who might be trying to read him. It also explains why Chalno was so much on his mind. He knew that everything he was doing would be exposed if someone with the Stone of Knowing got to Chalno."

Will frowned. "Why did he keep Chalno alive?"

"Chalno constantly asked himself the same question. He's quite skilled at sounding mysterious, and he worked hard to foster the idea that he had a unique ability to make sense of ancient scrolls. He also concluded that Rheibas wanted to be able to talk to someone about the stones. Apart from Chalno no one was safe."

"We can't tell the emperor any of this," said Will. "He wouldn't believe it anyway."

"No," agreed Thomas. "The emperor is a reasonable man. Probably a bit too reasonable to take any of this seriously, even if we were willing to expose the existence of the stones."

Will wasn't too dismayed. "At least we're no longer groping about in the dark," he said. "We understand what we're up against, the three of us in particular. We know that the Grand Vizier isn't going to stop until he gets the stones, and we know we can't let that happen, because the consequences are too terrible to contemplate."

"What can we do?" asked Thomas miserably.

Will shrugged. "We have until tomorrow afternoon. I'll think of something."

36

____

Thomas watched gloomily as Captain Bezai's ship drew closer to the Varasan vessel hosting the conference.

A tight knot had begun to twist his stomach. Heartening as it was to have the Grand Vizier's plans exposed at last, it had left him with nothing but apprehension about the future. Once more the Stone of Knowing threatened not only his peaceful existence but his life. He longed for Elena's calming presence, and he would have given a lot for the enthusiastic embrace of his children.

At least this time he faced the uncertainties of the future with Will and Brother Ander at his side.

Thomas had no idea what Will was thinking. The commander had been pensive and distracted throughout the return journey, leaning on the rail staring out to sea for much of the time. Brother Ander seemed his usual placid self, which meant he had very little to say.

"Why are there no servants to groom me appropriately?" demanded a petulant voice from across the deck. "I can't possibly be presented to my father with my hair like this!"

Princess Neira had been roused well before dawn to allow the ship to get underway when the sun rose. She had been moody and disagreeable ever since. Thomas knew her reaction to be little more than nerves—she had, after all, been separated from her father for months, enduring some truly harrowing circumstances during that time. It didn't make the strident edge to her voice any less grating.

Uman, her long-suffering personal guard, hovered at her side as ever, his face inscrutable. Being unable to speak, he offered no comment on her behavior.

Having reached the Varasan vessel, the sails were reefed and anchors released. A boat was lowered, and all of them climbed down to it. Before long they were scrambling up a rope net toward the deck of the Varasan ship.

The princess was first over the rail, closely followed by Uman. Thomas heard a squeal of joy, followed by the sound of the princess bursting into tears. He reached the deck in time to see her lose herself in her father's embrace.

Following the others to the side of King Krasmir, he was able to hear a translation of the emperor's interaction with the princess.

"My daughter! You are safe at last!"

"I have missed you so much, Father!" she managed. Having said it, she immediately dissolved into tears again.

The emperor gave her a few moments to recover herself, then he gently held her at arm's length, looking into her eyes. "I have been told you were left to die on a remote island, Neira. Is that true?"

For a long moment she hesitated. Bringing the stone into contact with his skin, Thomas witnessed the battle raging within her. Notwithstanding her lofty heritage, the princess felt small and insecure, of little value either to her father or to the empire. She harbored no doubts about what Rheibas wanted her to say. Absolving the Grand Vizier would place him in her debt, increasing her esteem in his eyes. The lure of such an outcome dazzled and enticed her.

At the same time, she despised him. The lower status of his birth predisposed her to look down on him, but she had also discovered from bitter personal experience that he was deceitful and dishonorable.

As she lingered, undecided, Uman gave her a sharp nudge. The reproachful expression on his face spoke as plainly as words.

His intervention seemed to decide her. A pout came to her lips. "It is true, Father. I survived only by a miracle. Rheibas is unusually skilled at deflecting blame, but he was the one responsible."

The emperor kissed her lightly on the forehead. "Good girl. Rheibas has been very useful to me for many years, and I would not cast him aside without good reason. Nevertheless, having been presented with all the evidence, I no longer have any doubt about the truth. But I wanted to hear it plainly from your own lips."

He turned to King Krasmir. "Thank you for keeping my daughter safe, Your Majesty. I am in your debt." It was the first time the emperor had addressed the king with such an honorific.

"It was both an honor and a pleasure, Your Majesty," returned the king, managing to keep any trace of irony from his tone.

"For now I will withdraw with my daughter," said the emperor. "Do not imagine I have forgotten the provocations of Rheibas though. I will deal decisively with him as soon as you have your daughter and her friends back."

With that he left, taking Princess Neira and her guard with him.

The moment they had gone, King Krasmir called Will, Thomas, and Brother Ander aside. A desolate look covered his face. "There's no good way to communicate this," he said. "Before the emperor arrived, we were visited by Kahrlin, the Grand Vizier's man. He said his master demands that I deliver the three of you to his ship for "negotiations", using force if necessary. He says one hostage will be released for each of you. He made it clear that if I refuse we will never see the hostages again. He also said that the Grand Vizier will kill them without hesitation if I try to involve the emperor."

The king regarded them with a haunted look in his eyes. "It need hardly be said that I refused his demands outright. Kahrlin said I would be offered one final chance. He would return in three hours for my decision. If his boat is empty when it reaches the Grand Vizier's ship, all three hostages will be executed immediately."

"I will go," said Brother Ander without hesitation. "I will appeal to him to release Princess Teylee in my place."

Thomas stared at the monk wide-eyed.

"It seems we have little choice," said Will grimly. "I will go too."

"This is madness!" protested the king. "What guarantee is there that he will release any of the hostages? What prevents him from simply adding you to his collection?"

When none of them replied, the king continued. "He has abandoned subtlety entirely, which surely means he is becoming desperate. He must be aware that the emperor is no longer deceived by his posturing. There is no telling what he is capable of."

Will nodded. "If he suspects the emperor is turning against him, he knows he's running out of options. He won't go quietly—he'll come up with a new strategy, and it might be one that doesn't require the hostages. We need to get them back while we still can."

His heart pounding, Thomas was struggling to breathe. Memories flooded into his mind. In Drettroth's fortress he'd been given an impossible choice between handing the stone to a madman or dying a horrible death. He'd chosen the costly path, and incredibly, he'd survived, but only because first Simon and then Brother Vangellis had willingly sacrificed their lives. Was it finally his turn to make the ultimate sacrifice?

By agreeing to go, his friends had backed him into a corner. Resisting the temptation to feel resentful, he acknowledged he could never live with himself if he shrank back out of fear and allowed them to go alone. As much as he questioned the Grand Vizier's sincerity about releasing the hostages, there was no way to be certain. He could not ignore a genuine opportunity just to save his own skin.

With a sigh of resignation, he made his choice. He and his friends would die together.

Knowing that the power of speech would abandon him if he didn't respond soon, he somehow ground out the words. "I will go."

The king covered his face with his hands. After a few moments he took a deep breath, then exhaled slowly. "I offered myself in place of my daughter," he told them frankly. "Kahrlin laughed at me." He threw up his hands in exasperation. "I don't understand what the Grand Vizier is hoping to achieve! Please pardon my bluntness, but I cannot see why he wants any of you. His current hostages give him vastly more leverage. And surely I am more valuable to him than my daughter!"

"He undoubtedly has his reasons," Will replied. "I imagine we'll find out soon enough what they are."

"I will call for the emperor to join me," cried the king. "Together we can easily overcome him!"

Will shook his head firmly. "You can't give him an excuse to follow through on his threat. As long as there's the faintest chance of the hostages being released, you must avoid even the appearance of provocation." His face became grim. "If you don't get the hostages back by sundown, destroy him without hesitation! Do not allow him any opportunity to escape!"

King Krasmir stared at them with haunted eyes. "So you are willingly going to your deaths?"

Will remained undaunted. "If there is a way to win free, we will find it. But if it costs our lives to end this, then so be it."

The king's face set hard. "I swear to you that I will not rest until every one of you has been released, or the Grand Vizier is dead!"

THOMAS STOOD TENSELY beside Will and Brother Ander as Kahrlin's longboat drew closer. Leaning toward Will in agitation, he exclaimed quietly, "Agreeing to go to Rheibas is one thing, but surely we can't take the stones with us! It's much too risky!"

Will shook his head. "Rheibas wants the stones, and we want the hostages. If we go without the stones, we'll have nothing to bargain with, and he'll have no further reason to keep the hostages alive. Besides, the stones might give us an edge, and we're going to need all the help we can get if we want to bring him down."

"But there are so many things that could go wrong!"

Will remained unmoved. "Don't forget that Rheibas has read the scroll. He knows that the stones will be useless to him if he takes them by force. He needs us to give them to him."

"We can't give him the stones for any reason!" protested Thomas.

Will gazed back at him calmly. "Of course not. If it comes to the worst, we'll throw them into the sea." He looked at them both. "Agreed?" he asked quietly.

Thomas and Brother Ander nodded their agreement.

THOMAS SAT in the prow of the longboat watching absently as the rowers bent to their task. Will and Brother Ander sat before him. Kahrlin sat at the stern steering the boat, a satisfied smirk lingering on his face.

Once his decision lay behind him, a surprising sense of calm had settled over Thomas. He didn't want to die. He wanted to grow old with Elena in the serenity of Newhaven, to dandle grandchildren on his knee. Nevertheless he was determined to play whatever role he could in setting the hostages free.

And the situation surely wasn't entirely hopeless. This time he was not alone, and Will must have some kind of a plan. In any event, he knew Will wouldn't stand passively by if the Grand Vizier proved faithless. Thomas was no soldier, but he would do anything he could to support his friend.

As they rounded a point, Thomas glanced behind to find that the Varasan ship had disappeared from view. Beyond the next point he spotted a three-masted ship lying at anchor. It quickly became clear they were nearing their destination.

A rope net had been lowered for them, and Kahrlin waved them toward it. Will ascended first, followed by Brother Ander and Thomas. Emerging onto the deck they found the Grand Vizier awaiting them, his face unreadable. The stone was touching Thomas's skin, and after his previous experience he found himself reluctant to look at the Grand Vizier. He needn't have worried. This time no barrage of horror awaited him. Rheibas was no longer bothering to mask his thoughts.

The language barrier did not prevent Thomas from seeing his

purpose clearly. Before he could whisper a warning to Will, a group of guards emerged from the hatch. Behind them trailed King Rupert, Princess Teylee, and a woman Thomas did not recognize, their hands bound before them. Their faces were defiant, but they did not appear to be in good condition. Then another figure appeared, similarly bound, wearing the garb of a priest of the dark gods. His hood had been thrown back. The many scars and the blue paint that covered his face did not entirely obscure the deep wrinkles that spoke of great age. Even without having previously met him, Thomas knew he was looking at the High Priest.

Rheibas shouted an order, and all except ten of the guards followed Kahrlin below decks. Three guards stood protectively around the Grand Vizier, another four positioned themselves behind the three captives and the priest, while the other three took up positions behind the new arrivals.

The stone revealed Kahrlin's frustration at being excluded from what was about to happen. He might have seen it differently if he realized that Rheibas intended to ensure total secrecy by killing every witness.

The interpreter standing beside Rheibas had no more idea of his fate than the guards, and he proceeded to relay the Grand Vizier's words in Arvenian. None of the guards understood what was being said—none of them spoke Arvenian, and Rheibas spoke to the interpreter too quietly for them to hear.

"I imagine that you have spoken to my former prisoner," Rheibas began, addressing the three newcomers. After a pause, he added, "I can see from your faces that you have. I believe I can therefore assume you understand my purpose in coming to this region."

When none of them denied it, he continued. "Unless I am greatly mistaken, I have assembled a most unusual group of people. One of you has exercised great authority over a number of years, to extraordinary effect." He nodded at Will.

"One of you has built a remarkable reputation, and not just as a healer." He dipped his head in the direction of Brother Ander. "I understand a mob savagely beat you and left you for dead. You got up and walked away." He shook his head in wonder.

"Your companion," and here he paused and surveyed Thomas curiously, "appears to be unexceptional in every way. Yet he hides a rare gift of exceptional insight. At our recent meeting with the emperor, it unexpectedly emerged that you were the one who found Bolnyk's hidden document." He bared his teeth in the semblance of a smile. "We have a servant's indiscreet glance to thank for identifying you. I must say that finding the document was a truly marvelous achievement on your part!"

He turned toward the High Priest. "I freely acknowledge that the presence of the priest may be little more than a distraction, although I would never dismiss the possibility that anyone with such unusual longevity is hiding secrets of their own. But I honor agreements when I make them, and that is the primary reason he is here. I won't go into details of this agreement, but it's fair to say it will reshape Rogand in significant ways. None of that need concern us now, though."

Rheibas was clearly enjoying himself. "Did you realize I set a test for you? You will remember Kahrlin's first meeting with King Krasmir, because all three of you were present. When Kahrlin briefed me later, imagine my surprise when he reported that the audience included a monk and a commoner. He couldn't account for it, and I didn't enlighten him with my guesses. He attended that meeting knowing the exact location of the island where our friends had been placed." He waved toward the three hostages. "Remarkably, Rogandan ships soon appeared at that very location. I had already moved the three royals, of course, but I left someone behind on the island to watch for visitors. I was not disappointed. The incident offered great encouragement to me. It showed me I was steering the correct course."

He frowned. "I must confess that one thing remains a mystery to me. Every indication suggests that each of you is aware of the others' gifts. Why hasn't one of you found a way to appropriate them all for yourselves? I can only imagine what you might have achieved, for example, Lord Torbury. You might have begun with the throne of

Arvenon, and I don't doubt it would have proven little more than a stepping stone. I find such hesitancy unfathomable. I would never have shown the same indecisiveness."

He shook his head. "No matter. It is time we made a beginning. I think you know what I want. A voluntary gift from each of you will save the lives of the captives. Who is going to be first?"

It came as no surprise to hear him speak of a voluntary gift. Having read the scroll, Rheibas understood that the stones would be useless if taken by force. But he was a fool if he expected them to simply give him what he wanted.

None of them moved.

Rheibas issued a sharp command. Drawing his sword, the guard behind the High Priest ran his prisoner through.

The priest crumpled. He did not cry out, but his face revealed his agony. The stone revealed to Thomas an abrupt and tormented end to the celebrated longevity of the priest.

Anger warred with compassion on the face of Brother Ander. Before the guards could react, he hurried across the deck to the fallen priest and knelt beside him. Placing a hand on his wound, he mouthed a fervent prayer.

As Thomas watched, life stirred in the old man. The grimace cleared abruptly from the priest's face, and he opened his eyes. Standing up, Brother Ander reached down a hand and helped him to his feet.

Rheibas applauded enthusiastically. "Splendid! Truly splendid! A remarkable performance!"

Then he scowled. "Do not think to test my patience. I will not tolerate any further miraculous recoveries." He waved a hand to the guard previously assigned to Brother Ander, and the man escorted the monk at sword point back to his original place. Two other guards converged on them, and the monk's arms and legs were securely trussed.

Another sharp command to the guard standing behind Princess Teylee resulted in the appearance of a knife at her throat. "If I hear nothing from any of you in two minutes, the princess will die."

37

Everything had been happening far too quickly for Thomas. Able to foresee Rheibas's intentions as he issued each command, the knowledge came too late for him to warn Will or to think of a way to prevent what was about to happen. Once more Rheibas had succeeded in distracting him, as he had during the meeting with the emperor. This time, instead of using images of horror, the Grand Vizier had flooded his own mind with images of everything he had instigated. The revelations had been as over-whelming as they were revealing, screening his next steps until he was actually carrying them out.

Thomas wasn't going to let Rheibas have it all his own way though. There was one thing he could do.

Lifting up his voice, Thomas spoke loudly enough for all to hear.

"The Grand Vizier has credited me with a rare gift of exceptional insight. For once he is telling the truth! However, I need no unusual perception to assure you he has no intention of ever releasing his hostages, or of letting us live—not even if we were able to give him what he wants. So much for honoring his agreements! No one witnessing this little drama—and that includes the interpreter as well as every guard present on the deck—will live to see another dawn. He plans to have every one of us killed! That is the reason he sent Kahrlin below with most of the guards. He still needs them once he is finished here."

The interpreter had gone pale. When Rheibas demanded a translation of Thomas's words, the interpreter did more than just comply —he shouted it for the benefit of the guards.

Rheibas decided in a moment that no further translation would be needed. At his barked command, one of the guards ran his sword through the interpreter. Then, with the help of a second guard, the killer threw the interpreter's body overboard.

It was too late. The damage had been done. Many of the guards were becoming noticeably restless.

Rheibas commanded one of them to fetch Kahrlin. When the guard boldly refused, Rheibas immediately ordered the others to kill him. Most hesitated, but the two who had disposed of the interpreter obeyed, and another body was soon disappearing over the side into the water.

One of the two loyalists ran to the hatch and opened it, calling for Kahrlin. The agent soon appeared, a host of guards at his back, with sailors following them onto the deck. In a fury, Rheibas commanded him to kill the nine remaining guards. The two men fool enough to carry out his orders were not to be spared.

All nine were soon fighting for their lives. A few of them had the sense to band together, and others fought back to back. Many of the guards from below deck milled around uselessly, unable to reach the fighting.

Thomas had won the prisoners a brief reprieve. Will had come aboard armed, and no one had attempted to remove his weapons. He now cut the ropes binding Brother Ander. Handing him a knife, he said, "Free the hostages!"

Both Brother Ander and Will weaved their way through the fighting, reaching the three at the same moment as three of Kahrlin's men. Will held off the guards while Brother Ander cut the bonds of King Rupert, Princess Teylee, and the Varasan agent masquerading as Queen Essanda.

Hastily retrieving discarded weapons, the king and the agent hurried to the support of Will.

Thomas cowered alone on the other side of the ship. Fighting now raged across the deck. Having been sentenced to death, the besieged guards fought with the desperation of men with nothing to lose. Nevertheless, there could be no doubt about the final outcome.

As the last of the guards finally went down, Rheibas bellowed a command. Moments later, Thomas felt a knife at his throat.

Rheibas spoke again, this time to Will and his companions. No one remained to translate his words, but his meaning was clear enough. He was warning that Thomas's life would end unless they laid down their weapons.

At that moment a splintering crash sounded, and the ship shuddered violently. Thomas was thrown to the deck, along with the guard holding the knife. In the sudden movement the blade nicked his throat, and he felt warm blood seeping down his neck. Frantically exploring the wound with one hand, he concluded the cut wasn't deep. His body went slack with relief.

The clasp around his neck had twisted, removing the stone from contact with his skin. He didn't care. Too much was going on around him to make sense of its revelations anyway.

The ship shook again, then slowly began moving through the water. The anchors had broken free, or else their cables had broken.

A shower of water sprayed the deck as a huge whale—almost the same length as the ship—breached beside them before disappearing into the depths. The whale was not long gone before gigantic tentacles appeared over the rail. Thomas watched with mouth agape as a tentacle swept the deck, barely missing him. Giant suckers fastened onto two guards as it passed. They disappeared with it over the side, screaming in terror.

The remaining guards had lost all interest in the prisoners. Thomas spotted Rheibas crouching warily beside the main mast, scowling helplessly as chaos engulfed his ship.

Peering about in search of his companions, Thomas glanced up as mighty tentacles wrapped around the mizzen mast. Unable to withstand the force, the mast gave way with a resounding crack. He scurried frantically out of its way as it came crashing down onto the main deck, bringing spars, sails, and lines with it. Anyone unfortunate enough to be caught in its path was crushed. The tentacles that brought it down now ranged freely about the ship, adding to the madness.

Will and Brother Ander were crouching beside the rail on the other side of the deck, the High Priest and the freed hostages beside them. Thomas set out for them, dodging flailing tentacles and falling timbers. He was halfway there when a figure rose up before him. It was Kahrlin. Recognizing Thomas, he drew his knife and stepped menacingly toward him. Before Thomas could react, a broken spar still attached to the rigging swung down and knocked the agent senseless. Trembling uncontrollably, Thomas stepped over him and resumed his journey.

Somehow he reached his friends unharmed.

Relief showed on Will's face. "You found us, Thomas! I couldn't see you!" Then he saw the blood. "Are you hurt?" he asked in alarm.

"It's nothing. Just a scratch," Thomas replied. He leaned closer to Will, pointing a finger toward the huge squid. "Did you do this?"

Wild-eyed and disheveled, Will surveyed the scene. "I summoned the creature," he confirmed quietly. "I have no control over it though! We're in as much danger as anyone else!"

As if to emphasize his assessment, Princess Teylee screamed in terror. Glancing in her direction, Thomas saw a huge eye peering over the rail. The entire head rose into view, alien and dreadful. Then the creature abruptly sank out of sight beneath the vessel, its tentacles gliding away behind it.

"I've heard tales of giant squid attacking ships," breathed King Rupert in awe. "I never believed for a minute any of it was true."

A strange calm settled over the crippled ship. Dazed men wandered aimlessly, picking their way among fallen spars, shredded sails, and the tangles of unidentifiable debris that lay strewn across the deck.

Thomas, Brother Ander, and Will stood warily beside the former captives. King Rupert and the counterfeit queen stood at the ready with drawn swords, but no one paid them any attention.

Almost no one. Humbled by forces beyond his control, Rheibas had not forgotten them. He glared toward them with calculating eyes from his refuge beside the main mast. Even now he had not abandoned his schemes to relieve them of the stones.

But the nightmare was far from over. The tentacles returned, rising lazily from the deep on the opposite side of the ship and bringing a sudden end to the respite.

A damaging hail of spars and tangled lines rained from above as giant limbs claimed the foremast and tore it down. Missing the deck, it crashed sideways through the hull not far from Thomas, leaving a gaping hole behind it.

This time the creature seemed more intent on tearing the ship apart than on hunting down the terrified fugitives cowering on its deck. Planks flew through the air as great tentacles clawed at the breach.

The ship had been drifting out to sea, and for the first time Thomas noticed it was beginning to list. Their side of the deck was slowly sinking.

"Can't you do something about this creature?" pleaded Thomas.

"I'm working on it!" Will replied tensely.

After falling into the sea, one of the ship's boats now floated peacefully on the seaward side of the vessel. Before anyone could seek refuge in it, the huge whale reappeared, surfacing behind the ship. Launching itself backward from the water, it landed squarely on the little boat. Water sprayed in every direction, and splintered pieces of wood soon littered the surface.

The whale hit the side of the ship with a jarring thud, knocking Thomas from his feet. He looked up to see the tentacles finally disappearing from view.

Moments later he saw the reason for the giant cephalopod's retreat. Fighting for its life, it had wrapped itself around the snout of the whale. They all stared in fascinated consternation as the two giants of the deep joined battle. Tentacles flailed wildly while the great tail of the leviathan slapped the water. Then the whale sank beneath the waves, dragging its intended meal with it. Soon nothing remained except a trail of bubbles.

The tiny humans perched precariously on the tilting deck had little to celebrate. By now all of them were acutely aware that the vessel was sinking. They eyed the water uncertainly, fearful of what else might be lurking in its depths.

Continuing to settle lower, the ship abruptly lurched of its own accord, leaning at an alarming angle. Men began sliding across the deck toward the rails, a few falling into the water. Thomas soon spotted figures dragging themselves onto chunks of floating debris.

Then with a creaking and groaning of timbers, the ship keeled over. Tossed carelessly into the ocean, Thomas surfaced to see the ship towering above him. Desperately swimming away from it, he tried to ignore the objects large and small splashing down around him. Wooden yards and booms, tangled lines, pieces of sail—anything not secured to the ship—plummeted into the water. There was no way to escape the deadly rain. Somehow emerging unscathed, he began scanning the surface anxiously, hoping his companions had also escaped injury.

Even before he spotted them all, a huge piece of sailcloth came down, suspended between broken spars. Rupert and Tasha were directly in its path, and it settled over them like a shroud. Thomas waited impatiently for them to swim out from underneath it, but he saw only signs of their struggles. Gradually it occurred to him that they must have become ensnared.

Brother Ander apparently reached the same conclusion, because he dived below the cloth, Will's knife poised in his hand. Fully expecting Will to join the monk, Thomas glanced about for his friend. When he finally located him, he saw the Varasan agent helping him onto a large piece of wood. Will seemed dazed, his head covered with blood. One of the falling objects must have picked him out.

Only the aged High Priest seemed aware of the drama below the sailcloth. Floating nearby on a support of his own, he stared at Thomas as if waiting for him to do something.

Shamed into action, Thomas took a deep breath and dived. Coming up beneath the cloth, he saw both the king and the princess entangled in lines. The monk had just succeeded in cutting the princess free. Seeing Thomas, he waved him to her aid, and moved to help the king.

Frantic for air, the princess seemed confused. Thomas grabbed her and led her beyond the enveloping sailcloth and upward. She broke the surface gasping desperately. Impatient to return to the others, he saw to his relief that her struggles had attracted the attention of the Varasan. As the agent moved to the aid of the princess, Thomas took a deep breath and dived back down.

Neither Brother Ander nor the king could have survived this long without air, yet he saw the monk still working frantically to free the king. Then Thomas discovered how they had continued so long. Stretching up, the king tilted back his head to claim a small pocket of air above him. The trapped air was now exhausted though, and no other pockets were in sight. Swimming toward the king, Thomas managed to free one limb from entanglement at the same moment the monk severed the final line. As Thomas led the king to freedom, Brother Ander set out after them, his attempts noticeably feeble.

The king surfaced, gasping weakly. The Varasan woman was ready. Grasping hold of him, she pulled him to safety.

Not pausing for a minute, Thomas filled his lungs and dived back under the water. The monk had not cleared the sailcloth, and his arms were flailing ineffectually. He clearly had no resources left.

There was not a moment to lose. Ducking back under the sail, Thomas grabbed him and pushed him clear. With the last of his strength he thrust him toward the surface. Dimly he saw an ancient arm reach down to grasp the robe of the monk and pull him with surprising strength toward safety.

Attempting to swim out from under the sail, Thomas felt resistance. Looking down he saw that his own leg had become entangled. Reaching down, he fumbled endlessly with the twisted lines. Finally succeeding in freeing his leg, he knew it had taken too long. The surface wasn't far away, but he no longer had the strength to reach it.

Thomas had passed beyond the limit of his own endurance. He struggled weakly as water filled his lungs, but he struggled in vain.

His fading thought was not one of regret, but of gratitude for a life rich beyond his imagining.

———

A FACE APPEARED, one he should have recognized. Words sounded, but he could not grasp their meaning.

Then, accompanied by much coughing and spluttering, everything came rushing back.

Thomas found himself lying on a flat piece of wood, large enough to accommodate his whole body. Brother Ander, astride his own piece of wood, was bending over him. The monk looked barely able to function himself.

Brother Ander turned to address the Varasan woman. "Thank you for retrieving him. I couldn't have done it."

Then the monk's eyes moved away, and a smile lit his face. There was nothing wry about it. It was a heart-felt smile, without reservation, reaching to his eyes. Following his gaze, Thomas was astonished to see the ghost of a smile on the High Priest's face, softening the deep lines of his ancient visage. With an effort he turned away, sensing it was not his place to intrude upon the moment.

Other voices reached him, and he turned his head to see the newly freed king propped up on an elbow, talking to the princess. Both of them rested on floating debris. Facing the other direction, he found Will floating beside him, stretched out on his own little raft. Blood had stained his hair a deeper shade of red. His eyes were closed, but his chest rose and fell rhythmically.

Will's eyes fluttered open. Seeing Thomas, his lips parted in a feeble smile. "Welcome back," he managed.

The monk paddled over to them and leaned in to examine Will's head. "My apologies for taking so long to notice this, Will," he said.

Laying a hand on the wound, he prayed simply, then leaned back. "How does that feel?"

"My head has stopped pounding," reported Will. He explored the wound with his hand. "It doesn't hurt at all. Thank you, Brother Ander!"

The monk smiled wearily and moved away.

As time passed, Thomas gradually became more aware of his surroundings. The ship lay crippled in the water, but much of it was still visible. Other survivors clung to floating objects of their own.

Not far away Thomas spotted Kahrlin kneeling atop a substantial piece of the hull. Reaching down, the agent dragged a dripping Grand Vizier from the water. Rheibas appeared to be bleeding freely from a gash on his leg, but he was alive. His wound was staining the water red, and Kahrlin knelt beside his master, apparently trying to staunch the flow of blood.

Thomas shook his head in bemusement. How was it possible that the person responsible for all the trauma, all the grief, had managed to survive?

Twisting the clasp of the stone, he peered at Rheibas once more. No distractions blocked his explorations this time; such tactics were beyond the chief minister in his current state. Hidden ambitions welled up at last—a mental image of Rheibas sitting in state upon an imposing throne in the heart of what Thomas didn't doubt was Kat Ahket. Whatever his eventual plans for Rogand, it seemed that after acquiring the stones Rheibas intended to begin with the Empire of Ahr. In light of this information, his plan to dispose of Princess Neira took on a new significance.

Returning the stone to its usual position, Thomas reached over and nudged Will, pointing out Rheibas and his lackey.

He soon discovered that other eyes were on the two Ahrans. A voice nearby rang out in a language Thomas didn't understand. Twisting around to identify the speaker, he saw it was the Varasan agent. From the tone of her voice, she had been taunting the two men.

Kahrlin was staring back at her in shock. Unconcealed hatred showed on Rheibas's face.

A fin appeared in the water near the beleaguered men, drawing their attention away. The Ahrans watched wide-eyed as it circled their tiny wooden island ominously. Then the island rocked violently, pitching both men into the water.

A head emerged, jaws yawning wide to reveal rows of razor-sharp teeth. Snatching Rheibas, it sank out of sight. Kahrlin's cry of dismay was cut short as he too disappeared, carried off by a second predator.

Thomas stared aghast at the empty platform, now rocking gently in the swell.

He faced Will. "Was that you?" he whispered.

Haunted eyes stared back at him. "I had nothing to do with it." Will's brows drew together. "Somehow, though..." he began.

"It seems fitting," Thomas finished for him.

The Varasan agent had witnessed the demise of the Grand Vizier with evident satisfaction.

"What did you say to Rheibas earlier, when you were calling out?" Will asked her.

"I told him he'd promoted the wrong bootlicker. I said that Bolnyk abducted two royals, and Kahrlin didn't even manage one. I was speaking in Ahran, which would have made it clear I wasn't Queen Essanda."

Will grunted in approval. "They weren't as clever as they thought, and it's satisfying to know they discovered the truth before the end."

The agent stared into the water where Rheibas had disappeared. "It wouldn't shock me if that shark gets indigestion," she growled. Seeing Thomas looking at her quizzically, she told him, "I've dreamed of bringing the Grand Vizier down since I was a child. Now he's gone, and not by my hand. The shark cheated me, although I suppose I should be grateful."

"Why did you want to bring him down?" asked Thomas.

She briefly described Rheibas's role in the unjust execution of her parents. "Suddenly my parents were gone," she added bitterly. "There was no dignity in their deaths. They'd been sentenced for sedition, so their bodies were thrown into a mass grave. There was no ceremony to remember them, and no opportunity for a confused and horrified child to grieve their loss."

Thomas stared at her, appalled.

"I found myself an orphan, left to fend for myself on the streets. Fortunately a widow found me and took me in. She was a good woman who set about raising me and loving me. She told me the day would come when I needed to forget him and focus my energies elsewhere."

The Varasan smiled wryly. "It seems she was right. About needing to focus elsewhere, at least. Whatever the future might bring, the time has finally come for me to find a new expression for my energy."

Brother Ander had been listening. "Invest your energy in pursuits that bring life and hope," he said with a weary smile. "Make sure your legacy counts for something when your time comes."

"I will ponder your words," she promised.

As they fell silent, Thomas peered numbly around him, weighed down and overwhelmed by what he had heard and witnessed.

The Grand Vizier had inflicted damage exceeding anything Thomas could comprehend. Countless lives had been destroyed at his whim. And once he learned of the stones, entire kingdoms had been thrown into turmoil. All to satisfy his rapacious appetite for power.

Now he was gone, snatched away in a moment. After having such a significant role in the affairs of the world, his departure from it had been undignified and without ceremony. Very few would miss him.

So much upheaval. So much destruction. And what had been the point of it all?

Everything went quiet, apart from the slap-slap of the water on the floating debris. Clinging stubbornly to his makeshift raft, Thomas continued to drift. Other predators were undoubtedly prowling below, but the knowledge didn't move him. He had stared death in the face and survived. For that moment at least, he remained undaunted.

As they continued to float, something nudged him from below, reawakening his alarm. Then a gray body surfaced beside him, and the unforgettable smile of a dolphin greeted his startled gaze. The creature chittered once, then submerged its head again.

It took another gentle nudge before he finally grasped what was required of him. Remaining perched on his little raft, he grabbed hold of the dorsal fin and allowed the dolphin to propel him through the water. Glancing back a couple of minutes later he saw his companions strung out behind him, similarly conveyed. A large pod of the creatures surrounded the little group, sporting about them before leaping joyfully above the waves. Their exuberance washed over him, buoying up his spirits and chasing away his memories of the darkness.

After a few moments his mount disappeared and another took its place. When he glanced behind once more, he saw that the remains of the ship were already far away.

A profound sense of serenity began to settle over him. Having refused to yield to the paralyzing embrace of fear, he had set foot on a path that promised only a terrible death. By a miracle he had avoided the looming disaster, only to be snatched away to an abrupt ending he never anticipated.

Having passed through the gates of death, he had been restored, beyond expectation and beyond hope. And now, in the most improbable of conclusions, he was returning home, borne along joyfully by the sublimest of earth's creatures.

In later years he remembered this journey as one of the purest joys of his entire life.

Leaning sideways to lay his head on the body of the dolphin, he allowed the last of the tension to drain from his body.

He was at peace.

38

____

Spotting the castaways, a fishing boat diverted from its course to pick them up. As the boat approached, their dolphin escorts glided silently away and headed out to sea, presumably in search of fish.

Will climbed aboard with the others, warmly expressing his appreciation to the fisherman and his son for rescuing them. The fisherman was well aware of the presence of the Rogandan and Ahran fleets, and confirmed that they were still in the area. He readily agreed to take them all to King Krasmir.

Will positioned himself in the bow, away from the others.

Thomas soon joined him there. "Thank you," he said quietly.

"For what?" asked Will.

"For that magnificent experience!" Thomas replied.

Will responded with a wink.

The others were distracted, none of them able to stop talking about the dolphins. Will understood perfectly. After the horrors they had endured, the timely arrival of the gentle creatures had done more to lift their spirits than he could have believed possible.

"I was astonished at how effectively you enlisted the aid of the dolphins," Thomas told him.

"They are intelligent creatures," Will replied. "It was much easier than I expected to convey what I needed them to do."

"You seemed to have a connection with them when we first sailed to Rog," Thomas observed.

"Yes. I needed to work on it though. If I seemed distracted when we sailed back from Rog, it was because I was concentrating on strengthening my links with sea creatures, particularly larger ones. I had no clear idea what I might do with those links, but couldn't see any other way to make use of the Stone of Authority."

"The opportunity arose, and you made good use of it."

Will nodded. "When the Grand Vizier had us at his mercy, I summoned the largest creatures of the deep available. I was as surprised as anyone by the giant squid—I believe they are rarely seen in shallow waters. All I intended was to create a distraction, but it quickly spiraled out of control. I could easily have been responsible for our deaths!"

"You have no reason to reproach yourself. We survived."

"That had a lot to do with you and Brother Ander," Will told him. "You used the Stone of Knowing to good effect when you warned the interpreter, and Brother Ander once more achieved the impossible with the help of the Stone of Vitality."

A wry smile came to Thomas's face. "It's ironic that the stones played such a big part in the Grand Vizier's downfall. He got to see them at work first hand, but he'll never get his hands on them. The shark made certain of that."

"Yes, the shark did us a favor. It arrived without encouragement from me, as you already know. I could summon a shark, but I'm not sure I have the mastery to direct it to do exactly what it did. I'm sure the Stone of Authority would be capable of it in the hands of the right person. But in the end the Grand Vizier was brought down without our involvement, and I'm perfectly content with that."

Will wondered if Thomas had discovered anything new about Rheibas's intentions. "Did you learn anything more about what he was hoping to achieve if he managed to get his hands on the stones?"

Thomas nodded. "He had an unguarded moment just before the

shark took him. He had his sights set on the emperor's crown. The stones would have helped deliver it. Eventually he would have needed to dispose of the princess anyway, and he saw a way to use her to create a crisis that might bring the stones into the open. We're fortunate indeed that he didn't succeed."

Their conversation was cut short when the Varasan ship used for the conference came into view. Before long they had pulled along-side. Will was the last out of the fishing boat, and he didn't leave before sincerely thanking the fishermen once again.

They found King Krasmir still aboard. The king was stunned speechless when they appeared one after another over the rail. When he caught sight of his daughter, though, his joy could not be contained. No one witnessing their reunion could have remained unmoved by it. For Will it was especially poignant, knowing better than anyone what the king must be experiencing.

As soon as King Krasmir was able to detach himself, he sent a message to the emperor, inviting him to join them for a full debrief-ing. While they were waiting, he went to each of the other new arrivals, welcoming them and congratulating them on their safe return. Not surprisingly, he remained longest with King Rupert, but no one was neglected. He greeted the High Priest with appropriate deference, and earnestly expressed his gratification at his rescue.

When he came to Will, he did not hide his relief at his safe return. "Allowing you to leave this morning was beyond uncomfortable, and I'm immensely relieved to welcome you back! I can't begin to imagine what I would have told your king."

"Your daughter's life was at stake, Your Majesty, and there seemed at least a faint chance I could do something to secure her release. After what I went through with my son, I could never have lived with myself if I didn't try."

"I am forever in your debt, Lord Torbury." He dipped his head in salute. Then he glanced at Will's clothing, still wet from the time he spent in the water. "How did all of you manage to escape his clutches?"

"That is a surprising story, Your Majesty."

Before he could relate it, the arrival of the emperor was announced.

After welcoming his honored guest, King Krasmir introduced the released hostages.

"Your Imperial Majesty, it gives me great pleasure to introduce you to King Rupert of Castel. And this is my daughter, Princess Teylee, to whom he is betrothed. Their companion in captivity was not Queen Essanda of Arvenon as her captors believed. This woman impersonated the queen in order to protect her. As a result, she endured on the queen's behalf a brutal abduction at the hands of Kahrlin, the Grand Vizier's senior agent. I have not introduced her by name out of respect for her request that her anonymity be preserved."

The emperor's demeanor showed how he felt about his most senior official having placed him in such a position. "I can see at a glance that none of you have been well treated," he acknowledged. "I can only apologize most sincerely for what you have endured at the hands of my chief minister. He denied any involvement, suggesting the betrothed couple had eloped, then absconded. He claimed the queen later visited her brother of her own accord. In view of his abhorrent behavior and his deception, it need hardly be said that Rheibas is no longer my chief minister."

He addressed the princess. "I profoundly regret the ordeal you have suffered."

Princess Teylee bowed. "Thank you, Your Majesty. All of us understand that the Grand Vizier was acting only on his own behalf." She looked at her father. "Knowing that he invented a report about us eloping might help explain why the guards tried to force us together. At first they gave each of us a hut, but later they demolished one of them. When the weather was bad enough, we were forced to shelter together."

King Krasmir didn't speak, but his face had gone dark with anger.

King Rupert faced Krasmir calmly. "You can rest assured that the Grand Vizier's efforts were in vain, Your Majesty." He grinned at the princess. "That isn't because our ordeal did anything to diminish my affection for your daughter."

She returned a grin of her own.

"Perhaps the Grand Vizier was hoping to reinforce his version of the truth," suggested Lady Tulinay with a frown.

"More likely he was looking for ways to further increase his leverage," scowled Krasmir.

King Rupert nodded. "That occurred to us as well. Any child we produced would be heir to the Castelan throne, as well as being Your Majesty's grandchild."

The emperor appeared more uncomfortable than ever. "Where is Rheibas now?" he asked.

"He is dead, Your Majesty," Will replied bluntly.

Both the emperor and King Krasmir regarded him in astonishment.

"How did that happen?" asked the king.

"As you told us, Your Majesty, the Grand Vizier sent Kahrlin to say that the hostages would only be released if the Arvenians visited him on his ship for what he called 'negotiations.' He was referring to Brother Ander, Thomas Stablehand, and me. We agreed to go in the hope that he would honor his promise and release them. When we arrived he claimed we had something he wanted. He didn't say what it was. He said unless we gave it to him, he would kill the hostages immediately."

Lady Tulinay was shaking her head. "It sounds like he was making a demand none of you could satisfy, thereby giving himself an excuse to kill the hostages."

"No doubt he intended to kill you as well," added King Krasmir. "Not least because the three of you witnessed Bolnyk's murder of Lord Torbury's son."

"It quickly became obvious to us that he intended to kill us all," agreed Will.

"How did you escape?" asked the king.

"Before he said anything to us, Rheibas sent Kahrlin and most of his men below deck, leaving behind an interpreter and a few armed men. He clearly didn't want witnesses. After killing us, he was going to have the interpreter and the others killed as well. Thomas announced that to the interpreter, who then told everyone else. Rheibas immediately had the interpreter killed and recalled Kahrlin and the others. When they arrived, he told them to kill the men on deck. A battle broke out. It didn't last long, but it bought us some time."

The emperor was clearly appalled. "How was Rheibas killed?"

"At this point nature intervened in a remarkable way," Will continued. "Incredible as it sounds, the ship was attacked by a giant squid. The squid in turn was attacked by a huge whale, but not before it had damaged the ship so badly it sank. While we were in the water, we saw a shark take Rheibas. Another shark took Kahrlin almost immediately. We stayed together and were eventually picked up by a fishing boat."

Will made no mention of the dolphins. The story was incredible enough already.

He turned to the emperor. "We don't know what became of the other survivors, but I'm sure that most of them are still in the area. It isn't far away. They will confirm my account."

The emperor immediately spoke to one of his aides. The man left the ship at once. After excusing himself, the emperor then spent a considerable time consulting quietly with other aides. He continued until a boat pulled alongside the ship and the missing aide returned. After a whispered conversation, the emperor once more addressed his hosts.

"The survivors are being rescued," the emperor explained. "An investigation is underway into their behavior. While they have not conducted themselves in a manner worthy of their emperor, I recognize they were following orders. They will be given a proper opportunity to explain themselves before I decide their fate."

He shook his head in astonishment. "I confess your tale is so bizarre it defies belief, Lord Torbury. Nevertheless, the other survivors have confirmed your account. It seems that justice has been served on Rheibas for his misdeeds, the sentence having been carried out by nature itself. I have never heard of such a thing!"

"What of Bolnyk, Your Majesty?" asked King Krasmir. "His crimes were committed against the empire as well as against Rogand and Arvenon. I am willing to hand him over to you for judgment if you are willing to take him."

"Gladly, Your Majesty," the emperor replied. "You have my promise he will be held to account."

Before the emperor left, he approached King Krasmir with one final suggestion. Will was one of the few within earshot. Neither of them seemed to object to his presence.

"I am told that your oldest son is of marriageable age, King Krasmir. It has not escaped my attention that any alliance between the empire and Rogand might be strengthened by a union between your son and my daughter."

The king's mouth opened, then he snapped it shut.

His dilemma was painfully obvious to Will. "As someone with no vested interest, might I offer a thought on the subject, Your Majesties?" he asked.

"Of course," said the king at once.

The emperor nodded as soon as the request was translated.

"It strikes me that events have conspired in such a way that Princess Neira's experience of Rogand has been profoundly disagreeable. After being rescued from certain death on a remote Rogandan island, she was fortunate to survive her initial attempt to reach Rog by sea. When she did arrive, it was necessary to confine her for her own protection. Rheibas found a way to contact her anyway. The letter he entrusted to Bolnyk exposed his attempts to manipulate her."

His eyebrows drew together. "I'm not sure if Your Majesty is aware of the full impact of Rheibas's scheming. In addition to the abductions and murder carried out by his agents, he has been actively stoking fears of an Ahran invasion, drawing upon an ever increasing naval presence to reinforce his threats. From the beginning he targeted the surrounding kingdoms as well as Rogand, both with his threats and his abductions. That is the reason King Steffan sent me to Rog. As a result Her Highness spent months in the capital in a climate of fear and uncertainty toward Ahrans in general, with no clarity about her own future, all the while cut off from the familiar comfort and security of her father's authority.

"I have no doubt she would not hesitate to do anything required of her for the sake of her father and the empire. However, if she marries the crown prince she will face a lifetime in Rogand, with her best years spent in service to the kingdom as its queen. In light of all she has endured, I fear that the prospect might seem disheartening. It might even seem to her like a heavy sentence."

He dipped his head respectfully. "I know I speak on behalf of my own king when I say that the arrival of Your Majesty has transformed our situation. A catastrophe has been averted, and you have lifted us from despondency to hope. It is not necessary for you to yield up your brightest jewel to secure the gratitude and friendship of the kingdoms of the region. You have achieved that already."

He bent low. "I have spoken very freely. Please pardon me if my words appear in any way presumptuous."

The emperor addressed himself to King Krasmir. "Do these sentiments echo your own thoughts, Your Majesty?"

The king nodded gravely. "Lord Torbury's analysis of the situation is perceptive, and I can only concur. In particular, I agree that all of us are in the debt of Your Imperial Majesty. Having come here with a willingness to search out the truth, you at once saw to the heart of it, in spite of a determined attempt by Rheibas to deceive you. No greater token of your goodwill is necessary."

The emperor nodded. Turning to Will, he regarded him thoughtfully. "You have given me much to consider, Lord Torbury. I compliment you on your diplomatic skills. It is not difficult to see why your sovereign appointed you as his representative."

He turned to the king. "In view of what both of you have said, it might be wisest to allow Neira to return to Kat Ahket."

With that, he bade them farewell and departed. He left with a promise to leave behind an official with authority to commence negotiations on trade agreements and a mutual assistance treaty.

As soon as he was gone, King Krasmir turned to Will. "It seems there is to be no end to my indebtedness toward you, Lord Torbury!" he exclaimed. "I could see no way to refuse the emperor's request without causing him grave offense, and no way to accept it without forever alienating my son—not to mention my wife—no doubt along with the rest of the kingdom! You have neatly extricated me from a very delicate situation."

"It is the least I could do, Your Majesty. There is one other matter I wished to raise with you. A former prisoner of Rheibas is currently being held in your dungeons. Having met with him and questioned him closely, I do not believe he has done anything worthy of punishment. Could you please ask one of your people to examine his case?"

"I will follow it up," the king promised.

Then he frowned. "Do you have any idea what Rheibas wanted with the High Priest?"

Will shrugged. "He said he was honoring an agreement. He didn't offer details, but he said it would result in significant change for Rogand. Do you have enemies among the priesthood, Your Majesty?"

"My agents believe that the Archprimus, the second in charge, thinks I am not sufficiently in thrall to the dark gods."

"In that case, if I had to guess, I'd say that the Archprimus agreed to deliver the High Priest to Rheibas, although for what purpose I cannot say with any certainty. In return, Rheibas promised the Archprimus he'd get rid of you and your family. Presumably the Archprimus would further benefit by stepping into the role of High Priest. That might have allowed him some measure of influence over who replaced you."

The king reacted with fury. "I have been careful never to interfere with the priests, but I will not tolerate insurrection!" he snapped.

"It may not be necessary for you to do anything, Your Majesty. I suspect the High Priest will be more than eager to deal with the matter."

Glancing toward the priest, Will found him talking with Brother

Ander. "I haven't mentioned it, but after we arrived on Rheibas's ship, he decided to show he was serious by ordering the High Priest killed. One of his men ran him through. Before anyone could stop him, Brother Ander hurried over and restored him. The High Priest later returned the favor by pulling Brother Ander from the water when he was about to drown. We might be witnessing the beginning of an unlikely friendship."

The king looked at the two men in amazement. "This has been a day of surprises!" he exclaimed.

BISRI AHUZZA STOOD at the rail of the emperor's ship, watching the water foam about the bow as the vessel plowed through the swell. Rogand lay behind them; they were returning at last to Kat Ahket, the imperial fleet clustered around them.

Looking up, he saw the emperor approaching. He bowed low.

"I have a request for you, Bisri. You seem to have reached an understanding with the Rogandans and their allies. It's apparent to me that they trust you. I wish to appoint you as my ambassador to the region."

Ahuzza bowed again. "You do me great honor, Your Majesty."

"I imagine you will need to learn both Rogandan and Arvenian," the emperor observed.

The bisri tried not to sound too eager. "I will apply myself diligently to the task," he promised.

The emperor gazed off into the horizon. "It seems I will be much distracted in the near future. Spending time with my daughter is long overdue."

Ahuzza looked at him quizzically.

"I proposed a marriage alliance with the Rogandan crown prince," the emperor told him with a sigh. "Lord Torbury said some pretty words to deflect me from my purpose, but it was nevertheless apparent that the notion terrified King Krasmir. I can only conclude that Neira has not left a favorable impression."

"I am sure Her Highness will both appreciate and benefit from your attention, Your Majesty."

"I see you share their opinion," observed the emperor gloomily. "The situation is clearly worse than I realized."

Horrified, Ahuzza opened his mouth to protest.

The emperor waved him to silence. "Don't bother to deny it, Ahuzza. You will be of little use to me as an ambassador if you're too frightened to tell me the truth." He frowned. "One thing puzzles me. Why did you travel to Kat Ahket to see me, when I had already received a message from Krasmir requesting a meeting?"

"It was Lord Torbury's suggestion to employ a backup plan, Your Majesty. Captain Gharpin and I sailed together to meet with you. But in case something went wrong, King Krasmir sent a message with a merchant as well. It seems the message reached you first."

"I would not have expected a merchant to reach me," the emperor told him. "These have been challenging times for merchants. Ahrans have not been welcome in Rogand, and few Rogandans have dared to travel to Kat Ahket."

"The Rogandans located a merchant who was unusually capable and persistent."

The emperor snorted. "Such qualities are hardly surprising in a smuggler. I had this so-called merchant thrown into jail as soon as he had delivered the message."

A look of horror played across Ahuzza's face before he could prevent it.

"Don't trouble yourself, Ahuzza. I arranged for him to be released with a stern warning after a couple of days in the lockup." He shook his head stoically. "I doubt it will make any difference."

Ahuzza looked at the emperor tentatively. "If I may raise a different matter, Your Majesty, I believe I will owe the crown prince an explanation when I return."

The emperor's eyebrows went up inquiringly.

"When I arrived in Kat Ahket he graciously agreed to receive me. I warned him about the chief minister and expressed my concerns about a possible threat to you. He told me I was raising serious allegations that needed investigation. He then placed me in protective custody. He explained it was for my own safety."

"And he later changed his mind and released you?"

"No. I escaped."

The emperor burst into laughter. "There is more to you than meets the eye, Bisri! I am delighted!"

He studied Ahuzza shrewdly. "And you have been wondering if my son might have been in league with Rheibas?"

Ahuzza felt color rising to his face. "The thought did occur to me, Your Majesty."

The emperor chuckled. "You needn't trouble yourself. My son hated Rheibas more than most—he despised the man. Much as I appreciate your concerns on my behalf, the young whelp does nothing without my knowledge. He never sneezes without me finding out about it!" A wry grin came to his face. "As for you escaping from under his nose, set your mind at rest. I will deal with the matter."

He slapped Ahuzza heartily on the back. "There's something refreshingly transparent about you, Bisri. I hope you never lose that quality!"

39

———

Rupert stood in a palace garden, holding Tasha's hands lightly in his own and gazing wistfully into her eyes.

"This has felt like the longest week of my life," he said with a sigh. "Harrowing as our captivity was, at least I was able to spend every day with you. Now I have to make an appointment to see you. And even then we're never truly alone." He threw a sideways glance at the chaperone hovering nearby. "I've been missing you, Tasha!"

"I've been missing you, too." She took a step closer, and his heart began to pound. "I want to spend the rest of my life with you, Rupert," she breathed.

He gazed at her in helpless longing. If it were possible, he'd marry her tomorrow and never leave her side again.

Both of them knew it wasn't that simple.

"I need to leave for Castel tomorrow," he told her, reluctantly bringing the moment to an end.

"Does it have to be so soon?"

The crestfallen look on her face tugged at his heart, but he couldn't escape his responsibilities.

"I've been away from my kingdom far too long. My subjects must have wondered if I'd ever return. And they believed that my sister—the last of our line—had been taken from them as well." He shook his head. "I can't delay this any longer. But I will return the moment our wedding has been arranged. After that we can be together always."

"We'd better talk to my parents," she said.

Leading him inside, she took him to a room in the royal apartments where they found both of her parents sitting restlessly.

Queen Deka jumped up when they appeared. Seeing the look on Tasha's face, she cried, "Whatever is wrong?"

"Rupert is leaving tomorrow," Tasha told them. "He won't be back until the wedding."

"There, there," the queen said, wrapping a comforting arm around her daughter.

Before long she began sniffling herself. Drawing back, she gazed at Tasha mournfully. "I thought I'd lost you!" she said. "Then at last you were restored to me. But now you'll marry and go away, and I'll never see you again!"

"Don't be silly, Mother," Tasha replied. "We'll visit Rog whenever we can."

"And you'll always be welcome at Castel Citadel," Rupert added. "You can stay for as long as you like."

Their efforts were in vain. After a brief attempt to rally, the queen abandoned herself completely to despondency. Dissolving into tears, she buried her face in Tasha's shoulder.

The king raised his hands helplessly. "We completely understand, Rupert. You must do your duty to your kingdom. I'm sure I don't need to tell you that you will always be welcome here."

After saying his farewells, Rupert excused himself. Tasha accompanied him out of the royal apartments.

"Will I see you tomorrow before I go?" he asked.

"Of course," she assured him. "And I will wait impatiently for your return."

A RED-TINTED SUNRISE SAW WILL, Thomas, and Brother Ander gathered at a small dock in Rog Harbor. The little group had come to farewell Kamash and his friend Gharpin. King Rupert had departed for Castel by ship the previous day, accompanied by much pomp and ceremony, and Will knew that an official send off would also have been arranged for Kamash if the old man hadn't firmly rejected any such notion. He also knew that King Krasmir had found time to express his thanks and say his goodbyes in private.

"So you're finally going back to your island again, Kamash!" said Thomas. "But not alone this time."

"I am joining him for one month only," said Gharpin. "I am helping him get a start."

Brother Ander grinned at the former captain. "Your Rogandan has improved a lot!"

The Ahran shrugged, jerking his head in the direction of Kamash. "I like him better when I do not understand him."

His remark drew a chuckle from Kamash. "Rude as Gharpin might be, it will be good to have some company while I get established again."

"What will happen when the month is up?" asked Will.

"The emperor sends a ship. To bring me to Kat Ahket," Gharpin replied. "Then he gives me a new ship. I am Captain Gharpin again!"

"Congratulations!" they all cried in unison.

"Even after he leaves we won't entirely lose touch," Kamash told them. "He's promised to look in on me whenever he's in the region."

"That's excellent news! We wish you well—both of you. All of us owe you a lot!" Will told them.

The others echoed his sentiments.

After a final round of farewells, the two men climbed into the boat and guided it toward the channel. Will and his friends stood and watched until they had sailed out of sight.

Thomas stared after them. "Partings never seem to get any easier," he said, a catch in his voice.

"No, they do not," agreed Will.

Turning their backs on the dock, the three Arvenians headed back toward the city.

———

DELMAR STOOD AT AN OPEN WINDOW, gazing absently out across the city of Varacellan to the sea beyond.

A knock sounded, and a servant appeared. "You have a visitor, Your Majesty," he announced, before silently departing.

Delmar looked up to find Maive standing hesitantly at the door. Their eyes met, and Delmar's heart skipped a beat. The day had finally come.

"Maran said you wanted to speak with me, Your Majesty," she said. Her cheeks colored faintly as she faced him.

"I can't tell you how relieved I am to find you safe and well! Our parting was awkward, and I'm very sorry for that. I've often wished I could have our time over again."

She didn't respond, so he continued. "You saved my life, and I never thanked you properly. Worse, I left you feeling awkward and uncomfortable."

"You have no need to apologize, Your Majesty. I said things I regret too."

He tried to read her eyes. Was it possible she had also dreamed of a different outcome?

"The significance of your service cannot be overstated, Maive. I understand that both King Rupert and Princess Teylee are alive only because of you. Castel and Arvenon, as well as Varas, are deeply in your debt. None of us will forget it." He paused. "Are you planning to continue as an agent now that the threat is behind us?"

She shook her head decisively. "I'm hoping for a more peaceful life in the future."

He smiled. "Does that mean you can tell me your real name now?"

After a moment's hesitation, a dimpled smile transformed her face. Had he imagined she wasn't a beauty?

"My name really is Maive," she told him.

He beamed at her.

A question had been plaguing him. "You've needed to impersonate a queen, Maive. Did it sour you on everything royal?"

"I have never confused pretense with reality," she replied carefully.

She hadn't answered his question, but the faint blush on her cheeks told a tale of its own.

"I hope you will pardon my directness, but I would like to get to know you, Maive. You as a person, not as an agent. Would you be willing to let me do that?"

She looked uncertain, and he took a deep breath. "Something happened when we were together," he told her plainly. "I can't pretend to understand it, but I felt like I came alive." He looked her in the eye. "You told me it meant nothing to you. Were you speaking the truth?"

She looked away, remaining silent for a long moment without responding. Then she shook her head, unable to meet his eyes.

His heart soared. "Whatever was awoken back then might not survive the experience of us getting to know each other properly. But I would like to give it a chance."

The tension had slowly been easing from her face. "I would like that too, Your Majesty."

Taking a step toward her, he reached out and took her hand. "Please walk with me. We have some attractive gardens in the palace grounds, and I would like to show them to you."

She nodded shyly but seemed content to walk hand in hand beside him.

"If we are going to get to know each other properly, you'd better begin by calling me Delmar," he told her with a smile.

THOMAS HAD BECOME restless to return to his family, and he knew that Will was no less eager to be gone. Eventually Will managed to conclude his business with King Krasmir, and they prepared to leave.

To their delight, Brother Ander had decided to join them for at least part of the journey. He was planning to return to Arvenon after spending some time in Aen-irac. Since Thomas and Will planned to make their journey on horseback, it made sense for him to travel with them for a while.

"Is the king planning to give you an official farewell?" Thomas asked Will.

"He would if I'd let him. Lord Kulferan and Lady Tulinay seem to have tolerated me well enough, but the other nobles must be smarting at the special attention I've received from the king. I have no interest in adding fuel to that particular fire."

Nevertheless, as they were about to depart, King Krasmir himself rode up, escorted by a detachment of royal guards. Dismounting, the king approached them.

"We are grateful to you for the gift of the horses, Your Majesty," said Will.

The king waved it away. "It is the least I can do. I owe you more than I can possibly repay, Lord Torbury." He regarded Will frankly. "A king chooses his friends carefully, and I hope you know that I have come to regard you as a friend. It need hardly be said that you are welcome here at any time."

Will bowed low in response. "I am humbled by your words, Your Majesty. For my part, I hold you in high esteem. Rogand is fortunate indeed to be led by you, and I value your friendship greatly."

The king turned to Thomas. "I confess you are a mystery to me, Thomas Stablehand. I cannot shake the feeling that things would have turned out very differently if you had not been here, but I cannot explain why. In any event, you will also find a welcome in Rogand should you ever decide to return."

Thomas thanked him sincerely.

Lastly King Krasmir addressed the monk. "I wish I could convince you to make your home in Rogand permanently, Brother Ander.

Nevertheless, you have assured me that you intend to return at some point, and I will hold you to that. Everyone who knows you will look forward eagerly to that day."

"I thank you for your kindness, Your Majesty," the monk replied. "God willing, I will visit often in the years to come."

Greatly heartened by the king's words, they left the palace. After riding through Rog, they guided their horses onto the main trade route heading south.

There was no shortage of things to talk about.

At one point Will asked Brother Ander, "Have you been to see the High Priest?"

"Yes," he replied. "Several times."

"Inside the temple?" Will asked in surprise. "The place sounds horrific from everything I've heard."

The monk shook his head. "I went inside briefly on my first visit. I found it so oppressive I had to leave. The High Priest was gracious enough to meet with me in the temple grounds."

Will's eyes grew wide with surprise. "That's totally unheard of!" he exclaimed. "He never leaves the temple! Everyone knows that."

Brother Ander shrugged. "We met with him on Rheibas's ship."

"Those were exceptional circumstances," Will returned. Abruptly changing the subject, he asked, "Do you know how he got to be so old? We know he doesn't have the Stone of Vitality."

Thomas grinned. "I suppose he could have invoked the ritual in Drettroth's scroll—the one that relied upon a bargain with the dark gods."

"I believe the explanation is much more simple," the monk replied calmly. "He told me that many of his forbears were long-lived. Apparently it runs in the family."

"Not an especially attractive explanation," said Will disappointedly.

Brother Ander smiled. "My mentor, Brother Elias, used to say that a simple explanation rarely draws a crowd, but it most often turns out to be the truth."

"Did you find out how he came to be on Rheibas's ship?" asked Thomas.

"He didn't say a lot about it, but I believe it was a power play on the part of his second-in-command, the Archprimus."

"Presumably he's had the man removed."

"There was no need. The High Priest told me a struggle broke out among the priests during his abduction. The Archprimus succeeded in taking him, but he was badly wounded in the process. It seems he didn't make it through the night."

"Thereby ending the power struggle," observed Will. "I'm sure the High Priest has rooted out the other conspirators by now."

"I believe so."

"What did the two of you talk about?" asked Thomas curiously.

"Many things," the monk replied, "but mostly theology."

"Do you think you'll see him again?"

"I hope so. He invited me to visit him again next time I'm in Rog."

When they reached the borders of Aen-irac, both Thomas and Will were sorely tempted to divert with Brother Ander to visit old friends. But a long journey lay ahead of them and their families drew them onward. They parted after the monk promised to pass on their greetings.

As soon as he found a suitable moment, Thomas asked Will, "What will you do with the Stone of Authority?"

"Return it to Amyra," Will replied without hesitation.

"Will the two of you share it?"

"Perhaps, under exceptional circumstances. Only if it involves animals though. To be honest, I'll be glad to see the last of it." A grimace came to his face. "However hard I try I can't get the memory of that giant squid out of my head."

Pressing on to Arnost, they arrived to an enthusiastic welcome from their families. Swarming around Thomas and Will eagerly, their children left no room for Amyra or Elena to even reach their husbands. However, as soon as both men retrieved gifts from their saddlebags, the children ran off in great excitement to enjoy their new prizes.

For a while Thomas lost sight of all else in the joy of his reunion with Elena.

A short time later a dazzling burst of sunlight drew Elena's attention heavenward. "Someone's pleased to have Will back again," she said with a smile.

Up to that point the day had been overcast, with dark clouds blotting out the sun. Sunlight was now streaming through a large opening in the clouds above them, shafts of light picking out the two couples.

"I see you've handed it over already, Will," Thomas exclaimed.

"I completely forgot to bring a gift for Amyra," he returned, "so I had to give her something."

She punched him in mock anger.

"What about you, Elena?" Amyra asked.

Elena patted her bodice with a grin. "Thomas was just as eager for a handover. But he's assured me he didn't only bring gifts for the children."

Chatting happily, the four of them wandered into the palace.

KING STEFFAN WAS NO LESS delighted to see Will and Thomas return safely. He was greatly relieved to hear that all of the hostages had been released, not least because it meant that Queen Essanda could come into the open at last. Hiding herself away might have been essential to preserve the fiction that she had been abducted, but it had also become increasingly difficult for the king to bear. He wasted no time in sending a message to Newhaven.

As soon as an opportunity presented itself, the king sat down with Amyra and Elena to hear an account of the dramatic conclusion to the saga in Rogand. All of them listened with amazement as Will and Thomas laid out the unlikely outcome of the Grand Vizier's scheming.

Amyra shook her head in wonder. "Perhaps we'll finally be able to enjoy an extended season of peace." She eyed Will and Thomas shrewdly. "I have a feeling that both of you understated your own role in what happened. I'll look forward to quizzing Brother Ander next time he visits."

The king nodded. "I'm eager to see him and hear his account myself. Brother Ander has become more remarkable than ever—if such a thing were possible."

He addressed himself to Will and Thomas. "What are you planning to do now?"

"Return home with our families, Your Majesty," Will replied.

"I could use your input on a few matters while you're here, Will," the king observed. "But I know what my wife would say. I can almost hear her telling me that after everything you've been through, the only pressing need for both of you is to spend time with your families."

He gazed at the two women. "I'm sure Amyra and Elena must have been starting to wonder if you would ever return!"

They said nothing to contradict him.

He sighed. "I managed without you while you were in Rogand, Will, and there's no reason I can't continue to do so."

AFTER A SINGLE NIGHT IN ARNOST, the two families set out for home, accompanied by a group of soldiers. Both Will and Thomas tried to decline the protection, but the king wouldn't yield.

When the time came to part ways, Thomas insisted that the soldiers continue on with Will. "You know how strongly Anneka and Rellan feel about Newhaven's privacy. And we don't need the protection. Not here."

"I scarcely know how to thank you, Thomas," Will told him. "I dragged you into danger once again, and it could so easily have been the end of us this time."

"You've never done it for your own sake," Thomas replied. "And we needed to be there—all three of us. It could have ended very badly without the help of the stones."

They parted with a confused mixture of regret and eagerness to reach their homes.

THE SUN WAS SINKING low in the sky when Thomas and Elena and the children finally reached Newhaven. Voices rose up to greet them, and they responded with cheery greetings of their own. Reaching their hut, the children raced inside, eager to rediscover everything they had left behind.

Stepping inside, Thomas took Elena in his arms. "We're home at last!"

He kissed her deeply, ignoring the noisy reaction of the children. "As soon as the children are asleep we'll find a quiet corner," he promised. "There's so much I still haven't heard about your time in Arnost."

She smiled up at him, a sigh of contentment passing her lips.

"I've never wanted fame or palaces, Elena," he whispered. "This is where I belong—right here with you."

40

———

30 years after the death of the Grand Vizier

With the Arvenian delegation drawing closer to Rog, a guard rode up to Lord Torbury's carriage, bringing an end to Thomas's conversation with his friend.

"A messenger has arrived from King Rimek, My Lord," the guard announced, addressing himself to Will. "The king is planning to greet the delegation in person. We expect to reach Rog by mid-afternoon."

"Thank you, Captain," Will replied.

The guard bowed and rode away.

"King Rimek." Will shook his head. "I'm still not used to it."

"It isn't surprising," Thomas replied. "You and King Krasmir were good friends over many years."

"I'm finding it harder to accept change these days," Will acknowledged. "I'm getting too old to be bothered with it. Still, young Rimek deserves his opportunity. He's waited long enough."

"He's certainly needed to be patient. And he isn't exactly young— he's in his early fifties!"

Will grunted. "Fifty sounds young to me."

Thomas laughed. "In that case I suppose you must think of King Aiden as a mere child. He isn't forty yet."

"He's a good boy," Will conceded. "His father would have been proud of him."

The mention of Aiden's father prompted Thomas to glance at the carriage behind them. Elena and Amyra were chatting enthusiastically with Essanda, the Dowager Queen of Arvenon since the passing of King Steffan two years previously at the age of 71. Elena might be a commoner, but preserving such boundaries held no more interest for Essanda than it had for her late husband.

"I suppose I'd better make myself presentable," said Will abruptly.

Thomas grinned. Will's appearance was always presentable, and his mind remained sharp as a dagger.

"I want you to take a good look at the Lestanorian ambassador, Thomas. He's certain to put in an appearance. I want to know if Lestanor is behind the recent trouble with the plains nomads." He looked at Thomas sharply. "You did bring it, didn't you!"

"Of course," Thomas assured him, patting his chest. As always, the Stone of Knowing rested securely on its clasp beneath his tunic. "I'll see what I can learn."

He glanced up at the sky. "Those dark clouds look threatening. We're incredibly fortunate to have avoided rain completely these last few days. I hope the weather doesn't intrude on the ceremony in a couple of days' time."

Will waved a hand dismissively. "Being fortunate has nothing to do with it. Rain won't interrupt the coronation any more than it did our journey."

Thomas's eyes went wide. "Do you mean to say you badgered poor Amyra into using the Stone of Authority—just to keep yourself dry?" He shook his head. "You're an old tyrant."

"Me? A tyrant? Ha!" he snorted. "Don't waste your sympathy on Amyra—she's more than capable of looking after herself!"

Thomas just grinned at him.

"Besides, it was never about me," Will insisted. "The queen is traveling with us. She's too old to be caught in the rain."

"She's younger than any of us," Thomas reminded him.

"Everyone's younger than us these days," grumbled Will.

The arrival of King Rimek brought an end to their conversation. Climbing down from the carriage, all of them bent at the waist.

After greeting the dowager queen and her companions, Rimek turned to Will and Thomas.

"Lord Torbury, Thomas Stablehand, you are both very welcome."

"Our sincere condolences on the loss of your father, Your Majesty," said Will. "He was a worthy king and a good man."

"He held you in high regard, Lord Torbury. He especially looked forward to your visits."

"It was an honor to know him."

"I trust that Arvenon understands that I value our alliance no less than my father. These are uncertain times."

"Lestanor?" asked Will.

The king nodded. "The new king has been flexing his muscles."

"The nomad tribes have been restive of late," Will told him. "We have wondered if Lestanor is behind it."

"Rogand also shares a border with the plains in the southwest," Rimek observed, "and we have noted similar stirrings. Whatever ambitions Lestanor's king might harbor, I am confident he will show restraint while we stand firmly together." Rimek smiled. "I am hopeful we will not need to draw upon your tactical genius anytime soon."

"My son Ethen might be of more use, Your Majesty. He shows considerable promise."

"I will gladly meet with him as often as King Aiden is willing to release him," the king replied. "In the meantime, I hope you will join me later. I find myself confronted with a number of strategic challenges, and I would value your wisdom."

"It would be an honor."

After a smile and a quick nod, King Rimek remounted and returned to the city.

As they rolled into Rog and headed for the palace, Thomas mused on Will's effortless transition from blustery old rogue to smooth-talking diplomat. The strange thing was that both identities reflected who he was. Thomas knew better than anyone how much the world needed men like Will, and he could only appreciate him in all his guises.

Dark clouds brooded heavily as the morning of the coronation dawned, but, just as Will had promised, the sky cleared well before the event got under way. The palace boasted extensive grounds, and the ceremony would be taking full advantage of them. In addition to nobles, officials, and envoys, King Rimek intended to admit a large contingent of commoners to the palace grounds to observe the coronation. Accordingly he made arrangements for a broad area to be cordoned off to accommodate the common people. Thomas had heard that refreshments would be freely provided to all after the formalities were over.

The coronation would also be the official commissioning of the new family crest, featuring a bear on a field of green. Even in the absence of visible opposition to his rule, Rimek understood that he needed to build a popular base of his own. Krasmir had often been likened to a bear, both before and after his coronation, and Rimek intended to use the symbol both to honor his father and to leverage Krasmir's popularity with commoners and nobles alike.

Thomas and Elena were led to preferred seating along with other members of the Arvenian delegation, and Thomas was delighted to discover Brother Ander among the group. He couldn't suppress a grin when he noted that the monk had been positioned as far away as possible from the large contingent of priests of the dark gods.

Brother Ander might have established a remarkable bond with the former High Priest, but his friend was long gone. The priest's prolonged tenure had finally concluded just two years after the Grand Vizier's demise, ending once and for all any suggestion that the dark gods had granted him immortality. Thomas had no doubt that the current incumbent wanted nothing to do with a foreign monk.

Other members of foreign delegations were positioned nearby, and Thomas was delighted to catch sight of an older man he recognized as Bisri Ahuzza. He decided to greet the Ahran as soon as he had an opportunity. A sullen faced man sat apart from the others. Bringing the stone into contact with his skin, Thomas confirmed he was looking at the Lestanorian ambassador. In a matter of moments he had mentally compiled a substantial list of observations to pass on to Will.

The ceremony got underway, commanding Thomas's full attention. In spite of his proficiency in Rogandan, Thomas understood very little of it, presumably because it relied upon archaic words no longer in common use. When it finished, loud cheering arose.

The king and his wife together raised high a staff featuring the new royal emblem, prompting a new round of applause. The flag rippled in the breeze, revealing a bear standing upright with arms outstretched.

Then a movement behind the king brought the cheering to an abrupt end.

Extensive woodlands fringed the grounds in which the ceremony was being held. To Thomas's amazement, two bears emerged from the trees, trotting purposefully toward the official party. Everyone backed away except the king, who stood boldly in their path. Guards belatedly hurried forward with drawn swords, but he waved them back. One of the bears was little more than a baby, and it held something between its teeth. The other bear was large and intimidating.

Bypassing the king, the baby bear shuffled toward the observers in the front row. Sitting on the very end of the row was Queen Deka, clad in mourning attire following the recent death of her husband, King Krasmir. After lifting its head high for all to see, the little bear opened its mouth and deposited a large white flower at the feet of the astonished dowager queen. Then it turned and ambled back to the forest.

Approaching the king, the large bear raised itself high on two legs and released a loud roar. Then it bent low, as if in homage, before spinning around and shambling off after its offspring.

For a moment complete silence reigned. Then a mighty shout arose as the people paid noisy homage to their king, enthusiastically affirming the honor bestowed by the bear. The commoners were delirious with excitement, and even the nobles were visibly impressed.

The king began to circulate among the people. As he passed nearby, Thomas overheard him say to one of the nobles, "I was as surprised as you!" Reaching the barrier separating the nobles from the common folk, the king horrified his guards by stepping over it to mingle with his people. He was soon swallowed up by a cheering mob.

With many old friends close at hand, Thomas still found time for a warm and informative interaction with Bisri Ahuzza. He was gratified to hear that the connection with the empire remained as robust as ever.

The festivities continued unabated as the day wore away. The sun was setting before the grounds were finally cleared of revelers.

That night Thomas and Elena sat with Will and Amyra in a palace apartment.

"The visit from the bears was very impressive," Thomas told Will. "Was Amyra in on your little surprise?"

Amyra opened her mouth to speak, but Will got in first. "I thought Rimek deserved a bit of a boost—just to get him started," he said. "It will be up to him from here."

"I was most definitely *not* expecting anything like that," Amyra assured Thomas. "He claimed he needed the stone in case the horses were unsettled." She cocked an eyebrow in Will's direction. "I should have known he'd pull some kind of stunt!"

"I knew exactly what to do with the bears, because Amyra's been trying to train me for years," said Will with a cheeky smile. "With little success, I'm sorry to say."

All of them burst into laughter except Amyra, although she didn't seem too displeased.

Queen Essanda and Brother Ander appeared, and loud voices and laughter quickly filled the room.

Before long King Delmar and Queen Maive joined them, prompting an enthusiastic greeting.

"Did you bring your children?" asked Amyra hopefully. "It's much too long since I saw them last."

"No," replied Maive with a smile. "They're not little anymore. The two of them are well able to fend for themselves."

"And we needed to leave someone in charge during our absence," added Delmar.

The energy level increased even more with the arrival of King Rupert and Queen Tasha.

"How are the twins and their sisters?" asked Essanda eagerly.

"All grown up," Rupert assured her. "I expect we'll be calling you over for a wedding or two before long."

"You hardly look a day older!" Elena told Tasha. "What's your secret?"

"I credit my husband," she replied with a grin. "He manages to keep a smile on my face no matter what happens. I must say you look remarkable yourself, Elena!"

"To me she's as beautiful as the day I first saw her face," said Thomas. He gazed fondly into Elena's eyes, dismissing with a grin the hoots from the other men.

"It's so good to see you all!" cried Essanda. "There was barely an opportunity to greet one another at the ceremony. When did you arrive in Rog?"

"Not until last night," Rupert replied. He indicated Delmar and Maive. "The four of us sailed together, and unfortunately we were delayed by adverse winds."

"I hope you weren't visited by a giant squid," quipped Amyra.

"That's no way to refer to Her Imperial Highness Princess Neira," chided Will, setting them off into gales of horrified laughter.

Animated conversation continued well into the night. As they reminisced, they discovered that their shared history had been transformed into memories of narrow escapes and ultimate triumph. Real as the horror had been, it had been left to wither in the past, blotted out by the vitality that flowed from their deliverance.

THE DAYS FOLLOWING the coronation proved to be a busy time for Brother Ander. His assistance with physical ailments was in heavy demand among both rulers and common folk, and he responded to them all without distinction. Wherever possible, he drew in local healers, intent on supporting rather than supplanting them.

Having developed significant friendships with every royal in the region, including the new king of Rogand and his wife, he also found himself taken aside for consultations on a wide range of topics. Giving freely of his time and wisdom, he received gratitude and friendship in return.

Intending to remain behind in Rogand for a season, he bade each of the visitors farewell as they departed, promising to come to them as soon as he could.

Thomas made a point of taking him aside as he was about to leave.

"All of us are getting older, Brother Ander. Apart from you, that is," he added with a grin. "Would you please be willing to conduct our funerals when the time comes? We'll try to send a message when the end seems to be getting close. I'm speaking on behalf of Will and Amyra, as well as Elena and myself."

"Of course," Brother Ander replied without hesitation. "I will pray that such necessities are long delayed!"

After embracing him one last time, Thomas joined the others. Their carriage rolled away, slowly dwindling in size. A distant waving of many arms provided the monk with a final glimpse of his friends before they were lost to sight.

EPILOGUE

Brother Ander stood silently before the open grave, his mind rich with memories. Fifteen years had passed since the coronation of King Rimek, fifteen years filled with unnumbered joys and griefs.

As so often seemed to be the case, he had sensed that the time was near. He had arrived at Newhaven in time to see Thomas Stablehand end his life at peace, surrounded by his children and grandchildren. Thomas had attained a great age, and he left the world grateful for a final blessing from his oldest friend—the man who had taken up the mantle laid down by another treasured friend, the long-departed Brother Vangellis.

A final expression of respect remained for Brother Ander to perform. Standing before the grave he began the committal, surrounded by grieving children, grandchildren, and many others from the Newhaven community.

Brother Ander aside, Thomas was the last of his generation. Both Anneka and Rellan were gone, leaving the Newhaven community to thrive under the leadership of their children. Four years previously, Thomas and Elena had traveled to the Torbury holdings to comfort Amyra as Brother Ander buried Will. They laid him to rest near his lifelong friend Rufe Sarjant and Rufe's wife Peggy. Amyra had passed away the following year, joining Will and her mother Dahra in the little graveyard.

Elena had hung on for two more years, eventually departing at the age of 78. Thomas had never recovered from her loss.

Now he was being laid to rest beside her, near the graves of her father Rubin, their friend Haldek, and his own parents, Axel and Marya.

Thomas and Elena left behind their three children, Tamara, Andy, and Delia. The monk had watched them grow from their infancy, conducted their marriages, and celebrated as between them they bore ten children of their own.

Dragging his thoughts back to the present, he addressed the gathered mourners.

"Thomas Stablehand was a simple man—a man of integrity and honor. No hidden agendas lay behind his ready smile. Simple as he was, he made a monumental contribution, not just to the lives of those he knew and loved, but to Arvenon and the kingdoms surrounding it. He was known and respected by kings, queens, and nobles, as well as countless commoners like himself. More than once he faced almost certain death without flinching, solely for the sake of others. He never spoke of the full darkness and horror of those times. I was present on one of those occasions, and I saw first hand his bravery and his willingness to sacrifice himself. A great evil was averted that day, in no small part because of his involvement. Perhaps he was never appropriately honored for his deeds, but he was content with that.

"None of that is why you are here today. You are here to honor the memory of the ordinary man you knew and respected—a man who loved his wife, cared for and provided for his children, and worked tirelessly in support of this community. Many of you learned to ride and to handle horses under the patient guidance of Thomas Stablehand. Thankfully, he has passed on his gift with the animals to his daughter Delia." He smiled in the direction of Thomas and Elena's youngest.

He gazed around him. "None of us live forever, however worthy our lives and contributions might have been. Thankfully though, we can enter eternity without fear or dread. One has gone before us, one willing to forgive our wrongs and discharge our debts if we will trust him to do so. It is into his loving arms and his gracious care that I commit Thomas Stablehand today."

Flowers were scattered lovingly over Thomas's remains as his body was slowly lowered into the ground. The grave was then sealed with fresh earth.

When the burial was over, the monk led the mourners away, encouraging them to celebrate Thomas's life as they reminisced together.

BROTHER ANDER REMAINED with them for several days. As he was preparing to go, Tamara took him aside.

"My father asked me to remind you of something he requested you to do. Apparently he spoke to you about it after my mother's funeral."

The monk smiled. "Yes, I remember the conversation. I will do as he asked." After thanking her, he said his farewells and left.

At the time, Thomas had drawn him aside. "Could you please do me a favor?" he had asked. "When I'm gone, go to the place where you used to sit with Brother Gerome to chat and watch the sunset. You'll find a package there, buried beneath a large rock. Please take it with you when you leave Newhaven."

Searching out the location, Brother Ander found the rock and dug up the package. He took it with him when he departed.

Two full days passed before he opened the package. He found in it a letter written by Will, and two pieces of tightly wrapped cloth. Unfolding the pieces of cloth, he discovered the Stone of Knowing hidden inside one, along with its clasp and chain. The Stone of Authority lay within the other.

Unrolling Will's letter, he sat down to read it.

Brother Ander,

I am writing this on behalf of Thomas, Elena, Amyra, and myself.

We have long agonized over what to do with the stones after our passing. We have seen the enormous good that can flow from their use. We have also seen the chaos that follows when a truly evil person gets as much as a sniff of them. I myself experienced the terrible consequences of Agon acquiring the Stone of Authority. Both Drettroth and Rheibas came uncomfortably close in their pursuit of the stones.

A number of options presented themselves.

We could each pass our stone to one of our children, leaving it to them to deal with the burden. The scroll indicated that others before us had followed this path, although the outcomes it reported were far from encouraging. And how would we choose between our children?

We could hide them where no one could find them. None of us were able to convince ourselves that this option would prove effective in the long term.

We could try to destroy them, perhaps by crushing them into tiny grains. Who could guess what might happen if we scattered the grains? If the powers of a stone reside in many of its grains, the effect might be to greatly expand their reach, and more unpredictably than ever.

After pondering and discussing these matters over many years, we together agreed on the simple plan of bequeathing the stones to you.

All three of the stones now rest in your hands. Had it been Rheibas, he wouldn't have wasted a minute before setting out to rule the known world. Perhaps you might decide to embark upon a great endeavor of your own. Perhaps you will simply use them for good, like the original Goodman Tomas in the scroll. Perhaps you will hide or even destroy them.

You must decide. We have no desire to encumber you with requests, recommendations, or even suggestions. We trust you to do with them as you see fit.

In taking this course, we recognize we are placing a great burden
on you. We can think of no one better able to shoulder such a burden.
This letter comes with our grateful thanks and sincerest regards,

Will Prentis,
  also for Amyra, Thomas, and Elena.

BROTHER ANDER SAT without moving for a very long time, pondering what he should do.

The stones had been entrusted to him. Nevertheless, even before he finished reading Will's letter he knew he would not keep them for his own use.

It wasn't a question of doubting himself and his motivations; there were practical considerations he could not ignore. Trouble had found him from the moment he used the Stone of Vitality without constraint. Any person bold enough to use all three stones would draw conflict as surely as honey attracted bears.

That would not have deterred Rheibas. Someone like him would wield the power of the stones without hesitation or moderation, ruthlessly destroying any who dared oppose him. But Brother Ander was not Rheibas. Nor was he unique. He felt sure that responsibility for all three stones would quickly become a heavy burden for most reasonable people.

The situation also forced him to confront a decision he had been deferring. How much longer could he continue to use the Stone of Vitality? With the monk's own generation little more than a memory, his longevity was already becoming proverbial. How could he possibly explain it as the years continued to stretch on?

Some kind of decision would be needed before long, although he saw no immediate urgency. He could be certain only of two things: he would not keep the stones himself, and he would not burden one person with all three of them. Beyond that he could not be sure of anything.

Eventually he placed the Stone of Knowing around his neck, making sure it wasn't touching his skin. Then he carefully secured the Stone of Authority within his robe.

Finally he put the stones from his mind and resumed his wanderings.

OBEDIENT TO A TIMELESS RITUAL, the sun reached down once more to kiss the horizon. Another day was drawing to a close.

Settling himself on a grassy hillside, Brother Ander gazed into the heavens, eager to savor the extravagant display already claiming the sky.

Wondrous as it was, it left him restless. That day, like every day before it, had known when its span was over. Yet here he was, five years after receiving the stones, still without a conclusion.

He could sidestep the issue no longer—the time had come. He would resolve it in the morning, before he did anything else.

Stretching himself out on the grass, he abandoned himself to sleep.

He woke well before dawn, confronted immediately with the troublesome question. What should he do with the stones?

Throughout his life he had seen evil in many of its guises, and he well knew the propensity for wrongdoing that had dogged humankind from the beginning. Allowing the stones to pass into unknown hands seemed risky at best, and grossly irresponsible at worst.

Hiding them seemed attractive if it could be done effectively. After all, the talismans had emerged in his lifetime after lying hidden for countless years—perhaps centuries. He had passed through many lonely regions in his tireless wanderings. One of them would surely do as a new hiding place.

And yet he could find no peace with such a conclusion. The more he pondered it, the more he realized that basing a decision entirely on fear required him to elevate evil more highly than it deserved.

Familiar words from his Holy Book came to mind.

> "As for man, his days are like grass.
> As a flower of the field, so he flourishes.
> For the wind passes over it, and it is gone.
> Its place remembers it no more.
> But the Lord's loving kindness is from everlasting to
>   everlasting with those who fear him."

No human endured for long—he well knew it, having conducted more funerals than he could count. Evil sometimes far outlasted the one who initiated it, but his own experience confirmed that the grace and mercy of the Almighty outlasted everything.

Why should he be afraid?

He saw at last what should have been clear from the beginning— he needed to dispose of the stones in a manner consistent with their original purpose.

No human artisan had crafted the stones. They were neither his, nor anyone else's, to hide or destroy.

Nor were they to be shunned. Malign intent had played no part in their origins. Fashioned by one who was unfailingly good, they had always been intended to be used.

It occurred to him to wonder if Will and Thomas and the others would have seen it the way he did. He had no way to be certain, but they knew him well, and Will's letter made it clear they trusted him to do as he saw fit.

Choosing to embrace hope, he decided at last. He would pass them on to three different individuals.

All that remained was to choose the recipients. In recent times the stones had rested in the hands of Thomas and Elena, Amyra and Will, Kamash, and himself. All of them were ordinary people, and none were prepared for what awaited them. Yet each had risen to the challenge. There was no reason to think others would do any less.

He felt confident he would recognize the right people when he came upon them. They would be no more perfect than the previous stewards, but the responsibility for final outcomes rested in the hands of the one who had fashioned and sent the stones.

A time would come for him to yield up the Stone of Vitality. Like Kamash before him, he would do so without regret. Having already exceeded a normal lifespan, he had no desire to live on endlessly. He would miss the familiar surge of joy as the sick unfailingly responded to his prayer, but he was content. Another could take up where he left off.

A great weight had been lifted from his mind. With a nod of satisfaction, Brother Ander shouldered his meager possessions and rose to his feet.

A pre-dawn glimmer had begun to lighten the sky. The sun was ready to burst forth, resurrected, like a butterfly released from its cocoon.

Turning toward the east, he set off with his face to the rising sun.

The End

The saga of *The Stone Cycle* ends with this final installment

Ready for more?

Don't miss the first novel in Allan N. Packer's second epic fantasy series!

The Hard Edge of Magic (The Ruptured Kingdom Book 1)

NOTE FROM THE AUTHOR

Thank you for reading *The Hope of Vitality*. Huge thanks for staying on the journey to the very end of the series!

Don't forget to leave a review. Reviews make a huge difference to me as well as benefiting other readers.

I also very much appreciate feedback from my readers. I'd love to hear what you thought of the series—please feel free to send me an email.

This release ends the saga of *The Stone Cycle*. If you haven't read *The Seer: A Prequel to The Stone of Knowing*, see below for more information.

What's next? Having thoroughly enjoyed my years in Arvenon and the surrounding kingdoms, I decided it was time to move on. The result is my second epic fantasy series, The Ruptured Kingdom! Check out the first novel in the series now: The Hard Edge of Magic, described below.

To be kept up to date on new releases, sign up to my mailing list at *allanpacker.com*. New subscribers will receive exclusive bonus novelettes, including a novelette prequel to *The Cost of Knowing*. The novelette, *The Rending: A Prequel to The Cost of Knowing*, is a complete story four chapters (13,000 words) in length. It provides background information on Anneka and her community. The novelette is described below. Paperback and audiobook versions are also available from online bookstores.

Hungry and desperate, Kylen knows what it's like to be an outcast. Plucked from the streets by a tight-lipped stranger, he begins to dream of a better life. But his rescuer turns out to be a renegade mage. In an instant Kylen finds himself transformed from a person of no account to a dangerous fugitive.

But much more than his life might be at stake. Dark forces are stirring, and an ancient evil is poised, ready to be unleashed on an unsuspecting kingdom. Comfortable and arrogant, the kingdom's mages are bent on destroying the one person capable of saving them.

On the run with his mentor, Kylen tries to ignore the voices whispering about his destiny. Of what use is a fabled destiny when you're struggling to survive?

If you enjoy epic fantasy with gripping action and relatable characters in a compelling coming of age saga, then try the novels of The Ruptured Kingdom *now!*

Endings may be beginnings in disguise

Anneka is comfortable and confident, a noblewoman of consequence living a life of privilege. Until the day her world is torn apart.

After losing everything she most cares about, she must abandon her home and her way of life in an attempt to secure the future of those who depend on her.

No one, least of all Anneka, could anticipate a deeper significance to her struggle. Yet her journey will one day influence the fate of kingdoms.

How did the stone come to be where Thomas found it? The answer can be found in a prequel to *The Stone of Knowing*.

The Seer is a novelette, 5 chapters (13,500 words) in length. It is a standalone story, and as such can be read independently of other books in *The Stone Cycle* series. The novelette is described below.

Eyes see no more than a glimpse

Sheylha is a seer—a woman with unique and extraordinary abilities. Powerful men want to control her, to use her to dominate others.

Kalvor is a warrior of unusual tenacity, a hunter who never gives up. Driven by his past, he has become a dangerous enemy.

When Kalvor is sent to find and capture the seer, each of them will be tested in ways they could never have imagined.

In time the outcome will determine the fate of kingdoms.

LIST OF CHARACTERS

- *Agon* - previous king of Rogand
- *Ahreitas* - imperial crown prince of Ahr
- *Ahuzza* - Ahran bisri (nobleman), special envoy of the emperor of Ahr
- *Aiden* - crown prince of Arvenon, son of Steffan and Essanda
- *Akohlsa* - Ahran agent working with Kahrlin
- *Ander* - a monk; former Arvenian soldier who traveled with Will and later commanded soldiers at the Battle of Torbury Scarp
- *Andy* - son of Thomas and Elena
- *Ashloh* - princess of Rogand, daughter of King Krasmir and Queen Deka; younger twin of Crown Prince Rimek
- *Atmek* - Rogandan priest reporting to Goultzar, the Archprimus
- *Amyra* - wife of Will Prentis; holder of the Stone of Authority; formerly Ahnya, daughter of Sheylha
- *Anneka* - former noblewoman who leads a community hidden away in the forest near Erestor
- *Bolnyk* - senior Ahran agent

- *Bezai* - Rogandan naval captain
- *Boedwyk* - eccentric Rogandan nobleman
- *Charlotte* - princess of Arvenon, daughter of Steffan and Essanda
- *Dahra* - mother of Amyra; formerly Sheylha, the Seer
- *Dannhur* - Rogandan soldier assigned as a guard to Brother Ander
- *Deka* - queen of Rogand; wife of Krasmir and mother of Crown Prince Rimek, Princess Ashloh, Princess Kyla, and Princess Teylee
- *Delia* - daughter of Thomas and Elena
- *Delmar* - king of Varas, a neighboring kingdom to Arvenon, and ally of King Steffan of Arvenon
- *Dessue* - Ahran guard leader
- *Drettroth* - high-ranking Rogandan nobleman who commanded the Rogandan army during the invasion of Arvenon; known as Vilkami during his childhood
- *Eisgold* - Castelan nobleman formerly commanding the Castelan army; exiled after the Battle of Torbury Scarp for ignoring orders at a crucial moment in the battle
- *Elena* - wife of Thomas Stablehand
- *Essanda* - Queen of Arvenon, formerly a princess of Castel
- *Ethen* - son of Will and Amyra
- *Galvas* - Varasan agent
- *Gharpin* - captain of an Ahran ship
- *Ghonik* - Rogandan soldier assigned as a guard to Brother Ander
- *Giddel* - Castelan envoy, based in Rogand
- *Goultzar* - Archprimus, second in command to the High Priest of the Dark Gods of Rogand
- *Haldek* - former Rogandan soldier who unwittingly helped Will on more than one significant occasion; living in a tiny forest community with Elena, Rubin, and Thomas
- *Hennis* - Arvenian army captain serving under Rufe Sarjant

- *Hourahn* - emperor of Ahr
- *Kahrlin* - senior Ahran agent in Castel
- *Karevis* - Varasan nobleman and commander of the Varasan army; played a key role at the Battle of Torbury Scarp
- *Kamash* - Rogandan who chose to exile himself to a remote island
- *Krasmir* - king of Rogand, formerly a wealthy and powerful Rogandan baron
- *Kulferan* - Rogandan nobleman and army commander
- *Kyla* - princess of Rogand, daughter of King Krasmir and Queen Deka
- *Kyleth* - Rogandan soldier assigned as a guard to Brother Ander
- *Leonid* - prince of Arvenon, son of Steffan and Essanda
- *Maive* - Varasan agent
- *Maran* - senior agent answering to King Delmar of Varas
- *Millie* - daughter of Will and Amyra
- *Neira* - imperial princess of the Empire of Ahr
- *Pultek* - Rogandan naval captain
- *Ranauld* - Arvenian count and a senior leader in the army at Torbury Scarp; a close confidante of King Steffan and a friend of Will Prentis
- *Rellan* - Arvenian soldier from Erestor who led a cavalry force to the battlefield at Torbury Scarp with his twin brother Kuper; married to Anneka; lives at the Newhaven forest community
- *Rheibas* - Grand Vizier of the Empire of Ahr
- *Rimek* - crown prince of Rogand, son of King Krasmir and Queen Deka
- *Roethen* - rich Rogandan merchant living in Rog
- *Rubin* - father of Elena
- *Rufe Sarjant* - respected and physically imposing Arvenian soldier; a close friend of Will Prentis and a key leader in the army

- *Rupert* - king of Castel, brother to Essanda, son of King Istel
- *Shallam* - Rogandan agent, fluent in Ahran
- *Shulkahr* - Ahran leader
- *Steffan the Second* - king of Arvenon
- *Talmon* - Varasan envoy, based in Rogand
- *Tamara* - daughter of Thomas and Elena
- *Teylee* - Rogandan princess, daughter of King Krasmir and Queen Deka, also known as Tasha
- *Thomas Stablehand* - possessor of the Stone of Knowing
- *Thorsel* - Castelan nobleman
- *Torbury* - title granted to Will Prentis by King Steffan; Will Prentis was elevated to the Arvenian peerage as Lord Torbury in honor of his efforts in defeating the Rogandans
- *Tulinay* - Rogandan noblewoman; head of King Krasmir's spy network
- *Uman* - guard and servant to Princess Neira
- *Vangellis* - Arvenian monk who became a key mentor to Thomas; role model to Brother Ander; killed at Lord Drettroth's stronghold
- *Vholahr* - senior Ahran general
- *Will Prentis* - commander of the Arvenian army, greatly respected by his soldiers as well as King Steffan due to his remarkable qualities; fluent in Rogandan and widely traveled
- *Yetvar* - leader of Rogandan shepherds
- *Zattu* - senior Rogandan priest
- *Zhukha* - Ahran agent

RESEARCH NOTES

The reader is advised to avoid this section before finishing *The Hope of Vitality*.

Rappelling with a single rope

In helping Bisri Ahuzza to escape from his room five floors above the ground, Shallam used a technique similar to the Dülfersitz. The technique is demonstrated live here:

- https://www.youtube.com/watch?v=j23eZhTOv3s
- https://www.youtube.com/watch?v=CLQoIltdYdo

From Wikipedia: https://en.wikipedia.org/wiki/Dülfersitz

The Dülfersitz (named after its inventor, mountaineer Hans Dülfer), also known as body rappel is a classical, or non-mechanical abseiling technique, used in rock climbing and mountaineering. It is not used frequently any more, since the introduction of belay devices. In the Dülfersitz, the rope is wound around the body, and the speed of descent is controlled using the friction of the rope against the body.

The advantages of the Dülfersitz are that one can descend without a climbing harness or belay device, and because the rope is not kinked or subjected to concentrated forces, it does not experience as much wear. The major disadvantage of this method is that intense heat is generated by the friction on the shoulder, neck and thigh, which can be painful, and can damage clothing.

Giant Sea Creatures

Giant squid and sperm whales are described below, as are sailing ships similar to those depicted in *The Stone of Vitality* and *The Hope of Vitality*. In each case, the source is Wikipedia. A few general observations follow.

• It's easy to lose sight of how small three-masted medieval sailing ships were, especially by modern standards. The carracks used by Christopher Columbus, Vasco de Gama, and Magellan typically measured around 20m in length, less than half as long as many modern superyachts.

• At 16m to 20m from end to end, sperm whales are almost the same length as the carracks used by these explorers.

• Giant squid are smaller, measuring 10m to 13m from the tip of their tentacles to their posterior fins, but not by a lot.

Giant Squid

From Wikipedia: https://en.wikipedia.org/wiki/Giant_squid

The giant squid (Architeuthis dux) is a species of deep-ocean dwelling squid in the family Architeuthidae. It can grow to a tremendous size, offering an example of abyssal gigantism: recent estimates put the maximum size at around 12–13 m (39–43 ft) for females and 10 m (33 ft) for males, from the posterior fins to the tip of the two long tentacles (longer than the colossal squid at an estimated 9–10 m (30–33 ft), but substantially lighter, due to the tentacles making up most of the length). The mantle of the giant squid is about 2 m (6 ft 7 in) long (more for females, less for males), and the length of the squid excluding its tentacles (but including head and arms) rarely exceeds 5 m (16 ft).

The known predators of adult giant squid include sperm whales, pilot whales, southern sleeper sharks, and in some regions killer whales.

The elusive nature of the giant squid and its foreign appearance, often perceived as terrifying, have firmly established its place in the human imagination. Representations of the giant squid have been known from early legends of the kraken through books such as *Moby-Dick* and *Twenty Thousand Leagues Under the Sea* on to novels such as Ian Fleming's *Dr. No*, Peter Benchley's *Beast* (adapted as a film called *The Beast*), and Michael Crichton's *Sphere* (adapted as a film), and modern animated television programs.

In particular, the image of a giant squid locked in battle with a sperm whale is a common one, although the squid is the whale's prey and not an equal combatant.

Sperm Whale

From Wikipedia: https://en.wikipedia.org/wiki/Sperm_whale

The sperm whale or cachalot (Physeter macrocephalus) is the largest of the toothed whales and the largest toothed predator.

Mature males average 16 metres (52 ft) in length but some may reach 20.7 metres (68 ft), with the head representing up to one-third of the animal's length.

Sperm whales usually dive between 300 to 800 metres (980 to 2,620 ft), and sometimes 1 to 2 kilometres (3,300 to 6,600 ft), in search of food. Such dives can last more than an hour. They feed on several species, notably the giant squid, but also the colossal squid, octopuses, and fish such as demersal rays and sharks, but their diet is mainly medium-sized squid.

Medieval Sailing Ships

From Wikipedia: https://en.wikipedia.org/wiki/Carrack

A carrack is a three- or four-masted ocean-going sailing ship that was developed in the 14th to 15th centuries in Europe, most notably in Portugal. Evolved from the single-masted cog, the carrack was first used for European trade from the Mediterranean to the Baltic and quickly found use with the newly found wealth of the trade between

Europe and Africa and then the trans-Atlantic trade with the Americas. In their most advanced forms, they were used by the Portuguese for trade between Europe and Asia starting in the late 15th century, before eventually being superseded in the 17th century by the galleon, introduced in the 16th century.

Famous carracks:

Santa María, in which Christopher Columbus made his first voyage to America in 1492.

- Tons burthen est. 108 tons BM
- Estimated hull length 19 m (62 ft)
- Estimated keel length 12.6 m (41 ft)
- Beam est. 5.5 m (18 ft)
- Draught est. 3.2 m (10 ft)
- Propulsion sail
- Complement 40

São Gabriel, flagship of Vasco da Gama, in the 1497 Portuguese expedition from Europe to India by circumnavigating Africa.

- Tons burthen ~ 100 tons
- Length 25.7 m (84 ft 4 in)
- Beam 8.5 m (27 ft 11 in)
- Draft 2.3 m (7 ft 7 in)
- Propulsion sail
- Complement ~60

Victoria, the first ship in history to circumnavigate the globe (1519 to 1522), and the only survivor of Magellan's expedition for Spain.

- Tonnage 85
- Length 18 to 21 metres (59 to 69 ft)
- Complement 55

ACKNOWLEDGMENTS

With the series now at an end, it's time to offer series-wide acknowledgments.

First, my wife Merilyn has graciously persisted as my alpha reader through multiple revisions of every novel, with changes having often been instigated by her feedback. The stories are invariably better for her input.

Heartfelt thanks to the beta readers who've stuck it out throughout the series: Merilyn, Andrew Menzies, Deborah, Ray, and Cherilyn White. In spite of his busy schedule, Stephen only missed once. Roly Edwardes joined the team for the final novel. I'm grateful to all of them for their feedback. It always makes a difference.

As the series progressed I have come to increasingly appreciate my developmental editor, Mary Novak. Her keen insights and helpful critiques have always proven invaluable.

Karri Klawiter has been wonderfully creative with the covers and always a pleasure to work with throughout the series.

Brian Plush managed some final additions to his excellent map in time for this novel, and I'm grateful for his skilful contribution.

Deborah's time has become ever busier with her growing family and her own writing, and I'm thankful for her meticulous proofreads throughout the series.

When I published the first novel, I had no thought of audiobooks. Since Greg John agreed to narrate them, I have been fortunate to connect with an appreciative and growing audience. I am very grateful to my ever-reliable beta listener, Arpenny Hart, who has consistently offered valuable and encouraging feedback. I thoroughly agree with her assessment that Greg has narrated the stories "with great clarity, energy and emotion."

I published *The Stone of Knowing* in early 2019, but almost three decades have slipped away since I first started writing it. Through it all, I've been a grateful recipient of the grace and mercy of God. Seasons come and go, but his steadfast love never changes.

ABOUT THE AUTHOR

Allan Packer writes epic fantasy. The novels in *The Stone Cycle* comprise his first series.

Allan grew up surrounded by books and became an avid reader during his childhood. In his university years fantasy displaced science fiction as his favorite genre, thanks primarily to J. R. R. Tolkien. He later shared this love with his four children by reading *The Lord of the Rings* to them aloud—a three-month marathon he completed twice during their formative years.

Born in Australia, Allan has lived and worked on three continents, and spent one quarter of his working years abroad. Having worked as an IT professional throughout his career, he was first published as a technical author.

Today he lives with his wife in Adelaide, South Australia, near their children and a small but growing band of grandchildren.

Allan is currently working on his second epic fantasy series.